The Ring of Light

The Ring of Light

by
L. Miral and A. Viger

Translated, annotated and introduced by
Brian Stableford

A Black Coat Press Book

ISBN 978-1-61227-756-1. First Printing. June 2018. Published by Black Coat Press, an imprint of Hollywood Comics.com, LLC, P.O. Box 17270, Encino, CA 91416. All rights reserved. Except for review purposes, no part of this book may be reproduced or transmitted in any form or by any means, electronic or mechanical, including photocopying, recording, or by any information storage and retrieval system, without permission in writing from the publisher. The stories and characters depicted in this novel are entirely fictional. Printed in the United States of America.

TABLE OF CONTENTS

Introduction

L'Anneau de lumière, signed "L. Miral and A. Viger," here translated as *The Ring of Light*, first appeared as a feuilleton serial in the daily newspaper *Le Petit Parisien* in 89 episodes, from 6 November 1921 to 4 February 1922. The story was reprinted in book form by Hachette in 1922 as *L'Anneau de feu*. At the time of the serialization *Le Petit Parisien* still claimed on its masthead to have the largest circulation of any newspaper in the world—approximately 400,000, down from a peak of two million—and the feuilleton might well have had a larger readership than any other item of speculative fiction published in France in the first half of the twentieth century. *Le Petit Parisien* published two further feuilletons under the same joint by-line: *La Bataille de l'or* [The Battle of Gold] ran from 14 August to 8 November 1923; and *La Loi de Mars* [The Law of Mars], a sequel to *L'Anneau de lumière* from 20 August 1924 to 16 October 1924.

The Bibliothèque Nationale catalogue records two novels signed Léon Miral published in the 1890s and a number of plays in which the same signature appears as a joint author after the turn of the century, but offers no further data regarding the author in question. Recent print-on-demand reprints of the latter two feuilletons in book form, issued via Lulu.com by Jacques Olliveau in 2015, however, offer the data—perhaps taken from *Le Petit Parisien*'s records—that "L[éon] Miral" was the pseudonym of one Léon Jacob (1858-1942), and that "A. Viger" was the pseudonym of Alphonse Berget (1850-1933)[1].

Alphonse Berget was famous in his own right, but none of the biographical articles written about him during his life or after his death list the Miral/Viger titles among his works, or give any indication that he ever wrote any fiction. The details of his career, however, make the attribution very convincing. Born in Sélestat in Alsace, Berget completed his education at the Sorbonne and went on to make a name for himself as a geophysicist and oceanographic physicist, as well as a notable popularizer of science, publishing texts on such topics as the discovery of radium, wireless telegraphy, astronomy and the conquest of the air: a career profile that fits the person behind "A. Viger," in accordance with the suggestions of *L'Anneau de lumière*, like a glove. Berget's exploits included a public demonstration of Foucault's pendulum in the Panthéon in 1902, on the classic experiment's fiftieth anniversary, in the presence of Camille Flammari-

---

[1] The notices in the two reprints give Berget's death date as 1934, but he actually died on 28 December 1933; the death might not have been officially registered until a few days later, and most obituaries would probably have appeared in January, which might explain the quoted date.

on, Henri Poincaré and many other notable scientists—an occasion given elaborate press coverage, in *Le Petit Parisien* and the other major Parisian newspapers.

Berget was presumably the instigator of the collaboration, and there is evidence in the story—pointed out in the footnotes—that his part of it might have been written some years earlier. "L. Miral" was presumably recruited in order to provide the melodramatic and romantic elements of a plot primarily designed to contain his sciencefictional ideas; the resulting hybrid is a rather odd chimera, which has elements of adventure fiction, spy fiction and utopian fiction as well as its elaborate scientific extrapolations. As to how and why "Miral" was selected to fill that role we can only speculate, but it might have been that case that he was a fellow Alsatian whom Berget had known for a long time. At any rate, Léon Jacob obviously shared with Berget a deep and abiding loathing of Germans and Germany.

The willingness of *Le Petit Parisien* to publish a work of interplanetary fiction in feuilleton form—which would have been regarded as an exceedingly risky move by normal journalistic standards—might have been due to the fact that Berget was undoubtedly acquainted with Paul Dupuy (1878-1927), a member of the Senate who was one of the paper's major shareholders in the early 1920s. Dupuy had a keen interest in science; he was the founder of the popular science magazine *La Science et la Vie*, in which Berget published a controversial article about the reality of Atlantis in 1926, and he had a particular interest in wireless telegraphy and the possibility of radio broadcasting.

However the collaboration and its publication came about, however, the circumstance makes the novel of considerable interest with regard to the history of French speculative fiction, especially interplanetary fiction. It is one of the earliest, and certainly one of the most extravagant, responses to the popularizing endeavors of the French aviator Robert Esnault-Pelterie (1881-1957), an enthusiastic propagandist for the notion that space travel might become practicable with the aid of rockets, and particularly the notion that they might be propelled by atomic power derived from radium or some other radioactive substance. He too might well have been personally acquainted with Berget, and his popularization of his ideas in 1912-13 is cited in the novel.

The Miral/Viger novel was published more than a year before the publication in Germany of Herman Oberth's *Die Rakete zu den planetenraümen* [By Rocket into Interplanetary Space] (1923), which stimulated various fictional endeavors, including Otto Willi Gail's *Der Schuss ins All* (1925; tr. as *The Shot into Infinity*). The next French novel to propagandize the potential of rockets as a means of space travel was Jean Petithuguenin's "Un Mission dans la lune," serialized in the *Journal des Voyages* in 1926 and reprinted in book form in 1933 as *Une mission internationale dans la lune* (tr. as An International Mission

8

to the Moon).[2] Berget could not have been aware when he wrote his own novel of the pioneering work done on the subject in Russia by Konstantin Tsiolkovsky, but might well have been aware of a novella published in Paris as a booklet in 1913 bearing the signature "André Mas," entitled *Les Allemands sur Vénus* (tr. as "The Germans on Venus"),[3] the heroes of which did not employ a rocket, but which nevertheless strives for an unusual level of scientific verisimilitude and included an elaborate bibliography of fiction and non-fiction dealing with the notion of space flight.

Nothing is known for sure about the entity of "André Mas," but hints dropped in the booklet suggest that he was a Germanophilic Alsatian resident in Paris who had a strong interest in aviation—which makes it credible that Berget knew the person behind the pseudonym. If he did, one has to presume, on the basis of the text of the Miral/Viger novel that he would have detested him on principle; it might or might not be significant that there is not a single mention in *L'Anneau de lumière* of the planet Venus, even though the astronomers of Mars are careful to show the hero of the novel all the planets of the solar system beyond Mars, including the as-yet-undiscovered Pluto. *L'Anneau de lumière* contrasts very sharply with both the Mas and Petithuguenin titles, the former stridently proclaiming that the destiny of Germany is to conquer the universe, while the latter is insistent in its scrupulous internationalism; for Miral and Viger, at least in the feuilleton if not the original version of Berget's part of the narrative, the legacy of the Great War is still exceedingly raw, and the German invasion of 1870—which resulted in the annexation of Alsace—far from forgotten; theirs is a story that displays its hatred proudly, only slightly disguised by a patriotism as transparent as the costumes it attributed to Martian women.

If that component of pure hatred can be set aside, however, the involvement of Alphonse Berget, a professional scientist of considerable reputation, with the planning and execution of a work of interplanetary fiction published as a feuilleton in the best-selling Parisian daily newspaper is a fact of some interest, perhaps all the more so because the fact was kept so quiet that nearly a century passed before anyone realized that it had happened. That presumably says something about the extent of Berget's anxiety that his reputation in the scientific community might be compromised by such an association.

It has to be admitted that *L'Anneau de lumière* is not a very successful work, viewed as a novel. It has all the typical faults of feuilleton fiction, being repetitive, rambling and full of inconsistencies, combined with all the typical faults of pioneering speculative fiction: logical fudges and oversights that were not obvious at the time but have become glaring now that we know so much more about the theory and actuality of space flight and space exploration. To make matters worse, there are distinct signs at certain points in the story that the

---

[2] Black Coat Press, 978-1-61227-466-9.
[3] Black Coat Press, 978-1-934543-56-6.

two collaborators are singing from markedly different hymn sheets, frankly at odds as to how to steer the story-line and what to incorporate within it—unsurprising if Miral was trying as best he could to adapt a story published some years earlier, in which the Great War played no part.

The very prominence of those defects, however, serves to illustrate that the undertaking really was an exceedingly bold one, and its audacity has a certain winning bravado. One cannot be surprised that the two novels with which the collaborators followed it up were far more modest in scope, their plots remaining safely earthbound, but nor can one help regretting that unheroic retreat. *L'Anneau de Lumière* cannot, in all honesty, be reckoned a good book, but it is certainly a remarkable one, and the belated revelation of the identity of "A. Viger" helps to testify to exactly how remarkable it is that it exists at all.

This translation was made from a Word copy of the text kindly supplied by the invaluable Jean-Daniel Brèque, to whom, not for the first time, I am profoundly grateful.

Brian Stableford

THE RING OF LIGHT

PART ONE: A JOURNEY OF NECESSITY

I. In which it will be seen that, in spite of its name, the Pacific Ocean can sometimes be angry.

On 21 February 1911, a frightful tempest—a cyclone, to use the correct term—was raging in the Pacific Ocean east of New Zealand.

Since the day before, the blue sky had been covered by clouds, light at first, then thicker, and finally completely dark. The wind had freshened gradually; from a gale, it had become a hurricane.

The sea, rising in enormous waves, had become utterly tempestuous. Veritable liquid mountains attained a height of sixteen meters, which is only rarely surpassed. It was one of the rotating storms that are produced at during fixed seasons in certain parts of the globe, the violence of which causes the most terrible catastrophes on land as well as at sea.

And yet, in the midst of that tempest, a ship was struggling against the unleashed elements. It was a three-mastered schooner carrying the French flag.

The spars had been taken down, the boom lowered. It was tacking to port, which is to say that it was receiving the wind from the left. Its sail was reduced to a fore lateen and a triangular "bad weather sail" on its mizzen, only offering a minimal surface to the action of the wind, but the violence of the latter was so great that the ship was still moving forward. An oil-powered engine, which could have been heard throbbing but for the din of the tempest, would, in any case, have permitted it to hold its course if its sail had been torn away by the fury of the hurricane.

The ship was moving in such a way as to flee the center of the cyclone, which is, as is well-known, a redoubtable region to be avoided at all costs. All the crewmen were at their posts. On the captain's bridge, two men were hanging on to the guard-rail, enveloped in their oilskins and sou'wester hats.

"I believe we're at the peak of the cyclone," said the senior officer, Captain Le Corvec, to the first mate.

"Yes, Captain," replied the other, Lieutenant Kohfornik. "The barometer has been going down all morning, but it seems to have stopped in its descent."

"How far has it gone down?"

"All the way to 690 millimeters, Captain."

Le Corvec reflected. "I've never seen such a low, and yet I've been in several of these South Sea storms." After a pause, he added: "Still, we have to keep our weather eye open."

At that moment, the door that gave access to the deck-house opened; four people, three men and a woman, appeared in the opening, clinging to everything that came to hand in order not to be blown over.

As soon as he saw them, Le Corvec descended rapidly from the bridge.

"Go back, Madame la Marquise; go back, gentlemen," he said to them. You'll expose yourselves to unnecessary risks and hinder the maneuvers, already difficult. Go back—that's an order!"

The moment that Le Corvec expressed himself with such energy and summoned his authority as captain—the "master after God" aboard the ship he commanded—the situation became serious. The passengers understood that, and were preparing to go back inside when another individual, also clinging on, appeared at the door of the deckhouse, with a napkin under his arms.

"Tea is served, Madame la Marquise!" he said, tottering.

In spite of the gravity of the situation, the four passengers could not help laughing at that announcement. But the man who had made it, losing his balance, had fallen on to the deck. He got up immediately, saying: "Oh, dear! These things only happen to me."

And they all went back into the deck-house, the door of which the wind slammed noisily behind them.

The tempest was not slackening however; quite the contrary. The waves were becoming higher and higher. The noise of the wind blowing through the rigging had reached its paroxysm.

"I believe that we might well drink from the big cup!" said a Provençal sailor whose comrades called him "the Maucot."

"If we had some tafia, at least!" said a Breton named Guénézan. "But there's only frogs' rum, and that's weak for Christians."

"You think about nothing but drinking," said the Maucot.

"Possibly! But I believe that we might well say a prayer to the Good Mother, because, if she doesn't throw us a lifeline, we're in the process of threading our last sheet."

"Silence, you lot!" said crew-master Le Floch, in a voice that dominated the racket of the tempest.

Meanwhile, the ship was lifted up like a dinghy on the crests of immense waves. The wind did not decrease, and Le Corvec was wondering how he could get out of it without serious damage, when Guénézan, who was on watch at the starboard davit shouted: "A ship! A ship in distress!"

"Where?" said Le Corvec and Kohfornik, simultaneously.

"There, to windward of us!"

In fact, a ship appeared in the direction indicated by the sailor, disabled, its masts ripped away. Its engine could no longer be functioning, for at every pitch, its propeller appeared, motionless. On the remaining stump of a mast, a flag was dangling.

"The German flag," said Kohfornik, looking through his binoculars.

"It doesn't matter," said Le Corvec. "It's necessary to do everything humanly possible to save those people."

The captain ordered a slight change of course, and his ship was already approaching the ship in distress when a monstrous wave fell upon the unfortunate vessel. The latter was undoubtedly holed already, for it was seen to heel over on its side and sink without it being possible to get to it in time to render assistance. The passengers, alerted, had come up on deck again and watched the terrible maritime drama with anguished hearts.

The captain and crewmen bared their heads. Le Floch made the sign of the cross.

"May God receive their souls," said the old Breton. "They're doomed."

But then the voice of Guénézan was heard again. "A boat! A boat!" cried the mariner.

Binoculars searched the sea. The sailor's piercing eyes had not been deceived. A boat had survived the shipwreck. It was bobbing like a cork on the foamy crests of the waves. A man could be seen within it, waving a shred of cloth on the end of a gaffe.

"We must save that poor fellow," said Le Corvec. "Put a launch to sea."

"Captain," said Kohfornik, "that would be risking the lives of five men needlessly. Since that dinghy is afloat, let's get closer to it and try to hoist it aboard."

"You're right, Kohfornik. We're about to come within range. Have the davits extended.

The men carried out the maneuver ordered; the davits, crossbars from which boats are suspended in order to be put to sea or brought back, were turned outwards. The maneuver was carried out at the expense of countless difficulties.

"Now, look out for'ard!"

The ship approached the dinghy, moving at low speed under the impulsion of its engine. The shipwreck victim could be seen clearly, making superhuman efforts to maintain himself with the aid of a scull. An instant later, a second victim became visible, lying in the bottom of the boat, seemingly lifeless.

"Hang on!" howled Le Floch, when they arrived within earshot.

The castaway waved his arms. The ship got closer and closer. Finally, just as an enormous wave lifted up the boat to the height of the starboard rail, Guénézan and the Maucot, each skillfully handling a coiled rope, dropped it into the dinghy. The man seized one of the rope-ends and moored it to the prow of his boat. In the meantime, Kohfornik deployed the lifting-tackle destined to haul it aboard.

The shipwreck victim had understood the maneuver to be made. He hauled gently on the rope that had been thrown to him in order to come alongside the ship. Finally, he reached one of the lifting-cables, the one at the rear. He seized it, and engaged the hook in the suspension ring. Half the work was done; it was a matter of connecting the second pulley-block.

"Let me do it," said a voice with a strong southern accent; and before any-one could stop him, the heroic Maucot, seizing the second lifting-cable, had swung over the side, suspended above the furious waves. The men held on to the rope.

"Let her out!" shouted the Maucot.

Two brasses were paid out.

"Hold hard! That's it, damn it!"

In fact, the brave Provençal had succeeded in descending into the dinghy and securing the forward hook; from then on, the shipwreck victims were saved. There was no more to do than hoist the dinghy aboard and bring it to the deck. The passengers, breathless with emotion, followed the phases of the drama.

The men started hauling on the two davits. It was then that it was under-stood how necessary it had been for the Maucot to risk his heroic maneuver; with the aid of gaffes, he and the castaway, at the prow and the stern respective-ly, warded off the battering blows to which the waves would have subjected the boat by smashing against the side of the ship, which would inevitably have bro-ken it.

Finally, it arrived level with the rail.

"Saved!" said all the watchers, with one voice.

The boat was brought on to the deck and secured. It was then possible to fetch out the second shipwreck victim, the one lying inanimate in the bottom of the dinghy.

One of the passengers leaned over the moribund man.

"Well, Doctor?" said the woman that Le Corvec had addressed as Madame la Marquise.

"He's alive, Madame," he said, simply.

"Take him to one of the free cabins. We'll give him the necessary care."

In the meantime, Le Corvec interrogated the shipwrecked sailor, in French, English and Spanish successively, but without success."

"But my dear Le Corvec," said one of the passengers, "since his ship was carrying the German flag, it's in German that it's necessary to speak to him. Being half-Alsatian, I know our enemies' language."

He advanced toward the sailor. "*Deutsch*?" he asked.

"*Jawohl*," the man replied.

"That's good," said the passenger. "Have some warm food given to this man, and some clothes. I'll interrogate him fully later."

While these words were exchanged, the ship had resumed its route. The worst of the tempest appeared to have passed; the wind seemed to be slackening slightly. The clouds, tearing, allowed little chinks of blue sky to become visible through holes in their somber mass. The barometer began to climb again.

Meanwhile, Kohfornik, aided by Le Floch, took stock of the launch so miraculously snatched from certain doom. There were a few stones in the bottom of the boat, doubtless ballast. There was nothing else there except an iron box, sealed by a rope wound around it twice.

The mate undid the knot and opened the box; it was full of mineral specimens.

"A matter for study by those Messieurs," said Le Floch, closing the box again and reknotting the rope that served to seal it. He went to take it down into the ship's lounge.

Then life aboard resumed its normal course.

As the wind died down, Captain Le Corvec had the sails hoisted again, minimally at first, and then, gradually, in their entirety.

The spars were hoisted to their positions again the next morning. Two days after the terrible "blow," anyone who saw the beautiful yacht, with the hull as white as its sails, would never have suspected that the lovely ship that was cleaving the blue waves of the great ocean with her prow had just escaped the very grave danger of a cyclone in the South Pacific.

II. In which we make the acquaintance of the yacht Coulomb, *its passengers, officers and crew.*

What ship was it, then, that we have just seen struggling against one of the greatest atmospheric cataclysms and snatching two shipwreck victims from death in near-miraculous circumstances?

It was a superb yacht, displacing six hundred tons, fitted out as a three-masted schooner, with an auxiliary engine fueled by oil. Its name was *Coulomb.*

The purity of its lines, both fine and robust in form, was appropriate to provoke the admiration of connoisseurs. It progressed primarily by means of the wind, which was its principal motor; under the action of its immense sails, it could easily attain thirteen knots in a fair wind; its engine was only there in order to permit it, if need be, to overcome periods of calm or to enable it to hold its course in a tempest, as we have seen in the previous chapter.

The tricolor flag that flapped at the horn of its mizzen mast announced that it was a French ship; a starry tricolor pennant at the top of the main mast indicated that it was part of the fleet of the Yacht Club of France; and finally, there was a pennant at the top of the mizzen mast bearing two blue stars on a yellow background.

The *Coulomb* belonged to Marquis Henri de Valsorres, who was aboard with his young wife, Marquise Marie de Valsorres. She was Alsatian, the daughter of the celebrated Strasbourg industrialist Jules Kessler.

Also aboard was one of the most distinguished engineers, Paul Espéret, a former student of the École Polytechnique, where he had been the classmate of Marquis Henri—for the Marquis and his friend Espéret were both scientists, in the full meaning of the term. The latter had graduated in second place from that celebrated scientific academy, closely followed, a few points behind, by his friend Henri.

Both of them, after graduation, had gone on to the École des Mines, and, on emerging therefrom, had each handed in his resignation, for Henri possessed a large fortune inherited from his father, further augmented by his wife's, and Espéret, the son of a rich Central landowner, also had the means to devote himself freely to scientific research.

At the moment when this story begins, Henri de Valsorres was thirty-four years old, and his friend Espéret was the same age. Both had already made themselves known by brilliant work crowned by the Académie des Sciences. Henri specialized primarily in geology and geophysics; Espéret had devoted himself to mechanics and astronomy but they both provided evidence of the expression that science is all one, so completely did they complement one another. For Espéret, Henri was the necessary collaborator—and vice versa, as one says in geometrical demonstrations.

The problem of the most complete utilization of the forces of nature, that of the conquest of space, preoccupied them both equally.

"You'll see," Espéret had said to his friend one day, "that humans will eventually be able to visit the worlds that gravitate in the heavens around the sun that illuminates them."

"Yes, I certainly believe so," Henri replied, "but what a prodigious force will be necessary to animate the vehicle destined to carry out that improbable voyage!"

"It will certainly require a powerful accumulator of energy. And where can that accumulator be found? Where can one even search for it?"

"Patience," said the Marquis. "The terrestrial crust has not yet delivered all its secrets. It contains substances like radium, which we have only known for a short time; perhaps it imprisons others even more energetic beneath the super-imposed strata that constitute it."

"Perhaps, indeed."

"Let's study, then, old man, swotting relentlessly. You'll see that we'll get there."

And Henri de Valsorres, with the aim of "swotting," as he said familiarly to his inseparable companion, had ordered the construction, two years before, of the yacht aboard which we see them today, in accordance with his own plans and personal ideas.

In fact, if the ship resembled, in its external features, all ships of the same type, it offered particularities that might have appeared strange to a specialist. Thus, all the hawsers, and all the "dormant equipment," instead of being made of steel cable, as on all modern ships, were made of phosphor-bronze threads. The anchors and their chains were also bronze, hardened by a special alloy. It was the same with the windlasses installed at the foot of each mast in order to hoist the sails. The axle of the propeller and the propeller itself were bronze. The engine, an internal combustion engine running on heavy oil—fuel oil, as they say nowadays—was entirely made of bronze, compressed by a special punch. All the pegs, braces and bolts of the hull were similarly made of the same phosphor-bronze. The hull itself, like that of modern ships, was entirely made of teak.

Captain Le Corvec, an old Breton long-haul captain, who commanded the ship, and had supervised its construction in a celebrated shipyard in Paimpol, could have affirmed that, except for the blades of the crewmen's and passengers' knives, not single piece of iron or steel had entered into the construction of the magnificent yacht, which Valsorres had named *Coulomb* in honor of the French scientist of genius who, during the reign of Louis XVI, had first discovered the fundamental laws of electricity.

Such was the vessel, simultaneously elegant, powerful and curious.

Its total length was fifty-two meters, with a breadth of eighty meters fifty, and a draw of three meters seventy. As we have said, it displaced six hundred tons, and it could make thirteen knots by sail and eight knots under its four-hundred-and-fifty- horsepower engine.

On the deck between the masts were two constructions—deck-houses, to use the maritime term. One contained a small lounge, the stairway to the interior of the ship, and a vast room, a veritable laboratory, in which instruments of all sorts could be seen: electrometers, magnetometers, compasses, sextants, chronometers, and a wireless telegraphy receiver. It was there that Valsorres and Espéret spent almost all their time. The other contained the galley, the larder and the large dining-room.

Although the scientific installations had been made with particularly care aboard the *Coulomb*, that did not mean that the comfort of the passengers had been neglected On the contrary, all that the most refined luxury can imagine to render life aboard a ship agreeable had been combined in the installation of the cabins.

The cabins of the Marquis and the Marquise, separated by a dressing-room and a bathroom, occupied four meters of the length and the entire breadth of the ship, immediately in front of the engines. Then came a vast lounge, artistically furnished, with rare engravings ornamenting the walls; glass cases enclosed precious works of art, secured by frames in order not to be displaced by the pitching of the vessel. A superb grand piano occupied one of the corners of the large room, which gave rise to the supposition that music was in honor among the passengers of the *Coulomb*.

Beyond the lounge was a broad corridor giving access to six cabins, with two bathrooms. One of them was occupied by the Marquise's chambermaid, Catherine, a beautiful young woman, Alsatian like her mistress, upon whom the chief engineer, the taciturn Breton Le Bris, looked with the most sympathetic eye. Another was Espéret's room; needless to say, it contained a profusion of books and scientific instruments of every sort.

A third was occupied by a passenger that we only glimpsed in the course of the story of the tempest, a young physician full of merit, Dr. Portier, the son of the late physiologist of the same name, a member of the Académie des Sciences, and himself a very distinguished scientist, already known for fine research on anaphylaxis. Dr. Portier, a friend of the family, had joined the *Coulomb* in Auckland, in New Zealand, and had embarked two days before the terrible cyclone of which we have told the story.

To complete the passenger list, it is now necessary to introduce Thomas. Who was Thomas? He was a worthy fellow, the engineer Espéret's valet, who was as devoted to him as a dog to its master. Valsorres had taken him aboard the *Coulomb*, where he combined the functions of valet with those of butler. Thirty-six years old, very robust in constitution, never suffering from seasickness, always in a good humor, he was a type specimen of the perfect domestic. He served at table with Catherine, whose solid stomach was equally insensible to the pitching and rolling of the ship.

18

Behind the engine-room were the cabins of the officers, the captain, Le Corvec, and his first mate Kohfornik, a "Breton's Breton," a native of the Île d'Arz in the gulf of Morbihan, who had sailed all the seas of the globe. Two engineers, Le Bris and Kermoisan, completed the general staff. Those four officers took their meals in a large ward-room, around which their cabins were grouped.

Finally, there was the forward "post" where the eighteen crewmen slept; two cabins adjacent to the post sheltered the crew-master Le Floch, an old mariner from Douarnenez, and the ship's cook. All the mariners were seasoned men; with the exception of le Maucot, all of them were originally from Finistère or Morbihan, and the Marquis de Valsorres could say that he had an elite crew. Those admirable mariners have, in any case, just given fine proof of their intrepidity and their composure during the tempest.

The reader is now acquainted with the yacht and its personnel.

III. In which the reader will begin to comprehend
why the Coulomb *is a ship constructed without iron.*

The day after the one on which these events took place, the passengers of the yacht gathered in the lounge with Captain Le Corvec, around a table where an excellent mocha was fuming in Sèvres porcelain cups bearing the *Coulomb*'s flag. Boxes of cigars had been offered to the four smokers, and even the Marquise de Valsorres was holding a cigarette of blond tobacco between her fingertips, from which she took an odorous puff from time to time.

"God, how glad one feels to be alive after such a shock," said the young woman, after having absorbed the contents of her cup.

"Yes, certainly, my dear Marie," said the Marquis. "And I believe that it's necessary to have passed through such moments in order to appreciate the real value of existence, *non bis in idem*,[4] as the Latin motto has it. Let's hope that the cyclones leave us in peace for the rest of our voyage, and that we're vaccinated against them, as the doctor might say. In fact," the Marquis continued, addressing the young physician, "how is your patient?"

"As well as can be expected, my dear friend. He's been rudely shaken up; he got a bang on the back of the head. Like all Germans, though, he has a particularly hard head and he'll get away with a few days of forced rest."

"Can he talk? Has he said anything?"

"Not yet. He's in a sort of torpor. But I think that tomorrow evening he might be in a fit state to answer your questions."

"And the sailor from the dinghy? What has he said?"

"Oh, that one seems to be a somber brute," said Captain Le Corvec. "Catherine, Madame la Marquise's chambermaid, who is also Alsatian, has tried to make him talk, at my request, but he only replies *ja* or *nein*."

"It's necessary to admit that the poor fellow has the right to be a little... troubled."

"Yes, evidently. Oh, he's a true German. If you'd seen, Madame, how he threw himself on the food we gave him and wolfed it, No, I haven't even seen negroes in the Congo eat like that. After that, he went to sleep, and he's been snoring for twenty hours."

"Well," said the Marquis, "Send someone to let me know when he wakes up. I'll question him fully."

"Now, my dear Marquis and my dear Espéret," said Dr. Portier, "it's time, after the excellent lunch we've just had, to keep your promise and tell me why

---

[4] Literally, "not twice for the same thing": the phrase that encapsulates the principle of double jeopardy in legal jargon.

we're aboard the *Coulomb* and why your beautiful ship is constructed without a single piece of cast iron or steel figuring in its masts, its engine or its hull."

"I'll satisfy you, my dear Portier, and in a moment, you'll know as much as we do about the objective and the means of our voyage."

The passengers and the captain lit new cigars, after the Marquise had poured each of them a small glass of 1879 brandy "from under the counter."

Then the Marquis, turning to the doctor, spoke to him in the following terms.

"You're not unaware, my dear Portier, that in my quality as a Frenchman, the son of a general, and the son and husband of an Alsatian, that I don't much like our enemies the Germans. We seem in France to be asleep with regard to that predatory people. While their Emperor talks about peace and wants to be heard preaching the union of peoples, their generals are organizing, training and equipping the most formidable of armies. At the same time, their factories are manufacturing war materials of unprecedented power, and others are mass-producing merchandise that their traveling salesmen—another army, as redoubtable as the army of soldiers—are going to sell all over the world, with thrusts of obsequiousness and insinuation, and blows of catalogues and intelligent discounts, gradually supplanting the commerce of France, England and Italy.

"If I tell you this it's because *I know it*, from my sojourns in Germany—the language of which I speak like a native—from the reports of our engineers and the pressing appeals made by a few friends that France still has abroad, who are begging us to react by a supreme effort against that veritable annexation by Germany of the commerce of the world. In addition, I have another reason to detest the Germans; in 1870, they had my grandfather executed by firing squad. It's too long a story to tell you now, and I'll only mention that sad and bloody memory.

"That said, I've observed the formidable power of Germany in all industrial directions: in chemistry, metallurgy, electricity, toys, optical instruments and machinery, they dominate all markets. They're invading the finance of Paris, and even London. As for the United States, I won't talk about that; a third of its immigrants are Germans, who are spreading their 'spirit' there. Alongside that, it's sad to think that the majority of the discoveries whose exploitation is enriching them were made in France.

"The first dynamo was the work of a Frenchman, Gramme. All of organic chemistry is the work of two Alsatians, Würtz and Gerhardt. Thermodynamics is owed to Carnot and Amagat. Microbiology is the immortal work of Pasteur, physiology that of Claude Bernard. The microscopes of which they have made a specialty were realized in their definitive form by the French inventor Nachel.

"I could pass in review all the scientific discoveries of the nineteenth century, but I'll stop at two final examples: wireless telegraphy, due to the genius of our compatriot Branly, and the phenomena of radioactivity, discovered by the illustrious Becquerel in 1896, which led the Curies, who made a brilliant corollary of it, to the discovery of radium in 1898.

"Now, on that last point, the Germans seem to have remained behind. Perhaps the flash of genius that stimulated the discovery made by Becquerel has been blocked by the spectacles that usually ornament the noses of their scientists."

"It's evident, my dear Marquis, that you know them well," the doctor interrupted.

"Oh yes, I certainly know them, my good friend, and in all their aspects. I know their crafty manner, their affable manner, and their arrogant manner, but all those disguises, all those masks, still hide the same ignoble, coarse, avaricious, thieving, underhanded and, above all, ferociously brutal individual."

"Bravo, Henri," said the young Marquise. "You're making my Alsatian heart beat joyfully."

"Well, my dear, I'm only telling the veritable truth. But let's get back to our subject, which is to say, radium. I told you that, on that point, the Germans are weak. Certainly, since the discovery, their chemical factories have started manufacturing radium salts, which they sell primarily to physicians; you must know something about that, my dear Portier."

"Alas, yes. They sell it to us, and at what a price!"

"But it seems that their effort stops there. They haven't understood, fortunately, what a formidable reserve of energy radium represents, if that accumulated energy can ever be fully utilized.

"I don't want to give you a lecture in physics; I'll simply tell you that, according to the calculations of the greatest physicist in England, Lord Kelvin, a single gram of radium, the radiation of which seems to be continuous and inexhaustible, emits in one hour a quantity of energy sufficient to raise its own weight to a height of thirty-four kilometers. In one hour—and it has been calculated that its radiation would take a thousand years to diminish by half.

"On that basis, a gram of radium represents a sum of energy of several billion horsepower. Imagine what power an individual—or a society or a country—that had a means to produce large quantities of radium would have at his disposal!"

"What an admirable picture you're painting there, Marquis—but it's a dream, isn't it?"

"A dream, my dear Portier? Yes, a dream yesterday, but tomorrow that dream might become a reality, and it's to bring about that reality that we're aboard the *Coulomb*, and that the *Coulomb* itself has been constructed."

"I confess that I don't see..."

"You're about to understand, momentarily. I'll resume my discourse. "There are better things even than radium. Becquerel discovered radioactive phenomena in uranium, whose activity is very weak. The Curies, concentrating uranium ore by degrees, obtained radium, the activity of which is two thousand times greater. Well, Espéret and I, by progressively concentrating radium salts, have obtained a substance ten thousand times more active than radium. We've only obtained a few centigrams of it, it's true, but that has sufficed for us to discover and measure all its properties."

"That's simply marvelous!" said the doctor, penetrated by admiration.

"I accept—we accept—the compliment, because it's merited. So, we've discovered virium—that's the name we've given it—but having discovered it isn't everything; it's necessary to be able to manufacture it."

"And that requires minerals of an exceedingly rare substance."

"Precisely, and that's where we come to our voyage. The center of the Earth, according to the latest theories of physicists, is the seat of chemical reactions in which, under the influence of enormous temperature and pressure, the atoms of radioactive substances are constituted. Now, matter in fission beneath the terrestrial crust escape through the shafts of volcanoes when they erupt, and one of the privileged regions of vulcanism is the Pacific, almost all the islands of which are volcanoes sprung from the sea bed. Is that understood?"

"Perfectly. Go on."

"I'll continue. Among the regions of the Earth where the resistance of the crust is minimal, there is an immense fissure that circles the globe, like a girdle, in the vicinity of the equator. Geologists call it the intercontinental depression. It's therefore along that line of least resistance that we have a chance to fining recently-emerged volcanic islands, and, in consequence, radioactive minerals of recent formation. Do you understand?"

"Marvelously."

"On the other hand, there is a second line of weak resistance, along which the terrestrial crust is subject to a veritable crease, which has, as an inevitable consequence, fissures and thus volcanoes, and that is the cordillera of the Andes. Are you still following?"

"Better and better; you're as clear as rock crystal."

"On that basis, it's in the vicinity of the intersection of those two lines—which is to say, in the equatorial portion of the American coast, that we have the best chance of encountering a new island. That's why we're cruising in the Pacific, and why we're approaching the equator, which we're going to follow for almost the entire width of the ocean."

"Perfect. Now, explain the construction of the *Coulomb* to me."

"You'll see. These radioactive deposits freshly emerged from the crust have intense electrical and magnetic qualities; they can and must cause the needles of compasses to deviate, and they have the same effect on the sensitive electrometers that can be constructed nowadays. That's why I've had this ship constructed without iron—which is to say, without anything capable of influencing a compass. We have two excellent compasses, one being the route compass placed on the bridge under the eyes of the helmsman, the other the standard compass installed with the instruments in the chart room—a sort of laboratory installed in the center of the ship. Those two compasses always ought to be, and always are, in accord. In addition, they ought to be in accord with a third compass, independent of terrestrial magnetism: the gyroscopic compass."

"The gyroscopic compass? What's that?"

"It's a discovery of our friend Espéret here,[5] and a discovery that will make his reputation, although he hasn't yet made it public. You're familiar with the gyroscope, the marvelous top that, freely suspended around its center of gravity in its double frame, seems to defy the law of gravity. Curious toys have been made with it, which prude seemingly paradoxical equilibria."

"Yes, certainly, I'm familiar with it."

"Do you also know that Foucault, who made use of it in 1852, concurrently with the pendulum, to demonstrate the rotation of the Earth, showed that the gyroscope, left to its own devices, places itself in the plane of the meridian?"

"No, I didn't know that."

"It's easy to understand, though. The rotational movement of the gyroscope combines with that of the Earth, and the resultant of the two rotations has the effect of placing the gyroscope in the plane of the meridian. You see?"

"Yes, I'm beginning to see."

"Give that, Espéret has constructed a gyroscope whose movement of rotation is maintained electrically. The instrument orientates itself within the meridians, and thus becomes a veritable standard compass."

"That's admirable!"

"Wait: that compass, based on a mechanical phenomenon, is not affected at all by the electrical or magnetic influences that act on the magnetic needle of ordinary compasses. Thus, as long as our compasses are in accord, we have no intense radioactive deposit in our vicinity; but if we observe a discord, even slight, between the two indications, it's because, not far away, a disturbing influence is making itself felt, which is acting on the magnetic needles of the compasses. In addition, the observation of our electrometers ought, in that event, to confirm the conclusions drawn from the discord of the two compasses."

"I understand everything now. Marquis, Espéret, you're two great scientists."

---

[5] In fact, the first gyrocompass was patented in 1885 by Marius Gerardus van den Bos. The first practicable model was developed in 1906 by the German Hermann Arnschutz-Kaempfe and was widely employed by the German navy. The American Elmer Sperry patented an improved design in 1908, which was adopted by the US Navy in 1911. It is unlikely that Alphonse Berget would not have known that in 1922, and it raises the possibility that he had actually written his part of the novel some years before, and that it was given to Miral belatedly for adaptation into a feuilleton; that might account for the awkward fashion in which the plot steers around the Great War.

"We're simply two seekers, dogged in the discovery of the truth and devoted to the grandeur of our homeland."

"But when you've discovered—if you discover—a radioactive island that will deliver its minerals to you, what will you do with them?"

"I'll package them up in the hold of the *Coulomb*, a part of whose ballast is formed of thick sheets of lead and the rest of stones. I'll replace the stones with the mineral, but I'll enclose the latter in a triple envelope of soldered lead, which is impenetrable to all radiations, and will preserve our delicate instruments from any ulterior perturbation. After which, I'll disembark them in Europe and process them, in the greatest secrecy, in a laboratory that I'll have constructed in the Valsorres park—because, for the rather audacious applications I have in mind, it isn't a gram of virium that we need but kilos."

"What are these applications, then, which you have no hesitation in qualifying as audacious?"

"They're the possibilities of attempting the conquest of a world and finally making a voyage in..."

At that moment, there was a violent knock on the door of the lounge.

Le Corvec went to open it, and found himself in the presence of crewmaster Le Floch, whose features displayed the utmost astonishment.

"What's the matter, my dear Le Floch?" said the Marquis.

"It's that the compass is out of kilter. It's no longer pointing north."

"What's that you saying? The compass is no longer pointing north?"

"It's the truth, on the heads of my wife and children. The lieutenant took the point this morning; he's made calculations to find the meridian, and the compass is no longer pointing north."

"What about the standard compass?"

"That one's even worse. One might think it had gone mad; it's turning one way and the other, like twirling dancer."

"Let's go see this, Messieurs; it's becoming interesting."

The four men, followed by Le Floch, went up to the deck, and from there to the bridge, in order to observe the indication of direction given by the compass. Going to the instrument room thereafter, they observed that the gyroscopic compass gave an entirely different indication, and the second compass, the standard compass, was completely crazy.

"Damn!" said Espéret. "It's really too good."

"What is it?" asked the Marquis. "Do you think...?"

"I think we might be much closer to the goal than we could have expected."

They went back on deck, where Kohfornik, his sextant in his hand, was measuring the height of the sun again, in order to confirm his previous point. The Maucot was at the helm.

"And to think, damn it, that all this has happened since those accused Germans came aboard with their damned rocks!"

The Marquis and Espéret looked at one another. The mariner's reflection had suggested the same thought to both of them at the same time. What if the mineral specimens that the Germans had had in their boat were radioactive?

But in that case, others were also in search of those deposits, and, more seriously, those others were enemies of France! And not only had they searched, but they had also found.

"Messieurs," said Valsorres, "let's go to the instrument room."

The Marquis, Espéret, the doctor and the captain ran down there.

Valsorres ran to the iron box. He untied the rope and took out a specimen that he brought toward the compass; the needles spun around several times. He carried out a similar test with the electrometer; the instrument deviated with such an intensity that its needle was blocked.

There was no more doubt; the Germans had found a radioactive deposit in the Pacific. The ship that had sunk before their eyes had probably been loaded with mineral, and the two shipwreck victims had been determined at least to conserve a few specimens, which they had placed in the box in the bottom of their boat.

Valsorres' face was somber. "Silence about this, Messieurs," he said. "I'll go and interrogate the injured man first. Would you like to prepare him for my visit, Doctor?"

IV. In which the reader will be able to convince himself that frankness is not the Germans' forte.

The Marquis de Valsorres was anxious, with good reason, as will easily be understood. To founder thus in sight of port! To see, as they say, the grass cut from under his feet as he was about to reap it—that was plenty to render both the patriot and the scientist anxious.

Then again, what had the Germans intended to do with those radioactive rocks? Had they, perchance, had the same idea, and the same project, as him? Were they, too, thinking of the conquest of a world?

At that thought, his teeth clenched and his brow furrowed; but he mastered himself quickly.

"Let's interrogate the sailor first," he said to Le Corvec. "Would you have Le Floch bring him to the lounge for me."

A few minutes later, the crew-master introduced the German sailor into the presence of Valsorres, alongside whom Le Corvec had taken a seat on the sofa.

"What is your name?" Valsorres asked him, in German.

"Hans Helmert."

"What is the name of the ship that sank?"

"The *Borussia*, out of Hamburg."

Valsorres, who spoke the Alsatian dialect admirably, had immediately recognized, by his accent, that the sailor was originally from the duchy of Baden, whose patois has much in common with that of Alsace. He therefore continued his interrogation in that dialect, which brought a beaming smile to the German's face.

"Where was the *Borussia* coming from when it capsized?"

"From the east, Captain." He evidently mistook Valsorres for the captain of the *Coulomb*.

"What cargo was the ship carrying?"

"Stones that we'd taken from an island where we'd disembarked, and where we worked for a fortnight. Then the stones were taken on board, where they were locked in lead-lined crates and put in the hold."

"Was the island inhabited?"

"No, Captain, it was a desert island."

Valsorres was visibly aggravated. Evidently, the man was telling the truth; not knowing anything about the objective pursued by his chiefs, he had no personal interest in lying; but the Marquis saw in his answers complete confirmation of his suspicions and anxieties. The Germans had certainly had, as he had, the desire to find a radioactive island, and they had found one.

After a momentary silence, he went on: "And who is the passenger who was with you, whom we were able to save?"

"It's His Excellency."

"His Excellency? Which one? What is his name?"

"I don't know, Captain. In the crew, we only knew him as His Excellency. He lodged in a cabin at the rear, and took his meals with Commandant von Steinmetz."

"Very good," said Valsorres to the shipwrecked sailor. "Have you recovered from your distress and fatigue?"

"Yes, Captain."

"Well, you can go. Le Floch, have this man given a good meal, to finish putting him back on his feet."

"Very good, Monsieur le Marquis," said the crew-master.

When the sailor had gone, Valsorres said to le Corvec: "Well, what do you think, Captain?"

"My word, Monsieur le Marquis, I think these people have, as they say, jumped the queue and arrived before us."

"Fortunately, their damned ship is at the bottom of the Pacific, and the bottom is a long way from the surface in these parts."

"Yes, indeed: on the chart the bottom is more than nine thousand meters down."

"That's true—we're over one of the largest ocean trenches in the world. But it makes no difference; I still have to interrogate 'His Excellency.'"

"With that one, it might be more difficult than with the sailor," replied Le Corvec. "And with your permission, Monsieur le Marquis, it's me who ought to talk to him. My status as Commandant of the *Coulomb* obliges me to draw up a formal account of the rescue, and I have an idea that that fellow must speak French like you and me—it's only if he doesn't speak French that I'll ask you to question him in his own language."

"You're right, my dear Le Corvec. Go and do your best."

The captain headed for the cabin occupied by the injured man, by whose side Dr. Portier was sitting, taking his pulse.

When the Captain arrived, the doctor stood up. "Here's the Captain," he said.

Le Corvec approached the bunk. "Monsieur," he said, "We picked you up two days again, in dire peril. My duty as commandant of the *Coulomb* is to draw up an official account of the event, and I've come to ask you to furnish me with the necessary information."

"Of course, Captain," the German replied, in excellent French. "I'm entirely at your disposal."

"Doctor, do you think that the questioning might fatigue your patient too much?"

"No, Captain, provided that it doesn't go on too long. In any case, I'll be here, and if I see any signs of fatigue I'll ask you to interrupt your conversation."

"Thank you, Doctor." Addressing the injured man, he said: "How do you feel? Are you beginning to recover?"

"I'm much the worse for wear, but very glad to be alive."

"You're certainly had a narrow escape. You were taken by surprise by the hurricane, then?"

"Yes, completely."

"You can't have been unaware, though, that you were in the region and the season of south Pacific cyclones."

"That's true; we knew that. Unfortunately, our ship was too heavily laden."

"With what as it laden?"

At that question, "His Excellency" paused to reflect for a moment, and then replied: "Nickel ores that we took aboard on a Pacific island."

"Which island?"

"An island in the archipelago of the Solomon Islands. One of our engineers was prospecting an important deposit of nickel ore there, and we had gone to embark the mineral."

While transcribing the injured man's replies, Le Corvec reflected. The man was indicating an island situated to the north-west, whereas the sailor had said that the ship was coming from the east. Did he have something to hide, then? That seemed evident.

The German then addressed the captain: "Is the ship that has rescued me a French ship?"

"Yes, Monsieur," Le Corvec replied. "It's the yacht *Coulomb*, belonging to the Marquis de Valsorres."

At the name of Valsorres, a slight tremor agitated the wounded man, who stared at the captain. "And the Marquis is aboard this ship?"

"Yes, Monsieur," Le Corvec replied.

"Do you know, Captain, whether he was able to save a small iron box that was in the boat?"

"Indeed, Monsieur. It's in the chart-room, at your disposal."

A smile of satisfaction illuminated the invalid's face. Le Corvec carefully refrained from telling him that a few fine highly radioactive specimens had been abstracted from its contents.

The captain went on: "Now I'll conclude where I ought to have begun, by asking you for your name, forenames and qualities, in order to record them in my official statement."

"My name is Baron Karl von Osterwald, attached to the general staff of His Majesty the Emperor of Germany. I had taken passage aboard the *Borussia* in order to travel to Australia, and from there to embark for Europe. The hurricane swallowed the ship, along with its cargo, its crew and its passengers, with the exception of myself and one sailor."

"The sailor is here, safe and sound," said the captain.

"Thank God," said Baron von Osterwald. "It's him who saved me, and without his devotion, I'd now be at the bottom of the sea."

At that moment, Dr. Portier intervened. "I think, Captain, "that your conversation has lasted long enough; any longer would risk fatiguing Herr von Osterwald, who still has great need of prolonged rest."

"Very good, Doctor. In any case, Monsieur has furnished me with all the information I need for my official statement. I have the honor of saluting you, Monsieur."

He left the cabin, where the doctor remained with the wounded man. Having arrived on deck, he found the Marquis and Espéret waiting for him impatiently. He gave them an account of his conversation.

"No doubt about it," said Valsorres. "These people have been searching and have found what we're looking for before us. Fortunately, they're now in no condition to continue their research, from now on and for some time we have a good start on them. It's all a matter of finding the island."

"But that's easy," replied Espéret. "We know—and had already suspected—that it's in the eastern Pacific. With our dual system of compasses, we'll be informed of its proximity by increasing perturbations of the magnetic needle and the electrometer, and I think we'll succeed, without too much groping, in finally setting a French foot on that promised land deflowered by the Germans. But there's still that box which, with its radioactive minerals, is hindering us by disturbing our instruments. That's most annoying!"

"But aren't we going to make a landfall a few days hence at Noumea," said Valsorres, "where I hope to find a letter from my sister, Madame d'Estrelles. We'll disembark the Germans and their box there, and we can continue our voyage of discovery without encumbrance."

"That's perfect," said Espéret.

"In that case," said Le Corvec, "we're setting a course for New Caledonia?"

"Directly, and with all sails aloft."

V. In which the reader will learn, via a letter from
Madame d'Estrelles, that one can make interesting
acquaintances in diplomacy.

For a fine sailing ship like the *Coulomb*, it was child's play to cover the distance of eleven hundred miles that separates Auckland from Noumea. It is well-known that a nautical mile represents a distance of 1,852 meters.

That distance of eleven hundred miles ought, therefore, to have been crossed in four days, and indeed, on the morning of the fifth day, which was 27 February, Captain Le Corvec dropped anchor in the bay of the isle of Nou.

Scarcely had the anchor bitten the sea bed than the yawl was put into the water, Valsorres, Espéret and Le Corvec went ashore, the last-named to fulfill the customary duties with regard to the maritime authorities.

The Marquis de Valsorres went to the post office in quest of a letter from his sister, the Vicomtesse Germaine d'Estrelles—a letter that he was expecting impatiently. That was because his sister Germaine occupied a large place in his affections. His father, General Valsorres, had long been a widower with two children, himself and Germaine; both of them had been raised by the general's sister, Mademoiselle Hélène de Valsorres—"Aunt Hélène," as they called her. She had served as their mother, having always refused to marry, even though the most brilliant suitors had presented themselves to ask for the honor of an alliance.

A little less than a year ago, Germaine had married a young diplomat with a great future, Vicomte Georges d'Estrelles. The young couple lived on the second floor of the Hôtel de Valsorres, situated by behind the Invalides, occupying half of an islet of terrain with vast gardens. The first floor of the house, as well as the ground floor reception rooms, were occupied by the Marquis and Marquise de Valsorres when they were resident in Paris.

It is understandable that, having a great affection for his sister, Marquis Henri was awaiting Madame d'Estrelles' news with impatience.

As soon as he arrived at the post office and identified himself, the clerk handed him a voluminous bundle of correspondence, from the middle of which, without any hesitation, he took a letter on which he recognized his dear Germaine's handwriting in the address.

Unsealing the missive was the work of a moment, and this is the letter that his sister had written to him:

Paris, 22 December 1910
My dear Henri.
As you recommended me to do, I'm writing to you poste restante *at Noumea, where I hope that the sojourn in the city of convicts won't diminish your*

31

good humor and won't bring you by contagion any difficulty in the execution of your projects.

First of all, let me give you news, great news.

Open your ears wide, big brother: for two months I've been the mother of a family; and when I say "a family" I'm not exaggerating, for I've given birth to two delightful twins, a boy and a girl. Naturally, their names are Henri and Hélène, with the result that, eighteen years from now, I can see myself provided with a polytechnician and a daughter to marry!

After having given you my news, I'll give you my husband's. Naturally, Georges is overjoyed at the double birth, which fulfills all his wishes; however, he wants to have another boy, firstly, he says, to increase the French population, and secondly because, so he claims, two boys and a girl constitute the dream of kings: two boys to ensure the perpetuation of the dynasty, a daughter for alliances.

I have, in any case, no reason to oppose to oppose the realization of that perfectly legitimate desire; a realization with which I'm entirely ready to...collaborate in all conscience. Look! Now I'm beginning to say silly things.

At this moment, Georges is very busy, otherwise he would have put a letter in this envelope for you. He's the director of correspondence at the Ministry of Foreign Affairs. He's working with a staff of clerks responsible for decoding messages from abroad that might be intercepted. Now, you know—or, rather, you don't know—that concerning us there have been "leaks." I don't know and I don't want to know any more, but what I can tell you is that the Chancellery is changing the cipher used in the messages sent to Paris from our embassies and legations. Georges is in charge of the key to that cipher, and he's thus in competition with Saint Peter, but that competition, honorable as it is, absorbs my dear husband singularly, and greatly restricts the number of hours that he's able to devote to his wife and children. Anyway, I console myself be thinking that it's for France!

Now I'll give you news of someone else that you love as much as me, our dear Aunt Hélène. She's still beautiful, that adored aunt; in fact, now that she has "salt and pepper" hair, she's even more distinguished than before, if such a thing were possible. She's a veritable grandmother for our two little ones, as she is still the best and most tender of others for me. She adores Georges, who returns the favor; he always says that he's found, in marrying, a charming wife (admire my modesty) and an ideal mother-in-law.

As if she doesn't have enough worries with the direction of our domestic affairs, of which she's assumed complete control, she's just passed the ladies' examinations for the Red Cross, and she now has the diploma of a nurse-major. And when we asked her with what objective she prepared for and passed that examination, she replied to us, with her delicate angelic smile: "My God, my children, if it doesn't do any good, it can't do any harm, and one never knows what might happen!"

In any case, we have no fear of war. Georges, who is well-informed at the Quai d'Orsay, is extremely optimistic. It appears that the Emperor of Germany—Lohengrin, as they call him at the Chancellery—is the most peace-loving man in the world. He receives the French who are introduced to him in Berlin admirably, and shows a very particular amiability for them. So, in that direction, I think that the horizon seems clear, and we have nothing imminent to fear.

After giving you news of people, I must also give you news of things. Let's talk first about our old family house. You know that, at the bottom of our garden, on the other side of the enclosing wall, there are two semi-detached houses, behind which the gardens unite their shade with our trees. Those two houses, which were unoccupied for more than ten years, have just been rented almost at the same time.

One of them is occupied by a celebrated foreign physician, German or Austrian—I don't know exactly—who appears to work marvelous cures for maladies of the nervous system. His name is Dr. Frank, and he lives in some seclusion, with a rather restrained manservant.

The other house has more worldly residents; it's occupied by a Scandinavian diplomat, Baron Lymstroem, the Finnish ambassador, recently appointed to Paris, where he's come to take up residence with the Baronne. Madame Lymstroem, who's said to be Polish by birth, is a woman of great beauty, a rather...imperious beauty. She's also said to be very rich; in any case, the household lives lavishly: horses, carriages, automobiles, numerous domestics—nothing is lacking, and their drawing rooms, in those circumstances, can't help but become a rendezvous for the elegant and select All Paris.

I've made the acquaintance of Baron and Baronne Lymstroem at a ball given by the Italian ambassador. The ambassador's wife, Comtesse Velletri—who is, as you know, amiability personified—introduced us. When we had learned that we're neighbors, the ice was quickly broken between the Baronne and me, Madame Lymstroem is a very well-educated woman, and truly seductive. We've exchanged visits and we now have the most cordial relations with those likeable neighbors. I'll introduce you to them when you return to Paris.

To give you an idea of the kindness of that charming woman, I'll cite you one example. You know my chambermaid Joséphine, a pure-blooded Alsatian. Unfortunately, the young woman has...how shall I put it?...slightly itchy feet, and she allowed herself to be abducted last week by a sergeant-major in the cuirassiers in barracks at the École Militaire. I was very annoyed. Just then, Madame Lymstroem was visiting me; on learning about it, she came to my aid. She told me that she knew a Swiss woman, an excellent domestic, who was highly recommended and immediately available. As you can imagine, I jumped at the providential opportunity. Immediately, therefore, I engaged Bettina Fuchs, who is indeed a model chambermaid, such as they don't make any more. It's a rare bird that the Baronne has found me.

My new chambermaid's face doesn't suit Aunt Hélène, though. She declares that she doesn't feel any sympathy for the excellent domestic—whose physiognomy, however, is not at all disagreeable, and whose service is absolutely perfect. Anyway, Aunt Hélène has instinctive antipathies. Would you believe that she doesn't like Baronne Lymstroem either? She affirms that she can't abide her. When I asked her the reason she simply said: "What do you expect? It's stronger than I am." In any case, with the perfect education that characterizes her, and which you know as well me, I have no need to tell you that, with regard to anyone except Georges and me, should doesn't let anything at all appear, and she receives her and her husband with the most perfect courtesy.

Baron Lymstroem is a type specimen of the Northern diplomat: tall, slim, very correct and very cold. He has an impassive physiognomy, in which it's futile to seek to glimpse any expression whatsoever. As a particular sign, I'll tell you that he's a keen bridge player—a game in which he's first class, and our friend Espéret, when he returns will find a worthy partner in him. Baron Lymstroem is also visibly much older than his wife; the age difference must be about twenty years. She's certainly no more than thirty-five, and he's surely well past fifty.

Kiss your wife, our dear Marie, tenderly, on my behalf, and tell me how much I'm looking forward to her return, in order to be able to introduce her nephew and niece to her. On behalf of both of us, give your—our—dear Espéret a firm and cordial handshake. Tell him that I'm thinking seriously about finding him a wife, for I don't want a man as perfect as him to end up as an aged bachelor.

I expect, my dear big brother, that this a long letter; forgive me my interminable loquacity, but when I'm chatting to you, even on paper, I feel that I can't hold back.

See you soon, then, my dear Henri, and receive an affectionate kiss from your little sister, who adores you.

Germaine.

While reading that letter, the Marquis' face had lit up with a joy that he did not seek to dissimulate. He had returned to the harbor, where the yawl as waiting with its four sailors.

Just then, Le Corvec returned from the Port Authority, where he had completed all the necessary formalities, and placed in the commissioner's hands the official statement regarding the shipwreck of the *Borussia* and the rescue of the two Germans.

Espéret, who had gone to take a stroll around the town, was waiting for them in a quayside café.

"All aboard!" ordered the Marquis.

All three took their places in the stern of the boat. Le Corvec took the yoke-lines. "Pull!" he said, curtly. The four oars fell into the water with a unison that proved how fortunately recruited the crew of the *Coulomb* had been.

Impelled by its four vigorous oarsmen, among whom was Guénézan, the boat cleaved the waves with its slender prow, and flew rapidly toward the yacht, on the deck of which the Marquise and Dr. Portier were visible, waiting impatiently for the travelers and chatting to the worthy Kohfornik.

As he climbed the ladder, Henri handed Germaine's letter to his young wife. "Here, Marie," he said. "There's great news from Paris." Then he addressed the doctor: "Can you disembark your patient soon, my dear Portier?"

"Whenever you wish, Marquis; immediately, if you desire. He's completely recovered and can support the disembarkation without the slightest risk.

"Well, you can tell him that he'll be able to return to Europe. The *Australien*, of the Maritime Mail, is due to leave in four days. He can book his passage and that of his sailor. Le Corvec will bring him ashore, where he can install himself in the hotel while awaiting the steamer's departure."

The doctor went to find the injured man, who had already been up on deck several times, and informed him of the possibility.

"Thank you, Doctor; I accept with pleasure. And after having thanked you for the merciful care with which you saved my life, I'd be very happy to address my thanks to the Marquis de Valsorres, for his admirable assistance and his gracious hospitality. But I'd like to leave a souvenir for the brave sailors who saved me."

"No need, Baron," replied Valsorres. "The devotion and heroism of French mariners isn't repaid with money. The sentiment of duty accomplished in the best recompense for them, the only one they desire."

In the meantime, the yawl had been equipped with a crew of four new sailors, in order to allow those who had just rowed ashore to rest. The Maucot was the "chief swimmer."

The two Germans had descended the ladder. As they passed through the coupée, The Marquis handed von Osterwald his iron box and said: "Don't forget your box, Baron; it's the only item of wreckage that remains from your disaster."

"Thank you, Monsieur le Marquis; it is in fact, a very precious souvenir. I'll take it with me." And he put it under his arm as he descended to the yawl, which sped rapidly toward the land, with Le Corvec at the tiller,

"A nasty fellow, that German," said Espéret.

"My word, yes," said the Marquise. "He has the head of an owl or an osprey, which has nothing engaging about it."

"Anyway," said the Marquis, "We're rid of him. Let him go be hanged somewhere else. Are you coming, Espéret?"

He took his friend to the instrument room. There, Espéret showed him a lead-lined box with a triple layer of metal.

"Here, old man. This is where I put the five or six mineral specimens that I removed from the German's box. "In this triple envelope of lead they can't affect our compass. In any case, for extra safety, I'll put them in a second lead case, and all of it in a sheet metal box."

"Yes, you're right, Like that, we'll be tranquil."

The evening was magnificent. After dinner, Madame de Valsorres, an excellent musician, sat down at the piano, and Espéret, who had a very fine baritone voice of which he made marvelous use, sang a few melodies by Gabriel Fauré and Duparc's masterpiece "*L'Invitation au voyage.*"[6] The Marquis and the doctor formed an attentive and competent audience.

"Bravo the artistes!" said Portier, after the performance of that strange but gripping melody.

"How beautiful the music is, and what horizons it opens up to whoever understands it!"

"Certainly," said the Marquis. "Then again, everyone finds in it what he searches for, in accordance with his own temperament. What is marvelous in that admirable art is that very imprecision, which permits everyone to find the form of his dream therein."

And on that philosophical reflection, they each went back to their cabins.

---

[6] A musical version of the famous poem by Charles Baudelaire. The composer, Henri Duparc (1848-1933) stopped composing in the 1885, suffering from an illness that had severe mental side-effects and eventually left him blind. He destroyed most of the music he had composed.

VI. In which the reader will see that it is always from the bosom of debate that enlightenment springs.

The next morning, Marquis Henri de Valsorres, who had got of early, was sitting at his desk writing a letter to his sister Germaine, which would depart with the *Australien*.

After having thanked the young woman for the details she had given him "about people and things," he gave her a vivid account of the tempest that had assailed the Coulomb, the sinking of the Borussia and the miraculous rescue of the two Germans. On the subject of the latter he asked her to seek information, by way of her husband's diplomatic relations, as to who the Baron Karl von Osterwald was that he had snatched from death, and who claimed to the attached to the general staff of the German Emperor.

After having given a rapid description of the island of Nou and Noumea, he recommended his sister to reply to him *poste restante*, via Colon-Panama, at Guayaquil, a port in the republic of Ecuador, where the *Coulomb* was sure to make a landfall.

After that, he went ashore with the Marquise, Espéret and the doctor, in order to feel a little firm ground beneath his feet and have lunch at the hotel.

We shall not describe the town of Noumea. We shall simply say that after lunch, followed by a two-hour excursion in a carriage, the passengers returned to the ship. There, in the yacht's lounge, around a table laden with charts, with compasses, rulers and set squares within easy reach, an important discussion took place, to which Le Corvec was invited.

"Now, my children," said the Marquis, addressing the people gathered in the lounge, "let's chat a little, but chat seriously. Our persistent, hereditary and pitiless enemies, the Germans, are on the same track as us, and even have an incontestable material advantage over us."

"Say that they *had*," Espéret put in.

"That's true; their ship and its cargo are at the bottom of the Pacific; but it's nevertheless true that they've found a radioactive island, of which Osterwald knows the exact longitude and latitude. In consequence, they can send a second ship there and embark a second cargo of minerals."

"Right," said Espéret, "but for that, it's necessary for Baron von Osterwald to return to Europe: say, sixty days; he'll need to organize a second expedition to the Pacific: say, three months, at least. That makes, if I can count, a minimum of five months. Now, in five months, it'll be damnable if we haven't, with the means at our disposal, the *Coulomb* and its crew, discovered their island and also taken aboard a cargo of those precious minerals."

"Your words are golden, my dear friend," said the Marquis. "That's my sentiment too, and it's to submit it to you that we're gathered around this table. Let's first examine, as our steward used to say, *the state of affairs.*"

And the Marquis unrolled a magnificent map on the table, a masterpiece of French hydrography—which, let it be said in passing, has always published charts infinitely superior, in precision and execution, to the most celebrated charts published in Germany.

"Pay close attention," said the Marquis.

The listeners gathered around the table, standing up and leaning over the maps displayed before their eyes.

"You know, as I've already told you, that not far from the equator, the line of least resistance that geologists call the intercontinental depression runs around the globe."

"Yes, old chap," said Erséret. "Go on."

"It's at the intersection of that line with another 'crease' in the crust consti-tuted by the Andean cordillera that we have a good chance of encountering is-lands freshly 'erupted,' if I might coin a phrase, from the bed of the Pacific."

"That's correct."

"In consequence, my intention is to follow the equator, slightly to the south, heading directly eastwards, carefully observing the concordance or dis-cordance of our compasses, heading in that fashion toward the coast of South America. What do you think?"

"Personally," said Espéret, "I approve on all points. But what does Captain Le Corvec think?"

The captain, thus addressed, leaned over the map, over which he ran the tip of an index finger jaundiced by tobacco.

"If you want my advice, Monsieur le Marquis, I think that it won't be as simple as that. The *Coulomb* is a fine sailing ship, of course; she can do thirteen knots easily—but in order to do that she needs the wind. Now, if we follow the equator we'll be caught by the doldrums and we won't advance any more than a mist. So, if it's a matter of making headway, that route doesn't please me."

"My dear Le Corvec," said Espéret, "you'd be right if we were to follow the equator rigorously from west to east, but we'll navigate parallel to that line and slightly below it. Now, as an old traveler of all the seas of the globe, you're not unaware that the so-called equatorial doldrums are situated slightly to the north of the line. In consequence, we'll avoid them."[7]

"Indeed, Monsieur Espéret," that captain replied, "but then we'll have a headwind, for those trade winds blow from the south-east to the south of the

---

[7] In fact, the parts of the Pacific affected by the Intertropical Convergence Zone, where the intersection of two trade winds causes long periods of calm, nick-named the doldrums by sailors, extend both north and south of the equator.

equator, so they'll be almost directly contrary to our route, and will hinder us considerably."

"You're right, my dear Le Corvec, in principle," said Espéret, "but I believe that in practice, you're no longer right."

"Why is that, Monsieur?"

"It's quite simple. The trade winds are contrary, you say. That's true; but trade winds are still wind, and the sole dread that a ship like the *Coulomb* can have is not to encounter any. As soon as it finds some, if necessary by tacking, it can advance in the desired direction."

"Then too," said the Marquis, "We have our engine."

"Yes," said Le Corvec, "but our supplies of oil won't get us as far as America."

"I understand that," said Valsorres, "but we won't have to use the engine all the time, and I'm counting on good trade winds to help us on our way."

"In those conditions, Monsieur le Marquis, I give in. We can go forward."

"Permit me," said Marquise Marie de Valsorres. "You know that a woman is always a little curious. In the midst of your savant conversation, there's one point that I don't quite understand."

"What's that, my dear Marie?" asked the Marquis.

"This: you said that, in spite of contrary winds, the *Coulomb* can still navigate in the chosen direction. That, I admit, I don't grasp very well, which troubles me slightly."

"It's quite simple, though, my dear Marie. A ship, with its sails, represents a solid body partially immersed in the water and floating on the surface. When the wind blows, one orientates the sails in such a way that it encounters them obliquely. Are you following?"

"Perfectly."

"Well, the effort of the wind on the sails is divisible into two: a force that pushes the ship forwards and a force that tends to make it move sideways, transversally—to make it drift, as mariners say."

"Go on."

"But that force is cancelled out by the great resistance that the water opposes to the transversal movement of the ship, because of the large surface area that the ship presents side on. In those conditions, there only remains the force that pushes the vessel forward and causes it to advance."

"Against the wind?"

"Not in a directly contrary direction, but obliquely. Good sailing ships like the *Coulomb* can advance by making an angle of forty-five degrees with the wind—four quarters, to use the technical term. The ship thus follows a series of zigzags and progresses, in sum, against the wind."

"I understand, my dear Henri. Captain, you can engage me in your crew as a sailor."

"Well, my dear Le Corvec, it only remains to give the course to the helmsman."

"I'll go do that, Monsieur le Marquis."

"Wait. Since we've just decided the certain outcome of our voyage, we'll empty a glass of champagne to the success of our crossing. Call Thomas, Marie."

The Marquise pressed a bell-push. The faithful Thomas appeared.

"Thomas," said the young woman, "bring up two bottles of champagne and wafers."

Thomas disappeared, only to reappear a few moments later carrying two gold-capped bottles, glasses, wafers and ice.

The Marquise filed the glasses.

"To our triumph!" said the Marquis, lifting his.

"To our triumph," his interlocutors responded.

"And to the annihilation of the Germans!" Valsorres continued.

"To the annihilation of the Germans and Germany!" replied the four persons present.

The glasses were emptied.

Then Le Corvec stood up. "I'll go set the course, Monsieur le Marquis."

"Go on, old chap. Eastwards."

"Eastwards," replied the Captain. And he ran to the stairway in order to go up to the bridge.

VII. In the course of which the reader will see that
a diplomat can sometimes allow himself to be
"led by the nose."

We have left the passengers on the *Coulomb* in the vicinity of New Caledonia. Let us transport our reader, in the blink of an eye, to a point on the globe almost directly opposite—the Antipodes—which is to say, Paris.

Nearly two months have gone by since the events that we have related, and we have arrived at 15 April 1911. We shall penetrate into the Hôtel de Valsorres. Let us go up to the second floor, where the apartments of the Vicomte and Vicomtesse d'Estrelles are, and let us go into the Vicomte's study.

Germaine is sitting in a comfortable leather armchair, facing her husband, near the hearth, in which a log fire is blazing, combating the last cold spell of a belated winter.

In another armchair, Mademoiselle Hélène de Valsorres—Aunt Hélène, as her nephew and niece call her—is working silently on a piece of embroidery.

Germaine is finishing reading the letter from her brother Henri, in which the latter recounts the dramatic details of the voyage, the cyclone, the sinking of the *Borussia* and the rescue of the two Germans.

She brings up the identity of Baron von Osterwald, on the subject of whom her brother asks her for information.

"What if you were to ask our neighbor Baron Lymstroem for that information?" she says to her husband.

"Nothing easier, my dear Germaine. I'll call on him at home and ask him to furnish me with the required details."

"Then I can give them to Henri by writing to him at Guayaquil, in accordance with the directions he's given me."

Then Aunt Hélene, who had not yet said anything, spoke. "Why bring Baron Lymstroem into this business and get a foreigner mixed up in it? Aren't you going to spend a few days in Berlin imminently, Georges, carrying important correspondence?"

"Yes, my dear Aunt."

"Well, nothing would be easier than for you to inform yourself on the spot, directly, which is always better than doing so at a distance, via intermediaries that one only knows, after all, quite superficially."

"Perhaps you're right, Aunt, and I'll do that."

"And I believe you'd do well."

"There goes Aunt Hélène again, manifesting her…mistrust with regard to the Lymstroem household. They are, however, very respectable people of a rare amiability."

"But my little Germaine, I've never said the contrary. Incontestably, he and she are very correct—even too correct. I don't dispute that. But if you want the reason for my antipathy, which was initially instinctive, it's that neither he nor she has a frank gaze."

"Get away! Now you're going to put their eyes on trial!"

"My dear children, I have always said: the eyes are the mirror of the soul. Now, look at Baron Lymstroem's eyes: they're the eyes of a cat, with green irises, with an expression in which I find the reflection of a cold ferocity. And the Baronne, with her cornflower blue eyes, has no expression at all, which is particularly serious in a woman. No, believe me, my children, mistrust those overly amiable neighbors; it's me who's telling you that, and me who's begging you."

"However, my dear Aunt," said Georges d'Estrelles, "the Baron is particularly amiable toward you. When he inclines before you to kiss your hand, one might think that he were prostrating himself before a divinity, before a idol that he venerates."

"And it's precisely that veneration, as you put it, my dear Georges, that aggravates me in a very particular fashion. I'm obliged to make a violent effort not to give him a black look."

"My dear Aunt," said Georges, "make that effort this evening; the Lymstroems are coming to dinner here—don't show them too somber a visage."

"Oh, don't worry, my children; without throwing my arms around them, I won't transgress the inviolable laws of necessary courtesy."

That evening, in fact, Baron and Baronne Lymstroem were introduced into the Estrelles' drawing room, having accepted an invitation to dinner. In addition to the two households and Aunt Hélène there was a sixth guest, a young embassy attaché, a sort of secretary to Georges at the Ministry of Foreign Affairs; his name was Pierre Vernier. He was already in the drawing room when the Lymstroems came in.

The Baronne was a truly beautiful creature. Tall, her bosom opulent without being excessive, with a trim waist and splendid hips, she never failed to make a great impression wherever she went. Her features had a regular beauty, and her blonde hair framed them with a heavy undulating mass. As Aunt Hélène had said, her bright blue eyes were devoid of expression—but did everyone have the penetration of Mademoiselle de Valsorres?

The Baronne was wearing a splendid costume in black lace with flecks of silver; thus clad, with her sturdy torso and opulent bosom, she gave the impression of one of the Valkyries of northern legend. A diadem of diamonds sparkled in her hair, and a splendid pearl necklace wound around her neck three times.

The Baron, tall, cold and correct, simply wore the red rosette of the Légion d'honneur on his coat. He kissed Germaine's hand and bowed profoundly before Aunt Hélène, who extended her hand to him.

"How kind it is for you to accept our slightly impromptu invitation," Germaine said to the Baronne.

"My dear Madame," the latter replied, "you know how much pleasure I experience in your company—a pleasure shared by the Baron. In consequence, your kind invitation was accepted in advance."

"Would you permit me," said Georges d'Estrelles, "to introduce to you one of our young attaches, Monsieur Pierre Vernier."

The young man bowed to the Baronne; the Baron extended his hand, saying: "You're beginning your career, Monsieur, under the most fortunate auspices; it's very fortunate for you to be the collaborator of a diplomat as distinguished as Vicomte d'Estrelles."

At that moment a domestic came in to announce that dinner was served.

Germaine took the Baron's arm, Georges offered his to the Baronne. Pierre Vernier served as Aunt Hélène's cavalier. Everyone went into the dining room, where a table delightfully decorated with flowers and laden with precious silverware awaited the guests.

Georges had the Baronne to his right and Mademoiselle de Valsorres to his left. Germaine, sitting opposite her husband, had the Baron to her right and Pierre Vernier to her left.

The conversation was immediately engaged.

"Have you received good news of your voyagers?" the Baron asked Germaine, affecting the greatest solicitude.

"Yes, Baron, this very day. I received a letter from my brother sent from Noumea."

"And the voyage is progressing fortunately? Everyone is well?"

"Thank you, but our voyagers have had a rather eventful voyage."

"How is that?"

"Can you imagine that they endured a frightful cyclone in the vicinity of New Zealand."

"A cyclone? A true cyclone" said the Baronne.

"Yes, dear Madame, and my brother gave me the most dramatic account of it. When I say dramatic, that's really the word, for they witnessed a shipwreck and were fortunate enough to carry out a truly exciting rescue."

"That is, indeed, terrible," relied the Baronne, with a well-simulated emotion.

"Isn't it? Can you imagine that in the middle of the tempest, they saw a disabled ship sink into the ocean. Only two of the victims were able to escape in a dinghy. At the price of a thousand dangers, they were able to take the two unfortunates aboard the yacht."

"And what was the ship?" asked the Baron.

"A German ship, the *Borussia*, out of Hamburg."

At the name *Borussia*, Baronne Lymstroem could not retain a slight start, quickly suppressed. Slight as the movement was, though, it did not escape the perspicacious eye of Aunt Hélène.

"Oh everything isn't roses in long haul voyages," said Baron Lymstroem sententiously.

"Don't talk to me about it," said Germaine. "I'm not like my sister-in-law Marie, who is aboard the *Coulomb* with her husband; she'd go to the ends of the earth. She rides a horse and fires a rifle like a cowboy. I'm much more home-loving, and adore being indoors."

"When one has a home like yours," said the Baronne, "a charming husband and delightful children, I can understand one loving it. Are the dear little angels still well?"

"Yes, Madame; they're growing marvelously."

After a brief silence, the Baronne resumed: "And are the names of the two people that Monsieur de Valsorres' ship saved so miraculously known?"

"Yes. One is a crewman, the other Baron Karl von Osterwald."

At that name the Baronne started again, and this time, Aunt Hélène , who was watching attentively, thought it useful to intervene. "Do you know him, Madame?" she asked, giving her voice the most amiable tone.

"Oh, only the name. Yes, while we were passing through Berlin, I believe I remember that we met him at a reception given by the Russian ambassador, and he was introduced to me by a functionary of the Imperial court."

"And in addition to the two persons," said the Baron, "were they able to save any objects or documents?"

"No, nothing, according to what my brother says…oh, yes, though, a small box containing mineral specimens."

The Baronne experienced another slight tremor, imperceptible to everyone except Aunt Hélène, whom it did not escape.

"In sum," said the Baron, "those two unfortunates owe a great debt to your brother the Marquis, who snatched them from death."

In the meantime, the Baronne, changing the topic of conversation, asked Germaine: "Are you quite satisfied, my dear Madame, with the chambermaid that I had the good fortune of enabling you to procure?"

"Oh, delighted. Bettina is an ideal domestic. She performs her service per-fectly, and without the slightest sound. She glides; one doesn't hear her."

"That's absolutely true," said the Vicomte d'Estrelles. "Sometimes, when I'm working in my study, somewhat absorbed, I find her behind me without having heard her come in. And I can't thank you enough, Madame, for having found my wife that exceptional chambermaid."

They got up from the table and went into the drawing room. The three women stayed there, chatting about people and things; the three men went to smoke in the Vicomte's study.

"Do you know, Monsieur," said the Baron to Georges d'Estrelles, "that the German military attaché is about to be changed?"

"Yes, I learned it at the Quai d'Orsay this morning. Who are they sending us?"

"General von Kriegar-Menzel, I believe."

"Isn't he the Emperor's senior aide-de-camp?"

"Yes, I believe he is. He's said to be very distinguished. And you're still very busy, very taken up by your functions?"

"Certainly—but in sum, it's necessary to devote oneself to one's country. You know something about that my dear Baron."

"Alas! As if I didn't have enough to do with the current service of the embassy, my government has just changed the cipher of its secret messages. It's an entire education to remake. Fortunate are the diplomats whose encryption doesn't change. They don't know how lucky they are."

"But my dear Baron, I'm stuck with the same education as you; we too have just changed the cipher."

The Baron manifested a sharp astonishment. "Since when, my dear Vicomte?" he asked

"Since it became certain that there had been leaks in the correspondence."

"And it's recent, the discovery of those leaks"

"Quite recent—a few weeks."[8]

Pierre Vernier listened with astonishment to the Vicomte d'Estrelles giving that information to a foreigner, for whom, like Aunt Hélène, he had no sympathy.

At that moment, the clock chimed eleven.

Outside it was raining heavily.

"I believe, my dear Vicomte," said the Baron, "That it's time to go home. I'll go look for my wife and take my leave of the Vicomtesse, thanking her for a delightful evening."

They returned to the drawing rom. The Baronne stood up to make her farewells.

"But you're not going home in this abominable rain?" said Germane.

"Oh, you know that the two houses are neighbors, and we only have fifty paces to take."

"It doesn't matter! At least permit me to send a domestic to accompany you with a big umbrella."

"You're truly too kind. Well, I accept, in order not to get my clothes wet. Bettina can shelter me as far as my house." The Baronne put on her cloak, which Bettina was holding for her, in the antechamber.

"Bettina," sad Germaine, "Take the big umbrella and accompany Madame the Baronne to her door."

"Very good, Madame."

Everyone shook hands; Baron Lymstroem bowed religiously before Aunt Hélène, and left with his wife.

---

[8] This does not tally with the announcement of that item of news in Germaine's letter, dated four months previously.

When they arrived at the door of their house, the Baronne said to Bettina, in a dry tone: "I have to talk to you this evening, at midnight. It's serious."

"I'll be there. Madame la Baronne can count on me."

And the Lymstroems went inside.

After their departure, Pierre Vernier said to Georges d'Estrelles: "Truly, Monsieur, you astonished me this evening."

"How's that, my dear friend?"

"By telling that foreigner that the cipher has been changed at the Ministry."

"Oh, you think so?"

"I believe that it might be an in imprudence. With these exotics whose wives are of bizarre nationalities, one never knows to whom one is speaking, and into what ears the words might fall."

"Perhaps you're right. Fundamentally, your anxieties would be well-founded if I had given him the new cipher, but fortunately, he doesn't have it and we're keeping it preciously." He pointed to a mahogany cabinet in the Louis XVI style. "It's in there, and where it is, my dear Vernier, it's sheltered from any indiscretion. On that note, my good friend, it's late; I'll see you to the door, for we're all going to bed."

And the Vicomte d'Estrelles took his leave of his secretary, Pierre Vernier.

VIII. In which two Germans of noble birth wash their dirty linen in private and converse with a domestic.

Let us follow Baron and Baronne Lymstroem into their house, which they have just reentered after spending the evening in the home of Monsieur and Madame d'Estrelles.

The Baronne, escorted by the Baron, has gone up to the first floor, where her apartments are situated.

When the chambermaid presented herself in order to perform her service and help her mistress undress, the latter said, dryly: "You can go, Lina; I'll undress alone.

The soubrette disappeared silently.

The Baron had let himself fall into a low armchair in his wife's bedroom. The latter threw her cloak aside, and said: "That imbecile Osterwald has probably allowed his important discovery to be filched!"

The Baron remained silent. The Baronne began to undress slowly, taking off her bodice first.

"You're not replying to my question," she said to her husband.

"My God, my dear Emma, it's not certain, but it's at least probable."

After removing her bodice the Baronne let her dress and its underskirt fall, which spread a circle around her like the petals of a flower around its pistil. Her splendid figure, emphasized by the corset that raised up her cleavage and made the most of the abundance of her hips, appeared in its opulent beauty. A special perfume made of a mixture of aromatics and natural scents emanated from the captivating creature.

The Baron was not insensible to that very material seduction, and could not help saying to the Baronne: "Decidedly, my dear Emma, it's fortunate that Saint Anthony is no longer of this world, for on witnessing a spectacle as flavorsome at the one you're giving me at this moment, however virtuous he was, he would certainly have succumbed, by sight, the sense of smell, touch and..."

"Oh, enough, my dear, I beg you!" Then, after a pause, she resumed in a dry one: "I believe you've said clearly, once and for all, that you'd give up these manners befitting a sergeant in the uhlans."

"But my dear beauty," said the Baron, "you can't prevent your husband— for I am your husband, after all—from being a man, and when a man has the good fortune to witness the intoxicating spectacle it has just been given to me to witness, no human force can prevent him, if not testifying by actions, at least affirming in words, the profound admiration in which the spectacle puts him, and the ardent desires that it inspires in him."

"Well, my dear, stuff your words back down your throat, and your desires...wherever you like. Don't oblige me to remind you of the agreements we made when we were married, and remember that I'm nothing to you: *nothing*, you hear? NOTHING, just as you're nothing to me."

"However, my beauty, you bear my name, and you have, I believe, been quite happy and very honored to become Baronne Lymstroem."

"Oh, my dear, let's not debate that point. I was happy to marry you because you brought me your name. I believe that you weren't sorry, either, to find me in your path."

"Oh, let's talk about it, my beautiful Emma. I don't want to remind you of the...doubts that were circulating regarding your birth and the right you had to bear the name you claimed to be your 'maiden name.'"

The Baronne had straightened up, splendid in her proud beauty; she had just put on a rich silk muslin peignoir.

"But you're forgetting, my dear—come on, hands down! Remember the agreement, will you?—you're forgetting that, in marrying you, I saved you from the suicide to which ruination had condemned you, in consequence of your long life of gambling, orgies, debauchery of every sort and in all milieux. You're forgetting that you had to pay a gambling debt within twenty-four hours, failure in which would have disqualified you in every drawing-room in the German aristocracy."

"In sum, beautiful Valkyrie, you mean, quite simply, that we're quits?"

"No," said the Baronne, bending down to take off her fine satin shoes. "No! You're forgetting, my dear sir, that with my beauty, on the one hand, and most of all, with my fortune on the other, I could always have found a husband, if necessary in a princely family seeking to regild its crown. While you...oh, let's not talk about that!"

"All right," said the Baron, calmed down by the cold shower that his companion had just launched over him. "Let's not talk about it anymore. But all that doesn't tell us whether the Valsorres have been able to take possession of the discovery of that animal, that imbecile Osterwald, may Satan adopt him for all eternity."

"Why are you attacking poor Osterwald like that, who nearly perished in the most terrible of disasters? It's truly not very generous of you. While he was confronting all the dangers, you were warming yourself at your fireside."

"And why are you defending him with this truly incomprehensible vehemence? Doubtless because he's one of your lovers?"

"Even if that were so," said the Baronne, standing up straight, superb in her anger, "it's certainly not for you to reproach me, after making curtsies and genuflections before that gray-haired old woman, that Mademoiselle Hélène de Valsorres, whose hand you kissed just now as if she were an Empress."

"Oh, my dearest! Are you doing me the honor of being jealous?"

Ever more beautiful as her irritation increased, the Baronne replied: "Me, jealous! Jealous of *you*? Ha ha ha—let me laugh at my ease. God knows, you're comical today, my dear! Truly, you've missed your vocation; it's on the stage of a music hall that you ought to be doing a turn. Me, jealous! Oh, no—that's too funny!"

And the beautiful creature let herself fall on to a sofa, holding her sides. Then, after a moment of sarcastic laugher, she said to the Baron: "Well, what are you waiting for, in order to leave me to finish undressing tranquilly and go to bed?"

"Me, nothing. I'm retiring, my beautiful, utterly beautiful, fury. My God, how much better anger suits you than tenderness! Truly, you seduce me even more when you're annoyed than when you're calm. Goodnight, my admirable wife..." He made the gesture of taking her hand in order to kiss it, but she withdrew it. "...But by the way, now I think of it, aren't you expecting Bettina soon?"

"Yes, I've arranged to meet her at midnight."

"Well, scold her sternly. It's more than a month since she furnished us with any information. This evening I learned, in the course of a conversation with Estrelles, that the French chancellery's cipher has been changed, and that stupid creature hasn't informed us of it."

"Don't worry," said the Baronne, "I'm going to stimulate her appropriately tonight." She headed for her dressing-room and opened a large cupboard, which contained her riding costume. She took out a slender and supple riding-crop with a golden handle.

"This," she said, returning to her bedroom, "is the best means of reawakening dormant zeal, and the skin of the so-called Bettina will make the acquaintance of this little instrument, in a fashion that will incite her not to risk exposing herself to its again. As long as she can get out and come to my rendezvous..."

"You know full well that the porter at the Hôtel Valsorres is devoted to her and opens the door at her request. It was a fine idea you had, in parentheses, my beautiful goddess, to place the excellent Oberstein there!" But I can see that I'm embarrassing you. Your modesty is doubtless alarmed by the thought that your husband might witness your nocturnal toilette. Goodnight, adorable Emma, and calm your anger on the back of that Bettina, whom I hope you won't spare!"

The Baron withdrew, blowing his wife a kiss. She responded with a scornful glare. She put on a pair of light slippers.

A few moments later, someone knocked on the door timidly. The Baronne went to open it, and found herself in the presence of Bettina.

Bettina was a lovely young woman of the German type: tall and strongly-built, with large breasts. She presented herself in the most humble attitude.

"Come here!" said the Baronne, dryly.

The poor creature advanced into the middle of the room. With a sideways glance, she had perceived the riding-crop on the bed and, doubtless instructed by experience, she suspected the punishment reserved for her.

"Tell me, infamous vermin, is this how you intend to earn the money we pay you?"

"But noble mistress, how have I incurred your ladyship's wrath?"

"She has to ask, great God! By the Devil and his horns, don't you know that you haven't finished the Baron with any information for a month!"

"Noble mistress, I've indicated the appointment of the new secretary to the French ambassador in Berlin."

"A fine affair! All the newspapers announced it the next day. And you didn't even inform us that the Ministry's cipher had just been changed."

"The cipher! But noble lady..."

"It was necessary for the Baron, thanks to the marvelous skill he deploys in conversation, to extract that confession from your master, Monsieur d'Estrelles. Are you blind and deaf, then? Have you forgotten what you owe me, and the extent to which you belong to me?"

"Oh no, most noble lady, I haven't forgotten."

"You remember, then that you've committed the sin that dishonors a woman! A child was born, and you drowned that child in the Iser! Do you remember, abject vermin?"

"Yes," said Bettina, falling to her knees and bowing her head.

"And in order to save you from the law, and the gallows that was waiting for you, I hid you in my schloss and smuggled you into Switzerland, where I gave you papers that permitted you to live tranquilly under your new name of Bettina Fuchs. Is that true?"

"Yes, most noble mistress. Yes, alas, it's true."

"And do you remember that in exchange for the salvation I gave you then, you swore to be mine, body, soul and will—in a word, to be my thing."

"Yes, noble mistress."

"And, to recognize that benefit, after which I placed you as a chambermaid in the household of the Vicomtesse d'Estrelles, you don't even know that the cipher has been changed, you can't even tell us what became of the mineral specimens collected by Baron Karl von Osterwald?"

Bettina opened astonished eyes,

"That's enough of that," said the Baronne. "For two months you haven't furnished any serious information. My patience has run out and you're going to receive the punishment you deserve. Take your clothes off."

The chambermaid took off her bodice, slowly.

"Strip!" ordered the Baronne, in an even more imperious one.

The unfortunate woman, trembling with fear, finished undressing.

"Now lie down there."

With the tip of the riding crop, which she had picked up, the Baronne designated a chaise longue positioned near the bed. Bettina lay down upon it. Then the Baronne began striking her with great strokes of the riding crop, addressing to her the qualifications that German officers of the highest nobility employ when speaking to their sergeants and soldiers.

"There, whore! There, vermin! There! There! Stupid animal! There!"

Madame Lymstroem whipped her furiously. Every blow marked the skin of the recipient with a long violet stripe. The unfortunate woman writhed in pain, but she had the strength of will not to scream, in spite of the suffering she was enduring; she scarcely uttered a faint whimper from time to time, quickly stifled.

The Baronne only stopped striking the chambermaid when she felt weary.

"Get dressed now," she said to her, "and try, in future, to show more zeal for the service of Germany and our august Emperor."

"Yes, most noble mistress," she said, getting up and kissing, respectfully, the hand that had just inflicted such a terrible correction. The unfortunate woman put her clothes on, rapidly, and after having bowed very deeply to the Baronne, left the room.

Left alone, Madame Lymstroem looked impatiently at the small glided bronze clock placed on the mantelpiece.

"He's not coming! What can have happened to him?"

Suddenly, faint footsteps became audible behind the wall against which her bed as set. She immediately hastened in that direction, moved the night table, approached a panel covered in silk cloth and pressed a button hidden beneath the tapestry. The panel, turning of its own accord, unmasked an opening that communicated with a secret passage giving access to the adjacent house, that of the celebrated Dr. Wilhelm Frank."

An individual appeared in that opening: tall, slim, with a cold gaze, severely but elegantly dressed; his features offered a strange resemblance to those of Baronne Lymstroem.

The latter had run swiftly to the bedroom door in order to bolt it. She threw herself into the arms of the new arrival, who returned her kiss.

"Wilhelm!"

"Emma!"

"My brother!"

"My sister!"

And, pushing back the mobile panel, which resumed its place with the slight click of a latch, she drew her brother to the chaise longue and sat down beside him. The she took his hands and looked into his eyes, tenderly.

"Tell me, dear brother, is there anything new?"

"Yes, my sister."

And a conversation commenced, long and doubtless very interesting, for Emma was literally drinking her brother's words.

What were they saying? We shall know in due course. For the moment, let us go, in the blink of an eye, to fly over the Pacific Ocean once again, and rediscover the yacht *Coulomb* and its passengers, continuing their adventurous cruise.

IX. In which it is proven that, when one in following up a good idea, one is always recompensed.

We left the *Coulomb* setting forth in an easterly direction, after having disembarked Baron Karl von Osterwald, the German seaman Hans Helmert, and the iron box to which Wilhelm II's orderly officer seemed to attach such a high value.

To begin with, the *Coulomb* had headed due north until it arrive at a latitude of five degrees south, below the equator. From that moment on, tacking in stages, it had set an eastward course, without ever deviating by more than a degree to the north or south from the line defined by the fifth parallel.

The radioactive specimens that they had taken from the German's box, enclosed in their triple envelope of lead, did not have any perturbatory influence on the two magnetic compasses on board; those, always in accord with the gyroscopic compass, showed that they had not yet arrived in the interesting region: the one where radioactive actions ought to make their perturbatory effects felt.

The crossing was, in any case, splendid.

Always navigating flat out, the *Coulomb*, carrying all its sail, made its thirteen knots gallantly, under the regular action of the south-eastern trade winds, which blow south of the equator in the austral hemisphere. The breeze was remarkably constant, and the speed maintained by the yacht was as uniform as if it had been propelled by its engine and its screw.

The days passed in delightful conversations on deck, in which the travelers, gently lulled by the movement of the ship, which was scarcely rolling, well supported by its sail, chatted *de omni re scibili et quibusdam aliis*.[9] They talked about Paris, Germaine, her husband, her children and Aunt Hélène. They always came back, however, to the objective of the voyage; every hour, Espéret or the Marquis, and often both, went to the instrument room to consult the compasses and the electrometer, but they had not yet given any indication of perturbation.

They had arrived on 25 March 1911. The distance, following the arc of the great circle, that separates New Caledonia from the American coast at the height of the equator, is approximately 7,200 sea miles, which is nearly 14,000 kilometers. The Coulomb, by dint of tacking—for Le Corvec was conserving his oil for "unforeseen circumstances"—traveled about 200 hundred miles in an easterly direction in twenty-four hours. It ought, therefore, to cover the distance it had to travel in thirty-six days.

---

[9] "All the things that can be known and many others besides": a sarcastic comment made by Voltaire about the scope of the knowledge of the polymathic Pico della Mirandola.

On the evening of 16 April, after an excellent dinner served by the excellent Thomas, the passengers were listening to Madame Valsorres, who was playing delightful pieces by Cherubini on the piano. Valsorres had gone out momentarily in order to consult the instruments. Suddenly, he reappeared in the lounge, with a satisfied expression. He tapped Espéret on the shoulder.

"What is it?" said the latter.

"There's news. Le Corvec has observed a slight discord between our compasses, and I've just observed the electrometer, which is showing a slight but incontestable deviation.

"Oho!" said Espéret. "Let's go take a look at that quickly."

They headed for the instrument room, and approached he electrometer. There was no doubt about it; the instrument's needle had deviated slightly from its equilibrium position, which corresponded to the zero on its dial.

Espéret delivered a few slight shocks to the instrument with his finger; after a few slight oscillations the needle always returned to the same position, slightly to the right of the zero.

"Very interesting, old chap," said the Marquis.

"Have you told Le Corvec?"

"We'll go and inform him. In any case, let's maintain the eastward course, guiding ourselves by means of the gyroscopic compass. Oh, my friend, what a stroke of genius you had in thinking of that and realizing that admirable instrument, without which we'd be almost disarmed!"

"All right, all right—you can compliment me when we set foot on our island. In the meantime, let's go give our orders to the captain."

They went up on to the bridge. Le Corvec was taking the height of the stars with a sextant, in order to maintain the same latitude.

"My dear Captain," Valsorres said to him; I believe we're reaching our goal. We're going to continue our eastward course. We'll observe our instruments every hour, and during the night, the officer on watch will also make an observation every hour."

"Very well, Monsieur le Marquis."

"Like that, you see, we're operating with almost perfect reliability. When we observe that the perturbation is at its maximum, we'll travel along the meridian from the place we've reached, from south to north, or north to south, until we observe a second maximum. Then we'll have every chance of being within sight of our unknown island. Is that understood?"

"Perfectly. For the moment, I'll set an eastward course?"

"Yes, still. We'll take observations continually and regularly."

Le Corvec gave his orders, and the two scientists went back down the lounge to announce the good news to the Marquise and the doctor, who did not hide their joy.

"Oh, my dear Henri, how proud of you I shall be if you succeed in this beautiful research, and if your anticipations are crowned with success."

"But they will be, my dear Marie. In any case, your presence aboard the *Coulomb* is a guarantee of success."

"Truly? I'm the expedition's mascot?"

"Certainly. Think about it. First of all, the cyclone that might have demolished us didn't do us any harm. Then the rescue of that Osterwald revealed our enemies' plans to us. Finally, today, the first clear symptoms are manifest of radioactivity acting upon our marvelous instruments. You see, thanks to you everything is going well: you're our tutelary divinity."

"Well, so be it; I've descended from heaven," said the young woman, laughing.

"While waiting for us to rise thereto," her husband replied, with a furtive glance at Espéret.

The doctor interrupted them. "How mysterious you are, Messieurs!" he said. "You're hiding something from me, and something very interesting. What is it, then?"

Valsorres and Espéret looked at one another. The latter spoke.

"My dear Portier," he said. "We've explained to you the goal—or, rather, the first goal—of our voyage, which is to find a radioactive island. But that's only one stage of a much longer voyage that we intend to undertake. The moment has not yet come to tell you its destination, but be certain that you'll be the first to be informed, for, however improbable the expedition we're planning might seem, I promise you that you'll be with us."

"Thank you, my dear Espéret—but all the same, you're putting my curiosity to a rude proof."

"Patience, dear friend, patience. Everything comes to he who waits. But what does Thomas want with us?" He pointed at the faithful domestic, who was advancing with a tray and glasses.

"Thomas," the Marquise replied, "is bringing us the nectar that the divinity is serving you, since it appears that I must inhabit Olympus. We're going to wash down with a glass of good Pommery the announcement that these messieurs have made of our imminent arrival at our goal. Let's drink, Messieurs, to the unknown island!"

And the charming woman filled the glasses with foamy liquid, and clinked hers against those of the passengers.

"What about the worthy Le Corvec. Aren't we going to summon him?"

Portier went to fetch the captain, who took a glass and emptied it in the blink of an eye.

"You see, Madame la Marquise," said he old mariner, "there's nothing like it at the beginning of a crossing, to cut off bad luck."

"Yes, my dear Captain," said the young woman. "Anyway, isn't it with a bottle of champagne broken on the prow of a ship that one summons the good luck of mariners upon it, after which, in baptizing it, the priest appeals to the blessing of heaven?"

"Indeed, Madame. Well, the *Coulomb* will simply have lots of luck."

"Let's accept that as an augury," said Espéret. "Come on, Le Corvec, another glass, and let's drink to our island."

"To the Île de France, Messieurs," said the Marquise.[10]

"To the Île de France," repeated the four men, in chorus.

They emptied their glasses joyfully.

"And now," said the Marquise, "let's go up on deck. From now on, it's necessary to have an eye fixed on the horizon in order to perceive the 'Île de France' that ought to be our promised land."

They went up on deck.

The worthy Thomas, picking up the glasses in order to return them to the larder, lifted up the two bottles of champagne delicately and held them between his eye and he light. The examination showed him that there was sufficient precious juice left in each of the two to satisfy his little passion—for the worthy Thomas liked wine, and nothing vexed him as much as taking back to the larder a completely empty bottle, whereas he was radiant when the receptacles he cleared away still contained appreciable quantities of liquid.

What do you expect? No one is perfect, after all, and everyone has his little weakness. Thomas' was, in any case, recommended by the old Latin proverb, which our lush Burgundy has adopted as its motto: *Bonum vinum laetificat cor hominis.*[11]

The *Coulomb* sped eastwards.

As it advanced in the direction of the sunrise, the symptoms of radioactivity became more intense.

The electrometer was now giving deviations attaining fifteen, and even twenty degrees to the right of zero. As for the discord between the magnetic compasses and the gyroscopic compass, it became larger every day, and the employment of the latter was now the only possible means of maintaining the ship in the precise direction that it had to follow over the surface of the sea.

It was now 18 April. Since the previous day, the deviation of the electrometer appeared to have reached its maximum, and the instrument, ceasing to deviate further to the right, now seemed to be returning toward the left. They had, therefore passed the meridian along which the most powerful action was produced. They were at longitude 105 degrees 30 minutes.

When Valsorres and Espéret had ascertained the fact they were overjoyed.

"I believe, old chap," said Espéret to the Marquis, "that we're on the meridian of our island."

---

[10] The name Île de France had previously been given to the island now known as Mauritius between 1715 and 1810, but had been freed up for possible reapplication since then.

[11] Good wine gladdens the human heart.

"I believe so too, my dear friend. Now we're going to sail along that meridian from south to north. I'll give the appropriate orders to Le Corvec.

The captain was on the bridge. The Marquis asked him for an exact point.

"We're at 105 degrees 30 minutes west longitude and 8 degree 25 minutes southern latitude."

"Well, old chap, set a course northwards."

Le Corvec gave the new heading to the helmsman: due north, by the gyroscopic compass, the indications of which were transmitted electronically to a dial—a rose, to use the technical term—set before the helmsman's eyes.

The *Coulomb* sailed northwards. It had a following wind for that; the south-easterly trade winds were impelling it generously, thanks to the orientation of its sails. As they advanced northwards, toward the equator, the indications of the electrometer became more emphatic and the discord between the compasses was augmented; in brief, the symptoms were becoming excellent

Valsorres and Espéret were radiant. Dr. Portier did not hide his admiration for the accuracy of the views of the two great scientists, who had been able to decipher one of the most obscure enigmas of the great book of nature, through the blurred line, which they had read as if it were child's play.

"Oh, mathematics is beautiful when one knows how to make use of it as you do," he said to the two friends, who were on the bridge alongside Le Corvec, scrutinizing the horizon with their binoculars.

"Yes, that's true," replied Espéret, "but it's necessary not to form too high an idea of mathematics. It's an error too generally widespread to consider it as a doctrine, when it's simply a language."

"Oh, you're right, my dear friend," replied Valsorres. "Yes, mathematics is a language, the most admirable and the most concise of all. But when one makes use of it, it's necessary not to forget that it's only a language, whatever virtuosity one can acquire in its manipulation. One only finds, in the second component of an equation, in a more or less modified form, what has been put into the first. It's like a parcel sent through the post; one only finds out on arrival what was put in it on departure."

"And not always then," murmured Espéret.

"Of course, conveyors, like scientists, make human errors. But I'll return to my point. If you put, in the first component of an equation, hypothetical givens, the result will always be stained by hypothesis. If, on the contrary, you put in hard facts, the results of indisputable experiments, you have every chance than the second component will give you results verifiable by experiment."

"And that's what you've done?" said the doctor.

"My God, yes," replied Valsorres. "So you'll see the result."

The result did not take long to become manifest in a triumphant fashion. At thirty minutes past midday on 20 April, Guénézan, who was on watch at the starboard davits cried: "Smoke to starboard!"

Le Corvec and Kohfornik looked through their binoculars.

"It's true," said the first mate. "It's necessary to alert the Messieurs."

The passengers were at lunch.

As soon as Le Floch, who has descended to inform them, spoke, everyone went up on deck with binoculars, which they aimed in the indicated direction.

"Smoke! I can see it!" exclaimed the Marquise.

"Yes, indeed, I see it too," said Valsorres.

"Me too," said Espéret.

"And me," added Dr. Portier.

"Oh, my children," said Valsorres, "If that's what we're looking for, what a great day it will be for us!"

In the meantime, Thomas, clearing the abandoned table rapidly, observed with joy that the bottles had only suffered light losses, so the worthy fellow blessed the discovery of the "Île de France."

As he ship drew closer to the smoke in question, they were able to see that it was escaping from a peak in the form of a near-perfect cone.

"The volcano!" said Espéret.

"Yes," replied Valsorres, simply, who was far more emotional than he wanted to appear.

The *Coulomb* approached rapidly. They could now distinguish a low-lying, rocky coast, devoid of trees, around the foot of the peak.

"I believe, old chap, that we're here," said Valsorres.

"I believe so too," said the engineer.

They both went into the instrument room; the electrometer had deviated all the way to the right. As for the magnet compasses, they were completely crazy.

"Well," said Valsorres to his friend, "I think we've hit the bull's eye."

"Yes, certainly, my dear friend. But let's go see, on land whether others have hit it before us."

"In any case," said the Marquis, "what is certain is that the island isn't marked on any chart. It's therefore a new island, and a fine success for our theoretical conceptions. Now, let's disembark as quickly as possible."

X. In which we can see that, when one discovers an island, it is necessary
to make haste to take
advantage of it.

Seething with impatience, the passengers wanted to disembark immediately. The wise Le Corvec moderated their ardor.

"You see, Monsieur le Marquis," he said, "it's necessary not to compromise our security. The island isn't marked on any chart, so we don't know the depths that will permit landing. In these diabolical regions, where islands emerge from the sea, one might well find submarine reefs as well on which we might run aground. I'm going to approach the island navigating with the engine, gently, taking continual soundings."

"Do so, old chap," Valsorres replied.

The orders were given to the engine-room. The engine was started and the propeller, rotating at low speed, caused the ship to advance very slowly toward the land. Crew-master Le Floch, placed at the starboard davit, threw the sound frequently.

"Thirty brasses!" he said.

"Forward slow," replied Le Corvec.

The passengers scrutinized the desired land through their binoculars. They could not see any living being.

"I believe that we're truly on a desert island," said the Marquise. "We've been transformed into Crusoes."

"Yes, my love, but favored Crusoes, for our ship, fortunately, hasn't been wrecked, and we don't lack anything."

"But when can we set foot on the enchanted island? I'm quivering with impatience!"

"Patience my dear Marie. Listen—can you hear Le Floch?"

The crew-master has just thrown the sound again.

"Nineteen brasses!" he shouted to the captain.

The bottom was rising. Le Corvec ordered the speed to be further reduced. At a sign from the captain, Le Floch threw the sound again.

"Fifteen brasses!"

"Stop engine!" Le Corvec commanded.

The propeller was deactivated; the ship was only moving on its own momentum. At a sign from the captain Le Floch dropped the sound for the last time.

"Ten brasses!"

"Reverse engine!" ordered the captain.

The propellers rotated in the opposite direction; the ship slowly came to a halt.

"Stop! Hold!" Le Corvec shouted into a mechanical loudhailer. "Drop anchors!"

The anchors tumbled into the sea and the chains rattled in the loopholes. The chains were stopped, precisely taut; the anchors had bitten the bottom.

"Now, Madame la Marquise, we can put the yawl to sea and you can disembark."

In the blink of an eye the yawl was put into the water. Four mariners took the oars. Le Corvec took the tiller. Valsorres, his wife, Espéret and the doctor took their places in rear,

At the moment when the boat was about to move off, a man carrying a basket launched himself toward the ladder in order to sit down at the top; it was Thomas.

"What are you doing there, Thomas?" Espéret asked his valet.

"I thought that Madame la Marquise and these Messieurs wouldn't be displeased, once ashore to empty a glass of champagne to celebrate the disembarkation. I've brought the necessary."

"What an animal!" said Espéret. "All right, embark with your basket."

Thomas did not need to be told twice. He descended into the launch, where he sat down a little more abruptly than he had intended; and under the vigorous impulsion of its four oarsmen, the yawl flew toward the land, which was two cables away.

When they were no more than a few meters from the island, Le Corvec, who had stood up in the stern of the boat and was searching for a favorite spot to land, ordered the oarsmen: "Let go!"

The men drew in their oars. The captain landed in a sort of little creek, on the edge of which the yawl came to rest. The mariners maintained the boat with their hands, clinging on hard to the rocks.

Valsorres leapt out first. As he set foot on the ground he had a smile of triumph. Raising his cap he cried: "We take possession of the Île de France!"

"Vive l'Île de France!" said the Marquise.

"Vive l'Île de France!" replied the passengers and the four mariners, in chorus.

The Marquise, aided by her husband's hand, disembarked in her turn. She had bought a Kodak, which she wore suspended over her shoulder. Espéret, the doctor and the captain leapt ashore after her. The boat was moored to a spur of rock. The four mariners came ashore on Le Corvec's order.

But a disagreeable surprise awaited the voyagers.

Scarcely had they disembarked than they saw visible traces of digging. Excavations, clearly of recent date, some of them quite deep, had been made at short intervals. Valsorres could not suppress a chagrined gesture.

"The scoundrels!" he exclaimed. "They've been here!"

"Well, old chap, you could certainly have suspected that. According to all the indications, I even believe that they moored in the same place as us."

"Well," said the Marquise, "they're no longer here and we are; that's the main thing. By the way, where's Thomas?"

The worthy fellow had opened his basket; he had taken out a small tablecloth, which he had set out on a rock that as almost flat. He had set down a pile of comfortable sandwiches and glasses; uncorking a bottle, he said gravely: "Madame la Marquise is served!"

Everyone started to laugh. Valsorres filled the glasses and lifted his own.

"My friends, to our success, the glory of France and death to Germany! To the Île de France!"

"To the l'Île de France!" they all repeated.

Le Corvec had filled glasses for the mariners and Thomas; everyone clinked hem against those of the Marquise and the passengers.

"Now," said Espéret to Thomas, "Pack up your stuff. And the rest of us, forwards!"

They climbed the rather steep slope that led to the interior of the island. They had scarcely covered a hundred paces when one of the sailors uttered a cry.

"What is it, Guénézan?" asked Le Corvec.

"I've found something, Captain," he said, "which surely didn't get here on its own."

The sailor pointed to a pickax, which he had spotted at the bottom of a hole.

Everyone drew nearer. Having taken the pickax from the mariner's hands, Valsorres examined it attentively.

"Look," he said, after a moment. "Here's the signature. Do you see this mark stamped in the iron of the implement?"

Everyone was able to read the words: *Krosenstein Eisen Fabrik-Hagen.*

"I believe if any further doubt remained to us, it's been removed," said the Marquis. "Here, Guénézan, take this pickax and deliver a few good blows at the bottom of this hole, to extract a few stones."

Guénézan obeyed. Several shards flew away under his vigorous blows. The marquis picked one of them up and approached it to a little pocket compass; the needle immediately went crazy.

"You see!" he said to Espéret.

"Splendid!" said the doctor.

In the meantime, the Marquise de Valsorres, who was searching for a viewpoint from which she could photograph the island, had climbed a little hill; she bent down swiftly and picked up an object that glinted in the sunlight. She waved it in the air and ran back in order to bring it to the group of passengers.

"I've also made a find!" she said.

The young woman had a long cylindrical copper container in her hand.

Dr. Portier leapt forward. "Excuse me, Madame; I believe that's a thermometer."

In fact, the doctor opened the container by sliding off the upper part, and he took out a thermometer, a marvel of precision, as only the Germans had the ability to produce in that era, alas. He examined the brand name with care.

"Look," he said. "*Füess, Steglitz bei Berlin*. I believe that this constitutes a visiting card."

"Yes," said Valsorres. "The thermometer and the pickax would dissipate all uncertainty, if any still remained."

"What can console us, after all," said Espéret, "is that we've seen that accursed ship, the *Borussia*, sink before our very eyes, laden with minerals that are, at this moment, at the bottom of the Pacific, while we're on the surface, with a good ship and a crew of worthy mariners, whom we're going to disembark in order to make us a provision of this precious mineral. And on that subject, we're going go back aboard immediately, to study those that Guénézan's pickax has procured for us."

"A German pickax! That's admirable," remarked the Marquise.

"Precisely, my dear Marie," replied her husband. "It's a just return of things down here. Now, let's go back aboard. We have serious matters with which to occupy ourselves."

All the voyagers went back to the yawl, which had rapidly rejoined the ship, solidly moored on its two anchors.

When they arrived on deck, Valsorres took Le Corvec to one side.

"My old Le Corvec," he said, "It's necessary to disembark as many men as possible tomorrow, with spades and pickaxes. We're going to collect as much of the mineral as we can, and replace with those precious stones all the ballast we have in the hold."

"Very good, Monsieur le Marquis," said the old mariner. "We'll arrange that tomorrow. At the same time I'll go over the island with a theodolite and a chronometer, and I'll calculate the longitude and latitude as precisely as possible."

"Perfect, old chap. Now, let's have dinner."

The following day, 21 April, early in the morning, the Coulomb's four boats put sixteen of the crewmen ashore. Armed with pickaxes, spades and shovels, they went to collect the mineral and embark it aboard the yacht.

At the same time, Le Corvec and Espéret had transported ashore the precision instruments, a theodolite and a chronometer, necessary for the exact astronomical determination of the longitude and latitude of the island, while the Marquis de Valsorres, equipped with a plane-table and a tripod, a surveyor's pole and a graduated telescope, set about drawing up a topographic map of the "Île de France.

"What inconveniences me," the Marquis said to his friend Espéret, "is that I can't make use of the compass to orientate my plane table; the needle is crazed by the minerals that constitute the soil of the island."

"Well, wait until Le Corvec and I have determined the direction of the meridian by solar observation; that way you'll have an even better reference point to orientate your plane."

"You're right, in fact. In the meantime, I'll go and install our signals at the principal points, and have poles transported there by two sailors.

In the meantime, a large and comfortable tent was erected on the flat ground of the isle, under which the voyagers would soon seated around a table, on which the faithful Thomas laid out the most correct place settings. Five folding chairs awaited the guests.

"We'll eat at ten-thirty," Valsorres had said, "so that we'll have finished half an hour before midday, in order to make our solar observations in good conditions." Naturally, the midday to which he referred was local time, deduced from the latest observation made at sea by Le Corvec.

The mariners, twelve in number, had already commenced their work as diggers; the cracked but rather dense rock burst into splinters under the iron of their pickaxes, and the stones thus extracted were already accumulating in piles of respectable dimensions.

At ten thirty, Thomas appeared at the flap of the tent, his napkin under his arm.

"Madame la Marquise is served," he said, taking a step forward.

But that step was a false one and the poor fellow fell, fortunately on the padded part of his person.

"These things only happen to me!" said the worthy fellow piteously.

Everyone burst out laughing when they saw that he had not come to any harm, and that he was laughing at his misadventure himself.

Everyone sat down at the table.

Another tent had been erected, under which the sailors, transformed into miners, went to take their meal.

Needless to say, the good humor was general.

"But you know, Messieurs," said the Marquis, drinking a cup of excellent coffee, "for castaways, we're provided with a certain comfort."

"Certainly," said the doctor. "Desert islands have their good points."

"You're forgetting, my dear doctor," said Espéret, "that since we're here, the island is no longer deserted."

"That's true. Oh, these mathematicians! How rigorously they reason! Don't talk to me about it."

In the meantime Thomas removed the bottles, and weighed them carefully, with an expert hand, to see whether the excellent wine they contained had left residues. What do you expect? The poor fellow had been distressed by his fall and needed to restore himself a little.

At eleven-thirty, Le Corvec made a sign to Espéret. "The point, Monsieur," he said. "It's time."

The engineer got up, holding a chronometer and a notebook. They both headed for the theodolite, installed on its tripod under the large parasol. The captain had regulated it in the morning.

After removing the parasol, Espéret began the angular observation of the sun, while Le Corvec made observations of the chronometer on his signals. Their labor lasted until half an hour past midday. Then they made a rapid calculation and deduced the exact latitude of the island.

"Five degrees two minutes south latitude," said Espéret.

"Perfect," said Le Corvec. "At three o'clock I'll take the height of the sun again, in order to have the longitude by means of the exact calculation of the time."

At the same time, Espéret had determined the meridian, in the direction of which he sent Le Floch to plant a stake. Valsorres thus had a reference point in order to orientate his plane table, which he immediately began to operate.

The voyagers followed the course of its displacements. By doing that, they discovered, on the flank of the smoking peak, a small spring escaping from a fissure in the rock. The spring gave off a sulfurous odor and abundant vapors

"Well, well," said the doctor. "Have we discovered a thermal bath? This spring seems to me to be very sulfurous and very hot at the same time."

"Bravo, Doctor," said the Marquise. "We'll found a Casino here, with a theater, concert halls, roundabouts and clay pigeon shooting."

"It will only lack bathers. But I fear that it won't receive any before the voyage is concluded. In the meantime let's see how hot the water is."

The doctor plunged a small thermometer into the fissure from which the water was escaping; the mercury of the instrument soon stopped, after a rapid climb, opposite the eighty-seventh division.

"Eighty-seven degrees!" said he young scientist. "That's a record for thermal springs."

"Did you say eighty-seven degrees?" asked Valsorres, interrupting his topographical drawing and approaching his companions.

"Yes, Marquis. See for yourself.

"Valsorres approached the thermometer, whose reading he was able to verify.

He returned to his plane table and his alidade, thoughtfully. "Eighty-seven degrees!" he said, in a low voice. "That indicates a very great proximity of the central heat. The island might be more volcanic than I hoped."

He was then seen to lie down on the ground and put his ear against the rock. He remained motionless momentarily, and then got up again in order to resume his work.

When he came to rejoin his companions in the evening, however, in response to the appeal of Thomas—who bumped his head on one of the tent-poles as he announced: "Madame la Marquise is served"—he looked worried.

His wife interrogated him on that subject. "Has something gone wrong with the drawing up of your plan?"

"No, my dear Marie. Everything's going well in that regard. And I think I'll have finished tomorrow. By the way, Le Corvec, were you able to make an observation of the sun at three o'clock and calculate the longitude of the island?"

"Yes Monsieur le Marquis. Monsieur Espéret and I calculated the horary angle. That gives us, for the longitude of the island, a hundred and five degrees thirty minutes.

"Perfect. So, a hundred and five degrees thirty west longitude, and five degrees two minutes south latitude; that's the exact location of our island. Let's verify one last time that it isn't marked on any map.

A Pacific chart was set out on the table, from which Thomas had removed all the bottles—making a slight grimace because they were all quite empty.

Nothing on the chart indicated an island at the longitude and latitude measured. The chart had been revised the previous year, as the figure 11-1910 engraved in the margin indicated. The "Île de France" really was, therefore, a new island.

"My children," said Valsorres, addressing his companions, "I believe that it's necessary for us to make haste to embark our cargo of mineral."

"Make haste?" said he Marquise. "Why is that, my love? Are we not delightfully situated in this little terrestrial paradise?"

"This terrestrial paradise, my dear Marie, might very well be transformed, not long from now, into an inferno, opening its flanks to torrents of igneous material, and might even sink into the ocean, by virtue of the same cataclysm that gave birth to it."

"What are you saying, old chap?" asked Espéret.

"Nothing is more reasonable. That thermal spring, the high temperature of which the doctor observed himself, shows us that the thickness of the solid crust that separates us from the ardent matter forming the Earth's central core is not very great. In addition, I thought I perceived certain subterranean rumblings that seem to me symptomatic. In consequence, the moral of the story is that it's necessary to work actively and not to linger on this island, which appears to me to be anything but a 'fortunate isle.'"

"You're scaring us," said Dr. Portier.

"No, my friends. But believe me—it's necessary to hurry. Tomorrow, we'll all set to work to help the sailors to extract and embark the mineral. The sooner we'll have finished, the better it will be, believe me."

The next day, and the following days, it was as Valsorres desired. Everyone set to work, Valsorres, Espéret and the doctor first of all—including Thomas, whom the Marquise replaced for table service with her chambermaid Catherine, an Alsatian from Ribeauvillé. The latter was still incensed by the thought that the "dirty Prussians" had already passed that way.

Thomas plied a pickax like everyone else. On the morning of the third day, the unfortunate fellow suddenly disappeared, uttering a terrible scream. Everyone ran toward him.

Thomas was plunged up to the neck in a sort of crevice that had been sealed by a thin layer of gravel, which had given way under his weight. He was pulled out safe and sound.

"These things only happen to me!" said the unlucky fellow, rubbing his painful limbs; and he headed for the tent where Catherine prepared him a toddy in order to reinvigorate him.

But the accident had attracted the attention of the Marquis. He took Espéret aside. "That crevice, whose sides I've just examined, is of very recent formation," he said. "It confirms my anxieties. Let's hurry, my friend, let's hurry."

They had all had picked up their tools and were working like laborers. The Marquise and Catherine laid and cleared the table, to the great despair of the worthy Thomas, who no longer had the resource of "adopting the orphans," as he put it, referring to the incompletely emptied bottles.

In the meantime, the ship's carpenter and the engineers made wooden crates lined with a triple layer of lead. As the mineral was extracted it was transported aboard by the boats and put in the crates, the lead lids of which were soldered shut. Then the crates were lowered into the hold.

A fortnight after the discovery of the island, all the mineral was on board the *Coulomb*, which had thrown its former ballast of stones, shingle and scrap iron overboard.

It was now 6 May.

The tents and the instruments had been taken aboard the yacht. The ship was ready to sail, its jibs hoisted. Le Corvec was on the bridge, Kohfornik beside the captain.

"Is it necessary to raise anchor?" the captain asked the Marquis.

"Yes, Captain," the latter replied.

Le Corvec gave his orders. The engine, activated, caused the capstan to turn slowly, which brought up the anchor chain. Kohfornik leaned over the side.

"The anchor's vertical," he said.

"Turn!" replied Le Corvec.

A last effort of the windlass freed the anchor from the bottom. It was brought back along the side and hoisted on to the davit.

"Let's go!" shouted the Captain.

The three main sails were hoisted, and then the staysails, and the Coulomb resumed its eastward progress, setting a course for the Ecuadorian port of Guayaquil.

They navigated thus for three days. It was the morning of 9 May. It was eight o'clock in the morning, and all the passengers were on deck before going to take their habitual cup of tea. They were chatting about one thing and another, including the imminent arrival in Guayaquil and the letters they hoped to find there.

Suddenly, the Marquise, who happened to be looking toward the rear of the boat, uttered a cry and pointed at the western horizon.

"Oh! What's that?" she asked her husband.

Valsorres aimed his binoculars at the horizon. He had scarcely put them to his eyes before he launched himself toward the ladder leading to the bridge, where Le Corvec as on watch.

"Have you seen that, Captain?" he asked, in an emotional voice.

Le Corvec looked in his turn.

"Ready to come about!" he thundered.

The rudder was lowered. The sailors get ready to haul in the sheets."

"Come about!" shouted the captain.

The jibs were changed, the sheets spun. The *Coulomb*, which had been heading eastwards, now directed its prow toward the west.

It was just in time.

Scarcely had the maneuver been completed than a monstrous wave, more than fifteen meters high, raced with enormous speed over the tranquil surface of the liquid plain, rising to assault the ship, which, thanks to its change of course, was presented to it head on.

It took the wave as if it were a cork, rising up to all the way to its summit and then descending into the liquid hollow that followed it.

The passengers had been knocked over. At the moment when the wave arrived, Thomas, his napkin under his arm, appeared at the door of the deckhouse to announce "Tea is served, Madame la Marquise!"—but the unfortunate fellow did not have time to finish the sentence. Under the violence of the impact, the spires of the masts had broken and they had fallen on to the deck, and the tip of the mizzen mast had knocked poor Thomas down; he lay there inanimate, perhaps dead.

The passengers had risen to their feet. Dr. Portier ran to the injured man, but the latter moved his arm slightly.

"He's alive!" cried Espéret, distressed by the accident that had overtaken his faithful domestic.

"Yes, Monsieur," said Thomas, trying to get up, with difficulty. "It's all right. These things only happen to me."

"Nothing's broken?" he doctor asked, palpating him.

"Yes, Monsieur, but I believe that all the crockery must have been smashed by that extraordinary lurch,"

Everyone laughed now that they knew that the fellow was out of danger. He got away with a sprained wrist.

Meanwhile, Le Corvec and Kohfornik occupied themselves with repairing the damage to the masts. There was no hope of replacing the spires, snapped at the root; the crew got busy disconnecting them. The ship would have to navigate with its lower sails alone. The outer tip of the bowsprit had also broken in the course of the extraordinary adventure.

"Fortunately," said Le Corvec, "We're no more than four days from Guayaquil; there's no more risk of running out of oil, and we can use the engine."

"Do it," said the Marquis. "But what's happened, and what was that huge and solitary wave that assailed us, and might have sunk us but for your prodigious maneuver?"

"A tidal wave," replied the captain.

A tidal wave! That response from Le Corvec was a flash of enlightenment for Valsorres. He knew what the redoubtable phenomenon known—very inappropriately—as a tidal wave was.

When, by virtue of a convulsion of the terrestrial crust, a portion of the sea-bed rises up, that elevation provokes the abrupt elevation of the mass of water above it, provoking the birth of a liquid tumescence, a veritable hill of water fifteen or twenty meters high, which engenders a wave like the ripples that the fall of a stone provokes in the surface of a tranquil pond; that wave constitutes the "tidal wave."

But because of its size, the wave is then transmitted over the surface of the sea with an enormous velocity. When the eruption of Krakatoa in the Sunda Islands occurred in 1883, the wave was propagated at an average velocity of 750 kilometers and hour, and it traversed the entire width of the Pacific in twelve hours.

That was what Valsorres remembered, and he wondered whether that solitary wave, necessarily having a submarine seismic phenomenon as its origin might not have been produced by a cataclysm that had also engulfed the "Île de France."

His first thought was to go back and see whether the island still existed. On reflection, however, he rejected the idea.

"Let's set a course for Guayaquil first and repair the damage. After that, we'll have plenty of time to return to see whether the Île de France is still in the same location above the surface of the Pacific."

And, without modifying the instructions that he had given his captain, he allowed the *Coulomb*, propelled by its engine and its screw, to cross the distance that separated it from the Ecuadorian port at low speed, in six days.

On 13 May, at nine o'clock in the morning, the Marquis de Valsorres' yacht dropped anchor in the harbor at Guayaquil, on the horizon of which Chimborazo proudly displayed its peak, the summit of which rose 6,310 meters above sea level.

Scarcely had the *Coulomb* moored in the harbor of Guayaquil than the Marquis and Marquise de Valsorres, Espéret and Dr. Portier disembarked on to the soil of the Republic of Ecuador. Le Corvec followed them, going to fulfill the usual formalities and make enquiries regarding the possibility of repairing the damage to his ship.

With regard to the latter point, there was no difficulty. Mr. Samuel W. Harford, shipbroker, indicated a carpentry yard where he could have the tips of the masts remade, the iron sockets of the old ones serving for the new.

In the meantime, the travelers first went to the post office, where they had not found any letter addressed to them *poste restante*. Their disappointment was great, but the director of the office, who spoke English, in which Madame de Valsorres was fluent, told them that he was expecting the mail boat from Panama the following day, which might perhaps bring the expected letter. It was necessary to be content with that hope.

The town is built at the mouth of the river Guayas, more than two kilometers wide at that point; opposite is the village of Duran.

The motor-launch was put into the water and took the *Coulomb*'s passengers for an excursion on the majestic river. After two hours, it brought them back to land where they were able to see and appreciate the "delights" of Ecuadorian civilization.

Guayaquil is a town of forty thousand inhabitants, the principal port of the republic, and it is from the village of Duran on the opposite bank that the railway departs that links the port to the capital of Ecuador, the city of Quito.

The *Coulomb*'s passengers had rapidly absorbed a poor lunch in a posada decorated with the pompous name of the Metropole Hotel in order to wander the ill-kept streets of the low town and stroll for a few moments along the river bank. After that, they went back on board, with the keenest satisfaction. The population, mostly formed of half-breeds, had nothing particularly seductive about it, so they appreciated the return to the comfort and tranquility of their beautiful yacht.

The next day, 14 May, they waited in vain for the arrival of the Panama mail boat. It was late; there was, in consequence no correspondence for which to hope. At four o'clock in the afternoon they had a new excursion in the motor-launch, this time heading down toward the sea,

Early the following day, 15 May, the port semaphores signaled the arrival of the *Cotopaxi*, the steamboat from Panama, with dispatches. To go ashore and to the post office was, for Monsieur and Madame Valsorres, a matter of minutes.

They spent a good hour in front of the counter, but their patience was finally rewarded and the clerk handed them, along with a voluminous correspondence for the ship, the expected letter from the Marquis' sister, Vicomtesse Germaine d'Estrelles.

This is what the letter contained:

Paris, 16 April 1910.
My dear Henri,

I received your letter from Noumea yesterday, and it has given us great joy, while filling us with emotion. What! You and Marie were nearly swallowed up by the vast cemetery of the ocean! I'm still shivering merely at the thought of it.

We palpitated at the story of the rescue of the two Germans whom you snatched from death. How very French it is, big brother, what you did there! To save two of our country's mortal enemies when you had only think of your own security to let them be engulfed by the deep sea! I'm proud of you.

By the way, I've passed on your request for information about the Baron Karl von Osterwald you resuscitated to my husband. George expected to obtain it in Berlin, where he's going in three or four days, but he met a military attaché at the Russian embassy this morning who had been in Berlin before coming to Paris, and asked him the question. By chance, the officer was able to furnish the requested tips.

Baron Karl von Osterwald is a most distinguished technologist, one of the finest graduates of the engineering school in Jena. He has played a major role in the improvement of German war materiel, in particular concerning large caliber artillery. For three years he has been attached to the Krupp factories on behalf of the Prussian Ministry of War. In addition to his technical skills, it appears that he is a considerable scientist, distinguished for important astronomical calculations. He had married a daughter of the high aristocracy of Silesia, the niece of Baron von Paschwitz,[12] colossally rich, so it's said. His wife died some ten years ago, so he's a widower, but—still cording to rumor—he consoles himself for his widowhood in the company of a great aristocratic lady, the wife of a foreign diplomat.

Those are the items of information that Georges was able to obtain. I'm passing them on for what they may be worth.

On reading the name von Paschwitz, the Marquis de Valsorres' expression darkened and his brow furrowed. What memories did the name that had suddenly appeared before his eyes recall to mind? We shall know in due course.

---

[12] This is not consistent with what we subsequently learn about the Paschwitz family, but as it is an item of hearsay, it might be the case that Georges' informant was simply mistaken.

After a momentary interruption, he continued reading his sister's letter:

Now, my dear big brother. I'll tell you about a terrible alarm I had last night.

We had had dinner with the neighbors I mentioned to you, Baron and Baronne Lymstroem, who live in one of the two houses whose gardens are adjacent to ours. Our guests had taken their leave at eleven o'clock and gone home. We had returned to our bedroom when the children's nurse knocked on the door violently.

"Madame! Madame!" she said. "Come quickly. Little Henri is terribly ill."

You can imagine the state I was in. I went to the little cot. The poor child was coughing; he was putting his hand to his mouth, and it appeared that he was choking. I was frightened.

I was asking Georges to fetch a doctor, when I remembered that the other neighboring house was occupied by a famous physician, Dr. Frank, and I asked my husband to go and find him. At that moment, through the trees, a light was visible in his window, so he hadn't gone to bed. Georges went downstairs.

Five minutes later he came back, bringing Dr. Frank.

He went to the cot and examined my poor baby impassively. After a few moments, he said: "It's nothing, We'll save him." Then, taking a syringe and a bottle from his bag, he gave the dear child an injection of serum.

"Don't worry, Madame," he said to me. "Your child is safe."

Oh, that man! How I blessed him for saying that, and for his miraculous intervention.

Georges saw him to the door. The physician is a scientist, very absorbed in his work, so, when my husband asked him whether he knew his neighbors, Baron and Baronne Lymstroem, he replied that he only knew them by sight.

Georges came back, glad to have gone to fetch him. We're going to invite him to dinner one day with the Baron and Baronne, whose complete acquaintance he will thus make.

I have no need to tell you about the devotion of dear Aunt Hélène during that alarm; she never quit the little invalid, and it was her who lent the doctor assistance when he recognized her competence. Curiously enough, though, Dr. Frank's face doesn't suit her either. She has these inexplicable natural antipathies.

After all, the physician saved my little Henri; that's sufficient for him to have a right to all our gratitude, and we won't spare it.

Those, my dear Henri, are the events that I have to announce to you; I wish you bon voyage, and a safe and prompt return. Kiss my pretty sister-in-law for me; give our best wishes to your faithful Espéret and receive an affectionate kiss from your sister,

Germaine.

The Marquis handed the letter to his wife, who read it.

When she reached the name of Paschwitz, she also started, and looked at her husband. "Always that accursed name, pursuing us all the way to the middle of the ocean!" she exclaimed.

"Yes, my love, yes. When shall we have reckoned with that execrable family?"

And they both remained thoughtful.

XII. In which the Marquis de Valsorres and his friend Espéret believe
that they can declare themselves
free of all anxiety.

A week had gone by, during which the damage to the *Coulomb* was repaired, the spires of the three masts and the outer tip of its bowsprit remade by
local carpenters. The Ecuadorian workmen were slow, but they had no more to
do than shape the topmasts, for fitting them in position the excellent mariners of
the yacht were there, and no artisan could have rivaled them in accomplishing
that task, in which they deployed marvelous skill.

The repairs were finished on 23 May.

The passengers had put their correspondence for Europe—via Panama-
Colon—in the post and the *Coulomb*, with its new topmasts, had set out to sea,
heading westwards. That was because Henri de Valsorres wanted to verify the
exactitude of his hypotheses regarding the tidal wave that had broken the rigging
of his ship, on the spot. In that case, perhaps the Île de France had either been
modified in its aspect by a particularly serious seismic event, or even swallowed
by the waters, like the island of Julia in the Greek archipelago at the beginning
of the nineteenth century.[13]

The *Coulomb*, his time impelled by following winds, made the journey
with the wind almost directly astern; it reached its maximum sped and showed
all of its brilliant nautical qualities. Less than six days after leaving Guayaquil,
the yacht was on the hundred and fifth west meridian, at a latitude of two degrees. They were, in consequence beginning to approach the Île de France,
whose position, the reader will doubtless recall, had been determined to be a
hundred and five degrees and thirty minutes west longitude and five degrees two
minutes of south latitude.

A course was therefore set south-south-west, and the speed moderated,
bringing in the topsails. At noon the following day, Captain Le Corvec, on the
one hand, and Espéret, on the other, each took the point with rigorous precision.
The result was: latitude five degrees two minutes; longitude a hundred and five
degrees five minutes. They were, in consequence, slightly to the east of the Île
de France.

The course was set westwards. The latitude did not change, and as they
were only twenty-five minutes—which is to say, twenty-five sea miles, the degrees of the parallel scarcely differing from the degrees of the meridian in the

---

[13] Julia was the name given to the island in question by the French; it appeared
above the surface of the Mediterranean after an eruption in 1831 and sank again
in 1832, after a fierce political controversy in which sovereignty was claimed by
four different nations. The English called it Graham Island.

vicinity of the equator—from the island, they surely ought to have perceived the island after two or three hours of navigation.

At two o'clock in the afternoon they had certainly covered twenty miles, and ought to have been within sight of the isle, or at least the plume of smoke escaping from the central peak; but nothing appeared on the horizon. The waters of the ocean were splendidly tranquil everywhere, brushed by the perpetual caress of the trade winds, fully meriting, this time, the name of Pacific.

Valsorres and Espéret were on the bridge beside the captain. The latter turned to the two scientists.

"Well, Messieurs," he said, drawing a formidable puff of smoke from his pipe. "I believe that our island has done a bunk."

"Oh, I hope that's true, Captain," said Valsorres.

"But I'm quite sure I'm not mistaken. The point that Monsieur Espéret and I took at noon gave us a latitude and longitude twenty-five miles east of the island. We've been traveling for a little over two hours at ten knots. We ought, therefore, to be within a mile of the island's location."

"In that case, we ought to be able to see it, and we don't," said Espéret. "In which case, old friend...."

"Oh, if that's so, if those accursed Germans, when they come back—for they will come back, that's certain—will no longer find it! What a disappointment for them and what tranquility for us! But it's necessary to be entirely certain of the disappearance of the Île de France. What do you think, Le Corvec?"

The captain reflected momentarily, and then said: "We can activate the engine, Monsieur le Marquis, and describe large circles around this point of the sea for a day or two. Every day, we'll take three heights in order to have the point as rigorously as possible. If, after that, we haven't found the island, well, we can set a course for Europe."

"Well, Captain, do as you say."

For two days the *Coulomb* described large circles on the surface of the sea around the location where the Île de France ought to have been. Three times a day, at nine o'clock, noon and three o'clock in the afternoon, Le Corvec and Espéret, with the aid of their sextants and chronometers, determined the lines of the sun's height whose intersection gave them the ship's exact position. The results were concordant; the yacht was circling the position where the island ought to be, and no longer was.

There was no doubt about it; the tidal wave that had assailed the *Coulomb* definitely originated from a cataclysm in the earth's crust, and that cataclysm had engulfed the Île de France with its layers of radioactive minerals.

It was four o'clock in the afternoon. Espéret and Valsorres could not hide their joy.

"Let's go down and announce the good news to the Marquise and the doctor."

The latter were on the deck. At the announcement of the disappearance of the island, they clapped their hands.

At that moment, Thomas, his napkin under his arm, appeared in the doorway of the deckhouse to announce that tea was served.

He did not have time to finish. A gigantic albatross, flying almost at sea level, had passed over the rail like an arrow and had butted the unfortunate Thomas in the stomach, knocking him over.

The doctor ran to him, but he got up immediately.

"It's nothing, Doctor," he said. "It's all right! These things only happen to me."

And now, let us take our reader back forty years. We are about to see characters appear whose names we have already heard, and read a story that will throw some light on the events with which we shall be occupied subsequently.

PART TWO: THE HERITAGE OF HATRED

I. In which we see how officers of the Prussian Guard amuse themselves.

On the night on 24-25 December 1870, a dozen Prussian officers were finishing getting drunk in the main hall of the magnificent Château de Herrenhof, situated in the vicinity of the village of Hochfeld, not far from Wissenburg, in the far north of Alsace.

Lying—or, rather, sprawling—on sofas, and armchairs in the purest Louis XVI style, they had eaten and drunk so much during that all-night party that they seemed absolutely incapable of drinking any more. And yet, one of them, who was smoking an enormous cigar, had stood up heavily, had rung, and had hurled at the orderly automaton who came running, in a thick voice, the single word: "Champagne!"

The orderly made an about turn, and the officer fell back in his armchair.

A few moments later, four soldiers appeared, each carrying a basket of bottles, which they had just taken from the cellar of the Marquis de Valsorres, the owner of the château.

The bottles having been uncorked and the glasses refilled, the soldiers withdrew briskly.

On hearing the corks popping, the officers had all stood up as best they could, and, staggering, had approached the table, on which there was an immense silver tray laden with glasses.

"To His Majesty!" said General von Barfeld, draining his glass with difficulty.

"Hoch! Hoch! Hurrah!" the officers responded. And they drank with a unison that denoted all the power of Prussian discipline.

"To the glory of our invincible army!"

"Hoch! Hoch! Hurrah!" responded the chorus of reiters. A further draught descended into the insatiable throats.

"To our definitive victory, the crushing of France and the French!" the general continued.

"Hoch! Hoch! Hurrah!" howled his subalterns, absorbing a third glass. Then they returned to their seats, with difficulty.

A thick cloud of smoke son enveloped those brutes, who did not take long to fall into a heavy sleep under the effect of the good food, alcohol and wine.

Suddenly, one of them, Major von Schwabach, gave a mighty thump to the sideboard next to his armchair, and shouted in a voice that woke everyone up: "Women! *Donnerwetter!*"

"Schwabach!" howled the general. "You ought to be ashamed to speak thus, you, a soldier on campaign!"

They a young rosy-cheeked blonde lieutenant replied: "With your permission, General, the Major has just expressed a thought that is common to us all."

"Von Paschwitz is right!" cried several officers.

The general became furious. "Gentlemen, gentlemen," he said. "I would like, by reason of the festival we have just celebrated so worthily, not to attach any importance to your extravagant words. But don't persist!"

"In that case," said Colonel von Trauwitz, who had not opened his mouth until then, "Let's have some fireworks, if His Excellency will permit?"

The general replied: "Go ahead."

Without waiting any longer, the colonel rang. Six soldiers came into the hall.

"Listen," said the colonel to one of them. "You know the three farmhouses at the bottom of the hill where the château stands?"

"Yes, Colonel."

"Well, you and three others will go and douse the roofs of those farmhouses and the surrounding trees with gasoline."

"Yes, Colonel."

"After which, you'll set fire to the lot. Understood?"

"Yes, Colonel."

"Go then, and quickly. Don't hang around!"

The soldiers went out.

The officers installed themselves next to the windows and continued smoking and drinking. Less than half an hour later, and immense sheaf of flames sprang forth in the dark night. The officers burst out laughing.

"Put the lights out!" cried the general. "They're preventing us from seeing the magnificent illuminations."

At that moment, the double doors of the main hall opened, and a vibrant voice cried in French: "Monsieur le Marquis de Valsorres!"

The officers turned their heads and perceived, standing on the threshold, the noble gentleman who had just been introduced like a stranger into his own drawing room.

"Still up at this hour, Monsieur le Marquis!" cried General von Barfeld, taking a few steps toward the party-pooper.

"Yes, General, and I don't understand your astonishment."

"Explain yourself, Monsieur le Marquis."

The Marquis gestured toward the window, indicating the conflagration.

"It's admirable, isn't it, that immense nocturnal illumination," von Barfeld continued. "Look how brightly its illuminating the whole area! One can almost see the church tower of Wissemburg. One could read a newspaper in this drawing room. Isn't it colossal?"

"Monsieur..."

"It's war—what do you expect, Monsieur le Marquis?"

"No, Monsieur. War doesn't consist of pillaging châteaux, sending the silverware and furniture to Germany, emptying the cellar and setting fire to farms, as you've just done."

"Of what does it consist, then, I pray you?"

"Of fighting loyally and sparing the occupied territory."

"Oh, good! That was the manner of your Emperor, the great Napoléon," added von Barfeld, with an ironic smile.

"And that of his generals," relied the Marquis. "They were not looters and bandits, like yours."

The officers had stood up and were already launching themselves toward the Marquis.

"Enough, Monsieur, and thank heaven for having spoken to me as you have tonight, for at any other time I wouldn't have been content to confine you to your bedroom with two sentinels at your door."

"Bravo!" said the officers.

"You're imprisoning me, then?" cried the Marquis.

"That's what I said." He rang, and gave orders to the two soldiers who came in.

Without responding to his ironic salute, the Marquis left the hall, followed by his two jailers.

"You spoke like a great leader to that insolent Marquis," cried Lieutenant Otto von Paschwitz. "And since he complains of our pillage, let's not belie him. When shall we take away the furniture of the Château de Herrenhof?"

"Tomorrow."

"In that case, I request the authorization to send the garniture of the mantelpiece of this hall to my schloss in Silesia."

"Pardon me, Lieutenant," said a tall, stiff major, "but I had exactly the same idea."

"Me too!" said several others.

The general imposed silence with a gesture. "That's enough, Messieurs. "I'll attribute to everyone what he ought to have. Now, gentlemen, I won't keep you any longer."

"At your orders, General!"

They got up, saluted their chief with characteristic automatic rigidity, and withdrew.

Von Barfeld darted one last glance at the farms that were still burning, and went to bed.

II. In which one can see how a French gentleman conducts himself with regard to barbarians.

The Marquis de Valsorres, followed by two soldiers, had returned to his story, where his daughter Hélène was standing; she too had witnessed, dolorously, the burning of the three farms.

By the light of the flames, the young woman was weeping on seeing that land, so rich and populous the day before, become wretched, abandoned and uncultivated as a result of the war. For, with the exception of the Marquis, his daughter, a few old domestics and the venerable curé of Hochfeld, all the inhabitants had fled before the invaders.

She was weeping in thinking that her maternal grandfather, Sébastien Holtz, the Maire of Lixheim, had been put in prison by those same bandits, some of whom before the war, had received the hospitality of the great Alsatian industrialist.

She was weeping in thinking that her country had been invaded, crushed and defeated. She wept in thinking that her brother Robert de Valsorres, a captain in the twelfth chasseurs, had not sent any news for more than a month, and that he had then been not far from Sedan.

Finally, she was weeping because the cries of joy and triumph of the soldiers had reached her, and had broken her heart.

The Marquis came in. He saw his daughter's beautiful face inundated with tears.

"Hélène!" he said, simply.

The young woman immediately wiped away her tears.

"Don't cry, my child. Sad as such a spectacle is, it's necessary not to be softened by it, for discouragement comes quickly. The wretches didn't want to put out that fire, which they lit with so much joy. I protested, and they've confined me, with two sentinels at my door.

"You're a prisoner, then?"

"Yes."

"Then I won't leave you, Father."

"That's also my intention, for I don't want to expose you alone, at any price, in the midst of these brutes."

"One of them, especially!"

The Marquis was stuck by his daughter's last words. "Has one of them lacked respect for you? Then woe betide him," he said, clenching his fists menacingly.

"No, They're all so basely, flatly polite that I'm astonished. But there's one I find more repulsive than the rest."

"Von Paschwitz?" asked the Marquis. "That Pole who's betrayed all the traditions of his fatherland in order to rally to the flag of the oppressors of his country?"

"Yes," the young woman replied.

"And that to obtain a commission and the confirmation of the property of his lands in Posnania and Silesia!"

"How do you know all that, Father?"

"From Prince Martorysky, who told me the story at the club some time before the war. He is, in any case, worthy of his new masters. But you're tired, my child. Go to sleep. Bonsoir, my Hélène."

The young woman went to offer her forehead to her father's kiss, and retired to her bedroom.

In the profound silence that hung over the country, she sat down in a large armchair near the fireplace and drifted into a reverie. The image of von Paschwitz haunted her. She saw him, obsequious and smiling, inclining his tall stature before her when she encountered him in the park or in a corridor of the château, and his gray eyes then fixed themselves upon her with a persistence that shocked her throughout her being, like an impure contact.

Finally, weary and exhausted, she fell into a deep sleep.

The next day after going down to the chapel in the early morning, she encountered the Prussian officer in the large vestibule. He gazed, with a sentiment that he did not succeed in dissimulating, at the pure oval of that beautiful blue-eyed face, crowned with magnificent blonde hair, the supple and slender figure, the shoulders whose perfection could be divined beneath the black neckline that hid them—in sum, all the beauty that made Mademoiselle Hélène de Valsorres the most adorable of creatures.

He bowed humbly before her and stammered a few words.

Hélène was walking upright and proud.

A distant burst of rifle fire then burst out.

Von Paschwitz shivered and listened.

"Pass, Mademoiselle," he said, standing side.

She scarcely nodded her head, and slowly went back to her father's study. At that moment, the fusillade, momentarily interrupted, resumed more forcefully,

"Do you hear?" said the Marquis.

"Yes, and Paschwitz, whom I encountered downstairs, seemed surprised just now on hearing that gunfire."

At that moment, a uhlan, a German cavalryman, came into the courtyard of the château at the gallop. Officers emerged in haste and ran toward the soldier, whom they questioned swiftly.

Silence fell.

The Marquis and his daughter were exchanging their impressions when the door of the study suddenly opened and Major von Schwabach appeared.

"His Excellency General von Barfeld wants you," he said, rudely, to Monsieur de Valsorres. "Follow me."

The Marquis looked at him proudly.

"I precede you," he said.

The reiter doubtless did not understand, and the Marquis, marching ahead, went into Barfeld's quarters. Without even offering him a seat, the latter said to him in a ferocious voice: "Do you know what's happening?"

"How can I know, since you're keeping me prisoner?"

"You don't know? This is it: snipers, bandits hidden in a wood, have attacked one of our cavalry patrols, killing six men and the commanding officer."

"Oh."

"If, between now and tomorrow, the murderers are not delivered to me, it's you, in your capacity as Maire of this village, that I'll hold responsible for the murder of those brave men."

"I don't know who they are and I don't know where they're hiding, and if I knew, I wouldn't tell you."

"That's your business. If you haven't delivered them by tomorrow, you'll pass under arms. I'll lift your arrest in order that you can carry out the necessary research." Turning to the two sentinels, he said: "This man is free, under your surveillance, and you'll answer to me for him!"

The Marquis went back to his study. He knew that he was condemned. When he found himself in the presence of his daughter, he looked at her for a long time.

"Hélène," he said, "I'm obliged to leave you."

She could not repress a sharp movement of surprise.

"Von Barfeld has charged me with a mission relative to the prisoners of war. I'll be leaving the château this evening."

The young woman stared at her father. "You're not telling me the truth, Father. You're hiding something. Take me with you; don't leave me alone here. I'm strong; I'm a Valsorres, and neither fatigues nor dangers frighten me—but don't leave me alone in the midst of these brutes."

"Impossible, my child. Now, let's kiss one another as if you were never going to see me again—for in war, you know, one never knows what might happen."

The young woman threw herself into her father's arms, sobbing. He held her for a long time. Then he looked at her, as if he wanted to fix in his memory, eternally, the cherished features of her pure face.

"Now," he said, "leave me, my dear child. I have instructions to give, papers to put in order and letters to write. Go, my daughter, don't worry; I'm not running any other risk than that of the journey."

Left alone, the Marquis reflected for some time. Then, after having made a gesture of despair, he sat down at his desk and began to write on a large sheet of paper

To my son... To my daughter...

Having concluded the testament, he rang and asked his domestic to fetch the venerable curé of Hochfeld.

In the meantime, Hélène, who had not been duped by her father's words, and had resolved not to quit him, made preparations with her chambermaid for her departure. She was putting the indispensable objects into a small valise when someone knocked on the door.

The maidservant went to open it, and came back immediately.

"It's Lieutenant von Paschwitz, who wants to speak to Mademoiselle."

"Tell him that I can't see him."

But then the officer pushed the door and came into the bedroom.

"Monsieur!" said Hélène, indignantly. "Get out! Your conduct is that of a..."

"Not when you now the imperious reasons that have led me to force your door, Mademoiselle." He turned to the chambermaid. "Leave us!" he said to her.

"Catherine," Hélène said to her maid, "stay in the little room next door."

"Oh, have no fear, Mademoiselle! If the circumstances weren't so grave, my respect alone would be sufficient to reassure you."

Hélène sat down, leaving her interlocutor standing.

"I'm listening," she said.

"You certainly know about last night's events," said the lieutenant.

"What? The burning of the farms?"

"No, the attack on one of our patrols by snipers."

"Well?"

"Well, General von Barfeld is holding the Marquis de Valsorres, as Maire of the village of Hochfeld, responsible for the murder of our men."

"Oh! So?"

"So, tomorrow morning, at eight o'clock, if the murderers aren't discovered, your father will be shot by a firing squad in their place."

"Ah! Wretch! cried the young woman. "That's a vengeance well worthy of the creature devoid of honor that you are! Swine! Coward!"

The lieutenant interrupted her. "Let's speak reasonably, I beg you, Mademoiselle. Do you want your father to be saved?"

"Do I want it? Oh, yes!" she said.

"Well, I can telegraph my uncle, Graf von Paschwitz, whose sole heir I am, and who is His Majesty's counselor, immediately. I can ask him to have the sentence annulled, and your father is saved."

The young woman put her hands together. "Oh, do that, Monsieur, I beg you."

"I'd like to—but on one condition."

"What?"

"Mademoiselle, like you I belong to a family of the old nobility. I'm not responsible for this war. I want you to cease regarding me as an enemy, and I ask you, in order to save your father, to consent to be my wife and call yourself the Gräfin von Paschwitz."

Hélène had a moment of revolt. A violent conflict took place within her. What, she the daughter of a lineage of heroic soldiers of France, become the Gräfin von Paschwitz, the wife of a Prussian officer! To figure in the court of Wilhelm of Prussia!"

On looking at the officer who was standing motionless before her, however, she understood that neither tears nor prayers could bend his implacable resolution. She stood up, straight and proud, and with an unparalleled nobility, she uttered the simple phrase that represented, for her, the most terrible of sacrifices:

"I accept."

A flash of triumphant joy shone in von Paschwitz's eyes. "Oh, Mademoiselle," he said, bowing deeply. "You have just given me a superhuman joy."

"Go, Monsieur," Hélène replied. Go—and if you keep your word, I shall keep mine...unless it is impossible.

"Everything is possible! Everything!" he said, as he withdrew.

III. In which it is seen that the heroism of the father cedes nothing to that of the daughter.

As soon as she was alone, Hélène ran to her father.

On seeing her, the latter understood at a glance that she knew the whole truth.

"Who...?" he asked her.

"Paschwitz."

"Naturally! Oh, the filthy swine! Oh, the bandits! To insult the dolor of a young woman whose father they're going to shoot!"

"No, Father, you're mistaken; on the contrary, Paschwitz wants to save you."

"Him!" The Marquis started at his daughter. "Hélène, the truth! I demand it!"

"Yes, Father, he'll save you if I become his wife," she said, blushing in shame and lowering her eyes.

"And you've consented?"

"I want to save you, Father, for my sake even more than for yours. Oh, I beg you, let me give you this proof of my affection and my devotion. What do you think will become of me if you die—you, my Father, my protector, my friend? I implore you, permit me to keep the promise I've made."

"I forbid you to do it," cried the Marquis, indignantly. "You, the wife of that renegade Pole, that accursed Prussian! Never! Never! I'd rather see you dead in front of me than know you were married to that wretch. A Valsorres, Gräfin von Paschwitz! No, no! Never! Never, do you hear! And I order you to go tell that incendiary that the Valsorres do not betray honor; that a life is not worth living if it is bought at the price of infamy. Go, my child, be courageous and receive the last adieu of your father, who blesses you and admires you. Be worthy of us until the end. Adieu, my Hélène! Adieu!"

Weeping, the young woman threw herself into her father's arms. He hugged her one last time."

"Tomorrow," he said, "When...it's all over, leave the château and go with the curé to the presbytery.. There, he'll make my instructions known to you. You'll follow them, won't you?"

"Yes, Father."

"Go, my child. Adieu."

On leaving her father's study, adjacent to the main hall, Hélène found herself face to face with the Graf von Paschwitz.

On seeing the distraught face of the young woman, her eyes filled with tears, the officer went pale.

"Monsieur," Hélène said to him in a firm voice, "My father has not authorized me to accept the offer you have made me."

"It is necessary, then, for me to renounce the project that would have made me the happiest of men?"

"It is necessary, Monsieur."

The lieutenant remained silent for a moment; then, addressing Hélène, he said to her, in a voice trembling with anger: "Very well, Mademoiselle. I love you; I adore you like a divinity. You have just inflicted the greatest dolor of my life upon me. I shall never forget it—never! You hear me!"

As she kept silent he continued: "Later, perhaps, much later, I might be able no longer to suffer from this amour to which you've given birth in me. But even if I live to be a hundred, I shall remember until my final hour the Mademoiselle de Valsorres refused to become the Gräfin von Paschwitz. And the bloody insult that you have made me will, I swear, be terribly avenged!"

And with the stiffness of an automaton, he bowed and disappeared.

The next morning, after a summary interrogation and a simulacrum of judgment, the Marquis de Valsorres was taken into the park of the château and placed in such a fashion that he was facing his daughter's apartment; von Paschwitz had wanted that refinement of cruelty.

His head high, his eyes fixed on the window behind which he divined the presence of the beloved child that he was leaving alone, the noble gentleman fell under the bullets of twelve German soldiers, commanded by von Paschwitz himself.

After having rendered her father the final duties, Hélène took refuge in the presbytery.

Disguised as a farm servant, she fled the same day and succeeded in reaching Luxemburg, passing into Belgium, and then to England, and ended up arriving in Touraine, at the Château de Valsorres, the cradle of the Marquis' family.

Before quitting Hochfeld in the evening, however, darting one last glance at the country she had loved so much, her heart had quivered dolorously. Flames springing from every window of the château were beginning to illuminate the landscape. She understood that after having pillaged the ancestral home, the men that history sometimes calls soldiers, but whom civilized people still call bandits, had set fire to the château in order to erase the traces of their thefts.

*IV. In which, while witnessing the last moments of
Graf von Paschwitz, the reader will make the
acquaintance of two characters in the present story*

Years have passed!

Oberlieutenant Otto von Paschwitz has become General von Paschwitz.

He has inherited the title and immense fortune of his uncle, as well as his magnificent castle in Silesia and the vast domains that surround it.

If he did not, in his twenty-five year military career—for it is now 1898—surpass the rank of Brigadier-General, it was because of his execrable character, for he rendered himself as insupportable to the army as to the court of Berlin. And in order not to be supported in those two milieux when one is the Graf von Paschwitz, it was truly necessary to be "a surly brute."

Retired to his castle, he no longer left it. He spent his life hunting, smoking, eating, drinking, playing chess and beating his servants.

One evening, after a formidable orgy, he fell, struck by an apoplexy, in the corner of his hearth. Thanks to his Herculean constitution, he got away with a slight paralysis of the right side. But three months later, scorning the pressing advice of his physician, he had recommenced his excesses; a second attack, much more serious than the first had been the consequence of his intemperance.

Seeing that he was doomed, his physician had not wanted to assume the sole responsibility for the catastrophe, and he had summoned to Paschwitz two medical celebrities from Berlin: Professor Scheisser and Professor Arschmann. But they had only been able to confirm their colleague's terrible diagnosis.

All three had gathered around the dying man's bed, examining him appropriately, when the latter, who had been mute and motionless for three days, suddenly raised himself up on his elbow, to the great stupor of the three heirs of Aesculapius, and, blinking one eye, said to them in a faint voice: "How many days have I to live?" And, as the physicians remained silent: "Reply, *gott verdammt!* If you aren't asses, as I believe."

"In four days, You Excellency will no longer be of this world."

For a short while, the Graf did not say a word, deeply immersed in somber thoughts. After a few minutes he said: "Call Arnold!" And he turned his back on his physicians, who withdrew in order to carry out the wish of the invalid by ending up old Arnold, the Graf's steward and confidant.

When the servant was in his master's presence, he latter simply said: "Do as I order you to do."

Three days later, in the large vestibule lined with the antlers of stags, the tusks of wild boar and hunting pikes, old Arnold is walking anxiously back and forth, looking out of a high window at the snow-powdered fir trees and the immense white carpet that covers the park and, in the distance, the entire landscape.

A light is burning in a window in the large tower; it is there, on an iron bed, that Graf von Paschwitz is about to die.

Two nurses are at the bedside of the dying man, whose gaze goes incessantly to a tall oak-framed pendulum clock. He murmurs: "They're not coming! As long as they arrive in time!"

Finally the noise of little bells resounds in the courtyard.

Arnold has run out.

A sleigh drawn by three horses, sliding over the hardened snow, stops in front of the perron. A tall young man gets down.

"I'm Wilhelm!" And, as Arnold says nothing, the young man adds: "The man the Graf is expecting. Then Arnold bows, with the greatest respect, and conducts the traveler into a drawing room on the first floor, where a copious collation has been set out on a table.

"You've come alone?" asks the old steward.

The young man seems astonished by the question, and replies affirmatively. Then, approaching the take, he pours himself a large glass of hot punch, which he drinks in a single draught.

On seeing his tall stature and his athletic build, Arnold found the gesture quite natural, and he would have been even less surprised had he remarked that, with his broad forehead, his powerful square jaw, his red hair and his gaze, simultaneously intelligent and malevolent, that the man could not be a ordinary individual.

While the traveler is restoring himself, another sleigh comes into the courtyard of the castle. A young woman of eighteen or nineteen gets out of it.

Arnold runs to meet her.

"I'm Emma, the woman the Graf is expecting."

The steward then introduces her into the drawing room where the young man who named himself as Wilhelm is already waiting.

With the same marks of respect, he withdraws, not without having noticed that the young woman possesses the strong and massive beauty of German women, that she has large blue eyes devoid of the slightest expression, superb blonde hair, an opulent bosom, a fine figure and seems, although distinguished, arrogant and haughty.

Left alone, the two young people, after ceremoniously greeting one another, examine one another curiously, without saying a word.

After a few moments however, Arnold comes back and asks them to follow him. Both obey, and they are introduced into the room where Graf von Paschwitz is dying.

The two nurses withdraw, the Graf and the two travelers remain alone. The newcomers' surprise, already great, increases as the dying man, whom they do not know, speaks, addressing them in a halting fashion.

"I'm about to die…! Before quitting this world…I wanted to see you both to tell you…that your mother's name was Wilhelmina… She was the daughter of Hans Frank, my gamekeeper… She was my mistress and…you are my children... Yes, my children!.... My children…*mine!*"

And as the two young people, amazed, remained silent: "Your mother, Emma, died giving birth to you."

Exhausted by sickness and suffering, he fell silent.

The two children looked at him with a curiosity as ardent as the one with which they had looked at one another.

As the voice of the invalid weakened, they drew nearer to the bed.

"Give me that potion on the table to drink…it will give me the strength to go on."

Emma handed him the glass, the contents of which he drank avidly.

"I didn't marry your mother because I had made an oath never to marry, but I have done everything to give you a brilliant existence."

"Father," said the young man, taking his hand. "I thank you from the bottom of my heart for what you've already done for me, in permitting me to study at the University of Jena."

"And you've become a distinguished physician…and a famous scientist, already…I know that!"

"And," said the young woman, "in having me brought up be the canonesses of Wittelsbach, with the noblest and richest heiresses in Germany, you've placed me in an elevated class of aristocratic society.!"

"You were my daughter."

"Father, I too thank you from the bottom of my heart."

They both considered him for a long time, in silence. Then, suddenly, lifting himself up painfully, he said: "Listen…come closer…what I have to tell you now that I sense death approaching, is of the greatest importance. I'm giving you my entire fortune, in equal parts…here's a duplicate copy of my will…"

"Father!" they exclaimed, interrupting him.

"Shut up and listen…both of you. I'm also bequeathing you the mortal hatred that I've always had, first against France, and then against a French family, one member of which once inflicted the most terrible of insults upon me."

"Its name?" asked the young man.

The Valsorres family. Read this!" he said, handing them a second sealed envelope. "I want you to swear to me to execute my last will!"

"We swear!"

"You, Wilhelm," he said, taking the young man's hand, "Will put your science and your fortune at the service of that double hatred."

"You will be obeyed, Father."

"You, Emma, must use all the means, all the seductions and all the resources of which an educated woman as beautiful and rich as you has at her disposal.

"I promise you, Father."

After a pause, the young man addressed the dying man: "Will you permit us Father, if it's useful, to conserve our mother's name? That might aid us in the accomplishment of the mission that we've sworn to accomplish."

The Graf had a smile of satanic satisfaction on hearing his son's words. "Good, Wilhelm...you're worthy of me! Keep your mother's name, under which you've already become famous, for as long as it might be useful to you. And on the day when you and your sister wish it, here is a document that authorizes you to take the title and name of von Paschwitz."

Again, he fell silent. Then, sensing that his end was near, he said: "Swear to your dying father to obey him!"

"We swear!"

"Go now, and leave me alone with my memories."

They each took one of the hands of the dying man, which they raised to their lips.

"Adieu...my children," said the Graf, in an even fainter voice. "Adieu...and remember!"

Slowly, they left the room.

Then, the two of them, finding themselves alone in the drawing room that preceded it, fell into one another's arms.

"My brother!"

"My sister!"

A few hours later, General Graf von Paschwitz rendered his soul to the Devil, after a frightful agony.

In 1898, several persons whom we know already, at least by name, are gathered in the Château de Valsorres, in Touraine.

First of all, there is the General Marquis de Valsorres, who, having been taken into captivity in Germany after the battle of Sedan, although he was then a simple captain, had had to suffer the harshest treatments as a result of the vindictive pursuit of Graf Otto von Paschwitz.

Returned to France, he had married and had two children, Henri and Germaine; at that time, Henri was twenty-three and Germane seventeen.

His young wife, whose health was delicate, had died in 1882.[14] Mademoiselle Hélène de Valsorres, the young woman we know, who was then twenty-

---

[14] The text I have has 1878, but that is clearly incompatible with Germaine being 17 in 1898, so I have amended the date to remove the inconsistency. Along with one or two other impossible dates, the error offers some support to the hypothesis that part of the text was written some time before 1822 and had a different chronology. The subsequent statement that Hélène is now forty-three might also be reckoned also dubious, as it implies that she was only fifteen or sixteen in the previous chapters, but I have not altered it.

four years old, declared to her brother that she would not marry and would serve as a mother to his two children.

At twenty, young Henri de Valsorres, who had entered the École Polytechnique sixth, had emerged first, as a pupil engineer in the Corps des Mines, and Germaine had become the most exquisite of young women. After the war, Captain de Valsorres, who had inherited the title of Marquis, had sold his properties in Alsace, and the family lived in Touraine, in the château that the general only left to attend sessions of the senior Council of War, of which he was one of the luminaries.

By an extraordinary coincidence, in that month of December 1898, General de Valsorres had only a few days to live, like the man who had been his father's murderer twenty-eight years before.

His sister Hélène, still beautiful in spite of her forty-three years, had asked the illustrious Dr. Portier to come from Paris. The latter had not hidden the gravity of the situation from the family. As the savant practitioner had promised the general a prompt recovery, the latter had shaken his head, like a man under no illusion.

A few days after the doctor's departure, he summoned his two children.

He recommended them always to have for their Aunt Hélène the affection they would have had for their own mother; never to forget that they had in their veins, as well as the blood of a lineage of noble gentlemen, the purest Alsatian blood; and always to remember that the Germans had shot their grandfather under the orders of a Paschwitz because their Aunt Hélène had refused to become the wife of that ferocious Prussian.

He made them promise always to love, above all, France, their great and dear fatherland, to which they ought, to sacrifice everything: family, fortune, life—everything except honor.

And, after having rested his gaze for a long time on the three individuals he loved more than anything in the world, Marquis de Valsorres quietly rendered his soul to God.

Le marquis de Valsohre

Zabeth

PART THREE: THE DEPARTURE

I. In the course of which the reader will be introduced to the Valsorres estate and make the acquaintance of the château and its dependencies.

Two years have gone by since we saw the yacht *Coulomb* make its curious and useful voyage in the Pacific Ocean.

The Marquis de Valsorres, having returned to France with his young wife, his inseparable friend Espéret and Dr. Portier, not forgetting the faithful Thomas, only stayed in Paris briefly before installing himself in the magnificent Château de Valsorres, his family's historic domain.

The Château de Valsorres is situated in Touraine, not far from the Loire; a small river, the Louchet, traverses its park, 1,200 hectares in area and completely surrounded by high walls, always maintained in perfect condition.

One penetrates into the park through a monumental gate, to the left of which is the house of the concierge, an old servant, who lodges there with his wife and his son Jérôme, one of the Marquis' gamekeepers. A truly royal driveway, bordered with plane trees, leads to a vast lawn surrounding a basin placed in front of the perron of the château, and the latter displays its grandiose, slightly severe but truly beautiful façade, at the end of the drive, this closing its seigneurial perspective.

Built under Louis XIII, the Château de Valsorres had been restored under the Second Empire by the savant architect Eugène Viollet-le-Duc, who had been able, while repairing "the insults of time," to conserve the style of the original construction in all its purity.

The main building is composed of a ground floor, raised up above the basement, to which one accedes by means of a monumental perron of ten steps, giving access, through a door with open panels, to the large vestibule. That vestibule occupies the anterior part of a central block, on either side of which extend two wings, each of which has a backward extension; those two extensions, with the central block, frame the courtyard of the château, from which, through a second gate, one reaches the main pathway of the park. To the left of the château, properly speaking, hidden by clumps of trees, are the outbuildings, the stables and the garages where the masters' vehicles are housed.

Let us avoid, for the moment, entering the sumptuous ground floor drawing rooms; let us take that pathway and follow it all the way to the vicinity of the surrounding wall; having arrived there and turning right, let us take a lateral path that we follow for about two hundred meters. We arrive in front of a wall constructed inside the park, hidden from indiscreet gazes by a thick curtain of trees.

That very high wall, the crest of which is bristling with "artichokes" in barbed iron to prevent any attempt at climbing over it, is only pierced by a single door, very tall, in cast iron, capable of resisting a 75mm shell. An electric bell is placed to the right of that door, which only opens to a ring effected in accordance with a determined rhythm.

Once through that door, one finds oneself in the enclosure so jealously guarded from all gazes. After traversing a small courtyard bordered by two hangars, under which numerous crates are piled up, one arrives at the door of a small pavilion raised by two steps. When one has passed through a square vestibule, one opens a door to the right, which gives access to a windowless room, the floor, walls and ceiling of which are covered with thick lead plates. Only the light of four large electric lamps, diffused by translucent globes, illuminates that room, which external daylight never penetrates.

On massive oak tables, precision instruments are installed: galvanometers, electrometers, spectroscopes, and various manometers. In one corner, a vast sink surmounted by shelves bearing numerous items of glassware, shows that chemical operations, or at least analyses, are also carried out there, which is confirmed by a precision balance placed on a stone tabletop.

On a stool in front of one of the tables, the Marquis de Valsorres, his eye applied to an ocular lens, is carefully observing the deviation of an electrometer, next to which is placed a small lead container, open at the top. After each observation, the Marquis writes a number in a notebook. An indefinable odor, heady and not disagreeable, fills the atmosphere of that special chamber.

The Marquis seems more and more satisfied.

At that moment, the door opens and Espéret appears on the threshold. Valsorres turns round. "Well?" he interrogates, in an anxious tone.

"All going well," replies Espéret. "The gaseous emissions are occurring with a marvelous regularity and rapidity. The pressure remains absolutely constant. For your part, where are you up to?"

"Everything's going equally well on my side. The electromotive forces have a remarkable constancy, and the analyses I've made, as many by chemical means as spectroscopic means, permit me to affirm that we almost have the pure metal."

"Virium?"

"Yes, the virium that you and I sniffed out, with the special flair of physicists and geologists: the metal to which we gave that name because it represents the greatest accumulator of force and energy of which we could dream. Now, our dream is finally about to be realized, and our hopes are about to become a reality.

"Oh, what joy, old chap!"

The two men shook hands warmly; emotion was legible in their features.

"Oh, what joy! And what glory for our country, which will be the first to make the conquest of an extraterrestrial world. This evening, we're finally going to be able to unveil our projects to my wife and our friend Dr. Portier. How many times I've been on the point of telling them everything—her, the companion of my life, and him, the faithful friend, the proven scientist—but I was held back by the fear of failure. I didn't want to make any promises without being sure of being able to keep them.

"And now we're sure of being able to keep them, as you say?"

"Yes, as much as certainty is humanly possible."

"We'll tell them everything this evening, then?"

"Yes, we'll go to the château; it isn't four o'clock yet, and our excellent chef will have time to prepare us a feast of Lucullus, for it's necessary to celebrate worthily a day in unique in our history, and perhaps unique in the history of the world."

"It's to be a great feast, then?"

"Yes, old chap. There will only be four of us, but we'll rejoice like forty. Let's go tell Marie to dress up; she'll be astonished, seeing that we're not expecting anyone, and Portier has already been in the château for three days. But we'll promise him an explanation at dessert.

The two scientists stood up. In the vestibule they found two men waiting for them. One of those men was the faithful Thomas, the other was a pure-bed Breton, Le Bris, the second engineer on the *Coulomb*, who had brought the two seekers the precious collaboration of his technical skill, his virtuosity as a technological constructor, which knew no difficulty, his blind obedience, his devotion, proof against everything, and his absolute discretion.

"Bonsoir, Thomas, bonsoir, Le Bris," said the Marquis and Espéret. "It's a good day, isn't it?"

"In truth, Monsieur le Marquis," said the engineer, "I believe you can be content and have a little rest; you've both been slaving away like convicts long enough."

"With your collaboration, my lads," replied Valsorres. "But don't worry; we'll all be recompensed for it."

"Oh, Monsieur le Marquis knows very well that it isn't for hope of a recompense that we work for him."

"Yes, yes, my dear friends, I know that, and that's why I love you both like veritable collaborators. By the way, this evening there'll be good wine in the parlor; you don't detest that, eh, Thomas?"

"Well, Monsieur le Marquis, it does good wherever it passes, isn't that true, Le Bris?"

"Of course," the taciturn Breton replied, laconically.

"Well, you'll be satisfied, for it's necessary to sprinkle today. But above all, discretion; hold your tongues; there are a great many people who would be glad to know what we're doing."

93

"Oh, Monsieur le Marquis can be tranquil; we'd be cut into pieces rather than tell anyone anything."

"That's good; I'm counting on you. Anyway, you alone have the key to the laboratory and the workshops; you both sleep up above, and you mount good guard day and night, don't you?"

"Oh, yes, Monsieur le Marquis; then again, there's the good dog Ravaut, who's worth his weight in gold for signaling any intruder. By night I release him inside the wall. You understand that, if we hear him bark, we can grab a revolver quickly and go down to see what's up."

"Perfect," said Espéret. "We're counting on you, lads. Until tomorrow morning!"

The two men went out and headed for the château, while Thomas grumbled to himself.

"As if it's common sense to ruin the temperament searching for heaps of drugs that burn your fingers as if they were matches, and which you can't touch without wrapping your hand in lead! Oh, poor me! As if it wouldn't be better, with that money, to empty a few good bottles of Burgundy! Fortunately, this evening, in the parlor, there'll be a party. Not true, Le Bris?"

"We'll see," said the Breton, laconically.

Let us follow the Marquis and Espéret; let us climb the perron of ten marble steps. We penetrate into an immense vestibule whose panels are decorated with admirable tapestries. Opposite the entrance, a staircase rises, the wrought iron banister of which is a unique masterpiece. Half way to the first floor it ends in a landing, from which the two staircases depart in their turn to reach that floor, where the bedrooms of the Marquis, the Marquise and their guests are located.

The reception apartments are on the ground floor. To the left, on going in, a magnificent drawing room, a boudoir and the Marquis' study communicate by means of a separate stairway with the bedroom on the upper floor, alongside that of the Marquise, from which it is separated by a dressing room and a bathroom. To the right is the dining room, with its tall glazed ebony dressers filled with old silverware, and, after the dining room a vast billiard room surrounded by comfortable divans, permitting players to indulge in games for all sorts, ranging from billiards itself to bridge, chess or poker.

On the walls of the drawing room, covered in antique woodwork with fine sculptures, paintings by Rigaut, Nattier, Madame Vigée-Lebrun, David, Winterhalter and Bonnat reproduce, in magnificent portraits, the features of Marquises and Marquises de Valsorres belonging to vanished generations. In a glass case, on velvet, are ancestral medals, from the Étoile du Saint-Esprit to the grand cordon de la Légion d'honneur. Other glass cases contain precious works of art. A magnificent Aubusson carpet covers the parquet, the marquetry of which constitutes an adornment in itself. Armchairs and sofas in antique tapestry are offered to the guests of the sumptuous dwelling; an Érard grand piano laden with scores allows a suspicion of the talents of the mistress of the house, and on a large Boulle table covered with precious marble, albums surround a bronze statue representing the Maréchal de Valsorres in his costume of the epoch of Louis XV. Here and there, in porcelain, rare flowers and plants with rich foliage delight the eye, reposing on the rich variety of their verdure and their bright colors.

Let us traverse the drawing room and go into the boudoir that follows it.

We find Marquise Marie de Valsorres there, in the process of bouncing a delightful two-year-old child on her knees. It was, in fact, shortly after the return of the *Coulomb* to France that the lovely Marquise gave birth to a son, thus fulfilling the dearest desires of her husband, who wanted and heir "to the name and arms." Little Philippe, in magnificent health, promises to be a strapping young fellow and a joy to his parents. The nurse, a robust Alsatian, has just brought him to his mother after a walk in the park. The Marquise's chambermaid, Catherine, whom we saw aboard the *Coulomb*, has withdrawn after having served tea to her mistress.

Now, the door opens.

Henri de Valsorres and his inseparable Espéret appeared. At the sight of them, the Marquise could not retain a burst of laughter.

"Well those are fine visiting costumes!" she said.

Valsorres and Espéret looked at one another. In fact, in the joy of their realized hopes and impatient to announce their results, they had forgotten to take off the white smocks that they put over their clothes in order to devote themselves to their laboratory work. They laughed at themselves. Then the Marquise noticed their beaming faces.

"You seem very content, Messieurs," she said. "What's rendering your faces so joyful?"

"My dear Marie," the Marquis replied, "we have indeed experienced today the joy that recompenses our long labors, and we're reposing momentarily from all our fatigues."

"What, Henri? Is it possible? You've found..."

"We've found, isolated and applied the virium, the extraordinary metal for the mineral of which we went to search in the Pacific."

"Oh!" said the young woman, throwing her arms around her husband's neck. "Oh, Henri, I'm proud of you. How wonderful! And you too, my dear Espéret," she added, extending her hand to the engineer, who kissed it. "I congratulate you and thank you."

"Now, at any rate, we're recompensed by your welcome my dear Marie," said the Marquis, more emotional than he wanted to appear. And I believe that our little Philippe won't have to blush at the name he bears." After a momentary pause, he went on: "But it's necessary to celebrate this memorable day with a feast worthy of it. Have you time to give orders for this evening?"

"Yes, yes, all the more so as we have visitors."

"Who, Portier?"

"No, not Portier, since he's already been here for three days. Guess,"

"Germaine and her husband?"

"No, Georges is retained at the Ministry, and you know that your sister never quits her husband."

"Then I give in."

"Well, it's Aunt Hélène, whose arriving with one of our Alsatian cousins, Elisabeth Kessler."

"Little Zabeth, as we called her! But she must be grown up now!"

"She's eighteen years old and she's charming. I've just received a telegram from Aunt Hélène, which announces their arrival for six o'clock. I'll have the victoria harnessed to go and fetch them from the station."

"Bravo! We'll have a serious feast then! And don't forget to have the finest vintages brought out, for I assume that, as is usual when Aunt Hélène is here, you've invited our dear curé, and the worthy fellow doesn't detest what he calls 'The Lord's benefits.'"

"Certainly I've invited out dear Abbé Travers; I know how you like to chat with him."

"Yes, that priest is a scholar; he has a remarkable intelligence and a vast knowledge. Rather ask Espéret, who, in his quality as a freethinker, isn't suspect from that point of view."

"I'm entirely of Henri's opinion," the engineer replied.

"Oh, you wretched miscreant," said the Marquise, menacing him with her finger. "And yet, I haven't despaired of converting you."

"Let's go clean ourselves up, old chap," the Marquis said to his companion, "for we're truly in no condition to receive ladies of quality."

The two men went up to their rooms while the Marquise summoned her cook and butler in order to give them orders for the evening's feast.

II. In which the reader will perceive Abbé Travers for the first time and see Dr. Portier make the acquaintance of a charming young woman, in the course of an excellent dinner.

On the evening of 21 March 1913 at half past six, an elegant victoria harnessed to two magnificent chestnut horses deposited Aunt Hélène and the young cousin Elisabeth Kessler in front of the perron of the château.

The Marquis and the Marquise helped the travelers to get down from the vehicle; there is no need to spell out the tenderness with which Mademoiselle Hélène de Valsorres was embraced by her nephew and niece. The exquisite woman still had the same distinction. Her gray hair was becoming increasingly silvery, further emphasizing her innate elegance, and her face, which did not age, remained young in spite of her fifty-eight years,[15] almost making her white hair a supreme coquetry.

As for her traveling companion, her young cousin Elisabeth Kessler, she was what might be called "a pretty girl" in every sense of the term. She was a typical Alsatian beauty: tall, with fine flesh, opulent without excess, with perfect breasts and hips. Her skin was very white, with pale blue reflections, absolutely indescribable; she had the hand of a fay, the foot of a Cinderella and, crowning the whole, a charming face with a pert nose and a smiling mouth, showing two rows of pearls that were certainly not false, and dark blue eyes beneath a forehead laden with rich golden blonde hair.

Such was the exquisite traveler that Mademoiselle Hélène de Valsorres brought with her. The Marquis and the Marquise gave her the most affectionate welcome; it was more than four years since they had seen her, and they scarcely recognized, in that beautiful young woman, the girl they had kissed in Strasbourg then.

"How tall and beautiful you are, my little Zabeth!" the Marquise said to her, kissing her again.

"Yes, she's beautiful, the little rascal," said the Marquis in his turn. "You're going to make all the young chatelaines in the vicinity green with envy; we'll be obliged to keep you in a cage."

"Oh, Cousin," said the young woman, cheerfully. "Your cages don't scare me; made by you, they can't be very terrible, can they?"

In the meantime, Mademoiselle de Valsorres was chatting in a low voice with the Marquise.

---

[15] The text I have has fifty-two years, but that is incompatible with Hélène having been fifteen, sixteen, or even seventeen in December 1870, so I have altered the figure accordingly.

"Isn't our little cousin delightful?" she asked her.

"Yes, Aunt: delightful is the word, and she'll surely have no lack of suitors, as a rich and pretty orphan!"

"Oh, she isn't precisely rich," replied Aunt Hélène. "She has a income of about thirty thousand francs, all told, but that ease, added to her beauty, will facilitate any union."

"I can believe it. But, in fact, where has she gone?"

Zabeth has simply been taken into the drawing room by the Marquis, where he had introduced her to his friend Espéret. The impression the young woman made on the engineer was the same as on her two cousins.

At that moment the nurse brought little Philippe, whom Aunt Hélène devoured with caresses.

"There's the heir to the name" she said, gravely.

"Yes Aunt," said the Marquis, "And we'll bring him up in such a manner that he'll be worthy to bear it."

"I'm sure of it," replied Aunt Hélène.

"But let's show our two travelers to their rooms," the Marquise interrupted. "They've spent the day on a train and won't be sorry to rest for a while." To Aunt Hélène and Zabeth she added: "All the more so as they have to make themselves beautiful, for we have a grand dinner this evening."

"What!" replied Mademoiselle de Valsorres. "You've already invited suitors for our young cousin?"

"Oh, no—we simply have, in addition to Dr. Portier, whom you know, Abbé Travers, the worthy curé of Valsorres."

"Why the feast of Lucullus, then?"

"Oh, that's a secret that Henri will reveal to us at dessert."

"If it's a secret," said Mademoiselle de Valsorres, "I won't insist, and we'll go and dress in order not to be late."

"It's for seven-thirty," said the Marquise, accompanying her aunt and her cousin to their apartments.

At half past seven that evening, the Marquis de Valsorres, Espéret and Dr. Portier were chatting in the drawing room when "Monsieur le curé" was announced.

Abbé Travers shook the hands that were extended to him sympathetically and sat down by the fireside with the three men.

Abbé Travers was a curious specimen. A pupil of the celebrated school of the Rue des Postes, he had been accepted at the École Polytechnique at nineteen and had emerged two years later to be one of the first entrants to the École de Fontainebleau, which made him a lieutenant in the artillery at twenty-three; he was sent to garrison in Vannes.

There he was received in an old "Bretonnian Breton" family, and in that family there was a young woman, as charming as she was serious, who made an impression on the young lieutenant that he had not sought to conceal. The young woman perceived it, as did her parents—which was not very difficult. The young artilleryman was easily led to confess his sentiments, and the two young people were engaged.

Then came the expedition to Tonkin. Lieutenant Travers wanted to take part in it, in spite of the young woman's supplications. "A soldier," he said, "is not made to rot in garrison." He departed, therefore, taking the promise from his fiancée that she would always think of him and would write to him as often as possible.

After being covered in glory, he was grievously wounded in the assault on Tuyen-Quan; he was even thought to be dead and that death was announced by the Indo-Chinese newspapers. He had simply been picked up, after having lost a lot of blood, by good indigenes, who did their best to care for him until a detachment of *marsouins* reached the village where he was, where they found him, picked him up and transported him back to Hanoi. There he embarked for France, still weak but happy; he had received the cross of the Légion d'honneur, and he was about to see his fiancée again and marry her.

Alas, woman is often fickle, and did the young woman not have the excuse of having believed her former fiancé to be dead? At any rate, when Captain Travers returned to Vannes, he learned that she had just married a rich local landowner. His dolor was great. Momentarily, he thought of suicide, but the memories of the religious education he had received at the Rue des Postes turned him away from that resolution. Nevertheless, he did not want to reenter "the world," which sickened him; he handed in his resignation. He had a small income, which permitted him to live in comfort, if not wealth. He entered the seminary of Saint Sulpice and was ordained as a priest.

With his name, his title as a former student of the X, and his scientific merit, he could have envisaged a brilliant career in the clergy, but that was not in his character. He solicited and obtained a small country parish, where he could do good without seeing evil done around him.

Then, it is necessary to say, he had been fortunate, on arriving there, to find the Valsorres family, where he received the most sympathetic welcome, the Marquise holding him in high esteem and the Marquis being delighted to find a former comrade of the X in his curé. Moreover, broadened by modern ideas without being a "modernist," and living well, Abbé Travers did not detest a good dinner.

When he was seen passing at a lively stride, with his hat slightly tilted, the red ribbon in the buttonhole of his soutane and a sturdy cane in his hand, everyone in the region, even the freethinkers, saluted him with a cordial "Bonjour, Monsieur le curé!" Even the schoolteacher could not charge the former pupil of our foremost scientific school with "ignorantism," so he saluted him deferentially when he encountered him. Thus, the good Abbé Travers was everyone's friend, even of those who "did not go to mass."

"Well, my dear Marquis," said the priest, rubbing his hands, "What's new? Is the scientific work still going well?"

"Better than ever, my dear Abbé. My friend Espéret and I are very happy today, in fact, for I believe that we have finally reached the goal that we've been pursuing for more than three years."

"Really?" said the curé.

"Yes, Monsieur le curé," said Espéret. "Today we can finally say: *Oof! I believe that's it!*"

"Bravo, Messieurs. I don't know exactly what the nature of your work is, but I'm certain that it's something quite remarkable, and above all quite disinterested—isn't that so, doctor?" he added, addressing Dr. Portier.

"Oh, Monsieur l'Abbé, I don't know any more than you do, for although I've witnessed a part of these Messieurs' research, I've not yet had precise information regarding the mysterious goal they're seeking to attain, the revelation of which has been promised to me for a long time."

"Well, my dear Portier," said the Marquis, cheerfully, "you won't have much longer to wait; this evening, after dinner, while smoking the good cigars that our dear curé likes so much, I'll tell you everything. You won't be out of place Abbé, for in your quality as a former polytechnician, you might be satisfied; in any case, I expect something other than compliments from you: objections and criticisms."

"Yes," said Espéret. "Above all, be pitiless. No polite admiration, eh?"

"Don't worry," said the priest. "I'll judge your experiments with complete impartiality."

"That's perfect. But here come the ladies, whose arrival announces that of dinner."

In fact, the Marquise appeared, splendid in a "moonlight" velvet dress, followed by Aunt Hélène, clad in black, following her invariable habit, but a black of supreme elegance, and Elisabeth Kessler, as fresh as a flower in an exquisite white costume.

Abbé Travers, Espéret and the doctor went to greet the Marquise and present their respects to the two travelers. The Marquis took Dr. Portier by the arm and brought him toward Elisabeth.

"My little Zabeth," he said, "you're the only one here who doesn't know our friend, Dr. Portier, already an illustrious young scientist; permit me to introduce you to him, with the hope that you'll count him among the number of your friends.

The young woman held out her small hand to the doctor, letting the gaze of her large blue eyes fall upon him. Under that gaze, the young man felt strangely troubled; he was only able to stammer a few unintelligible words, and timidly took the hand the young Alsatian extended to him, bowing deeply.

The doctor's disturbance had not escaped the infallible eyes of Aunt Hélène. She was sitting on a sofa beside the Marquise.

"Dr. Portier seems quite moved in the presence of our little Zabeth."

"My God," said the Marquise, "that's because little Zabeth is very pretty, and quite capable, as you put it, of *moving* a young man. But you're forging chimeras, Aunt; I believe that Zabeth isn't thinking about marriage for the moment, and in that case, you're giving yourself futile preoccupations."

"My dear Marie, believe in my old experience: either I'm very much mistaken, or Dr. Portier has just received the 'thunderbolt.'"

"Well, the future will decide," said the Marquise.

At that moment, the butler appeared solemnly in the doorway and, raising the heavy silk curtain, pronounced the sacramental words: "Madame la Marquise is served!"

Everyone stood up.

Espéret offered his arm to the Marquise; the Marquis was Aunt Hélène's cavalier; Abbé Travers marched alongside him, while Dr. Portier was utterly bowled over when Zabeth said to him, with a charming smile: "I'll take your arm, Doctor!" Those simple words made him shiver, and when the young woman's hand was placed on the arm that he offered, scarcely brushing it, he felt his heart beating in his breast with a greatly accelerated rhythm.

They sat down at table.

The Marquise had Abbé Travers to her right and Espéret to her left. The Marquis had Mademoiselle de Valsorres to his right and Zabeth to his left. Dr. Portier was placed between the young woman and the ecclesiastic.

As had been decided, the dinner was sumptuous.

The tablecloth that covered the long table was garnished with admirable silverware. A marvelous centerpiece in sculpted silver represented a mythological ship at the prow of which a naiad was brandishing a trident, while around its gull, emerging from silver waves, tritons with inflated cheeks were blowing into conch-shells. The vessel was filled with magnificent roses. Crystal decanters with silver trimmings contained red wine, white wine and water. A splendid Sèvres porcelain service, each item of which bore a golden V surmounted by the coronet of a Marquis, garnished the table, and the engraved crystal glassware also bore the Valsorres monogram. The butler, in a black coat and white cravat, supervised the service carried out by two white-gloved footmen clad in the dark blue livery of the château.

The inevitable moment of silence marked the commencement of the meal, but when the soup was absorbed and the precious Alsace wines, the authentic produce of the celebrated vineyard of Heiligenstein, at the foot of Mont Saint-Odile, was poured into their large Bohemian blue crustal flutes, the conversation soon became lively and animated.

Aunt Hélène was questioned about the incidents of her journey. The charming woman had no sensational events to relate. She had simply encountered, in the corridor of the carriage in which she was traveling, Baron Lymstroem.

"And I confess," she added, "that that encounter had nothing very agreeable about it for me."

"Still your prejudices, Aunt?" said the Marquise. "Georges and Germaine brought the Lymstroems here for the hunting season, though; they spent four or five days here, and didn't make a bad impression on me."

"What do you expect, Marie? It's stronger than me. And I'm not the only one. Ask Zabeth, who was seeing him for the first time, what she thinks of the Baron."

The young woman, thus put on the spot, replied with extreme frankness: "My God, Aunt, I confess that when I saw Aunt Hélène saluted by that still and stilted individual with dirty blond hair stuck to his skull, I had a vague an instinctive sentiment of repulsion, which was accentuated when I saw him trying to talk to her—and I experienced a genuine relief when I saw our aunt take her leave of him in a rather dry fashion."

"What do you expect, my child," said Aunt Hélène. "There are sentiments stronger than the will, over which we have no control."

"Yes, Aunt; on seeing that Baron Lymstroem, I had the impression of seeing a reptile, a snake or an enormous toad."

"Fortunately, he isn't venomous," said the Marquis, "And he didn't bite you."

"Oh, but in that case, Dr. Portier would have got me out of trouble, I think—isn't that so, Doctor?"

Poor Dr. Portier, thus questioned, blushed as red as a poppy. He was nevertheless able to answer: "Oh, Mademoiselle, in that case, as in any other circumstance, I would be only too glad to put all my modest science at your service."

"In sum," said the Marquis, "there's no bite. That's the essential thing."

"Is he married, that Baron?" asked Zabeth. "Is there a Baronne Lymstroem, and is she of the same species as her husband?"

At that question, all eyes turned toward Aunt Hélène

"Yes, my dear child, there's a Baronne Lymstroem, but she isn't, as you put it 'of the same species' as the Baron. Madame Lymstroem is a splendid woman, a professional beauty of the Parisian diplomatic corps. She's tall, admirably made, with superb hair and strangely blue eyes. I'll even say that it's her eyes that render me so unsympathetic to her."

"Oh, my dear Aunt, by virtue of the community of marriage, then, you put the Baron and the Baronne in the same basket?"

"My word, yes. Between ourselves, that household is the least sympathetic in the world to me, and I don't look with a very kindly eye on the intimacy that has been established between the Lymstroems and your cousins the Estrelles."

"Oh, are they as intimate as that?"

"Yes, the Lymstroems occupy one of the two semi-detached houses neighboring the Hôtel de Valsorres, which Georges d'Estrelles and his wife occupy, and their relations are frequent and cordial."

"Indeed," said the Marquise. "Every time we go to spend a few days in Paris, we're sure of dining three or four times with Baron and Baronne Lymstroem at Germaine's, and as I've said, yielding to my sister-in-law's insistence, we invited them once to spend four or five days at the château."

A pike was served, a freshwater monster that could have taken its place in the oceanographic museum of Monaco. The footmen poured a marvelous Haut Sauterne into the glasses.

"The sudden amity of my sister and brother-in-law for that household of resident aliens is curious," the Marquis said, while absorbing flavorsome mouthfuls of the "shark of ponds."

"But it isn't only the household that is in your sister's good graces; there's another resident alien, as you put it, who is constantly pushing his nose in: Dr. Frank, a kind of fake Pole or Czech, who lives in the other house next door to ours."

"And naturally, Aunt, you don't like him either?"

"No more than the Lymstroems. For him, however, there seems to be a reason. One night when Henri, Germaine's son, was seized by a coughing fit, Georges, going the shortest distance, rang Dr. Frank's doorbell asking him to come urgently. The doctor came immediately and gave the child an injection of serum, which saved him. It was the croup."

"Yes, I remember," said the Marquise. Germaine told us in a letter that she wrote to us in 1911, which we received in the Pacific, at Noumea, I think."

"That's right," said Espéret, "I remember the detail."[16]

"Me too," said Dr. Portier.

"You were on the voyage, then, Doctor?" asked Zabeth, looking her neighbor in the eyes.

"Yes, Mademoiselle," he replied.

"So you witnessed the terrible cyclone?"

"Yes, Mademoiselle."

"And you probably cared for and saved the two Germans who were shipwrecked before your eyes?"

"Yes, Mademoiselle."

That was all that the unfortunate fellow was able to reply, in his disturbance.

"My God," said the young woman, "how frightened I would have been! A cyclone! That must be terrifying!"

The Marquis laughed. "But everyone here has passed through cyclones: Marie, Espéret, Portier, me..."

"And me," said Abbé Travers.

"You too, Abbé?"

---

[16] In fact, it's wrong; it was in the letter received at Guayaquil.

"Yes; don't forget that I made the crossing to Indo-China twice, once during the monsoon season. I never recall that without a little shiver. It was at the autumnal equinox, 21 September. Oh, my word, at such moments, one feels very small in the hands of God, and one is very glad to recommend one's soul to him."

"You hear, Espéret," said the Marquise.

"Yes, Madame. Well, would you like a sincere confession? Although I'm a freethinker, during our Pacific cyclone, I recalled the prayers of my childhood and I believe I murmured an *Ave Maria*."

"Ah. I've got you! They're all the same, these strong minds: once in the presence of death, they summon the curé and confess."

"Well, when I'm dying, I'll summon Abbé Travers."

"At your service, my dear comrade," replied the abbé, "But as late as possible, eh?"

"My word yes, for life is good."

It was, indeed, good; a haunch of roe deer venison had just been served, washed down by Château Latour.

Young Zabeth was astonished by it. "But Uncle," she said to the Marquis, "I thought the hunting season was closed."

"Yes, child, but not for us. The park is entirely enclosed by walls, so we can hunt here at any time, even without permission. I'm sure Jérôme killed this one at the request of the cook?"

"It was, indeed, the worthy Jérôme."

"Who's Jérôme?" asked the young woman.

"He's the son of the concierge; he's the park gamekeeper. A handsome lad, parenthetically, who covered himself in glory in the Sud-Oranais. He has the military medal."

"Oh, yes," confirmed Abbé Travers. "Jérôme is a very worthy young man, who is as devoted to you as a dog. No one had better attempt to do anything against the château or its inhabitants; he'd have to deal with Jérôme's carbine, and the gamekeeper can shoot, I can tell you."

A toothsome aspic of foie gras had just made its appearance in the arms of the butler. A venerable Musigny filled the glasses. They did it honor, but the conversation continued.

"Jérôme is a good shot, then?"

"Yes, Mademoiselle," said the abbé, "and I know my marksmen, for in Indo-China, we had marsouins who were first class. Well, one day last winter, walking through the forest of Valsorres between the park and the Loire, I met Jérôme, his carbine on his shoulder, and walked with him for a while, chatting. Suddenly, he seized his rifle, grunting "Oh, the filthy beast!" and shouldered it. It was a hawk that was flying—and I mean flying—at a height of a hundred and fifty meters. The gamekeeper took aim for a second, and fired; the hawk fell like a stone, killed by Jérôme's bullet.

"Ah!" said Espéret. "He fired a bullet!"

"Yes."

"Damn! That's better than William Tell, what you're saying."

"It's as I say. With a gamekeeper like Jérôme and dogs like Ravaut and Ramonet, you can feel secure."

"In any case," aid the Marquise, "We don't have any enemies."

On that consoling word, a Russian salad strewn with truffles was served, the sight of which, although somber, was full of attractions for the guests. The salad was attacked with vigor and replaced by an ice cream of the most agreeable appearance. Champagne of a celebrated vintage had been poured into the glasses.

The Marquis raised his glass. "My children," he said, "We thought we ought to celebrate this unique day worthily. Today, in fact, my friend Espéret and I have finally reached the goal toward which all our efforts have been extended. In a moment, I'll tell you what it consists of, the means by which we've arrived at it, and the projects we're basing on it. In the meantime, let's drink to our hopes and our success."

"Yes, my dear Henri, said Aunt Hélène. "To our triumph!"

"To France!" replied Henri. "It's for her that we've labored!"

"To France!" the seven guests repeated, in chorus, their gazes illuminated by a patriotic flame.

The Marquise had risen to her feet, taking Espéret's arm in order to pass into the small drawing room where coffee was served.

Zabeth was on Dr. Portier's arm. "It's beautiful to labor for France!" the young woman said, in an ardent voice, "Isn't it, Doctor?"

"Yes, Mademoiselle. There are only two things for which one would give one's life without regret: firstly, one's fatherland, and..."

"And what?" said the young woman.

"And...the woman one loves," the doctor completed, awkwardly.

"But no, Doctor," said Zabeth, looking at him fixedly, "for her, it's necessary not to die; on the contrary, it's necessary to live, in order to make her happiness and render her proud of the exploits that one might accomplish for her."

"Exploits? Heroisms of chivalry?" said the young physician, bitterly.

"Exploits...or scientific works," the captivating creature continued. "Glory isn't only acquired on the battlefield; one can also harvest it in a laboratory, for example. Look at my cousin, look at Monsieur Espéret."

"So, Mademoiselle," said Portier, with a tremor in his voice, "you think that a scientist..."

"Would be worthy of inspiring passion in a young woman? Indeed, I think so very sincerely..."

"Thank you, Mademoiselle," said the doctor, bowing profoundly to his lovely neighbor, whom he had just ushered into the small drawing room.

The doctor had joy in his heart; it seemed to him that he was walking on roses, breathing the purest perfumes and hearing the sweetest music.

What's the matter with me this evening? he wondered.

What's the matter with you, my poor doctor? You're in love, for the first time in our life; you're in love without knowing it; you've fallen madly in love, and people like you only fall once. Oh, if you could open your heart to Abbé Travers, how rapidly that worthy man, with his experience of life, would open your eyes!

Zabeth, as a very well brought-up child, immediately fulfilled the office of "the young lady of the house." She served the coffee, and poured an 1887 cognac that can have had few rivals into the little glasses. The Marquis offered Henry Clays, which the men, including the abbé, lit with delight. The Marquise, Aunt Hélène and the young woman brought cigarettes of blond perfumed tobacco to their lips.

The Marquis rang. A footman appeared. "Bring the blackboard from my study, with chalk and a sponge," he said to the domestic.

The latter came back a moment later, bringing the equipment requested, with the aid of his colleague.

Everyone gathered around the board. Henri, standing next to it chalk in hand, looked at the door to make sure that it was firmly closed; everyone understood that the scientist, in exposing his work and his projects, did not want any indiscreet ear to pick up the smallest part of it.

Having observed that only his friends and relatives could hear him, he began to speak.

III. In which the reader will finally understand why the Marquis de
Valsorres went to the Pacific Ocean
to discover an unknown island.

"I want," said the Marquis de Valsorres, "to ask you for a few moments of sustained attention, in order that I can make you understand clearly what I'm going to reveal to you. You all know, because you've often heard us talk about it in our conversations, that life on Earth is necessarily limited.

"Isolated in cold space, it only receives external heat from the sun around which it rotates. The mass of matter in fusion accumulated beneath its thin crust only transmits an insignificant quantity of heat by comparison with that which the day star sends with its incessant radiation.

"But that solar radiation is not and will not be indefinite; the star will cool relative to the unfathomable space that surrounds it. It is possible to calculate, in accordance with the quantity of heat thus radiated by the star, the probable duration of the life that it remains to pass through. Helmholtz, in Germany, and Arrhenius, in Sweden, have made the calculation. Naturally, the results don't have the pretention of being accurate to the day, not to the year; their only ambition is to indicate to us the order of magnitude of the number of years for which the sun, which is presently the source of all life, can still 'live' before being extinguished and becoming a dead star."

"But it's the end of the world that you're announcing, Henri," said the Marquise. "Brrr! I'm shivering."

"It isn't us who'll witness it, my dear Marie, nor our children. But in sum, the eventually must be envisaged, for it will certainly occur. After a number of years that can be estimated at seventeen millions, the sun will have been reduced by cooling to a quarter of its present volume. Well, before that contraction is realized, the temperature of the terrestrial globe, insufficiently warmed by the cooled star, will not exceed zero degrees. Life on the Earth will doubtless not last as long, and the calculations of astronomers and physicists fix its ultimate persistence at about six million years. Six million years! Such is the time that still remains for human beings to accomplish the destiny of their species.

"What will then become of the Earth itself, deprived by a general death of the existence of all the beings that populate its surface?

"Will human beings have succeeded in postponing that fateful date by utilizing al the forces of nature, and bringing into play the new forces that science, driven to its ultimate, has yet to discover, capturing extraterrestrial energies if necessary? Or, at least, will they have succeeded in transmitting to other, younger worlds, the discoveries of their genius, which will, in the course of the centuries, have deciphered one after another the obscure enigmas of the mysterious book of nature?"

The Marquis de Valsorres paused for a moment.

His audience, penetrated by the grandeur of the idea that he was stirring before their minds, were listening without saying a word. Abbé Travers was pensive, his head in his hands; Dr. Portier was drinking in the speaker's words; Aunt Hélène and the Marquise were not hiding their admiration for the man who could give a form to such profound thoughts in that way.

Little Zabeth clapped her hands. "Science is beautiful when it's like that," she said, with a naivety that contained an accurate observation.

"My child," said the Marquis, "it isn't science that is beautiful; it's the eternal truth that it pursues incessantly and sometimes succeeds in glimpsing. But I'll go on.

"Do you not all think, as I do, that it's sad to think that after the mortal cooling on the Earth, all the discoveries that have been made in the course of its history by the men of genius who have been counted among its inhabitants will be annihilated? That the *Pensées* of Pascal, the verses of Victor Hugo, the plays of Shakespeare, the inspirations of Beethoven, the discoveries of Archimedes, Galileo, Newton, Pasteur and Becquerel will all find a definitive tomb, with no issue, in oblivion?"

"My dear Marquis," Abbé Travers put in, "I believe you're forgetting the eternal life?"

"No, my dear Abbé, I'm not forgetting it; like you, I believe, not in spite of being a man of science but because of being a man of science. Yes, I believe in an eternal life, better than this one, where the truth will be revealed to us entirely at a stroke. But that is a matter of conviction and not a matter of reasoning. Now, we're not dealing with faith, we're dealing with science, and nothing but science. It's therefore necessary to limit ourselves to the domain of acquired conquests and material possibilities."

"I understand," said the abbé. "Go on."

"So, struck by that idea, which has always obsessed me since my emergence from the École Polytechnique, I have always concentrated my thought of one subject: a voyage into the heavens and the conquest of distant worlds."

"But that's Jules Verne's voyage to the Moon!" exclaimed Zabeth.

"Patience, my little friend. You'll see exactly what it is soon enough. So, I always caressed my chimera, but I refrained from talking about it to anyone; I would have been treated as a madman. That idea, however, never quit my mind, and I was faithful to the motto: *Let us always think of it and never speak of it*, for I never talked about it, but I thought about it constantly.

"You reminded us just now, my dear Zabeth, of Jules Verne's cannon, which was both brilliant and impractical. It was brilliant from a mathematical point of view; the great scientific romancer had, in order to establish his project, called upon the enlightenment of one of the most knowledgeable mathematicians of our epoch, Joseph Bertrand, the permanent secretary of the Académie des Sciences. It was in accordance with the results of his calculations that Jules

Verne imagined his cannon and his shell containing the three voyagers, who were to disembark on the Moon."

"But in that case, Cousin. Jules Verne's project was serious, and not simply imaginary?"

"It was serious in theory, but in practice his shell containing passengers was simply unrealizable."

"Why?"

"Simply because, given the enormous velocity that it was necessary to impart to the projectile, the passengers would have been killed on departure."

"Killed! But they were inside the shell, not in front of it."

"Yes, my dear Zabeth—look, you can see Abbé Travers smiling, who remembers at this moment, that he was once one of our most distinguished artillery officers."

"What, Monsieur l'Abbé, you think, like my cousin, that I'm being stupid?"

"No, Mademoiselle," replied the curé of Valsorres, "you're simply sinning by ignorance. As the Marquis said, in order to reach the Moon, it's necessary to impart to a projectile a velocity that will permit it to surpass the zone of terrestrial gravity. So far as I recall from my course in astronomy at the École, that velocity has to be twelve thousand meters per second—isn't that so, Marquis?"

"Eleven thousand two hundred and eighty, to be exact."

"Well, in those conditions, given the instantaneity with which that velocity would be communicated to the shell and its passengers, being inside or in front of it is exactly the same thing."

"Oh," said the young woman, with a charming *moue*. "And I was already promising myself a voyage into the heavens!"

"Patience, my dear Zabeth. Let me continue, and you'll see that your voyage is perhaps less impossible than one might believe."

"I'm listening, Cousin."

"So," the Marquis continued, "the cannon solution is impossible, for that reason and also for two others. The first is the fall on the moon, which would be terrible and would annihilate the projectile and its passengers, even if they had been able to resist the shock of departure. But the real reason is the impossibility the voyagers would have of returning to Earth."

"Oh, that's true! It's necessary to get back."

"Yes, my dear child; one wouldn't find, on the Moon, a second cannon disposed to return the projectile. You see that, in spite of its elegant ingenuity, Jules Verne's solution is impossible."

"Alas, yes, Cousin."

"Don't lament, Zabeth. For want of the cannon, we might be able to find something else—and that something, Espéret and I believe that we have."

"And that is?" said the three women, the abbé and the doctor simultaneously.

"It's simply a rocket."

"A rocket!" cried the abbé. "Like the firework?"

"Yes," replied the Marquis; a rocket—but especially designed with a view to that extraterrestrial voyage."

"Ah!" said Abbé Travers, "I'm beginning to understand."

"Are you?" said, the Marquis, "Well, you'll soon understand completely.[17] It's frequently said that a rocket is propelled 'by reaction against the air' but nothing is less accurate. A rocket would be propelled just as well, and even better, in the void than the air. A rocket is, in fact, propelled through the air by the recoil of the gas originating from the combustion of the gunpowder and escaping through the rear. A very simple example will help you to understand."

Here the Marquis drew a diagram on the blackboard.

"Imagine," he said, "a machine-gun fixed to a wagon able to roll without friction along rails. With each shot fired, the wagon with acquire a movement of recoil that will accelerate it, for if the effort of the gas expelling each bullet is always the same, the total mass of the wagon with be diminished, at each shot, by that of the bullet and the charge of powder."

"So," said the doctor, "the velocity of the recoil of the machine-gun could increase indefinitely?"

"Yes," replied the abbé, "ardently following the discussion, which brought him back to his old terrain, "if the number of shots were itself infinite, and there were no resistance on the part of the rails and the air."

"That's perfectly exact," said the Marquis. But only the resistance of the air would impose a limit on the acquired velocity. Our rocket will behave like the machine-gun, and even better than the machine gun. In this case, the projectile is constituted by the gas of the powder, emitted in a continuous fashion by its combustion. If one is the master of that emission of gas, one will also be the master of the propulsion of the rocket; that velocity can be very moderate on departure, in such a fashion as not to affect the organs of the passengers."

"Oh, Henri!" said the Marquise. "You expect there to be voyagers, then?"

---

[17] Authors' note: "In November 1913 the engineer Robert Esnault-Pelterie presented a remarkable work to the Societé Française de Physique in which he examined the conditions of the possibility of a voyage into space with the aid of a rocket. The Marquis de Valsorres was evidently inspired by the ideas of the savant engineer, for the project that he explains here is identical to that of the distinguished physicist and aviator." The date given is some time after the present scene is set, but the note is odd anyway, given that the Marquis has supposedly been nursing his project for years. It is also incorrect; Esnault-Pelterie did publish his essay on the possibility of using a nuclear-powered rocket to travel in space in 1913, but the lecture he gave to the Societé Française de Physique was in November 1912 and was on a different topic.

"Certainly there will, my love: Espéret, myself and the doctor, to begin with."

"Great God!" said the young woman. "But that's terrible!"

"What! You, Marie, who have seen without shivering a Pacific cyclone rushing to assault our ship, are afraid?"

"Not for me, Henri, for you!"

"Then don't worry; we won't be afraid because we won't have any reason to be afraid."

"Fine! You say all that with a coolness that makes me shudder."

"Wait until you've heard everything. So, I was telling you that the rocket is the imagined projectile, on condition that one can dispose of a sufficiently powerful explosive, and the combustion can be graduated at will."

"Do you have that, Marquis?" asked the abbé.

"Wait, impatient Abbé, wait. Suppose, for a moment, that we have that hypothetical explosive, representing a formidable quantity of accumulates energy in a small volume, at our disposal. We can depart as gently as we wish, accelerating our velocity gradually as we go, in such a fashion that our organisms, thanks to that gradual acceleration, will not suffer; we can even alter our course whenever we desire."

"Ah! You expect to be able to steer?"

"Nothing is simpler. Instead of a single exit orifice for the gases, placed at the rear, with a view to propulsion, we'll have several, disposed laterally, which we can open at will. We'll thus have lateral forces that will allow us to deviate entirely at will."

"That's perfect," said the doctor, "but what speed will we need to attain in order to reach other worlds, and how long will our journey last?"

"I'll answer you, my dear friend. Let's suppose at first that we were proposing to go to the Moon. Let's consider the operation as divided into three phases. First of all, the projectile, gently escaping the Earth, is accelerated until it reaches the critical velocity it requires to liberate it from terrestrial gravity. At that moment, the propulsive effort is stopped; the vehicle continues its trajectory in space by virtue of its acquired velocity. Finally, it approaches the Moon; it is turned over, end for end, and the propulsive effort, resuming its action, acts as a brake and slows the velocity until it is nullified at the moment when the projectile alights on the lunar surface.

"In order to depart, we can apply to the projectile a force equal to eleven tenths of its weight, which is acceptable if it is to contain living beings. I'll spare you the calculations; I'll submit them to you, my dear Abbé, you'll see that they're exact. In those conditions, when the projectile arrive at the critical distance it will have a velocity equivalent to 8,180 meters per second."

"And how long will it take to reach that point?"

"About twenty-four minutes nine seconds," the Marquis replied. "From that moment on, the vehicle continues its route without propulsion, by inertia, solicited continuously by the opposed attractions of the Earth and its satellite. When it arrives at the point where those two attractions are in precise equilibrium, its velocity will be 2,030 meters per second. That is its minimum value, and when it arrived at the lunar surface its velocity would be 3,060 meters per second if its velocity were not braked."

"But how much time would be necessary for your rocket to complete that second phase?" asked the abbé.

"It can be calculated quite exactly; I make it forty-eight and a half hours."

"One two days!" said Aunt Hélène. "Two days for a voyage in the infinity of the heavens!"

"No, my dear Aunt, it's not infinity. The Moon is only a stone's throw away from us; its distance from the Earth is only thirty times the diameter of our globe. That's simply an excursion to the suburbs, so to speak."

"The suburbs! How you go on!"

"We're not there yet, but we're getting there, and we'll go much further yet. It remains for me to talk about the third phase, that of the fall on to the Moon, paralyzed by braking. All the calculations made, it ought to last three minutes forty-six seconds." The Marquis wrote the figures on the blackboard as he announced them. "That makes, in total"—he added up the three phases— "forty-eight hours fifty-six minutes, or, in round figures, forty-nine hours."

"And the return?"" asked the Marquise, anxious.

"The return journey ought to be effected in the same time as the outward one, following the operations in inverse order, employing the same propulsive forces."

The listeners were, so to speak, breathless in following the development of that powerful conception.

Abbé Travers was the first to break the silence.

"My dear Marquis," he said. "Let me first congratulate you on this great idea and the fashion in which you have so marvelously brought it to completion. But will you permit me to ask you a question?"

"One question, two—as many as you like."

"Your project is magnificent, supposing that you have the hypothetical explosive. Have you, then, discovered some new powder?"

"No," said the Marquis. "Supposing that the vehicle weighs a thousand kilos, of which three hundred kilos represent the consumable mass of the explosive itself, I calculate that a detonating mixture of hydrogen and oxygen would contain a hundred and thirty-three times too little energy to permit that celestial excursion. The most violent explosives, such as trinitrotoluene would be three hundred and sixty times too feeble."

"You're disarmed, then?" said the doctor.

"No, my dear Portier, no. You know the marvelous substance that is a corollary of the admirable discovery of our comrade at the X, Henri Becquerel?"

"Radium," said the doctor.

"Yes, radium, my friend."

"But you pronounced the name of Henri Becquerel," the Marquise put in. "I thought radium had been discovered by Monsieur and Madame Curie."

"Radium itself, yes; but that was a consequence of the more general and more immense discovery of the radioactivity of matter, made two years before by Henri Becquerel, the great and illustrious French physicist, and to give everyone the part that belongs to him, we can justly say that Henri Becquerel was the Christopher Columbus of the new world of the science of matter, and that the Curies, like Fernand Cortez, subsequently discovered its richest province."

"So radium will serve our purpose?" asked the abbé.

"You'll see. You've heard mention of the prodigious quantity of molecular energy accumulated in a gram of radium. That metal disintegrates spontaneously before our eyes, constantly emitting heat and incessantly producing radiations of several sorts. It has been possible to deduce from measurements presently made that 1,800 years are necessary to reduce its activity by half."

"That's prodigious!" aid Abbé Travers.

"Isn't it? In those conditions, one can calculate the energy contained in a given mass of radium. A kilogram of that substance would contain 5,760 times as much as would be necessary for our lunar excursion."

"So you have the engine," said Zabeth. "When are we leaving?"

"Patience, ebullient child. First of all, we don't have the engine, since radium is rare and a gram costs hundreds of thousands of francs. But even if we had, it wouldn't get us much further forward."

"Why not, Cousin?"

"It's quite simple. A gram of radium would suffice; it would even be five and a half times as much as we needed, but it would be necessary for the energy that it contains to be released at will, and not dissipated slowly in the course of several centuries."

"Adieu, beautiful dream, then."

"Not yet, child. We'll return to that point shortly. In the meantime, I recall that I treated the voyage to the Moon as an excursion to the suburbs; that's because, in fact, there's no interest in visiting our satellite; it really is too close, and thanks to today's powerful telescopes, we know very nearly what our companion is like: as bald as a egg, as arid as a desert, devoid of life, vegetation, water and air."

"So you'd like to go further?"

"So long as we're risking the displacement, it might as well be worth the trouble. There are planets to visit."

"Oh! The planet Mars, with Martians, as I read in that exciting book by Monsieur Wells."

"Yes, certainly. But Mars resembles the Earth too closely. In fact, Mars is doubtless a planet even older than ours. No, the one I'd like to reach is a much younger planet, closer to its origins—in brief, a planet that will live much longer than the Earth."

"Jupiter, then?" asked the abbé.

"No, Saturn," the Marquis replied. "Saturn is in its formation, perhaps in an epoch corresponding to the Tertiary epoch, or even the Secondary era, of our terrestrial geology. In consequence, we'll have the chance there of finding a world much fresher than our Earth, which is truly a rather mature individual."

"Don't speak ill of mature ladies," said Aunt Hélène. "Think of my white hair, my dear Henri."

"Your white hair, my dear Aunt, makes you ever younger, as you know full well. At any rate, it's on Saturn that Espéret and I have set our sights, and, word of a Valsorres, it's on Saturn that we'll disembark some day, and we'll thus be the first humans to have penetrated the interior of its beautiful Ring of Light."

"Let's go to Saturn, then," said the abbé, enthusiastically. "But how long will it take?"

"Ah! That's the thing. For Mars, in the conditions on the basis of which we calculated the lunar voyage, it would be necessary to count on a little more than ninety days, which is three full months, and as much for the return journey. For Saturn, whose distance from the Earth is seven times greater, it would be necessary to count on a duration of seventeen times three months—which is to say, fifty-one months, or four years and three months."

"That would be tempting God!" said the Marquise.

"But my dear Marie, I haven't yet said everything. Radium, admitting that one could dispose freely of its energy, would contain in a mass of one kilogram 5,600 times more than would be necessary. We could therefore employ the surplus of energy to increase the velocity of our projectile once launched, and attain velocities comparable to those of comets."

"Ah! But Marquis, I'll stop you there," said Dr. Portier. "The astronomer has spoken; let the physiologist speak in his turn."

"Go on, my dear friend. Raise objections—that's all I'm demanding—and I'll try to answer them."

"Have you reflected that, departing with a force equal to eleven tenths of the weight of your rocket, you'll be applying an acceleration equal to eleven tenths of that of gravity, until the critical distance is attained."

"Yes, certainly."

"But in that case, it's necessary to remember that, from that moment on, your voyagers will no longer weigh anything! Now, imagine life without weight! Walking would no longer be possible; liquids would no longer emerge from the receptacles containing them; the slightest vertical effort would draw you away indefinitely, until you bump into a solid wall, from which you'd rebound like a ball; the products of digestion, no longer having any weight, would

114

refuse to fall into the hygienic receptacles into which they ought to disappear, and I don't know what else. Have you thought of all that?"

"Yes, my friend, I've thought of it, and that's what now remains for me to explain to you."

A footman had just brought a tray. Zabeth offered fresh beverages again, with exquisite grace.

Then the Marquis, having moistened his lips in a glass of water, resumed his little discourse on a great subject.

"First of all," he said, "let's examine the question of the material existence of voyagers enclosed in a space as small as that of the rocket. Obviously, one can't envisage, for the voyage to Saturn, the duration of four years and three months that I mentioned to you just now; it's necessary to be content with a duration of a few days.

"On that subject, we can consider the problem as completely solved. The progress realized in submarines can allow it to be regarded, from now on, as quite possible to regenerate a confined atmosphere for least a hundred or a hundred and fifty hours. That will give us a possible delay of six days, and one could doubtless do even better were it to become absolutely necessary. I therefore think that, from that viewpoint, we can count on a sojourn of twenty to thirty days in our rocket vehicle.

"As our friend Portier says, however, after the critical distance, our voyagers would no longer have any weight; they would therefore be in conditions where life would become materially impossible."

"You agree, then?" said the doctor.

"Yes, my dear friend; I agree, and I've provided for it."

"By what means? I can't see any."

"By a mechanical means."

"A mechanical means? Marquis, you're bowling me over."

"Well, get up again, and listen to me carefully. Taking the first part of the trajectory, the force on departure being eleven tenths of its weight, the voyagers will, for their part, have the sensation of weighing eleven tenths of, or a tenth more than, their normal weight. Will that hamper their conditions of life greatly?"

"Not enormously, I suppose."

"Good, but once the rocket is free from the action of gravity, we can substitute for it by the creation of a constant artificial acceleration produced by the engine itself. If we regulate that acceleration in such a fashion that it equals that of gravity, the voyagers will constantly have the sensation of having their normal weight. Once arrived on Saturn, where the gravity, to within approximately a twentieth, equal to that on Earth, they would find themselves in their ordinary circumstances. Everything, therefore, depends on that artificial acceleration during the second phase of the voyage."

"I understand. But how will you do it?"

"How will I do it? I shall simply accelerate the speed of the rocket by allowing the propellant gases escape all the time instead of allowing the projectile to travel at a constant velocity in the second phase by virtue of its acquired velocity.

"Supposing that we maintain a force equal to eleven tenths of weight constantly, we can calculate that the projectile ought to turn about at a distance from the terrestrial ground equal to fifteen times the diameter of the Earth, if it were a matter of going to the Moon. At that moment, its velocity would be equal to 61,700 kilometers per second. After which, the vehicle, turned around, would be braking with a force equal to its terrestrial weight. In those new conditions of velocity, the voyage would be much shorter, and we would reach our satellite in three hours five minutes."

"That's an excursion of half a day," said Zabeth.

"Yes, Cousin. To reach Saturn, taking account of the distances, it would be necessary to count on a duration of 850 hours, and as much for the return; that would be 1,700 hours in all, or a little more than two and a half months."

"You're overwhelming me with your implacable precision," said the doctor. "But, setting the question of the explosive aside, what about the temperature? Have you thought that you're going to be traveling in sidereal space, at 273 degrees below zero.

"Yes, I've thought of that."

"You've thought of everything! What a man of genius you are! I admire you profoundly, my dear Marquis."

"Oh, reserve half your admiration for Espéret. For all of this, we've truly collaborated, in the strictest sense of the word. I was telling out that I've thought about the question of temperature. You'll see how simple it is.

"Firstly, I constitute aboard my rocket a metallic envelope with a double wall, a void being created between the two, as in a Thermos flask. After that, the external envelope is divided into two parts: one is black, the other polished metal. As we will be exposed to solar radiation all the time, if I make my rocket pivot around its axis in such a fashion that it turns its black side to the sun, it will warm up; if, on the contrary, I expose my polished side, it won't warm up. It's no more difficult than that—but it's necessary to think of it."

"Yes," said the abbé. "You have powerful brains, Messieurs."

"And you know how to make use of them," said Aunt Hélène.

"But you haven't yet spoken about your explosive," said the Abbé Travers. "You've only talked about radium, but while showing us the inconveniences."

"I'm getting there now, Abbé. To reach Saturn it would be necessary to dispose of 6,800 kilograms of radium, and it would also be necessary to extract the energy at will in a short enough time. With radium, that isn't possible—but it is possible with virium."

"Virium!" said the priest and the doctor at the same time. "What's virium?"

"You're about to find out. You remember, Marie, and you, Espéret, and you, Portier, the voyage we made to the Pacific, where we went to discover an unknown volcanic island. My work as a geologist had caused me to presume that if radioactive minerals are the minerals of heavy elements like uranium and thorium, that is because the integration of matter takes place in the center of the Earth under very high pressures. But if we could discover a volcanic island recently emerged from the ocean, then we had chances of finding younger and stronger radioactive minerals there—and our research was crowned with success. We discovered the Île de France, on which the Germans had already disembarked. We brought back nearly three hundred tons of superactive mineral in the hold of the *Coulomb*. At present, that mineral is here, under the hangars of our laboratory. Espéret and I have extracted a new substance from it, to which we've given the name of virium."

"Yes," said the abbé, "because of the Latin *vires*, which means force."

"Exactly. Today, we concluded our trials. Virium has an activity about 60,000 times stronger than that of radium, which would permit us to reach Saturn by augmenting the speed of our rocket gradually. Transporting two or three kilos of virium, we would be sure of arriving on the planet in less than thirty days, and above all, of being able to return by the same method—which, you'll admit, has its importance."

"Have you enough mineral to prepare that quantity of metal?"

"Yes, we already have nearly a kilo of virium bromide, and we've only used sixty tons of mineral. We're now in a position to attempt the enterprise."

"In condition, nevertheless," said the doctor, "that you succeed in extracting the energy accumulated in the virium at will."

"Well, my friends, that also has been found, and the author of the discovery is our dear and great friend Espéret."

All eyes turned to the engineer, who was drawing voluptuous puffs of smoke from his long cigar. All hands extended toward him. The abbé was exultant, with an overflowing enthusiasm.

"Oh, there's no great merit in that," replied the engineer thus complimented. "A simple laboratory reaction that permits the molecules of virium to disaggregate at our behest, to make it, so to speak, 'fire at will.'"

"Yes," said the Marquis, "a very simple reaction, but which it was necessary to seek and find. So, my friend, whether you want it or not, the glory is yours."

The Marquise had risen to her feet and advanced toward her husband. "So," she asked, in a slightly tremulous voice, "this almost unimaginable voyage, is really possible?"

"Yes, my dear Marie," the Marquis replied. "It's possible; it will be undertaken, for the greater glory of France and for the glory of the name that we have transmitted to our son."

A tear, a pearl of inestimable price, for it expressed simultaneously, dread, amour and a legitimate pride, shone for an instant between the young woman's long eyelashes. Then she threw her arms around her husband's neck, kissed him tenderly and said: "Henri, you'll depart, you'll arrive, you'll come back—yes, you'll come back as the greatest man the Earth will ever have known. Oh, I'm proud of you, my Henri! What pride there is for me in being your wife and bearing your name! Oh, Henri, I love you!"

The two spouses remained in the embrace for a long time. Espéret could not hold back a furtive tear, which saw the light between his eyelids. Abbé Travers did not dissimulate his emotion. Aunt Hélène was weeping.

Little Zabeth had instinctively placed her hand on Dr. Portier. "What a fine voyage, Doctor? Will you be going?"

"I hope so, Mademoiselle. Isn't a physician necessary to accompany the expedition?"

"Oh, my God!" How anxious I shall be!" said the young woman.

She had scarcely finished uttering that heartfelt carry than she blushed all the way to the ears. She tried to recover. "I shall be so anxious for my dear cousin Henri, and for Monsieur Espéret, and..."

"Who else?"

"And for you," she finished, almost in a whisper. But, immediately collecting herself, she said, pertly: "You'll bring me back a souvenir from out there, won't you, Doctor?"

"Yes, Mademoiselle; but on the other hand, when I depart, I'll leave you something."

"What?"

"My heart," said the young man, in a muted voice.

Quietly as he had produced those words, however, they had fallen into Zabeth's ears like delightful music. She looked him full in the face with her large eyes, so pure, and said, simply: "I accept the deposit, and I'll try to render it to you on your return."

And the two young people shook hands silently

Aunt Hélène had seen everything; an exquisite smile illuminated her beautiful face, and she murmured in a low voice: "Fortunate children! May life be clement to them!"

Everyone stood up and went back up to their apartments, prey to the most ardent emotion.

Abbé Travers, his cane in his hand and his hat tilted over his ear, went back to his presbytery at a rapid pace, murmuring: "On Saturn! On Saturn! And to think that I won't be there!"

Meanwhile, the dinner in the servants' parlor was even more cheerful than the one at the masters' table. As the Marquis has promised Thomas, a few good bottles had arrived to bring joy to the staff, who were marvelously able to take advantage of the windfall. The footmen, chambermaids, coachmen and chauffeurs were all banqueting joyfully, sitting around the long table where Monsieur Bernard, the butler, presided, opposite Madame Antoinette, the château's housekeeper and the Marquise's confidant.

When the warmth began to become interesting, the butler said to Thomas: "It's a pity that your beauty isn't here this evening."

"What beauty?" asked Thomas.

"Oh, don't play the innocent: the lovely chambermaid of Madame d'Estrelles, Monsieur le Marquis' sister. She came with her masters in November for the hunting. The Baron and Baronne Lèchetrône were here at the same time.

"Baron Lymstroem, the Finnish ambassador?"

"Something like that; I don't care. Well, my lad, that chambermaid, whose name was..."

"Bettina?"

"Yes, that's it, Bettina. Well, my lad, she had a crush on you. Oh, the way she looked at you—it was truly pleasing to see."

Thomas swelled with pride, caressing his chin.

"The fact is," he said, with a victorious expression, "that she was a fine girl, and not stuck up. Oh, no, not stuck up at all."

"You know something about that, eh, you old rogue!"

"That old chap, isn't for publication. If anyone asks you, you'll say that you don't know anything."

"No, but at times," said the blonde Adèle, a kitchen maid, "he doesn't want to say anything and it's exactly as if he'll tell us everything."

"Me?" said Thomas.

"Yes, you old fool. You have a way of saying things, without saying them, that's exactly as if you said them."

The butler filled Thomas' glass and the later emptied it immediately.

"What?" said Thomas. "Anyway, it isn't anything to dishonor a man or a woman; one wouldn't be the only one that had happened to."

"We're going to know everything!" cried Adèle.

The taciturn Le Bris become anxious on seeing Thomas' tongue thicken while becoming more loquacious. He got up and approached him.

"Hold your tongue, imbecile," he whispered in his ear. And he went back to sit beside Catherine, the Marquise's chambermaid, who was considered as his "promise."

In fact, the worthy daughter of Alsace had quickly appreciated the solid qualities of the Breton Le Bris, and she was, indeed, "engaged" to him. We cannot affirm that the two of them had not tasted dessert before dinner, a little—let him who is without sin cast the first stone.

Somewhat calmed down by Le Bris' reflection, Thomas nevertheless continued to talk.

"Yes, she's a lovely girl, and very amiable all the same, Mam'zelle Bettina, and she's always perfumed; she smells as good as at the hairdresser and has a way of looking you in the eyes that gives you chills in the spine."

"Well, my old Thomas," said the beautiful Julie, another kitchen maid, the "promise" of the gamekeeper Jérôme, "you're hooked! Beware of amour; it makes you do stupid things."

"Oh, not me, my girl. Amour gets up too late for that."

"Pretentious, you see!" said the housekeeper. "On that point he has no sermons to preach—you know, Thomas!"

People laughed covertly at the venerable housekeeper's quip; she must have been beautiful once; the residue of it could be divined under her gray hair. Julie was her "niece"; well-informed people claimed in low voices that she was her daughter.

"Oh, you, Madame Antoinette," Thomas replied, "you ought to know something about it. You can't have been bad in your time, to judge by the present, and well, when one is a lovely woman, one always finds a sock on one's foot, no?"

Madame Antoinette blushed beneath her silver fleece, which brought smiles to many mouths.

"In any case," Thomas continued, "on the virtue of Mam'zelle Bettina, I haven't said anything, myself: nothing. Come on, Monsieur Bernard, another glass—it's good."

And the dinner continued, increasingly cheerful.

When the meal was over and the diners got up, Jérôme and Julie were the last to leave.

"She seemed all right to me, that Bettina, when she came here with her master."

"She's a Boche!" replied the young gamekeeper.

"That's doesn't mean to say that she's no good…and she seemed to me to have wound Thomas round her little finger—he's completely hooked.

"Yes," said Jérôme, "that's unfortunate!"

"Why?"

"Because Thomas, who works with the masters, must know things that it's necessary not to say to anyone whatsoever, and, well, what gets in through the ear can get out through the tongue."

"You think so, Jérôme?"

"I don't know anything, but I'm afraid. Thomas likes skirts, and with a glass of wine, one can quickly get what one wants from him."

The two young people remained silent momentarily. The gamekeeper broke the silence first. "In any case, I'll keep my eyes open," he said. "I don't want anything bad to happen to the Marquis and the Marquise. They're so good to us, and everyone."

"Me neither," said Julie. "Well, Jérôme, it's agreed, we'll keep watch, me with my eyes and ears, and you…"

"Me?"

"You, if necessary, with your carbine!"

And the two young people went up the stairway leading to the servants' lodgings together,

IV. In which one can see that what makes the joy of some sometimes makes the despair of others.

The day after that memorable day, at ten o'clock in the morning, the Marquis de Valsorres, Espéret, Dr. Portier and Abbé Travers were gathered in the electric equipment room of the laboratory situated at the rear of the park, to which we once introduced our readers.

The Marquis and the engineer had rapidly brought the doctor and the abbé up to date with their research methods and had shown them the results. Both had marveled; both, having the minds of scientists and experimenters, had understood the merit of the discovery and grasped the importance of its possible applications.

The four interlocutors were sitting around a little table. The doctor was the first to speak.

"Now what are you going to do?" he asked the two scientists.

"We're here to decide that," the Marquis replied, "You, Portier, because you'll be on the expedition, you, my dear Abbé, because your advice will be as precious to us as your science."

"First of all," said the priest, "you're firmly resolved to attempt this voyage to the planets, the audacity of which almost constitutes a temerity?"

"Yes, certainly," relied the Marquis, while Espéret approved with a nod of the head. "As I told you yesterday evening, Saturn is the object of our 'raid.' On the way, we'll pass through the vicinity of Mars and Jupiter, but we'll only cast a rapid eye over them; the veritable object of our voyage is the marvelous planet around which ten moons gravitate and which is surrounded by a ring of light."

"You're going to occupy yourselves with the realization of your beautiful conception, then, and have a rocket constructed."

"Yes," replied the Marquis, "but it's necessary first to gather the means."

"From what point of view? Material or financial?"

"From both points of view—which are fundamentally only one: finding the money necessary for the enterprise."

"Will it need a great deal?" asked Abbé Travers.

"My God! 'A great deal' is saying a lot; I don't think the expense will be extremely high. In spite of that, I estimate that a sum of five or six millions will be necessary, as much to construct the machine as to gather all the indispensable accessories here, some of which might be costly."

"Damn!" said the doctor. "Six millions is quite a figure."

"I have no need to tell you, Messieurs," the Marquis continued, "that if necessary, I'll meet all the expenses of the enterprise myself. Madame de Valsorres and I have a fortune of about fifty millions; I'd willingly sacrifice an eighth in order to be able to realize this voyage, which will, I truly believe, be unique in the history of the world."

"Yes, certainly," Espéret approved.

"But couldn't we address ourselves to the State?" said the doctor.

"To the State!" replied the Marquis shrugging his shoulders.

"Yes, my dear Marquis," said the doctor. "The expedition you envisage has no other goal but procuring France the glory of being the first of all the nations to plant her flag in the soil of unknown worlds. So why not associate our country with the grandiose project, in order that, if it will obtain the primary honor, it will at least have the right to say that it has gone to some trouble?"

"Yes, my dear Portier," relied the Marquis, "your proposal is that of a good Frenchman—but have you reflected that, in order to have the collaboration of the State, it will first be necessary to have the assent of the Chambers."

"Well," said Portier, "we'll get it."

"We'll get it! One can see that you know nothing about parliamentary affairs. You've lived in your laboratory, with your eye to your microscope, and you have no suspicion of the inertia of the political world and parliamentary personnel."

"However, it's a matter of a project of genius, an admirable conquest that will make the glory of France!"

"Yes, exactly, but it doesn't have any electoral appeal. Think about the number of indifferent individuals to whom it will be necessary to lay siege and convince, and who'll reply to us: 'What purpose will it serve?'"

"You're absolutely right, in principle," replied Espéret, "but contrary to your opinion, I find something exciting in the very difficulty; there's no difficult in taking a poorly defended fortress by assault. 'A victory without peril is a triumph without glory,' as the great Corneille says. The Chamber will be indifferent, you say? Well then, let's turn it around. It'll be damnable if we can't succeed in convincing and enthusing a couple of ministers."

"Isn't the Minister of Public Works one of our former comrades of the X?" said Abbé Travers.

"That's true," said Espéret. "That's Bretonnaud, the former engineer of the Bridges and Highways, who became a député and now a minister. You're right. Abbé, I believe he's our man."

"My friends," replied the Marquis, "I'd like nothing better than to rally to our opinion. Like you, I believe that it's necessary, when we plant the tricolor in the soil of Saturn, that France—all of France—should be represented by the glorious symbol, for which so many brave men have fallen and will fall again under the blows of an implacable enemy."

"Yes, indeed, old chap," said Espéret, "I agree with you."

"In spite of that, however," the Marquis continued, "I can't forbid myself a great skepticism. Remember how indifferent scientific research is to many of our ignorant députés. Our laboratories are devoid of resources and our scientists have no means of working. The press has signaled this disastrous state of affairs in vain. *Le Petit Parisien*, for example, in an active and generous campaign, has set the poverty of our scientific establishments—whose annals are so glorious— before the eyes of its innumerable readers in vain. It leaves our politicians cold. In words, it's true, science is their great warhorse. They always have it in their mouth in their speeches and at their rallies, but when it's a matter, I don't say of rewarding, but merely of paying for that science, there's no longer anyone there."

"So you'll renounce asking the support of the Chambers?" said the doctor.

"No, my friend. I'll follow Espéret's advice and yours; I'll struggle conscientiously until the end."

"So?"

"So, this discussion is closed, and Espéret and I will leave for Paris tomorrow morning. This evening, we'll finish bringing you, my dear Portier, and you, my dear Abbé, up to date with our research, which you'll continue in our absence, for it's necessary that the manufacture of the virium doesn't suffer a moment's interruption."

"Don't worry, Marquis," replied Abbé Travers. "The doctor and I will try to do our best; and while you go out there to handle the parliamentary matter, we'll handle the radioactive matter. Every instant that the exercise of my ministry leaves me, I'll spend in our laboratory."

"That's agreed. And on that note, let's have lunch."

The four men stood up. As they went out, the Marquis gave a few technical instructions to Thomas and Le Bris, after which they all headed for the château.

While waiting for them, the ladies were taking a stroll in the admirable spring morning. When the Marquise perceived them she shouted to them: "Let's go, laggards! Come quickly; lunch is getting cold."

They all hurried in the wake of their gracious guides and went into the dining room, where they occupied the same places as before. The conversation began immediately.

"You know, Marie," said the Marquis, "that Espéret and I are leaving for Paris tomorrow?"

"No, my love, but I know now. Why, if there's no indiscretion in asking?"

"None, my dear. We're going to try to interest the government in our projects and obtain a State subsidy."

The Marquise made a disdainful moue. "Oh, the State!" she said, in a tone that marked her lack of confidence. "You think that our députés will be interested in your voyage to Saturn?"

The Marquis looked at his guests. "You see, I haven't said anything to Marie, but I can see that she shares my opinion completely."

"Me too," said Aunt Hélène. "I'm very skeptical."

"In spite of that, we're going to attempt the siege of the Chamber. It's necessary to be able to tell ourselves that we've done everything to enable the government of France to associate the country officially with our enterprise."

"Where and with whom will you begin?" asked Aunt Hélène.

"We have a former comrade of the École Polytechnique, Bretonnaud, who is presently Minister of Public Works; unless his state of mind has been completely transformed by politics, he'll be able to understand us."

"We expect so, or, at least, we hope so," added Espéret.

"And then, as he's in politics, perhaps he'll be able to indicate the influences of which we need to make sure in order to attain our objective."

"My children," said Mademoiselle de Valsorres, "I'll say my prayers for your success. Have you telegraphed Germaine to inform her of your arrival?"

"No, Aunt, not yet."

"Well, don't bother; I'll telephone her shortly to announce your visit."

"Is Georges in Paris at present?"

"Yes, still occupied with Foreign Affairs, where he's the Minister's uncontested right arm."

"In fact," the Marquis put in, "that's a second Excellency who might give us a serious boost."

"Indeed," replied Aunt Hélène.

"Well," said the abbé, "with two ministers up your sleeve, if you don't succeed in carrying the Chamber's voyage, it will be cause for despair."

"Are you taking Thomas?" the Marquise asked the engineer.

"No, Madame. Thomas is familiar with our laboratory research; he's supervising the chemical part of our operation—the 'cooking,' if you like—while Le Bris monitors the instruments and the mechanical part."

"You ought to finish bringing me up to date before you go, you know," said the abbé.

"And me," said the doctor.

"Don't worry. We'll just have our coffee, and we'll go to spend the rest of the day in the laboratory."

Lunch had concluded. They went into the small drawing room, where the coffee was served. The black beverage was rapidly absorbed. The four men got up.

"That's it, go work," said Aunt Hélène. "In the meantime, I'll telephone Germaine to tell her you're coming."

The Marquis, followed by his collaborators, had arrived in the laboratory, where Thomas and Le Bris were waiting for them, at their posts. There, for three long hours, he and Espéret brought the doctor and Abbé Travers up to date with their operations. The doctor was especially initiated into the chemical preparations, of which Thomas was the manual auxiliary, and Abbé Travers was enabled to devote himself to the electrical verifications inseparable from the preparation of the virium.

In that fashion the afternoon went by rapidly.

In the evening, everyone went to dinner at the château.

The Marquis had received his sister's reply; Monsieur and Madame d'Estrelles were expecting the Marquis and the engineer with the greatest impatience; their apartments in the Hôtel de Valsorres were ready.

Everyone had now rallied to the idea of soliciting the collaboration of the State. Espéret was full of confidence, as well as the doctor; the three women were still skeptical; Abbé Travers said nothing.

The next morning, at seven o'clock, a victoria took the Marquis and Espéret to the nearly Pont-sur-Ance railway station, escorted as far as the gate by vigorous good wishes. At eleven-thirty the two travelers disembarked at the Quai d'Orsay station, and at midday, the Marquis was embracing his sister in the small drawing room of the Hôtel de Valsorres.

"Finally, big brother, here you are!" the young woman said, throwing her arms around her brother. "But what have you been doing at Valsorres while you and Marie have been buried there for more than a year?"

"I'll tell you that over lunch. How is your husband?"

"He ought to be here already…and here he is."

Vicomte Georges d'Estrelles appeared at that moment, with a voluminous Russian leather briefcase under his arm.

"Bonjour Henri! Bonjour Espéret!" he said, extending his hand affectionately to the two new arrivals. "Well, what brings you here—or, rather, what's been keeping you out there?"

"That's what I asked a moment ago," said Germaine. "I was told that we'd be fully informed over lunch."

"Let's go have lunch, then!"

"How are your children?" asked the Marquis.

"Marvelously well, and growing like mushrooms."

"You haven't had any anxiety since the famous alarm that frightened you so much, my dear Germaine?"

"No, no; everything's fine; in any case, we still have Dr. Frank within arm's reach."

"That's true; I forgot that he's your neighbor."

"To table!" said the young woman.

They all went into the dining room.

"And your other neighbors, Baron and Baronne Lymstroem?"

"They're still there."

"The Baron is a man of merit, it appears, isn't he, Georges?"

The diplomat, thus questioned by his wife, replied: "Yes, the Baron is a very interesting man; although he isn't, I admit, very sympathetic in appearance, he gains in being known. He's a diplomat of great merit; he has a profound erudition on all international matters, and he's also an unparalleled bridge player."

"Oh, then I understand your relations with him," said Henri. "You and Pierre Vernier, your right arm, are fanatical bridge players."

"Anyway, tell us what brings the two of you to Paris," said Germaine.

"This is it," said the Marquis. "It's necessary to tell you that, since our return from the Pacific, Espéret and I have been in pursuit of an important discovery."

"In chemistry or mechanics?"

"Both," Henri replied. "For three years we've been seeking, and have finally found, a new substance, more than 60,000 times more powerful than the famous radium, of which you've certainly heard mention."

"What! You've surpassed Monsieur and Madame Curie?"

"Yes, and by far. It's the mineral of the substance in question for which we went in search, guided by Espéret's special ideas, and found on a Pacific island. For three years we've been treating that mineral patiently, and we've extracted the element we were seeking, which we've named virium."

"Oh, my dear Henri, my dear Espéret, that's excellent, what you've done, you know!" said the Vicomte d'Estrelles.

"My dear Georges, you'll have the right to say that when we've applied the virium to the purpose that we have in mind."

"Which is?"

"Simply a voyage to the heavens, specifically to the planet Saturn."

The Vicomte and Germaine looked at the Marquis for a moment without saying anything, but their gaze expressed a profound amazement.

"You're wondering whether we're mad, my friends. Don't worry, Espéret and I have all our reason. It isn't a utopia we're submitting to you, it's a project reposing on solid and scientific bases.

And the Marquis then explained to his sister and bother-in-law the project of the celestial voyage that we heard detailed at the Château de Valsorres.

Vicomte d'Estrelles and his wife were truly overwhelmed by the boldness of the conception, as much as by the beauty of the discovery that they had revealed.

When Henri had finished his explanation, there were affectionate congratulations.

"So you're really preparing to make this incredible voyage?"

"Certainly, my dear Germaine. Except that, because it will be rather costly, we've come to Paris to solicit the collaboration of the State."

"Oh! The State—which is to say, the intervention of the Chambers?" asked Vicomte d'Estrelles

"My dear Georges, I can see that you, too, don't have any great confidence in the sagacity of our honorable gentlemen. But I consider that it's our duty at least to solicit that collaboration, in order that no one can reproach us for not having associated the entire country with our voyage of discovery and conquest."

"That comes from the heart of a good Frenchman."

"Whatever happens, our conscience will be clear. We have, in any case, the Minister of Public Works, who is a former comrade of the X. With his support, I hope we'll be able to succeed."

"We wish you that success, wholeheartedly."

"I should think so," said Georges. "I'm well in with my Minister, Monsieur Le Vandier; he's one of the most open-minded of the entire cabinet. Would you like me to ask him to support your request?"

"Certainly, my dear friend, and I thank you very sincerely."

"Well, it's agreed. I'll be seeing my Minister soon, and I'll give you his response this evening."

With that, they went into the small drawing room to take coffee.

During lunch the service had been carried out by two chambermaids; Vicomtesse d'Estrelles, as she had often said, had a horror of the service of men, and except when she gave grand dinners, it was women who served at table. One of those two women was Bettina, the "camouflaged" German whom Madame Lymstroem, as we have previously seen, had placed with Madame d'Estrelles. As one can imagine, not one of the words pronounced at table had escaped her ears, trained to listen to everything, nor her infallible memory, equipped to retain everything.

At the first words spoken by the Marquis, all her attention had been concentrated on the conversation, and yet, such was her self-control, that nothing in her physiognomy had allowed the suspicion that she was interested in anything except the details of her service, which she carried out with perfect discretion.

When the guests had left the dining room, while clearing he table, she was thoughtful; she was wondering how she could let Madame Lymstroem know what she had just learned as quickly as possible.

Chance was about to serve her desire. The Vicomtesse rang; Bettina ran into the small drawing room.

"Here, Bettina," said Germaine. "This is a note for Baronne Lymstroem that I forgot to end her this morning; it's my reply to an invitation. Go take it to her right away."

"Very good, Madame," the chambermaid replied, taking the letter. She immediately left the Hôtel de Valsorres, thanks to the plausible reason, in order to go to the semi-detached house inhabited, as we know, by Baron and Baronne Lymstroem.

The chambermaid went past the concierge, who saluted her in a respectful manner, indicting the importance she had in the house. She simply asked him: "Is Madame la Baronne at home?"

"Yes, Mademoiselle Bettina."

"Please let her know that I'd like to see her immediately." She stressed the last word.

The concierge said a few words into a telephone, and then listened to the response, his ear to the receiver.

"You can go up, Mademoiselle Bettina. Madame la Baronne is waiting for you in her bedroom."

The chambermaid went upstairs and knocked discreetly on the indicated door.

"Come in!" replied a voice.

She went in and found herself facing the Baronne, who was lying on a chaise longue with a book in her hand, staring at her.

Bettina bowed almost to the floor before that woman, who was her only veritable mistress, and handed her Madame d'Estrelles' letter. The Baronne unsealed it and said, after having scanned it: "Is it for this that you've permitted yourself to disturb me, stupid idiot?"

"No, most noble lady," the chambermaid replied. "But I've learned today things of such interest and such gravity that I didn't hesitate to take advantage of the pretext of the letter in order to come and give your gracious ladyship an account of them."

"Will it take long?"

"Perhaps, most noble lady."

"Sit down on this cushion, then," she said, pushing a thick cushion placed before her with her foot.

The chambermaid was confused by so much honor.

"But before you begin, go and inform the Baron; I assume that what you have to say will interest both of us."

"Yes, certainly Madame la Baronne."

The chambermaid went out, and came back a moment later, followed by the Baron, who asked his wife: "What's this idiot telling me? She has something important to tell us?"

"Yes, my dear friend, and she's going to do so immediately. Sit down, Bettina."

The chambermaid sat down, not without the Baronne having made sure, with a rapid glance, that the doors were firmly closed.

Bettina then commenced the account of the conversation she had overheard during lunch. She had a prodigious memory and had retained everything that had been said, save for the lacunae in her eavesdropping occasioned by the necessities of her service at table.

Several times during the spy's narration the Baronne had shown signs of a violent anger. The Baron, by contrast, remained impassive.

When Bettina had concluded her report the Baronne stood up opened a drawer in a small desk and took out a thousand-franc bill, which she handed to the chambermaid.

"Here," she said. "Take this. Today you've rendered a great service, for which I want to show my gratitude."

Bettina took the banknote, and, curtsying before her noble mistress, kissed the hand she held out to her respectfully.

"You know from experience how I punish when I'm discontented," said the Baronne. "You can see today how I reward when I'm satisfied. Go, my girl, and continue your loyal services with as much success. Remember that you're serving Germany, great Germany, and our powerful Emperor."

The chambermaid withdrew, after bowing profoundly.

The Baron and his wife remind alone in the Baronne's bedroom. The latter strode back and forth, stamping her foot in rage.

"Please my beauty, calm down!" said her husband.

"Oh, how stupid you are, my dear! You can remain calm in the presence of such a revelation!"

"But it's still only a project, adorable wife!"

"Yes," she replied, angrily. "A project that is going to become a reality tomorrow. These accursed French! They want to steal from our glorious fatherland a glory that should have been reserved for her! The conquest of the world! To think that that idiot von Osterwald allowed his secret to be discovered in the Pacific!"

"No, beautiful friend, since the *Borussia*, which was carrying it, was shipwrecked and all its passengers perished, save for one sailor."

"And how do we know that the sailor didn't talk?"

"But the man doubtless didn't know anything."

"What about the mineral specimens that von Osterwald had with him in a box?"

"You know very well that he saved his box from the wreck."

"But how do you know that Valsorres and his damned soul Espéret weren't able to analyze the stones while he was unconscious? Oh, truly, you can remain calm in the presence of such a blow! So, the French are going to conquer Saturn, and Baron Lymstroem remains impassive! Not only is it the French, but it's a Valsorres, a descendant of the accursed family against which my brother and I swore an eternal hatred at my father's deathbed. And his Excellency Baron Lymstroem sits placidly in his armchair! Germany is losing the conquest of the world that ought to complete that of the Earth, and Your Excellency is content to twiddle his cigar-case between his fingers! Have you forgotten who you really are, wretch, beneath your appearance of a Finnish diplomat?"

"No, my dear, I haven't forgotten."

"Well, I'm reminding you again. When, ruined, you were facing suicide or dishonor, remember that one of the Emperor's aides-de-camp came to offer you both salvation and a fortune."

"By marrying you."

"Yes, by marrying me—but on the condition that you gave your signature—your *signature*, you hear—that wherever you were, to whatever residency you were sent, you would be a zealous but discreet servant of Germany and the Emperor."

"You've told me often enough for me to remember it."

"One would scarcely think so, given our impassivity before the project of a voyage that I consider as a catastrophe for our country."

"I'm not as impassive as you might suppose, and I'm even thinking about means to employ in order to avert it."

"Let's see he fashion in which you're going to keep your engagements."

"And let's see the fashion in which you're going to keep yours. A fair exchange. After all, I'm only your husband in name, and I want to be *in fact*. Without that, well, yes, I'll remain impassive and inert, as you seem to fear."

The Baronne looked scornfully at the man to whom she had riveted her life. A violent combat was engaged within her.

After a brief pause, she said: "All right, I'll consent to be your wife, once, but on condition that you prove to me the efficacy of the measures that you envision in order to thwart the projects of our doubly hereditary enemies."

The Baron cast a glance over the splendid creature into which desire put a gleam.

"Come with me," he said, simply.

The Baronne followed her husband, who went into his study and carefully bolted the door.

Having done that, he went to the door of a cupboard, which he opened with a special key. A complicated apparatus was then offered to Madame Lymstroem's eyes.

"What's that?" she asked, curiously.

"That my dear wife—I can now give you that name, since all hopes are permitted to me—is simply a wireless telegraph apparatus, a marvel twenty years in advance of any other, which Colonel von Metzen, the savant military engineer, installed here a month ago."

"While he was staying in the house?"

"Yes, my beauty. This long-wave apparatus permits me to communicate directly with His Majesty's military cabinet in Berlin."

"That's marvelous," said the Baronne.

"Isn't it, my blonde Valkyrie? Oh, aren't the French stupid? It's their Professor Branly who invented the means of wireless telegraphy, but they let his discovery drop without applying it, while our scientists, setting to work, improved it in an incredible fashion. And today, while Branly is continuing his work with difficulty, in a laboratory devoid of resources, our engineers have realized his masterpiece, which will be so useful to us!"

The Baronne was beginning to look at her husband with less scorn; her German heart opened to the contact of a man as German as she was.

The Baron started a small motor connected to the electricity supply. "That," he said, "is our wave-producer. You can see how silent it is." In fact, the motor was spinning, albeit at a prodigious velocity, almost soundlessly around its axis, mounted on steel ball-bearings.

The Baron pressed a button.

"That informs the Emperor's cabinet that I'm about to send a message."

Madame Lymstroem softened further. "But I don't see the telegraph antennae that require supports like the Eiffel Tower."

"That was necessary once. The only antenna I need is a copper wire hidden under the drapes, which runs around my room four times. Ah! Here's Berlin responding to me.

In fact, a discreet little bell made its carillon heard. The Baron put a telephone to his ear, and picked up a pencil with his right hand, which he approached to a white sheet of paper. He inscribed letters s he received the signals.

"They're asking what's up! They'll be satisfied."

And the diplomat spy, sitting down at the transmitter, sent signals without stopping for more than ten minutes.

He received the following response: *Wait half an hour, the time to inform You Know Who.*

All that, naturally, was transmitted in a cipher, to which the key was changed every day of the year, in accordance with a rule only known to people as important as the Baron.

The Baronne was beginning to look at her husband tenderly. After half an hour, the little bell began ringing again. The Baron picked up the telephone in his left hand and his pencil in his right. He wrote the letters down as the communication came in. When he had finished he translated it with the aid of the key, and handed it to his wife, who read:

Do everything necessary to prevent that departure. Unlimited credit. Failure inadmissible.

"Oh, Wilfrid!" said the Baronne, throwing her arms around her husband's neck. "I've misunderstood you, but now I understand you, and I'm entirely yours."

And she drew him into her bedroom, the door of which closed on them.

V. In the course of which the reader will see the welcome reserved for a man of genius.

Five days have gone by since the arrival in Paris of the Marquis de Valsorres and the engineer Espéret.

The two scientists had not wasted their time; for they had had a meeting with their former comrade Bretonnaud, the Ministry of Public Works, on whose scientific education they were counting to sponsor their project in the Chamber.

Was it the influence of life in parliamentary milieux? At any rate, the Minister welcomed the projects of his two comrades with a certain skepticism. In the end, however, confronted by the enunciation of precise facts and the offer of immediate and material verification of the results advanced, he began to wonder whether Valsorres and Espéret might be right, and asked them for time to reflect. In the meantime, Vicomte d'Estrelles had almost rallied the support the Minister of Foreign Affairs, Le Vandier, to the Marquis' project. The latter discussed it with his colleague Bretonnaud, who, seeing that he was not alone, already felt more courage to support the proposal.

A dinner had been arranged at the Estrelles' for the following evening. The two ministers were there. Valsorres was so eloquent, and his sister Germane so charming, that the two politicians were convinced, and, on leaving the Hôtel de Valsorres, the Minister of Public Works said, addressing the Marquis and the engineer: "It's agreed, Messieurs. I'll talk to the prime minister tomorrow morning, and in the afternoon I'll put before the Chamber a request for extraordinary credit, up to six millions, to permit you to attempt your audacious and magnificent enterprise."

That was done.

At first, the Council of Ministers was not very enthusiastic. However, on the observation that the government might appear "backward," in refusing to support the proposal submitted to it, the prime minister was authorized to put forward the request for credit.

While these efforts were attempted fortunately, Baron Lymstroem was not inactive. Thinking above all of disqualifying the Marquis' project, he thought of having it divulged in the press, in spite of the discretion with which its authors had surrounded it. To that effect, he telegraphed one of his agents in Berne, to tell him what steps to take.

The next day, a newspaper in Zurich with clear German tendencies announced that engineers beyond the Rhine had found a means of attaining the most distant planets with the aid of an apparatus propelled by an accumulator of energy of unprecedented power; the project of the Marquis de Valsorres was thus "deflowered."

Several newspapers in Paris and the provinces reproduced the article in their review of the foreign press, and two days later the same Swiss newspaper affirmed that it had it from "a reliable source" that the French government was about to allocate funds for the enterprise of an interplanetary voyage.

The maneuver was clever. It cast suspicion of the purity of the French scientist's intentions. People could wonder, on reading the information released in a perfidious manner, whether the Marquis de Valsorres might be secretly acting on the behalf of a neighboring government.

And the following day, after a tendentious article in which it claimed that Germanization was making immense progress in Alsace-Lorraine, the same newspaper insinuated cleverly that the Marquis de Valsorres, the author of the "French" project, had married an Alsatian.

There is scarcely any need to depict the indignation into which these underhanded lines threw Henri and Espéret. Unfortunately, reproduced in twisted fashion, they produced their effect; many députés had read them, and the fear of encouraging an enterprise whose origin, thus presented, might seem suspect, influenced their opinion, already hesitant, and pushed them toward voting "no." So, when the project came before the budget committee after having been submitted to the Chamber, it found a rather cold welcome.

The Marquis and Espéret had been summoned in order to explain the broad outlines of their project and its costs. Is there any need to say how eloquent Henri was eloquent and how precise Espéret in the scientific rigor of their explanation? No, of course not—our readers will not doubt it.

The members of the committee immediately divided into two groups with very distinct opinions. Some, engineers and technicians, understood perfectly everything that was magnificent, audacious and grandiose in the two scientist's endeavor—but they sensed that they were in the minority, and dreaded compromising themselves in the eyes of the majority, composed of professional politicians, by giving the project to much support; so they contented themselves with discreetly approving the Marquis' explanations with nods of the head. As for the others, they remained silent, some even affecting to write or read various papers while Henri was striving to convince his audience,

When the two scientists had completed their lecture, the president of the committee rose to his feet and asked the members present: "Does anyone have any supplementary questions?"

Not one voice was raised.

Then, addressing our two friends, the president said to them: "Thank you for your luminous and interesting communication, Messieurs. We have no further need of you. The Committee will study your proposal and pronounce for or against.

Henri and Espéret bowed and went out.

After their departure, the discussion commenced immediately. The project was sharply attacked by certain members, part of prominent groups in the

Chamber. It was described as fantasy, and one of the members even pronounced the words "scientific hoax." However, a député from Tarn-et-Moselle, Monsieur Mangin-Dutoit, defended it energetically. He replied indignantly to the insinuations that had been read in the press on the subject of the precise objective of the voyage. He affirmed that he knew the Marquis and Espéret personally and could guarantee both their ardent patriotism and their profound science. Finally, the député announced that he would defend the project with all possible ardor at the tribune in the Chamber.

A murmur greeted Monsieur Mangin-Dutoit's final words. There were whispers; animated words were exchanged in small groups.

"Does anyone else want to speak?" asked the president.

No one replied.

"Then I shall put to the vote the adoption of the request for extraordinary credit that has been submitted to us.

The members voted and the votes were counted.

"By a majority of five votes," said the president, "the committee rejects the request for credit deposed for the project of Messieurs de Valsorres and Espéret's expedition."

The evening papers announced the result of the committee's vote in their stop press. The Minister Bretonnaud had already informed Henri by telephone.

The Marquis said to Espéret: "You see, old chap, it's as I said; it's a check we could have avoided, for it was foreseeable."

"But it's only the vote of the committee," Espéret replied. "There's still the vote of the Chamber."

"Oh, I expect even less of that one than the other."

Espéret made no reply. He too sensed that the game was lost.

"I'm even inclined to ask Bretonnaud to withdraw the proposal; there's no point in having our project discussed in public session in these conditions, and exposing it to the attack of incompetent and systematically hostile people. What do you think?"

"I've ended up thinking like you, my friend."

"It's agreed, then. I'll call in at Public Works and ask the Minister to withdraw the proposal."

"I'll go with you," said the engineer.

It is almost superfluous to say that Baron and Baronne Lymstroem had been informed of the committee's vote. They were talking about what had just transpired, which they had so ardently desired.

A third person witnessed their conversation in the Baronne's bedroom. That was Dr. Frank. He never went through the entrance vestibule of his brother-in-law's house; he was unfamiliar to all the staff, simply a foreigner who was simply known to live in the house next door. When he wanted to see his sister, we have seen the method he employed, and the secret means by which he entered the Baronne's apartment.

That day, naturally, the three interlocutors were radiant, and satisfaction was legible in their faces.

"Finally," said the Baronne, "the horizon is clearing slightly." To her husband she said: "Oh, Wilfrid, you've worked well!"

"Haven't I, my love? Confess that the idea of having the pro-German press intervene was an idea of genius!"

"Yes, certainly," said Dr. Frank. "For it would have been impossible to buy the French press, which is not for sale. Whatever their opinion was, the Parisian newspapers wouldn't have bargained."

"Not to mention that the steps to take would have been too dangerous. It would have been necessary to uncover ourselves, and that would have compromised my position as a diplomat of a neutral country."

"Fortunately, we understand that neutrality fully," said the Baronne. And all three burst out laughing.

The beautiful Emma resumed speaking. "Anyway, if you wish, Wilfrid, we'll drop in on the Estrelles after dinner. We'll see the Marquis there, and you can present him with our felicitations and our condolences at the same time."

"Perfect. That way, we'll be able to take the temperature of the house."

"And add that perhaps we might know what they've decided, for I don't believe that those two obstinate individuals will admit defeat."

"Very good, my beauty. Decidedly, Emma, you're a perfect woman…in all respects."

"Truly?" the Baronne replied. "You see me very touched by your flattering appreciation."

In the meantime, Henri and Espéret had returned to the Hôtel de Valsorres.

Germaine was distressed by the news of the rejection of the request for credit. Aunt Hélène, who had returned from Touraine the day before, shared her indignation.

Georges d'Estrelles arrived in his turn. He had heard the result of the vote from his Minister. He was furious too.

"The idiots! The imbeciles!" he repeated, incessantly.

His wife put an end to his imprecations. "Let's have dinner anyway," she said. "It's not a reason to let ourselves die of hunger. Let's replenish our strength, Messieurs. We can talk about all this while dining."

"And we can discuss the matter of our future resolutions."

The dinner, naturally, lacked vivacity. The check, at the beginning of the period of realization, was a cold shower.

When the meal was over, the diners went into the small drawing room, where they were taking coffee when Bettina, lifting the door-curtain, announced: "Monsieur le Baron et Madame la Baronne Lymstroem." And she stood aside to let the two visitors pass.

It was, in fact, those two sympathetic individuals, who had come, as they had put it "to take the temperature of the house."

Germaine had risen to her feet in order to greet them.

"My dear Madame," the Baronne said to her, "the Baron and I didn't want to wait any longer to present to you both with our felicitations, and the expression of our astonishment on learning of the extraordinary vote of the budget committee."

"Oh, you've heard!"

"Like everyone, by reading the evening papers, which gave the news in the stop pres," said the Baron.

"All the same," added the Baronne, "who could ever have believed that such an audacious endeavor wouldn't find the support of parliament."

"Certainly not me," said the Baron. And, turning to Henri and Espéret, who were smoking cigars: "It's beautiful, Messieurs, what you have conceived. It's a project worthy of France, which you honor with your genius. Yes, I say to you sincerely: it's magnificent. Receive my most enthusiastic felicitations."

"Oh yes,!" said the Baronne, apparently enthused, "it's a truly grandiose conception."

The two men accepted the hands that their neighbors held out to them, and shook them gratefully.

Germaine looked at Aunt Hélène, who was keeping silent, and gave the impression of saying: *Well, you can see, dear Aunt, that you were mistaken about the Lymstroems You see what loyal and faithful friends they are.*

The young woman offered refreshments to her two visitors.

After a moment's silence, the Baron said: "The project will have a world-wide resonance, my dear Marquis."

"Oh, do you think so, Baron?"

"But yes, yes! Be certain that the telegraph, with and without wires, has already carried the news to every country in the globe."

"And perhaps even the planets," said the Baronne, "if they can receive wireless telegraph messages."

"In addition," said the Baron, "you've put all the scientists and astronomers on the alert."

"Not to mention the military men," said the Baronne.

"Military men?" Germaine queried.

"Certainly, my dear Madame. Isn't it a conquest of which these Messieurs have dreamed? Every conquest interests military men."

Aunt Hélène pricked up her ears, and did not take her eyes off the Baronne and her husband.

The latter continued: "And now your beautiful dream has vanished and your hopes are dashed."

"Oh, no," replied the Marquis.

"Are you going to return to the assault on the Chambers?"

"God preserve us!" said Valsorres.

"So?" queried Lymstroem

"So, my dear Baron, since France doesn't want to support us in this enterprise we'll by-pass the State and go to Saturn without it. After all, I prefer that solution; that way, we'll be our own masters and, not being submissive to any official control, we'll have elbow room. We'll be able to depart whenever we wish, as we wish. That's worth a good deal."

"In that case," said the Baron, "You're going to meet the expenses of the expedition?"

"Certainly."

"It's from your personal fortune, then, that you're going to take the six millions that you requested of the Chamber?"

"Yes," the Marquis replied, simply.

The Baron stood up. "Messieurs," he said, solemnly, "your character is at the height of your genius. Once again, receive the sincere felicitations of a man who admires you...and envies you. I wish that my own country had citizens who could reach your level. Yes, it's very fine."

And once again, he extended his hand to the two men. They shook it with their honest hands, far from suspecting that they were subject to the grip of a traitor.

The Baronne embraced Madame d'Estrelles. The latter was very emotional. "Thank you, my dear friend, for your affectionate sympathy," she said. "Your amity is doubly precious to me in these hard moments."

The Baron bowed profoundly to Aunt Hélène, to whom the Baronne held out her hand with great demonstrations, and the Finnish diplomat and his wife quit the Hôtel de Valsorres, to which they had come, as they had said, "as neighbors."

The man and the woman did not unseal their lips until they were in their apartments. Then the Baronne, after having checked that the doors were locked, let her rage burst forth.

"Well," she said, furiously, "that's fine work!"

"What's the matter, my dear?" asked her husband,

"What's the matter? You are! You, who've behaved like an idiot! You, who haven't succeeded in preventing those two Knights of Space from undertaking their expedition!"

"Permit me, gracious Emma, to say that I did everything in my power. Haven't I carried out Berlin's orders scrupulously?"

"That's true!" replied the Baronne "But what good will it do? Will it facilitate the voyage projected by Osterwald?"

"Always Osterwald! Is he so dear to your heart?"

"That's my affair," replied the daughter of Graf von Paschwitz. "He's still going to be outdistanced. He lost six months in consequence of his shipwreck; he had to go in search of new minerals in the Pacific, so he'll be beaten by that Valsorres in an accursed race!"

"You detest him greatly, then, that Valsorres?"

"Do I detest him? I hate him with all my German hatred, him and his wife and his sister and his brother-in-law d'Estrelles. You're forgetting that I swore, at my father's death-bed, to retain that hatred in the depths of my heart."

"Oh, dear heart, I know that it's sown in fertile ground."

"What do you mean? Is that irony?"

"Not at all; I mean what I say. But let's get back to the subject. You're lamenting seeing Osterwald outdistanced; me too. I'll forget for the moment that he was your lover."

"Stop insulting me, if you please!"

"I'm not insulting you, my beautiful and legitimate wife"—the Baron emphasized that word—"I'm simply recalling an undeniable fact. So, I was saying that I'm forgetting that he's your lover in order only to see him as a German hero, burning with the desire to conquer new worlds in order to subjugate them to our great fatherland and the authority of our august Emperor."

"Well, it seems to me that you can scratch that conquest of distant worlds from our program."

"Why is that, if you please?"

"But, triple idiot that you are, didn't you hear what that Valsorres—may Satanic woe engulf him—said: he's going to do the thing at his own expense. *At his own expense*, you hear?"

"Ta ta ta!" replied the Baron.

"Oh, you can joke; *they'll go*."

The Baron stared at his wife, who began to undress. "Well, my beautiful and dear Emma, I tell you—I, Baron Wilfrid Lymstroem, Finnish Ambassador, and German subject even so—tell you that *they won't*."

The Baronne stopped dead. "You say they won't go?"

"Yes, I say that, because I'm sure of it."

"Oh! A boast!"

"No, dear beauty. Grant me hospitality and I'll explain to you, in whispers, the means I count on using to put a radical stop to that voyage."

"Truly? Oh, Wilfrid, if that's true..."

"Begin by listening to me, doubter."

"All right! I grant you the requested hospitality." And the Baronne went to push the bolt that locked her in with her worthy spouse. It is necessary to believe that he was persuasive, because, at one o'clock in the morning, he went back to his bedroom, accompanied tenderly by the Baronne, who said to him in a voice that she rendered affectionate: "Oh, Wilfrid, I've misunderstood you. You truly are a great German."

The Baron entered his apartment rubbing his hands; he had not wasted his night.

The next day, he did not waste his day either, for he had announced to his wife that he was leaving for Berlin without delay, in the company of Dr. Frank.

VI. In which we make the acquaintance of an
industrialist who is also a good Frenchman.

The Marquis de Valsorres and Espéret deployed the greatest activity.

Early the next morning, furnished with all their plans and drawings, which they had brought with them, they went to see the celebrated Lorraine ironmaster François de Bourcelle, the director of the colossal factories at Voysange, near Metz. Fortunately, the latter was in Paris.

Informed by telephone, he was waiting for the two friends in the vast study that he occupied on the first floor of his magnificent house in the Rue Blanche. He knew the Marquis de Valsorres well, he was even distantly related to him. Relations between Alsatians and Lorrains are frequent and cordial. He therefore welcomed his two visitors cordially.

"What good wind brings you?" he asked.

"Can't you guess?" Espéret asked him

"I believe that I have, in fact, guessed; it's not difficult. You've come to consult me on the subject of the construction of your interplanetary vehicle, about which all the papers are talking this morning." And he pointed to the issues of the *Petit Parisien*, the *Écho de Paris*, the *Figaro* and the New York *Herald*, on an armchair.

"You've guessed it," said Henri replied, "but only in part."

"What do you mean, in part?"

"It's quite simple. We have, indeed, come to consult you first of all, and then to order the apparatus from you."

"Aha!" said the ironmaster. "It's an order, then?"

"And a firm order," the Marquis replied.

"Damn! It's serious, then." François de Bourcelle stood up, and went on: "Messieurs, after having congratulated you, permit me to thank you for the great honor you're doing me in coming to confide your projects to me, to our factories, and charging them with their realization." He shook the hands of his two visitors cordially; all three of them were visibly moved.

"Now, Messieurs, "said the industrialist, "let's not waste our time in unnecessary palaver, shall we?

François de Bourcelle's study overlooked, through three high windows, the magnificent gardens that separate the buildings in the Rue de Clichy, at the rear, from those of the Rue Blanche. The ironmaster could work there far from the noises of the street.

A magnificent mahogany Empire-style desk, decorated with marvelous bronzes, occupied one extremity of the room, the walls of which were garnished with bookshelves in the same style as the desk. At the other extremity was a vast drawing table on which were compasses, slide rules, planimeters and integrators—in sum, all the graphic instruments necessary to an engineer.

Sitting at a smaller table, a young female typist was tapping her machine.

"I don't need you any more, Mademoiselle Madeleine," the industrialist said to her. "I'll be busy all morning, and I'll give you leave until two o'clock."

"Thank you, Monsieur," the young woman replied, getting to her feet and bowing, with a smile. She went out.

The three men gathered around the drawing-table. Henri de Valsorres began to unroll his blueprints.

"First of all," he said to François de Bourcelle, "let me explain to you rapidly the objective of our affair, the principle on which the machine that we're asking you to construct is based, and the means we count on employing in order to assure ourselves of the necessary energy. "

And the Marquis gave the ironmaster the explanations that we have already heard at the Château de Valsorres, except that this explanation was more technical; his interlocutor was an eminent engineer, a graduate of the École Centrale, and differential equations and integral calculations did not frighten him.

When the Marquis had finished his explanation, Monsieur de Bourcelle simply said: "That's admirable, Marquis; I can't find any other word to translate my thought; but let me ask you one question."

"One question, two, as many as you wish."

"You've succeeded in preparing a kilo of virium; that's perfect. This virium is sixty thousand times more active than radium; that's understood. It therefore represents an accumulation of energy sixty thousand times greater than the Curie metal, I admit; but that energy will take thousands of years to dissipate. What you need is to make it develop at will, in a very short span of time."

"Exactly."

"Well, how will you do that?"

"Here I'll hand over to Espéret; he's the one who found the means you're demanding."

The engineer, put in the spotlight, turned to François de Bourelle. "Yes, it's me who found the method of liberating the energy in our new radioactive metal at will. You know that there exist, in chemistry, substances called catalysts, which act almost by their mere presence, without the quantity of the substances brought into play intervening in a appreciable fashion."

"Yes, I know that," replied the ironmaster. "We make frequent use of that property in the metallurgical industry."

"Well, I've simply obtained a catalyst, but instead of a chemical catalyst, it's a physical catalyst that I employ."

"A physical catalyst? Explain yourself, Monsieur, because I confess that I can't quite grasp..."

"You'll understand immediately," Espéret continued. "That catalyst is simply a beam of cathode rays."

"Cathode rays?"

"Yes, the rays that the cathode emits in the bulbs in which X-rays are produced."

"You're magicians, Messieurs!" said François de Bourcelle, marveling. "But tell me how..."

"You'll see. I discovered it by chance. One day, in Valsorres' laboratory, we had isolated our first decigram of virium; I had nearly pulverized into very fine grains that I had enclosed preciously in a thick lead bottle. Did a particle remain on my table? Probably, for this is what I observed. I had had the idea of comparing the radiation of virium with that of X-rays, and for that, I had started up the induction coil that was to produce the famous rays. Scarcely had he coil been activated, however, and scarcely had the effluvia traversed the vacuum tube than a vivid, almost blinding light suddenly filled the entire room; one might have thought that an enormous quantity of magnesium powder had been ignited. At the same time, the Marquis and I, as well as our aide Thomas, both felt a sensation of intense heat, almost a burn. The latter fell over, so intense and so sudden was the sensation."

"But how did you figure out..."

"Wait. At first we didn't know anything at all; we had been astonished, Valsorres and I. But you know Pasteur's great saying: 'Knowing when to be astonished appropriately is the first step on the road of discovery.' We thought about a spontaneous deflagration of our tiny provision of virium. In order to clarify the situation I took the bottle containing it outside and opened it. The provision was intact. It was, therefore, something else. I searched for three days; I made my induction coil function in a hundred ways: nothing. It was enough to make ne tear one's hair out. Finally, on the fourth day, I thought of resuming the comparison of the two radiations—that of virium and that of X-rays. I took a tiny pinch of virium bromide with forceps and, in order to see what effect cathode rays had on it, I fixed it with a little gum arabic to the wall of the vacuum tube."

"Fortunately," the Marquis interjected, "I had recommended that you enclose it in a lead bottle."

"Yes, certainly; without that, we'd no longer be here to tell you the story. I'll continue. Scarcely had I switched on the coil and sent the current into the tube than the same phenomenon of illumination and heat was produced. This time we were on the track."

"That's magnificent," said François de Bourcelle.

"Then I recommenced the trials, but gradually. I used less concentrated virium bromide; I regulated the intensity of the current producing the cathode rays. Finally, I arrived at the conclusion that cathode rays produced the molecular disintegration of the virium, even in infinitesimal doses."

"Like the fulminate detonator that provokes the explosion of the shell of a 305mm naval gun?"

"Exactly. So we have the means of disengaging at will, graduating it in accordance with our needs, the formidable quantity of energy contained in the virium. That's the principal point of our discovery; it's our secret, Monsieur de Bourcelle; I confide it to your honor as a scientist and a Frenchman."

"Don't worry, Messieurs. It will remain where it is and no one will have any knowledge of it."

At that moment the telephone on the desk rang.

François de Bourcelle put the receiver to his ear.

"Hello!"

...

"Yes, speaking."

The ironmaster listened with the greatest attention. After a few minutes, he pronounced into the apparatus the simple words: "Thank you for your communication, my dear friend; we'll take advantage of it." And he hung up the receiver.

Then he turned to the two friends. "Well, Messieurs," he said, "here's a very curious coincidence. One of our engineers has returned from Berlin, where he concluded an important deal, and do you know what he's told me? Simply that he recognized, in the uniform of a colonel in the Emperor's general staff, one of the former foremen of our factories, whom we had taken on with Swiss identity papers and diplomas."

"That's frightful!"

"Isn't it? We always have to be on the alert, for we're surrounded by spies."

The two friends remained silent.

"Now we know the principles, let's see about the means of realizing them. Nevertheless, I still have one question to ask you, for it relates to a point that's still obscure in my mind."

"Speak, dear friend," said the Marquis.

"This is it. I understand very well the principle of the propulsion of your rocket by reaction. I also understand that you've found in virium the accumulator of energy necessary to furnish you with force throughout the duration of your voyage through space. But have you thought about the prodigious quantity of heat that the disintegration of that substance will produce? That quantity surpasses all evaluation, and as the reaction and the escapement will be made of metallic elements, no metal will resist that heating: everything will melt in a matter of seconds, and even though your voyage will be taking place in intersidereal space, the temperature of which is 273 degrees below zero, I believe that your organs won't even reach those cold regions, and will melt before even traversing the terrestrial atmosphere."

Valsorres looked at François de Bourcelle, smiling.

"We've forgotten, my dear friend, to give you one important detail. In fact, with ordinary metals you'd be entirely correct, but the molybdenum steel that

143

we count on employing acquires special properties in the presence of the products of the decomposition of virium. Again, it's by chance that we were able to discover that.

"We had decomposed virium in a small cylinder of that steel. The metal began by reddening very rapidly, but, to our great astonishment, instead of melting, it rapidly became darker again. The experiment, repeated twenty times, give us the same result."

"So?"

"So, it's doubtless a molecular action of atoms liberated by the virium on the molecules of the incandescent metal. Are they atoms? Are they the 'electrons' that seem to constitute the atoms themselves, and which, liberated by deflagration, condense the constituent elements of the steel? Still a mystery—but the fact is certain. Not only does our steel not melt in the presence of virium but its conductivity of heat is diminished, with the result that the substances in contact with it hardly warm up. That's what renders our enterprise possible. Otherwise you'd be right: the apparatus would melt before having traversed the terrestrial atmosphere."

"It's admirable, more and more admirable," said the ironmaster. "Now, let's get to work and find the means of the material realization of your amazing machine."

The three men leaned over the blueprints that Valsorres had laid out on the table.

François de Bourcelle continually picked up a slide rule and made a rapid calculation, the result of which he inscribed in a notebook. The conference, begun at nine o'clock, did not finish until half past twelve.

As he showed his visitors out, François de Bourcelle shook their hands vigorously. "Messieurs," he said to them, "it will be the greatest honor for our factories to have been chosen by you for the construction of your machine of genius. Count on me, as on yourselves."

"And above all, the most absolute silence," said the Marquis.

"That goes without saying. We're surrounded by too many spies not to be on our guard. Didn't we have proof of that a little while ago?"

"That's true, alas," said Espéret.

"And when do you expect to be able to deliver the engine to us?"

"I hope that everything be completed within eight or ten months, Messieurs, But let me tell you the manner in which I expect to carry out me task."

"We're listening."

"Our Voyange factories are in annexed Lorraine. If we constructed the machine there I would have to fear the ever-open eye of the German police. Under the pretext of the inspection of the working conditions they have the right to enter everywhere. I have no need to tell you that those inspectors are not inspectors at all."

"Aren't they?" said Espéret.

"No, they're engineers, and expert engineers, disguised as policemen, who come to discover our manufacturing secrets, for the benefit of the Krupp organization. I have, at any rate, played a trick on them."

"What?"

"I pretended to put aside in the metallurgy laboratory, when they arrived, a flask containing metallic barium, and I deliberately left in view a specimen of steel stamped, in minuscule letters, with the words *Bar 17 0/0 AA H*. They stole the ingot, and the Krupp factories worked on that false trail for a year. They wasted twelve months and at least twenty million."

"Bravo! That's good tactics. But you were saying, with regard to the Voyange factories…?"

"This. We have other factories, in France. They're situated not far from the others, in Broeuf, but on this side of the frontier. It's there that I'll have construction of the pieces of your rocket started."

"Pieces, you say?"

"Yes, to avoid even the possibility of an indiscretion, the pieces will be made separately, each in a different workshop. They'll be sent to you at Valsorres, and it's there, in the shade of your park, that you'll assemble them in order to realize your marvelous rocket. In consequence, from now on, have the necessary premises and machinery constructed and fitted out, and hire workers. In ten months, at the latest, we'll be ready."

"Thank you, my dear friend," said Valsorres.

"Now, Messieurs," said the ironmaster, with emotion in his voice, "permit me to say one final word to you. I'm not alone in our forges. Without having shareholders, I have associates; all the partners in the Voyange factories are in my family. But I know the sentiment of all my partners; they're Frenchmen, Lorrains, and gentlemen. They wouldn't admit that we could take any profit whatsoever from a construction designed to attain such a noble goal. You know them all, Marquis; they're the families of Hautmont, l'Estoc, Halgan, Burel and us. I can guarantee their acquiescence, and I'm happy to tell you that your engine will be delivered to you strictly at cost price. I ask you to be good enough to accept that offer as it is made, simply and wholeheartedly. It's for France!"

"It's in the name of France that we thank you, my friend," said the Marquis, with tears in his eyes, enthusiastically shaking the hand that François de Bourcelle held out to him.

When our two men were in their automobile, Valsorres finally broke the silence. "That's some consolation for the budget committee, eh, old chap?"

"Yes, my dear friend." After a pause, he added: "What a pity that a man like Bourcelle isn't a député. If only there were twenty like him in the Chamber, things would be different."

"Certainly! It's necessary that he presents himself. My wife knows his wife intimately we'll try to get him elected."

"Yes," replied Espéret. "That might be the catalyst."

VII. In which one can see the danger there is in loving both wine and beautiful women.

The Marquis de Valsorres and Espéret had quit Paris the following day, taking François de Bourcelle with them, who wanted to take account personally of the two friends' endeavors, in order to be able to work, in full knowledge of his subject, on the construction of the marvelous rocket that was going to conquer worlds.

The Marquise was waiting for the travelers. She had learned the result of the parliamentary session from a telegram from her husband and the newspapers. She simply threw her arms round her husband, saying to him: "Well, it's over!"

"No, my dear friend; let's rather say: it's about to begin."

After the compliments of the arrival, François de Bourcelle was conducted to his apartment, where he only remained for a few minutes; he was in haste to find himself facing the marvelous results obtained by the two scientists.

They too were waiting for him impatiently; they were burning to set the fruit of their research before the eyes of the eminent engineer. They headed for the laboratory, therefore. The faithful Thomas met them at the door, which he only opened after having cast a wary glance over the visitors through a judas hole.

"Bonjour, Thomas!" said Espéret.

"Bonjour, Messieurs," replied the worthy servant. "Oh well! Those pigs— begging your pardon—voted against you!"

"Yes, my good Thomas," replied the Marquis. "But that won't prevent us from undertaking our little voyage."

"And you'll be in the party," said the engineer.

"Oh, my good master! Truly! What an honor for a poor devil like me." And the fellow began to execute a jig, throwing his cap into the air, which he caught while leaping up.

When he had concluded that choreographical interlude, the Marquis asked him: "Anything new?"

"Nothing, Monsieur le Marquis, except that we've obtained nearly a hundred grams of your accursed drug."

"Accursed drug! That's how you talk! Anyway, another hundred grams is always good to have. And Le Bris?"

"Le Bris has been working all the time with Abbé Travers, who no longer leaves here. Oh, he's a stout fellow too."

"Let's go see all that, my dear Bourcelle. I'll go on ahead to show you the way."

"Do so, dear friend."

All three penetrated into the laboratory that we have already described. A moment later, Abbé Travers, with a white smock over his soutane, came in and shook their hands.

"Abbé Travers, our savant curé, a former pupil of the X," said the Marquis, introducing him to Bourcelle. Then, addressing the priest: "Monsieur François de Bourcelle, the ironmaster of Voyange, in Lorraine."

The two men shook hands cordially. Then, addressing Bourcelle, the Marquis said: "Now, let's begin at the beginning. First, here are the mineral specimens." He took several stones extracted from the volcanic soil of the Île de France out of a lead-lined box.

Bourcelle examined them like a connoisseur. He had taken a folding magnifying glass with three lenses out of his pocket, and he scrutinized the mineral structure of the specimens in the smallest detail.

"Very curious," he said, returning the stone to Espéret.

"Wait," said the later. "You'll see better."

He then approached the specimen to the electrometer, after having opened a small orifice in the lead sheath that enveloped the instrument. The needle immediately deviated to the maximum and was blocked.

"What do you say to that?" asked Espéret.

"I say that it's truly marvelous."

"That's the origin of our endeavors. Now, this is what we've done with it."

The Marquis opened a formidable strong-box, on the shelves of which lead boxes were deposited that must have been of considerable thickness, given the foot required to transport them to the table.

He opened one of them; it contained grains of a clear substance the color of milky coffee.

Bourcelle leaned over curiously, and put out his hand in order to take a few grains."

"Stop, my dear friend!" said the Marquis. "You'll burn yourself grievously."

Then he took a very tiny grain with platinum forceps and deposited it in a small porcelain cup.

"That's virium bromide."

François de Bourcelle was going from one astonishment to another. "Messieurs," he said to the two scientists. "I'm seeing today the most surprising thing I've ever seen, which I would never have dared to imagine."

"Now, however, you're going to see something even more astonishing."

"What's that?"

"The manner of liberating at our will the formidable energy contained in the molecules of virium." He turned to the abbé. "My dear Abbé, have you been able to set up the new high-tension transformer?"

"Yes, Marquis."

"And the results?"

"You'll see. Follow me."

They all followed the abbé, who went into another room, after picking up the cup in which Valsorres had deposited a grain of virium bromide. The abbé placed it on a little support, the height of which could be regulated by a screw in proximity to a glass tube of the kind that is used to produce X-rays. A large induction coil was set on a nearby shelf, and the two wires ended with two electrodes of the vacuum tube.

"Messieurs," said the priest, "stand aside, please."

Everyone retreated as far as possible.

"Now I'll switch on the current."

The abbé turned the commutator of the coil.

Scarcely had the effluvium reached the interior of the tube than a fiery atmosphere filled the entire room, while a sensation of intense heat struck the marveling spectators in the face.

"Well, dear friend," said Henri to François de Bourcelle, "are you convinced?"

"Yes, certainly."

"And you can say that you've seen it."

"I will say it…or rather, I won't say it, but I'll get to work."

"We prefer that," said Espéret. He turned to Abbé Travers. "Well, my dear curé, you've worked hard in our absence. The reaction was produced with an astonishing surety."

"Oh," said the curé of Valsorres, modestly, "I simply had the idea of dosing the current; that way, we can now graduate the release of energy at will. That, I believe, is what you desired above all."

François de Bourcelle reflected. "Messieurs," he said, "let me renew the expression of my most profound and sincere admiration. I know now what a man of genius is, for I've met two of them. And now, let's get to work. If it won't abuse your hospitality, I'll stay here for two or three days, in order that we can discuss and settle together the details of the machine that I'll put under construction without delay in our French factories in Broeuf."

"My dear friend, you know that you're at home here."

"Well, we'll begin tomorrow morning. Unfortunately, I'm not a very good draughtsman."

"Me neither, unfortunately," said the Marquis.

"Nor me, alas," said Espéret.

"But I am, Messieurs," said Abbé Travers. "At the X I always obtained 19 in graphics, and at Fontainebleau, in truth, I even hooked the 20, with the general's felicitations."

Everyone applauded.

"My dear Abbé," said Valsorres, "you truly are an envoy of Providence."

"Well," said the curé, "let's just say that I come from paradise and say no more about it."

After that response, they all washed their hands and resumed the route to the château, not without the Marquis having said to Thomas and Le Bris: "Au revoir, lads—and mount good guard."

"Have no fear, Monsieur le Marquis," the good servant replied.

Dinner was cheerful; the impression of confidence and hope completely effaced the bitterness that the committee's vote had left.

As they went back to their apartments, the Marquis said to his wife: "How frightfully distracted I am!"

"Why Henri, what have you forgotten?"

"Simply to tell you that my sister Germaine is coming, and is arriving tomorrow."

"With her husband?"

"No, Georges is retained at the Ministry. Germaine is coming with her two children, their nurse and her chambermaid."

"Well, my love, fortunately you've remembered; otherwise poor Germaine wouldn't have found a carriage at the station tomorrow when she got off the train."

"Yes, but what do you expect? I have other things on my mind."

"I understand."

And with that, they separated.

The next day was devoted to work. Henri, Espéret, Bourcelle and the abbé spent all their time in the Marquis de Valsorres' study.

Abbé Travers had brought his rulers, set squares, drawing pens and compasses. Under the fingers of the expert draughtsman, the ideas of the marquis and the engineer, brought to practical perfection by the ironmaster, increasingly took on substance. Working drafts began to give a general idea of what the rocket would look like.

The workers only paused when the lunch bell rang.

Henri found his sister, who had just arrived with her two children. The latter were joyful at seeing their little cousin Philippe again, and the three children were playing happily together under the surveillance of their nurses.

After lunch, the toilers returned to their work.

When evening arrived, as they came down to dinner, Abbé Travers said to the Marquis: "I think that with two days' work I can make clean copies of the drafts and give you definitive plans for their execution,

"Thank you, my dear Abbé!" said the Marquis, shaking the savant curé's hand.

While the masters were appreciating the excellent cuisine of the Marquise's chef, the servants were dining joyfully in the servants' parlor, as usual, except that they had one diner more, and that guest was Bettina, Vicomtesse d'Estrelles' chambermaid, the spy placed in the house by Baronne Lymstroem. What is more, that guest was seated next to Thomas.

One might think that the genius of evil is omnipotent in favoring enterprises. At the very moment when Lymstroem was wondering how he could procure information regarding the endeavors of the two friends, the sister of the Marquis left for Valsorres, taking her chambermaid with her. Decidedly, Hell was on his side.

Needless to say, the chambermaid had been coached before leaving Paris. In an energetic conversation, Baronne Lymstroem had given her orders that admitted no discussion.

At all costs, it was necessary to bring back precise documents.

As the radiogram from Berlin had said to Lymstroem himself, failure was inadmissible. Either Bettina brought back useful information, in which case she would be royally rewarded, or she came back empty-handed, in which case she would receive the most terrible of chastisements from the Baronne's expert hands.

At the last threat, the unfortunate young woman had shivered; she still remembered the cruel correction that her pitiless mistress had administered to her with blows of a riding crop; she was too much under the thumb of that terrible woman not to obey her blindly. And yet, Bettina was not all bad; she sometimes felt regret and disgust at her own conduct.

But the Baronne had her in her power, by means of the confession of her past sin, and she made that Sword of Damocles shine, always suspended over the poor woman's head.

We therefore rediscover the German woman—disguised as Swiss, her Germanic origin not evident to the profane by virtue of any accent—in pursuit of her designs.

The naïve and worthy Thomas did not feel at ease next to his beautiful neighbor at table; there were no attentions that he did not pay to her in order to render her meal more agreeable. The other domestics had seen the performance and laughed at it; they saw it as the realization of their prognostications, and that amused them greatly.

Only Le Bris and Catherine, the Marquise's chambermaid, did not laugh; they observed the couple—Le Bris because, being a confidant like Thomas of the work and projects of the Marquis, feared an indiscretion of Thomas' wagging tongue after a glass of wine, Catherine because, being Alsatian, like her mistress, her perspicacity and mistrust had been alerted by Bettina. Under the Swiss, the Alsatian had sniffed the German; tiny details of pronunciation, which would have passed unperceived by anyone else, had struck the ear of the daughter of Alsace, habituated to the accents of the people of her homeland and its neighbors the Swiss.

She repeated to Le Bris: "You see, Yves, that woman appears to me to have been born much nearer to Berlin than to Geneva." And by way of conclusion she had added: "Keep an eye open, and the good one."

"Understood," the taciturn mechanic had replied.

Bettina responded with provocative glances to Thomas' attention, which put Espéret's faithful valet in a state of extraordinary enthusiasm. When the domestics' meal had finished, Bettina stood up in order to go and receive her mistress' orders.

"Shall I see you again, at least?" Thomas whispered in her ear.

"Yes, yes, my dear friend," was the beautiful German's response.

Thomas remained nonplussed by the temporary separation that deprived him of his idol for a while. The latter came back a few moments later.

"I've been given leave for the whole evening," she said. "Madame says that she'll undress by herself today. And she added, with a gaze that set her admirer's veins ablaze: "I'm entirely free this evening."

Thomas was in seventh heaven. *Is it possible?* he wondered. But a difficulty appeared to him. In what refuge could he shelter his happiness?

Thomas reflected, seeking without finding. He was walking along a deserted path in the park alongside his Dulcinea. The latter then said to him, with a caress in her voice: "So I'm going to spend the whole evening at your place, my dear Thomas."

The worthy fellow had not expected that.

"My place!" he said, bewildered. "My place?"

"Yes, my dear, why not?"

"You can't think so!"

"On the contrary, I do think so. Isn't that where we'll be most comfortable?"

"Yes," replied Thomas. "But I sleep in a room over Monsieur le Marquis' laboratory, and no one can go in there. Only Le Bris and I reside there—and Le Bris would know everything."

"Who's Le Bris?"

"He's the mechanic, he's Catherine's 'promise'—she's the Marquise's chambermaid, as you know, the one who looks at us in such a way that one might think that she's jealous, doubtless because she thinks you're too beautiful."

A strange smile passed over Bettina's lips. "Oh, he's Catherine's lover!" she said. "We can be tranquil, then."

"Why is that?"

"Because he won't be spending the night in his bedroom. I have sharp ears and I heard them just now, although they were whispering."

"Oh!" said Thomas, shaken. "That's another matter, then."

"Isn't it, my love?" said the lovely young woman, passing her hand through her admirer's hair. "The only thing that worries me is the means of getting out of the château and in again unperceived."

"For that you can be tranquil. The little side door at the bottom of the service stairs is never locked; there's nothing to fear at the château; in any case, the park is enclosed, and Jérôme mounts good guard."

"Who's Jérôme?"

"The gamekeeper. He does a round every evening at eleven o'clock."

Bettina reflected.

"My dear friend," she said, "give me careful directions to the path where I ought to meet you."

"Here," he said, "you go along the main path to the end and then turn right; there you follow a little path that will take you straight to the laboratory. I'll wait for you at the entrance, because of the dog.

"Oh," said Bettina. "There's a dog?"

"Yes, Ravaut, a fine dog who keeps good guard—but with me, there's nothing to fear; he won't even bark."

The chambermaid reflected. "It's necessary that he doesn't howl and wake everyone up! That would make a fuss!"

"Be tranquil, my dear Bettina. "I assure you that Ravaut will be quiet and you can come to join me without anxiety. Until this evening, then?"

"Until this evening," the German woman replied.

Thomas applied a burning kiss to her lips. They separated, the chambermaid putting on an appearance of returning to the château after "taking the air" in the park, and Espéret's domestic returning to the laboratory, as was natural. On the way he met Jérôme, who was making his habitual round with his carbine over his shoulder. The gamekeeper was escorted by his dog Ramonet, who was trotting at his heels.

"Well, Thomas," said the young man. "You're going home to bed?"

"Necessary, in order to be up early in the morning," Thomas replied.

"Well, old chap," said Jérôme, "you're content now—your beauty is here. Oh, she was giving you the eye during dinner! Damn it, Thomas—it only happens to you!"

Thomas swelled with pride.

"You don't have anything to complain of either, Jérôme," he replied. "Mam'zelle Julie is very friendly to you, and she's a fine sprig of a girl—anyone would be a liar who said anything different."

"Yes, that's true," replied the gamekeeper, flattered in his amour and his self-esteem. "And she'd make a fine wife, you know."

Thomas approved with a gesture. "You see, Jérôme," he added, in a doctoral tone, "that proves that there's someone for everyone."

"Yes, that's true."

"And the thing is to be able to be content with one's share, without seeking to take one's neighbor's, not true, Jérôme?"

"That's my opinion," replied the gamekeeper. He whistled to his dog, who was rummaging in the bushes. "Here, Ramonet," he said. "Let's go, old chap. Au revoir, Thomas, and goodnight!"

"Thank you, Jérôme, and the same to you."

The two men turned their backs on one another, Jérôme heading toward the château.

We have said that Hell seemed to have mobilized its forces in order to aid Baron Lymstroem's projects; we are about to have another proof of that.

The gamekeeper's round was early; that is because he too had a little rendezvous with the lovely Julie, who had decided to crown his flame while waiting for him to lead her before Monsieur le Curé and Monsieur le Maire "for the right reasons." The curé was Abbé Travers and the Maire the Marquis de Valsorres.

And that is why Bettina was assured, that evening, of not finding any obstacle in the accomplishment of her tenebrous projects.

It is midnight.

As if everything had made a decision to favor the work of treachery that was about to be accomplished, the moon, which had been shining brightly at the beginning of the evening, was veiled by clouds and was no longer illuminating the pathways of the park with its milky light. They became absolutely black under the shadow of the tall trees.

The little side door at the foot of the service stairs opened quietly; Bettina emerged, treading softly.

The German woman thought of everything in order to ensure her retreat in case of alarm. She took a small piece of wood from her pocket and placed it in the socket of the lock; that way, it was impossible to close, and the door, simply pushed to behind her, would open at the slightest pressure.

The chambermaid's head was covered by a mantilla; she had a small bag in her hand. Resolutely, she set forth among the main pathway of the park. When she arrived near its extremity, she found Thomas, who was waiting for her, escorted by the dog Ravaut.

The good beast uttered a dull growl.

"All's well, Ravaut," said Thomas, caressing the animal. "You can see that Madame is a friend."

That did not appear to be the dog's opinion, for, without barking, he circled the newcomer, growling dully.

"Come on, shut up!" said Thomas, giving him a little tap over the ears.

In the meantime, Bettina had passed her arm under her admirer's.

"Finally," said the latter. "I thought you'd never get here!"

"What a fool you are! You know Thomas, that I want it as much as you do."

"Then let's go in, and let's hurry; let's not waste any time."

Thomas drew his visitor away. He opened the door in the grille and released Ravaut in the enclosure; then he headed for the building and opened the door.

"Now we're at home," he said, taking Bettina by the waist and kissing her full on the mouth.

"Patience!" she said. "Wait till we're entirely in your place." Then, seeing the doors in the vestibule, she asked, distractedly: "What are all these doors?"

"The one on the right is Monsieur le Marquis' laboratory. The one opposite, on the left, is where my master, Monsieur Espéret, works."

"Oh, it must be a funny sight, those machines."

"Oh, it's not as funny as all that," said Thomas. "There are instruments, bottles and balances."

"I'd like to see what it's like, all the same," said the chambermaid.

"Soon. I'll show you that afterwards."

"No, before—it's a curiosity. And if you're very good..."

Thomas was all ears.

"If you're very good, I'll give you a taste of an extraordinary cognac, of which I was able to filch a little bottle from my bosses."

The fellow's eyes lit up with the double desire engendered in him by the proximity of the much-desired woman and the prospect of a "little glass."

"Let's go," he said, "since you want it."

He took a bunch of keys out of his pocket, and, taking a small "pump key" from it, he opened the door of the Marquis' laboratory.

The soubrette darted a rapid glance around.

"My word, no, you're right," she said, "it's not very funny. Is the other side any more amusing?"

Thomas extinguished the commutator. He closed the door and opened the one opposite, which gave access to Espéret's laboratory.

"But it's even less funny here," said Bettina, pulling the same face. "Let's go, my friend. Thanks for satisfying my curiosity—let's go up to your room."

They both went up to Thomas' bedroom. He closed the door behind them. The poor fellow was mad with joy.

With a feverish impatience, he covered his idol with ardent kisses. She pulled way, went to open her bag, and took out a little bottle.

"Do you have any glasses?" she said to her admirer.

Thomas opened a cupboard and took out two wine glasses. "Here, my beauty," he said.

Bettina filled one of the glasses entirely, and put a few drops of golden liquid in the other. It spread an absolutely provocative odor. Thomas breathed in the scents of the alcohol and the woman voluptuously.

"To our amour!" said Bettina, raising her glass.

"To our amour!" said Thomas, emptying his.

While drinking, he made the reflection: "Damn it! That's good, Bettina of my heart! I've never sucked such a velvet!"

"Well, don't stint yourself, Thomas; there's plenty left." And she filled her companion's glass again; he drank the second draught and fell into an armchair, taking Bettina on his knees.

"That's funny!" he said. "I feel very sleepy!"

"That's not astonishing, my dear friend," the chambermaid replied, caressing him with her hand. "Working as hard as you work, you certainly have the right to a little rest."

"But I want to go on looking at you, and my eyes are closing in spite of me!"

"Come on, make a little effort, my dear! Tell me again that you love me!"

She kissed him on the mouth.

But Thomas' head fell on to his shoulder; the poor fellow was profoundly asleep.

Bettina got up. First she swallowed a white pill; then she went to open her handbag and took out a minuscule photographic apparatus, a masterpiece of one of the most celebrated German firms. She also took out a little roll of magnesium wire and a box of matches.

Then, having made sure, by touching him, that Thomas was solidly asleep, she took the bunch of keys from his trouser pocket and, having taking off her shoes and walking in her stockings, she went down to the laboratories.

First she opened the door of Espéret's.

Having switched the light on, she searched to see whether there were any papers in evidence, but saw none. She retreated into a corner, lit her magnesium thread and rapidly took two photographs of the instruments disposed on the central table. The cathode ray tubes were there.

That done, she locked the door again carefully and opened that of the Marquis de Valsorres' laboratory. She carried out the same photographic operation, and after carefully locking the door again, she went back up to rejoin Thomas, who was still sleeping the sleep of the just. She took care to replace the keys that she had previously extracted in his trouser pocket.

At about four o'clock in the morning, Bettina shook her companion forcefully. He uttered a dull groan, but did not wake up.

"All right," said the chambermaid. "Let's employ stronger means."

She took a flask of smelling salts out of her handbag and put it under her companion's nose. Under the irritating emanations, the latter sneezed, and then opened his eyes.

"Well, old man," said Bettina, "You were fast sleep. You had to breathe in my smelling salts to wake up."

Thomas rubbed his eyes.

"What time is it?" he asked.

"It's gone four o'clock, my lad, and I only just have time to run away if I want to get back into the château without being seen."

The spy got dressed in the blink of an eye. Thomas tried to retain her, in vain. She refused herself to all his demonstrations. "And come with me, above all, because of the dog."

Thomas escorted his idol to the door. Ravaut growled a little, but in response to Thomas' voice he remained tranquil, while looking obliquely at the chambermaid in a manner that was not at all sympathetic.

As she went through the door she turned round and blew a kiss to her lover of opportunity. He went back to bed, his heads heavy.

Oh, unfortunate Thomas, what consequences your moment of weakness might have!

VIII. In which it can be seen what the first consequences of Thomas' weakness were.

The Marquis de Valsorres did not waste time.

Under his active direction and that of Espéret, a vast area had been cleared in the forest of Valsorres, the trees of which enveloped the walled park of the château on three sides. The clearing that created with axes, was bordered by the section of the enclosing wall to which the scientists' laboratory was adjacent. An iron door had been pierced in the wall and permitted the two friends to pass directly into the new area reclaimed from the forest. A high wall had been constructed around it, and the top had been garnished, not only with shards of broken glass encased in cement, but with a line of iron "artichokes" with sharp barbs, in such a way as to render any attempt to climb over it even more dangerous.

The enclosure this created had a surface area of about two hectares.

Inside the walls were vast hangars with high roofs, the frames of which had been furnished by the felled trees. At the back, opposite the communicating door, a large building closed by glazed panels enclosed forges, drills, workbenches and lathes—in brief, all the material necessary for an assembly plant.

It was there that the various sections that were to constitute the marvelous rocket, in which the heroes of this story were going to launch themselves into space to conquer a new world, were to be collected and fitted together.

The personnel had already arrived, and, under the direction of the worthy Le Bris, had proceeded with the installation of the machine-tools. That personnel was tried and tested. It comprised the two engineers and the two stokers of the *Coulomb,* and six sailors, under the direction of Jean Le Floch, the ship's crew-master. Those eleven individuals were lodged in a "barracks" constructed next to the workshop. It is evident, therefore, that in order to assemble his machine, the Marquis had elite men, as much from the viewpoint of devotion as those of technical competence, muscular strength and skillful ingenuity.

A vast iron door with two battens opened to a road driven through the forest and ending at the national highway. It was by that route that the pieces of the rocket fabricated in the Broeuf factories were to arrive, transported from the nearby railway station by trucks.

Letters from François de Bourcelle arrived two or three times a week. The ironmaster thus remained in constant communication with the two scientists, with the consequence that not a single rivet was placed and not a single hole drilled without him being advised and without him being able to ask for and obtain any modifications he judged indispensable.

All these works of installation had lasted three months. It was 15 June.

A few days after her arrival at her brother's house, Germaine d'Estrelles had returned to Paris with her chambermaid, her children and their nurse.

As one can imagine, Bettina was too wily to write from Valsorres to her true mistress, Baronne Lymstroem; in a small village, everyone would have seen her going to the post office. Even less had she sent the Baronne the photographs that she had taken, which, in any case, had not been developed.

She thought that her mistress would not stay long at the Château de Valsorres, and she was not mistaken. Six days after her arrival, Madame d'Estrelles had returned to the capital in order to rejoin her husband. Then Bettina took advantage of her first free moment to present herself at the Lymstroem house. The concierge, who knew her, let her go up after having confirmed that Madame was "at home."

The chambermaid knocked gently on the door of the Baronne's bedroom.

"Come in!" said the latter's voice.

Bettina went in, bowing down to the floor. She was holding her traveling bag in her hand.

"What is it, imbecile?" asked the Baronne.

"I've bought some information for Your Gracious Ladyship," replied the chambermaid.

The Baronne got up, curiously. "Let's see these precious documents," she said, ironically. As she spoke, she extended her hand.

Bettina took the little photographic apparatus out of her bag.

"Most noble mistress," she said, "I was able to penetrate, only for a moment, into the Marquis de Valsorres' laboratory and take some photographs there, in conformity with the indications that Your Grace had deigned to give me."

"Give them to me quickly!" cried Baronne Lymstroem, impatiently.

"They aren't yet developed. Following your instructions, I brought them back intact."

The Baronne pressed a button. A chambermaid appeared.

"Tell the Baron that I want to see him immediately."

The chambermaid went out. In the meantime, the Baronne had unhooked a small telephone apparatus and put it to her ear.

"Is that you, Wilhelm?" she said.

"Yes, Emma, it's me," replied the doctor's voice.

"Come right away, through the door to my bedroom. There's news."

A moment later, one of the panels of the tapestry rotated, unmasking the opening by mans of which, as we have seen in a previous chapter, Dr. Frank penetrated directly into his sister's bedroom. He had scarcely arrived when the Baron appeared in his turn.

"What is it?" the two men demanded.

"Tell them," the Baronne ordered Bettina.

The latter repeated what she had said to the Baronne and handed the little camera to her mistress.

"That's my affair," said the doctor, taking possession of the object. "In twenty minutes, we'll know what these plates contain. Wait for me here."

The German scientist returned to his house and shut himself up in his laboratory in order to develop the precious photographs there.

In the meantime, the Baron and Baronne pressed Bettina with questions.

"How were you able to introduce yourself into the laboratory, which must be well guarded?

"Noble Lordship, I tried to gain the good graces of the laboratory assistant, who had a bedroom there."

"Ha ha!" replied the Baronne, laughing loudly. "Mademoiselle Bettina has played the siren, it appears?"

Bettina lowered her eyes, blushing.

"Come on, tell us everything. Don't leave anything out."

"No," said the Baron, his eyes gleaming. "Give us all the details. It will be piquant to know how you got in."

The unfortunate young woman was covered with shame. At that moment, she truly felt that she was the plaything of those two tyrants. She remained silent.

"Come on, stupid imbecile, is it necessary to repeat what I've just said? You know that I have the means to make myself obeyed."

Then Bettina, understanding that it was necessary to say everything, recounted in the slightest detail her night with Thomas. The Baron's eyes were gleaming.

"Ha ha! How beautiful she is, the bitch," said the diplomat, stimulated by the chambermaid's story.

The Baronne looked at him scornfully. "If those details interest you, my dear," she said to her husband, "feel free to have them given to you."

At that moment, Dr. Frank returned, holding a porcelain dish, in which four photographic plates were bathing, in the condition of negatives.

"Here they are," he said. He lifted one of the plates up between his eye and the lamp. "This is the only one that contains any information, but I don't yet know how important it is. In any case, it's unexpected. Do you see, Wilfrid?" He showed the plate to the Baron.

The latter examined it for some time with a small magnifying glass, which he took from the Baronne's table.

"I can see, alongside a porcelain crucible, a kind of oval glass vase."

Frank did not say anything.

"And one might think," the Baron went on, "that two wires were attached to two buttons placed at its two ends.

"Ah!" said Frank. "You see the same thing that I do." He addressed Bettina. "Do u remember what was on the table when you took his photograph?"

159

"Yes, Milord. I remember now that there was a kind of big glass egg with wires attached to it."

"And to you remember where those wires came from?"

The chambermaid made a new effort of memory. "I believe I recall, without being entirely sure, that they came from a kind of big bobbin with pieces of copper."

Frank clapped his hands.

"That's it! Cathode rays!" He turned to the chambermaid again. "Bettina, today you've redeemed all your past sins. You've brought us an item of information that is priceless, and I'll recompense you for it."

He took his wallet from his pocket and took out a thousand franc bill. "Here, my beauty," he said. "Take this for yourself; you've worked well." And he kissed the spy on both cheeks. The honor confused her.

The Baronne, for her part, had taken a five hundred franc bill out of a drawer, which she gave to her slave, holding out her hand, which the domestic kissed with the marks of the keenest gratitude.

Even the Baron joined to all that a hundred franc bill, and, putting his arms round the beautiful girl's hips, he assured himself of the solidity of her anatomy. His wife did not manifest the slightest sign of jealousy.

Bettina withdrew, bowing profoundly.

As she went downstairs, she could have been heard to say, very quietly: "My God! Into what an ocean of shame have I fallen! To think that I belong, body and soul, to those brigands. What use is money to me, if I've lost honor?"

And the poor girl, wiping away a furtive tear, returned discreetly to the Hôtel de Valsorres.

When she had quit the Lymstroems and Dr. Frank, the latter spoke. "I don't know yet what that cathode ray apparatus is for, but in the hands of a Valsorres, it's nothing futile. But use can that tube be to him? I'm stumped."

The Baronne replied to him: "My dear Wilhelm, the best thing to do is to go see von Osterwald right away."

Frank reflected.

"Between the two of you," his sister continued, "you might be able to get the key to the enigma and utilize Bettina's information."

"You're right, my sister," said the physician. "I'll leave for Berlin tomorrow."

The Baron interrupted. "Isn't Osterwald at Krupp's at the moment?"

Frank slapped his forehead.

"That's true, my dear fellow, you're right. I'd completely forgotten that he's been at the Essen factories for more than a month, trying out the utilization of his minerals, without any great success. Oh, that accursed Valsorres will get ahead of us, and win the game in spite of all our trumps. Curse him!"

The Baron smiled. "My dear brother-in-law," he said. "Valsorres won't win the game. I've already promised your sister that, who wanted to recompense me for what I said to her on that subject—isn't that so, delicious Emma?"

"Delicious Emma" turned round.

"That's true," she said. "Wilfrid has found an absolutely infallible means of opposing his voyage."

"And what is it?"

"Ah," said the Baron, "that's our secret, isn't it, my beauty?"

"Yes," said the Baronne, smiling in a mysterious fashion."

The doctor took his leave of his sister and brother-in-law. As he closed the secret door he said: "I'll be at Krupp's tomorrow evening."

François de Bourcelle had not remained inactive.

As soon as he returned to Voyange he had announced to two of his best draughtsmen that he was taking them to the French factories at Broeuf, and that they would be spending several months there. They were, therefore, to make preparations to depart with him immediately.

There, François de Bourcelle had a long conversation with his principal engineer in the presence of the two draughtsmen, both brilliant graduates of the École Centrale. In the course of that conversation the broad outlines of the construction of the rocket were settled.

Three days later, the draughtsmen had put a preliminary plan on paper, which the ironmaster discussed with them and his engineer at length. Modifications to the first draft were decided.

The two young men set to work again. They were two Alsatians who had been immediately smitten with Henri de Valsorres' project, the grandeur of which they understood and in which they were proud to collaborate.

Four days later, they brought François de Bourcelle a plan that the master and his engineer judged faultless.

Then they passed on to the execution. Detailed designs of the various pieces were drawn up, and tracings were taken of them to be given to the chiefs of the various workshops where the sections of the rocket were to be made in isolation. None of the chiefs knew for what apparatus the part he was manufacturing was destined, much less did any suspect the goal to which that apparatus was to be directed.

Things went so smoothly that, three months after the first conversation, the metallic pieces emerged from the workshop, were packed up and sent by railway to the Château de Valsorres.

We have seen that, by virtue of the Marquis' efforts, everything had been prepared to receive them. As soon as the pieces arrived they were placed under the hangars in the order in which they were to be mounted. All the pieces of the assembly were carefully checked in the workshop; it could now be affirmed that, once the pieces were put in working order, the assembly could be completed in less than a month by the men of the *Coulomb*.

The Marquis, Espéret, Dr. Portier and Abbé Travers did not quit the laboratory, where they were working hard on the extraction of the virium bromide. They now had more than a kilo and a half. That was nearly ten times as much as was necessary to accomplish their interplanetary journey.

"But I'd rather have too much than too little, "said Espéret. "One never knows what might happen!"

"Then too," said the abbé, "you'd be very sorry to be obliged to remain in heavens; you'll be very content to return to Earth. This way, you'll have an abundant provision of fuel for the return journey."

Thus, by virtue of the continuous labor of everyone, the elements of success had been prepared in isolation.

Nothing had been left to chance; everything had been foreseen.

Yes, everything—except for the underhand maneuvers of Baron and Baronne Lymstroem; except for the "infallible means" that the sinister Boche had conceived for opposing irrevocably our heroes' departure.

What was that means?

IX. In which the reader will find a complete description of the transplanetary vehicle.

Things were moving swiftly at Valsorres.

Thanks to the admirable mariners of the *Coulomb*, led by Le Bris and the technical personnel, the pieces of the rocket were put in place as soon as they arrived.

With a great comprehension of the enterprise, François de Bourcelle had initially impelled the fabrication of the pieces of the basic framework, so to speak: those that were to form the skeleton and general support of the aerial vehicle.

In the middle of the enclosure where the assembly was taking place, a large area had been reserved, surrounded by robust scaffolding permitting the mariners to realize the positioning of the various parts as they arrived at the foot of the structure.

That was commenced on 25 March, and by 10 May, one could already have a clear idea of it. In the center of the system of scaffolding, a kind of huge cylindro-conical shell deployed its rounded form, perched on a metallic framework reminiscent, in its approximate dimensions, of the form of the inferior supports of the Eiffel Tower. Its exterior surface was divided longitudinally into two disparate parts; one was coated with a layer of brilliant nickel, while the other was covered with a layer of mat black paint.

Between the four feet of the substructure, a ladder is set up, thee rungs of which end in a "manhole" giving access to the interior of the engine, after an ascent by means of iron crampons placed along the walls of a sort of vertical tunnel or shaft three meters long.

Having arrived there, one penetrates into the "chamber" properly speaking: a circular space for meters in diameter and four meters fifty in height; it is there that the audacious scientists who are to set forth on the conquest of worlds must stay and live for two, or perhaps three, months.

The interior installations are not yet in place, but the Marquis de Valsorres or Espéret would say that they are ready to be put in; that they comprise couchettes superimposed in pairs, as aboard ships, with numerous drawers and a host of compartmentalized cupboards in which the utensils, instruments and weapons indispensable for the unprecedented enterprise can be lodged.

Only one thing is in place: that is a workbench with two shelves, tools and even a small portable and collapsible lathe, in order for an urgent repair to be made, if necessary.

On the ceiling of the room is a broad opening one meter fifty in diameter, containing a kind of shaft, narrowing toward its summit. It is at the upper extremity of that shaft, solidly inserted in bronze armatures, that the "porthole" is fixed, of thick Saint-Gobain glass, twenty-five centimeters wide, which will permit one of the voyagers—the one "on watch"—to perceive the point in the sky or the planet toward which the marvelous projectile will steer.

Other portholes, four in number, are pierced in the lateral walls of the chamber and permit observation through the sides. Finally, in the trapdoor closing the access shaft, a sixth porthole, ordinarily covered by a metal plate, permits a view of what is happening behind the rocket.

We have penetrated thus far into the chamber—the cabin, so to speak—which is not the most interesting part of the apparatus; we shall now see the essential organs.

The cylindro-conical surface, half-polished and half-blackened, is not the wall of the chamber; it is only the external envelope of the celestial vehicle. Between that envelope and the interior envelope, properly speaking there are two others, fitted with the greatest care by autogenic solder, in such a fashion as not to leave any fissure—for between those three envelopes there is a vacuum, the most perfect vacuum that humans can produce.

It is that evacuated envelope that ensures the protection of the voyagers against the terrible cold of interplanetary space. It is known, in fact, that the temperature of celestial space is absolute zero—that is to say, 273 degrees below the usual zero of thermometers.

It is to resist that cold that Valsorres and Espéret had the idea of concentric enveloped imprisoning an airless space; that is the artifice of Thermos flasks, in which aliments can be kept hot or cold, at the temperature of their introduction.

Thus, the entire shell is surrounded by two "sheaths of void," if one might put it thus, in such a fashion as to render losses of heat by conductivity minimal.

Below and above the cabin were two spaces, each having its destination. The space situated below the cabin and separated from it by several thick plates of steel was the combustion chamber. It was there that the virium was to be decomposed, under the action, variable at will, of cathode rays, and furnish the formidable dose of energy necessary to the propulsion of the rocket at the fantastic velocities that it had to attain in order to be able to arrive at its goal in the desired time.

That combustion chamber occupied a volume of approximately two cubic meters beneath the cabin, and it was terminated by three steel tubes that opened between the engine's foot-supports. Those three tubes made an acute angle between them, in such a fashion as to resemble a tripod; the motor effort was thus directed in accordance with heir axis when the gases were escaping through all three tubes simultaneously; but if one of them were closed, the effort became asymmetrical and the shell could be deviated in its trajectory.

In addition, three other vertical tubes departed from the combustion chamber and curved horizontally toward the exterior, in three directions, making angles of a hundred and twenty degrees between them. It was these tubes that served, by virtue of the reactions the gases produced at their emergence, for steering the rocket or, if necessary, turning it around in space. In the latter case, the release of the gas by the inferior tubes would brake and gradually deaden the fall on to a planet, on which the voyagers could alight very gently. Steel valves permit the closure at will of one or several outflow orifices; these valves are maneuverable from inside the shaft situated at the top of the rocket.

The "pilot" of the rocket would, therefore, at all times, be the master of its direction as well as its velocity.

Above the cabin is a space four meters high, divided in two horizontally by a rigorously airtight partition that traverses the upper shaft. It is in that space that the provisions of water and comestibles necessary to the expedition will be stored.

Valsorres was counting on making the complete journey in two months; he wanted to ensure a safety margin and to take enough food and water for six months. It was necessary to anticipate for each voyager an average of two kilos of solid nourishment and two liters of liquid per day. That made, for 180 days, 360 kilos of nourishment and 360 kilos of water; multiplied by four that gave 1,440 kilos of food and 1,440 liters of water. Valsorres would take 2,000 kilos of food and 2,500 kilos of water. The latter would be lodged in the superior space, the closest to the tip of the rocket, the food beneath. Doors permitted access to the circular space that contained them, and could contain other necessary objects: blankets, clothing, linen, bandages, pharmaceuticals, etc.

As for the heat indispensable to obtain hot liquids, there was nothing to worry about; a single particle of virium bromide represented more than the calorific energy necessary for cooking preserves and the preparation of hot coffee or tea.

Valsorres had thought about defense, in case of being attacked by Saturnians, if they existed. He was taking four automatic repeater Winchester carbines and two large caliber "express rifles" with explosive bullets, to combat any animals that might be encountered, and, in addition, two ordinary hunting rifles. Each of those weapons was amply supplied with cartridges.

Furthermore, each voyager was to be equipped with a Browning pistol and a sturdy hunting knife of American form, short and solid.

Finally, in order to foresee everything, the Marquis was taking a machine gun, and a provision of ten thousand cartridges. With that, the four Argonauts could "hold their own" against infinitely superior forces.

Needless to say, particular care had been taken in the matter of instruments. Astronomical telescopes with lenses and mirrors, "refracto-reflectors" of great power, in spite of their reduced dimensions, would permit the voyagers in the heavens to observe everything, close or distant, that appeared to their gaze. The most powerful of those telescopes had a magnification of two hundred times, the weakest a magnification of sixty. Each of them was to take, in addition, a set of prismatic binoculars magnifying twelve times, for relatively short-range observations once they arrived in the vicinity of Saturn.

The precision instruments—barometers, thermometers and manometers made by the best constructors—were carefully lodged in cases, themselves arranged in cupboards. Chemical products destined to emit oxygen and absorb the carbon dioxide originating from the respiration of the voyagers were stored in the compartment at the extreme front.

Orifices closed by spindle-taps traversed the concentric envelopes of the rocket and ended in tube inside the cabin; they would permit the travelers, before risking emerging from their vehicle, to determine the pressure of the atmosphere at the point of disembarkation, as well as the nature of the gases that they would have to respire there.

As can be seen, everything had been anticipated, even photographic apparatus of long and short range, for photographing distant stars as well as the closest objects.

No expedition had ever been prepared with such a determination to leave nothing to chance.

There was nothing more to do than put the furnishings of the cabin in place and remove the scaffolding used in the construction. Then, the rocket, free of its shackles, would be able to launch like a shooting star toward the new world that it was about to conquer.

X. In which the reader will see the means employed by Baron Lymstroem
to prevent the departure of the Marquis de Valsorres.

The last preparations were reaching their end. It was 8 June, and Valsorres had fired the departure for the twenty-fifth of the same month.

Is there any need to describe the emotion that gripped all the residents of the château?

Germaine d'Estrelles and her husband had come to Valsorres on 1 June; they intended to spend with the Marquis the final days separating him from his flight into the heavens. They had brought with them their two children and their nurse.

Naturally, Bettina, the Vicomtesse d'Estrelles' chambermaid, accompanied her mistress. Before her departure from Paris, the German woman had had long and mysterious conversations with Baron and Baronne Lymstroem. Every time, the spy left the house of the Finish diplomat with a more somber expression and a more dejected attitude.

Aunt Hélène had also arrived at the château, with her young cousin Zabeth. The latter no longer quit the construction yard; she had become the improvised aide of Dr. Portier and was doing her best, under his direction, to arrange and dispose all the items constituting the on-board pharmacy.

Valsorres had maintained the greatest secrecy regarding his enterprise. He had not wanted to see any journalist, and had not wanted to make any communication to the Press. However, in order to authenticate his departure, he had decided that it should take place before representatives of six great newspapers, three French: *Le Petit Parisien, Le Figaro* and *Le Temps*; one English, *The Times*; one Italian, *Il Secolo*; and one American, the New York *Herald*. He had expressly ordered that no German journalist be present at the departure.

It was, therefore, 8 June.

The voyage was, as can be imagined, the object of all conversations, in the drawing rooms as well as the servants' parlor. The audacious enterprise of the Marquis could no longer be dissimulated from the domestics, so the "voyage to the Moon" was the topic of conversation of all the servants. And the commentaries were lavish.

In the village, too, there was no talk of anything but the "voyage to the Moon"—for, like the servants of the château, the worthy peasants were unaware of Saturn and its ring of light.

Abbé Travers was the butt of the most incessant questions.

"Is it true, M'sieu l'curé, that M'sieu l'Marquis is going, like that, to the Moon?"

"Yes, my dear Mathieu, it's true."

If Mathieu was religious, he made the sign of the cross, saying: "But M'sieu l'curé, it's like someone trying to reach the good God."

"No, old chap" the curé replied. "On the contrary, it's to render better homage to him."

The schoolteacher had also questioned the savant abbé.

"Is it true, Monsieur le curé, as it's being said in the neighborhood, that the Marquis de Valsorres is going to make a voyage to the heavens?"

"Yes, Monsieur Barthon, it is."

The schoolteacher reflected.

"Well, I declare that it isn't possible."

"On what basis do you say that?"

"I'm speaking in the name of science."

"My god Monsieur Barthon, you'll see for yourself. At my request, the Marquis has decided that the authorities of Valsorres will be present at his departure, in order to draw up an official statement. There will be the deputy mayor, the municipal councilors, the justice of the peace, the town clerk, the notary, you, the local policeman, the director of the post office, the brigadier of the gendarmerie and his two men. So you'll be able to see. And then, like Saint Thomas, you'll be forced to render to the evidence and believe what you've seen."

The schoolmaster went home very pensive.

On the evening of 8 June the sky was overcast; the barometer had gone down considerably during the day; the wind had turned to the south. In brief, a storm was brewing.

Nevertheless, dinner had been very cheerful. The Marquise was trying to hide the terrible anguish that she felt as the hour of separation drew nearer. Germaine was striving to do the same, as was Aunt Hélène. As for the Marquis, Espéret and the doctor, they were talking about planets, satellites, orbits, ellipses, conjunctions, oppositions and occultations, all subjects as interesting for them as they were obscure for the other diners.

After dinner, they went to take coffee on the terrace of the château in order to breathe more easily, but the air was as stifling outside as it was in their apartments. Lungs were oppressed by a heavy, stormy atmosphere

The children, as always, were dining separately with their nurses, in a small drawing room on the ground floor. It was Bettina, that evening, who was providing the service in that "little dining room."

When the three children had finished, they were taken to say goodnight to their parents before going to bed

"Oh, I'm very sleepy," said little Philippe.

"Us too," replied the two d'Estrelles children.

"Come on, children, off to bye-byes," said Philippe's Alsatian nurse. Addressing the Englishwoman who was looking after Germaine's children, she added: "I don't know what's the matter with me, unless it's this stormy weather, but I'm falling asleep as well."

"Me too," replied the Englishwoman.

And the two women hastened to undress the children and put them to bed; then they went to bed themselves, and fell heavily asleep."

The Marquis' guests had not taken long, either, to go up to their apartments.

At eleven o'clock, the entre château was silent.

At half past eleven, lightning began to streak the somber sky; the storm began and son took on a terrible aspect. The thunderclaps succeeded one another without interruption. Large raindrops came to flatten against the hot earth. The terrible power of atmospheric electricity was manifest in all its grandeur.

Shortly after midnight, a door in the first floor corridor opened quietly. A woman came out wrapped in a dark mantle, carrying a package, which she concealed with the greatest care. She arrived at the door to the service stairway, which she went down cautiously. Having arrived on the ground floor she continued down to the basement, and found herself in front of the small side door by which we saw Bettina go out in order to go to her rendezvous with Thomas.

She went along the main path of the park, which she followed as far as the junction with the first lateral path. There she stopped beside an enormous oak.

A shadow detached itself from the tree trunk.

"Is that you, Hans?" she asked.

"Is that you, Bettina?" the man replied.

"Yes, it's me, and here's the object." She handed the man the package that she as holding under her mantle.

The man took it, and sheltered it under a vast cloak.

"Adieu, Bettina!"

"Adieu, Hans!"

Bettina went back to the château; anyone who had followed her would have seen her weeping, her shoulders shaken by long sobs, and would have heard her say: "Great God! When will this shame end? Oh, truly, I think I'd rather die than live like this!"

She went back into the château through the side door, which she closed carefully. As soon as she was in the corridor she took off her wet shoes, which she held in her hand in order not to leave footprints. Having arrived in her room, she changed her rain-soaked garments completely, replacing them with dry clothes. She cleaned her muddy shoes, threw her dress on to a chair, dissolved a pinch of white powder in a glass of water and drank it. A few minutes later, she was sleeping heavily.

As for the man we heard called Hans, he had taken the lateral path that ended at the enclosing wall, exactly where a breach was that was to be repaired the following day.

Behind the breach as a long, low automobile with its headlights out. A man was standing beside the vehicle, while the chauffeur was at his post. The motor was turning over gently.

The man approached the breach, through which Hans was about to climb.

At that moment, barking was heard between two thunderclaps.

"Damn!" said the man from the car. And, turning to Hans, who was coming through the breach, he commanded: "Hand it over, quickly!"

Hans handed him the package that he was holding under his cloak. At that moment, a flash of lightning illuminated the brief scene. At the same instant, a rifle shot rang out under the trees. Hans made a violent gesture and fell to his knees.

The man from the vehicle only just had time to put Hans' burden into it and run toward him to help him through the breach. He felt his fingers moist with blood.

"You're wounded?"

"Yes, Milord, but not dead, fortunately.

Both of them hurled themselves into the automobile, which pulled away at top sped.

A few seconds later a man and a dog arrived at the foot of the breach. The man was holding a carbine in his hands, still smoking.

"I hit him, though," he murmured, bending down. Addressing the dog, he said: "Seek, Ramonet, seek, seek! Go on, Ramonet! Go, go!"

The dog searched the brambles. Suddenly, he barked, and bent down to seize something in his mouth.

"Bring it, Ramonet, bring it!" said the man, who was none other than Jérôme. "Bring it, my good dog!"

After having stroked the dog, he took what it had picked up from between its teeth.

It was a cap with a leather peak.

"This will help the gendarmes pinch the thief who got into the enclosure!" aid the gamekeeper. "Now let's go back. The thief has fled, but they'll catch him."

And Jérôme went back to his little house, followed by Ramonet.

The next morning, the park resembled a battlefield. There was nothing but broken branches and uprooted trees. Two of the château's chimneys lay on the ground; the windows of the veranda had been smashed by hailstones as big as hazelnuts.

The servants, having risen early, were busy doing their best to repair the damage, while awaiting the arrival of the indispensable workmen.

The Marquise de Valsorres had been one of the first up, and she darted the sovereign gaze of the mistress of the house everywhere, wanting to measure for herself the extent of the ravages caused by the tempest.

When she went past her little Philippe's door, she opened the door quietly.

"Come on, little idler, it's time to get up," she said leaning over the cradle in which her son should have been lying.

But she had hardly finished the sentence when she uttered a loud scream.

The cradle was empty.

Philippe was not there.

Frightened, the Marquise turned toward the alcove where the nurse's bed was, and called to her. The nurse was sleeping heavily and did not respond to the appeal.

The Marquise shook her; nothing happened. She put a bottle of smelling salts under her nose; only then did the nurse start.

"Philippe? My son? Where's Philippe?"

The Alsatian rubbed her eyes.

"Monsieur Philippe? He's asleep in his crib."

"No, wretch," said the panicking Marquise. "He's not in his crib!"

The nurse leapt out of bed and saw that the child was not there.

"My God! she said. "My God! What's happened?"

The Marquise had pressed all the bell-pushes; the servants came running from all directions.

The poor crazed mother addressed all of them. "Philippe? Have you seen my son? Where is he?"

The domestics were struck with amazement. Philippe had disappeared. One of the valets had gone to inform the Marquis. He arrived.

"What is it?" he demanded.

"Philippe has disappeared! Look, his cradle is empty!"

The Marquis approached the sobbing Alsatian.

"Come on, Thérèse," he said. "Instead of crying, try to remember what happened last night. Come on, tell me everything."

The unhappy woman recounted what she could remember.

"Yesterday evening at nine o'clock I took Monsieur Philippe to his room, although he had had more sleep than usual. I put him to bed and he went to sleep immediately. And my eyes were closing too, so much that I went to bed and must have fallen asleep immediately."

"So you didn't hear anything?"

"Nothing, Monsieur le Marquis. I was sleeping as I've never slept before."

"And the thunder didn't wake you?"

"Thunder?" asked the nurse, astonished. "Was there thunder?"

The Marquis did not understand. "But there was a frightful storm last night, you silly woman!"

"My God! My God! What a disaster!" said the poor woman.

That was all that could be got out of her.

Germaine, attracted by the noise, came to join her sister-in-law. She was informed of the catastrophe in a few words. Moved by anxiety, she ran to her children's room—but the two little ones were fast asleep.

Vicomtesse d'Estrelles went to the Englishwoman's bed; but she too was sleeping like a log. As with the Alsatian, in order to wake her up it was necessary to employ smelling salts. Only then did she shake it off.

"Do you know what has become of Monsieur Philippe?" Germaine asked her.

Completely bewildered and only half awake, the Englishwoman did not understand what was being asked of her. Questioned, she told a story identical to Thérèse.

"But that's horrible!" said the Marquise, between sobs.

"Come on," said the Marquis. "Let's pull ourselves together. What is this story of sleep. What did you have to eat and drink yesterday evening?"

"As usual, Monsieur le Marquis, the children's supper: a little soup, broth and biscuits."

"Where did you have this meal?"

"In the little dining room, Bettina served us."

"Someone go and fetch Bettina," said the Marquis.

Germaine ran to her chambermaid's room. She came out uttering a cry. "She's asleep too, and can't be woken up!"

The Marquis understood less and less. "Wake her up, so she can tell her what she knows."

While Bettina was being woken up, Valsorres addressed the assembled domestics.

"It's a little implausible that someone was able to get into the château, go into a bedroom and take away a child without any of you having heard or seen anything!"

One of the valets came forward. "Perhaps it has something to do with the gunshot I heard at about midnight."

The Marquis stated. "A gunshot! Where? Speak, damn it!"

"Well, Monsieur le Marquis, I couldn't sleep because of the storm. I'd opened my window for a moment, and between two thunderclaps I heard, as I said, a gunshot, and a dog barking."

"You're sure of that?"

"Yes, Monsieur le Marquis. I thought that it was Jérôme making his round, who had fired at a poacher."

The Marquis had turned round. "Send someone to fetch Jérôme!"

The gamekeeper arrived at that moment; he had noticed the general hubbub at the château, and had come to make his report to the Marquis on the night's events.

"This is what I saw, Monsieur le Marquis," he said. "It might have been shortly after midnight, because I'd heard the church clock striking twelve during a lull; the wind carried it. I'd just taken the first path to the right and Ramonet was with me. It was black, and except for the lightning flashes you couldn't see three paces in front of you.

"Suddenly, the dog started barking, and in a lightning flash, I saw a man who was trying to get out of the park through the breach on the wall. 'Stop, or I'll shoot!' I said. "A terrible clap of thunder begins to roll, and then there's a second lightning flash. I see the man jumping through the breach. I fired a shot of the carbine—quickly, but I'm sure I hit him. This morning, I saw blood on the stones, and the dog brought this back."

As he finished, Jérôme took out of his game bag the object that Ramonet had picked up from the ground.

The Marquis seized it and examined it. "It's a livery cap," he said, "but there's no armory or monogram. He looked inside the cap. "Ah! It's a German cap!"

In fact, in the middle of the red lining inside the cap were words inscribed in golden letters: *Karl Steinmann, Hutfabrik, Kaiserstrasse 12, Breslau.*

The Marquis reflected. Suddenly, he turned to Jérôme.

"Let's go to the breach," he said.

But the Marquise grabbed her husband's arm

"Henri! Henri! Jérôme's bullet might have killed Philippe, if the man took him."

Vicomte d'Estrelles, who had also arrived at his sister-in-law's side, had heard the last words. "Don't worry, my dear Marie. These people have taken Philippe away alive, for they'd have no interest in taking him away dead. For me, your little one is alive, and we'll get him back."

Then he followed the Marquis and Jérôme, who departed with the dog.

In the meantime, Bettina had been woken up. The chambermaid too had been very difficult to bring round. She rubbed her eyes and declared that she did not remember anything.

"After serving dinner to the children, I went to dine myself. I felt a great need to sleep and went to bed. I heard absolutely nothing last night."

"Not even the storm?"

"Was there a storm, then?" the German asked, with a marvelously feigned naivety.

The Marquise saw that he girl knew nothing. She fell into an armchair, and gave free rein to her tears, which her sister-in-law's caresses tried in vain to dry up.

Meanwhile, the Marquis returned from his investigation.

"Well?" the Marquise asked, anxiously.

"Be brave, my dear Marie. It's definitely a kidnapping. Philippe has been abducted by two men in an automobile, which was certainly a German auto."

"The cap, then…?"

"The cap is that of the man who got into the park. How did he get into the château? How did he find the bedroom where the child was sleep? As many mysteries, for the moment, which it's impossible to explain. All that we know for certain is that the auto was German, for we've just found another proof. It must have been necessary to tighten a screw, the chauffeur must have taken out his tool-kit, and had probably just finished when Jérôme fired, for he left the kit by the roadside and must have leapt back into his seat in order to get the car moving."

"What about the car?"

"The car left a profound rut in the edge of the road soaked by the rain. It's a powerful vehicle with matching tires, at least forty horsepower. As for the tool-kit, here it is: look, it's German."

The Marquis showed his wife the leather bag containing the chauffeur's tools, all of German provenance.

"Then it's all over?" said the Marquise, in anguish.

"No, Marie, no. Before coming back here Georges has gone to the telegraph to mobilize the Paris police and the surveillance service of the Foreign Affairs."

"Alas," said the poor mother, "it will be too late."

"It's certain that they have a start. Leaving here at quarter past midnight with a forty horsepower and the roads deserted at night, if they knew the road they must have made at least fifty an hour; in eight hours they could have covered four hundred kilometers. But the police are fine sleuths. In any case, I'll leave for Paris with Georges, and I have no need to tell you that everything that it's humanly possible to do, we'll do. Don't despair yet."

As the Marquis finished speaking, a powerful automobile drew up in front of the perron. Henri got into it with his brother-in-law, after having kissed his sister and his wife, to whom he said, with a final kiss: "Be brave, my poor love. God is just!"

And the auto set off for Paris at top speed.

XI. In which it can be seen that Marquis Henri de Valsorres is worthy to bear the name of his ancestors.

As one can imagine, Henri de Valsorres had acted rapidly.

As soon as he arrived in Paris, he had gone to see the Prefect of Police, to whom he had given a detailed account of his son's abduction. He had brought the pieces of evidence with him: the livery cap of German manufacture and the tool-kit left by the roadside by the chauffeur, similarly of German origin.

The Prefect had promised to act diligently. Immediately, he had telegraphed all the frontier posts to stop any vehicle containing a child, unless the identity of the passengers could be established.

For his part, d'Estrelles had informed the Minister of Foreign Affairs of the incident. The Minister had immediately started wheels in motion among the French police abroad, while not dissimulating his scant confidence in the success of the enquiries launched. They were, in fact, to remain vain, by virtue of the infernal skill with which the abduction had been organized, in its slightest details.

The wretches who had kidnapped little Philippe knew that the abduction would be perceived in the morning. As the crime had been committed at midnight, they had eight hours before them, and with their fast auto, barring accidents, they could cover at least four hundred kilometers in that time. But the Swiss frontier is nearly six hundred kilometers from the environs of Tours, and a breakdown might have slowed them down and the frontier posts would have had time to be alerted. They had therefore made provision to put all research off the track and thwart the pursuits.

Instead of seeking to leave France with the child via the land frontiers, they had planned to depart by sea. As soon as the little prisoner was captured, the auto would head at top speed for Les Sables-d'Olonne, the distance of which from Tours by road is only 250 kilometers. They were therefore able to reach that port in less than five hours, and would have a margin of three hours in case of any unforeseen incident. A German ship would be waiting for them at Les Sables; the child was to be embarked on it and immediately put out of the reach of the French police, while the auto returned tranquilly to Paris.

That infernal plan succeeded completely. At half past five in the morning the automobile stopped on the quay of the deep-water basin of Les Sables, alongside which a steamer carrying the German flag, the *Bavaria*, was moored. That steamer was a commercial ship, a "cargo boat," but it possessed six cabins able to take passengers.

When the automobile stopped alongside the ship, Dr. Frank could have been seen getting out of it, carrying a sleeping child in his arms. That was poor little Philippe, in the power of his kidnapper.

As soon as the child was aboard, the ship, its boilers already under pressure, made ready to depart. Six o'clock chimed in the bell tower of the church of Les Sables-d'Olonne. The tide was high and the sea flat calm, the sluice-gates of the basin were opened. The *Bavaria* emerged slowly from the port, passing between the two jetties.

Philippe de Valsorres was now completely lost to his parents, and the kidnappers were out of range of French justice.

As for the automobile, having filled up with gasoline, it took the road to Paris at moderate speed. Between Les Sables and La Roche-sur-Yon, however, its chauffeur could have been seen to carry out a curious maneuver. Having got down from his seat, he changed the plate bearing the registration number of the vehicle. He had foreseen the possibility that the customs officers at Les Sables in service on the quay had made a note of the number of the auto from which Dr. Frank had emerged, carrying his victim.

In that fashion, everything had been foreseen, and the crime had not left the slightest trace.

Needless to say, no trail could be found. Enquiries were made about several automobiles that had passed through Valsorres in the course of the previous day; their chauffeurs or owners were able to prove their identity and the reasons for their journeys without difficulty.

After several days spent in Paris, the Marquis decided to return to the château.

As soon as he crossed the threshold of his family dwelling, the Marquise, who was dressed in mourning, hurtled toward him.

"Well?" she demanded, in anguish.

"Nothing, my poor Marie. Nothing."

"Weren't the police able to do anything?"

"The police went into action, but the indications we had were very weak and the Prefect didn't hide the scant confidence he had in the result of the investigation. The wretches had at least six hours start, and you can take it for granted that they took advantage of them."

The Marquise de Valsorres had collapsed on a bench in the vestibule.

Her husband, her sister-in-law and Aunt Hélène covered her with their caresses, but nothing could appease the poor woman's dolor.

Only Aunt Hélène had recovered her composure. She was the first to think that the Marquis had important matters to deal with. She therefore said to him: "A large envelope arrived here yesterday, addressed to you, with a German postmark.

"A letter from Germany for me? Where is it?"

"In your study."

Henri ran upstairs. A minute later he came down, his face convulsed with anger.

"Oh, the swine! Oh, the bandits!" he cried.

Aunt Hélène ran toward him. "What's the matter now?"

Henri handed her a sheet of paper. "Read that, Aunt."

Aunt Hélène took the piece of paper and read aloud:

The Marquis de Valsorres has no need to try to recover his son. He will not see him again on Earth or in the planets where he wanted to take a holiday in such an imprudent fashion. If he wants to know the reason that impelled the person who is writing this letter to take possession of the child, let him ask Mademoiselle Hélène de Valsorres to consult the memories of her youth. She will perhaps recall her disdain for the Graf von Paschwitz during the war of 1870.

The shade of Graf von Paschwitz is taking its revenge today.

There was no date and no signature, simply a Hamburg postmark on the envelope.

The piece of paper fell from Aunt Hélène's hands. "Oh, the villains," she murmured, also letting herself fall on to the bench beside her niece.

A profound silence reigned among the actors of the scene.

Espéret, who had just appeared, picked up the piece of paper and read it attentively.

"Nothing," he said. "Not one clue. The letter is typewritten."

The Marquis, however, had taken back the sheet of paper and reread it aloud. When he arrived at the third line he cried: "Oh! I understand everything! They want to prevent me from departing, and for that, they've abducted my son." The Marquis had raised his head. "Yes, that's the evident objective of the kidnapping. They think that they'll oblige me to expend my activity and my energy in researches that they've taken care to render futile..."

And he added, after a pause: "Well, they're mistaken." And he turned to everyone present. Portier and Abbé Travers had arrived in their turn. The Marquis, addressing them, said in a firm and assured voice: "Messieurs, I announced to you that we would depart for Saturn on 25 June. On 25 June, the rocket will leave the Earth and launch forth into space. The Marquis de Valsorres must not break the promises he has made. *Noblesse oblige!*"

Abbé Travers had advanced toward the heroic gentleman; tears were shining in his eyes and it was in a tremulous voice that he said to the Marquis de Valsorres: "You are what I thought: you are worthy of France, of which you are a child, worthy of the ancestors whose name you bear, worthy of the wife with whom you share it, and worthy of our old École Polytechnique, of which you are a glory." And he added, after glancing at the Marquise: "And worthy of the son you are mourning today, whom God, in his infinite justice, will return to you."

All hands were extended toward Henri de Valsorres; everyone was weeping. Even the domestics, who had hurried to the vestibule, did not hide their emotion.

Aunt Hélène advanced toward her nephew. "Yes, Henri, you're right; you are giving the greatest lesson that it is possible to give, for you are stronger than grief. You are great, Henri, and you are truly a Valsorres. Depart then, my dear child; depart and return glorious to the château of your fathers."

But the Marquise, who had thrown her arms around her husband, murmured in a low voice, while stifling her tears: "They've taken my son; my husband is going to leave me; what will become of me?"

XII. In the course of which we see the Marquis, Espéret, Portier and Thomas leave Earth, promising to return.

The days passed quickly at Valsorres, the final days that the Marquis and his companions were to pass in the midst of their friends before launching forth on their heroic enterprise.

It was 18 June. Only seven days separated the voyagers from the date fixed for their departure. Henri was actively carrying forward his preparations, keeping his eyes on everything in order to leave nothing to chance.

The voyage might last two months; he was taking provisions for six; he needed three hundred grams of virium to accomplish the planned trajectory; he was taking nine kilos.

The question of respirable air had been studied carefully. Considerable quantities of copper oxide, destined to furnish oxygen, were accumulated in the terminal section of the rocket, as well as caustic potash to absorb the carbon dioxide emitted by the lungs of the voyagers. On the advice of Abbé Travers, they were even taking a provision of compressed nitrogen in steel bottles especially fabricated by François de Bourcelle.

"I know that the nitrogen isn't 'used up' and serves indefinitely, in theory," said the polytechnician priest, "but if, as a result of an accident, the air from your rocket leaks into the interplanetary void, you'll no longer have nitrogen to temper the action of your oxygen. It's therefore necessary to take a supply."

And the Marquis had done as the abbé proposed.

Rid of its scaffolding, the rocket now stood up in all the elegance of its lines, given a simultaneous impression of lightness, security and power.

Henri de Valsorres spent his mornings and days in the assembly yard, checking all the instruments, provisions, weapons and garments. Trial elevations had been carried out several times and had shown that the apparatus responded exactly to its author's calculations. In the evening, the Marquis devoted his time to his wife, his beloved Marie, whom he tried as best he could to console for the disappearance of Philippe.

"Come on, my love," he said to her. "Philippe will be returned to us; I'm convinced of it." When the Marquise shook her head sadly, he went on: "There is a justice; the benediction of Heaven will extend over us; it will permit you to be a mother a second time; another son will console you for the loss of the first if we don't get him back—but we will get him back, you'll see!"

The four voyagers had, as they say, put their affairs in order.

Espéret had no family except for a few distant cousins; he made a will, which he deposited in the office of Maître Marly, the aged notary of Valsorres, who handled the affairs of the château, like his father and grandfather before him.

Dr. Portier was orphaned of both parents and had no brother or sister. He had put all his papers and scientific work in order, and had said to little Zabeth: "Mademoiselle, I certainly expect to return from up there, but if, by chance, I don't come back, I confide my modest endeavors to you. There's an entire program of research to carry out. If I remain on another plant, you can have your son do it, when you have one."

The young woman, her eyes moist with tears, had replied: "My dear friend, I won't give them to my son, because, if you don't come back, I shall never have a son..."

Portier interrogated her with his gaze. "...Because I shall never marry."

The doctor was pale with emotion. "Then, if I come back...?"

"I'll be your wife," Zabeth replied, putting her hand in that of the doctor, who covered it with kisses.

As for the worthy Thomas, he had no one on Earth about whom he could think. He had simply given Bettina his photograph, with a lock of his hair, saying to her: "Keep this, my dear Bettina, in memory of me."

The Marquis had written his last will and his testamentary dispositions in a copious handwritten document, duly signed, made in duplicate and enclosed in two envelopes sealed with his arms. One had been deposited personally with Maître Marly, the other had been given to the Marquise de Valsorres, who had placed it preciously in her jewel-box.

25 June arrived.

The day was solemn.

As if nature had wanted to celebrate the departure of the four heroes, the weather was splendid.

At eight o'clock in the morning, all the residents of the château had gathered in the chapel in order to hear mass said by Abbé Travers. The worthy priest, in celebrating the holy sacrament, could scarcely dissimulate the profound emotion that he was experiencing.

The day went by in veritable meditation. Everyone was thinking about the imminent separation while awaiting the departure, which was to take place at nine o'clock in the evening.

After dinner the abbé, clad in a surplice, escorted by a choirboy carrying holy water, proceeded with the blessing of the projectile. The ceremony was simple and moving.

The voyagers were at the foot of the apparatus. Behind them stood the Marquise, Aunt Hélène, Germaine, little Zabeth and Georges d'Estrelles.

François de Bourcelle had come from Paris to witness the departure of the machine whose pieces he had constructed.

The six representatives of the Press were with the family. As the Marquis had desired, the "authorities" of Valsorres were to witness the departure, in order to draw up an authentic official report. The deputy mayor was there; Mahaut, the Marquis' most important farmer, was there; there was the physician,

Dr. Gérard; there was the brigadier of the gendarmerie and one of his men; Maître Marly the notary was there, the local policeman and the schoolteacher. The domestics of the château and the mariners of the *Coulomb* were grouped in the rear. The inhabitants of the village and the surrounding communes had gathered outside the enclosing wall in order to watch the launch of the projectile.

The supreme moment had arrived.

The Marquis shook the hands of the witnesses. He kissed his aunt, his sister and little Zabeth. Then he clutched his wife to his heart in a long and passionate embrace. She could scarcely hold back her tears.

"Have confidence, Marie," the Marquis said to her. "We'll come back. And if we don't come back, the son that you'll bring into the world will continue the Valsorres line. You'll bring him up, giving him the example of his forebears, and talking to him about his father—who will, I'm sure, have the joy of holding him in his arms."

As for little Zabeth, she had been unable to hold back. She had thrown her arms round Dr. Portier and kissed the young man passionately. Then, turning toward the witnesses, she said to them with pride in her voice: "He's my fiancé, I love him, and I expect him to come back."

One after another, however, the passengers, climbing the ladder, penetrated into the shaft that gave access to the interior of the shell. The Marquis went up last, after having blown one last kiss to his wife.

The sound of the trapdoor closing was heard, and the grating of the screws that sealed it from the inside.

On the orders of Le Bris, the witnesses retreated sixty meters away from the rocket; it was about to take off.

In fact, a jet of incandescent gas was seen to depart from the inferior section of the apparatus, between the four supporting feet. The disengagement, calm at first, quickly took on a character of extreme violence, fusing forcefully, with a noise that increased dramatically.

The Moon, in its last quarter, rose above the horizon.

Abbé Travers showed the audience a brilliant dot in the sky. "That's Saturn!" he said, in a grave voice.

All the men had bared their heads.

The jet of gas was now whistling with an indescribable violence.

Suddenly, the shell was seen to rise up slightly; it quit the ground and broke any connection with the soil. Then its movement of ascension was accentuated; it surpassed the height of the tallest trees. Then its velocity accelerated; it was literally hurled into the sky, followed by a luminous streak of propellant gas.

The acclamations of the witnesses and the villagers were still resounding when it was no more than a brilliant dot against the dark blue sky.

The Marquis de Valsorres, Espéret, Dr. Portier and the faithful Thomas had now been launched into space.

Then the schoolteacher, Monsieur Barthon turned to Abbé Travers and said: "You were right, Monsieur le curé, they've gone. But it remains to be determined whether they'll come back."

The curé replied: "Certainly they'll come back; it's me who tells you so, in the name of science and in the name of the justice of God."

PART FOUR: IN SPACE

I. In which it will be seen that that voyagers of the Fusée *are able to perceive the Moon at close range, at the Earth at long distance.*

Our voyagers, therefore, departed at nine o'clock in the evening of 25 June 1914.

As soon as they were all assembled in the interior of the *Fusée*, the Marquis de Valsorres had said to his companions: "From now on, my friends, we only form a single body, we must only have a single soul. We must live for one sole objective: to plant the flag of France on Saturn and to return to Earth to rejoin the cherished individuals we left behind there."

"That's understood," said Espéret. "Let's not waste any time; its quarter to nine. Let's set an example of exactitude; it's necessary for us to be launched into space at nine o'clock precisely."

The Marquis activated the transformer, of small dimensions, which, via the intermediary of the cathode ray tube, was to liberate the energy of the virium. The voyagers, as a matter of precaution, were carrying twenty-four of those tubes, carefully wrapped up in corrugated cardboard.

Then Dr. Portier, bending down, opened a compartment in the bottom of the shell and, with tongs that he held in a hand clad in a glove fitted with articulated lead plates, he dropped approximately two decigrams of virium bromide into a cylindrical opening in the floor of the cabin and closed the lid again.

The lid was made of a thick sheet of quartz inserted in a bronze crown, the screws of which held it from the inside.

Valsorres looked at his watch; it was eight fifty-two.

"Begin the disengagement," he said.

Portier rotated the commutator of the coil; the gas began to escape, whistling; the entire metallic skeleton began to vibrate.

At eighty fifty-eight they had the impression that the system was lifting; the disengagement took place without interruption and with the greatest regularity. At zero hour precisely, they felt the apparatus rise of from the earth. Through the portholes the voyagers could see the tops of the trees falling away beneath them,

They had departed.

The velocity accelerated, but the Marquis did not want to go too rapidly in traversing the dense layers of the atmosphere, which, by virtue of their friction, might have heated the apparatus excessively.

At nine fifteen he estimated that the vehicle had traveled approximately sixty kilometers. The Earth, examined through the porthole, was scarcely visible, illuminated as it was by the pale light of the lunar crescent.

"Now let's bring the second element of reaction into play," the Marquis ordered.

Portier and Espéret repeated the maneuver they had made for a second opening. The velocity accelerated. All four of the voyagers were silent. The Marquis was observing the Moon through the upper porthole.

"Let's start the third element!" he commanded.

The maneuver was repeated a third time. Now the *Fusée* was operating with all its motors; inside the projectile, that was, so to speak, imperceptible.

The four men gazed at the sky through the portholes. Espéret was the first to break the silence.

"In about three hours, at this speed, we'll be in proximity to the Moon."

"Are we going to land there?" asked Dr. Portier.

"I don't see any need," Valsorres replied. "The Moon is close enough to the Earth for us to know that it has nothing very interesting to offer."

"In any case, Espéret observed, "we're going to pass close enough to it to be able to observe it at our ease."

"And even to see the side that is never visible from Earth, and which the sun must be illuminating at present, since the Moon, reduced to a mere crescent, is close to being new."

"That's perfectly correct," Espéret replied. "We can steer in such a fashion as to pass in close proximity to our satellite. Portier, my dear, deflect us slightly to the right."

Dr, Portier opened the valve controlling the lateral disengagement tubes opening to the left; immediately, by virtue of the reaction to the escape, the *Fusée* veered slightly to the right.

Valsorres observed the Moon through the upper porthole. After a moment, he said to Portier: "That's good, we're heading in the right direction. We're making good progress.

"How long will the Messieurs take to reach the Moon?" asked Thomas, always curious.

"Not much, my dear Thomas," Espéret replied. "It's a quarter of an hour since we left; I about three hours we'll have arrived in proximity to the Moon."

"That's good," replied the faithful servant, laconically.

While the *Fusée*, thus steered, continued its route, the Marquis addressed his three companions. "My friends," he said, "it's now necessary to regulate the employment of our time. We're three scientists and one good servant. It's necessary that one of the three of us is always on watch. Do you agree?"

"Perfectly," replied the others.

"So, we'll divide our days into intervals of eight hours, during which one of us, taking turns, will take over the direction of the *Fusée*, except for critical moments when 'all hands are on deck.'"

"Agreed," aid the Marquis' companions, in unison.

"From now on, we'll no longer have 'natural' days and nights, since, once we're out of the zone neighboring the Earth, we'll be illuminated by the sun's rays all the time, which will always penetrate the chamber through at least one of the portholes. We'll thus always have the impression that it's daytime."

"We won't go to bed, then?" said Thomas

"Yes, my lad, we'll go to bed, and you'll be able to sleep easy, because you'll have finished your day's work."

"But how will we know when it's finished?"

"Like this. We'll continue to use terrestrial hours. In two padded boxes I've brought five chronometers of the *torpillleur* type,[18] which have rendered such great services in navigation. Those five chronometers will be reset every day, two by Portier and the other three by me. By comparing them, we'll be alerted to the slightest irregularity in the functioning of any one of them."

"That's perfect," replied the doctor.

"In addition, I'll hang up a clock in the chamber, without a pendulum but with a spring escapement. The clock will be set, every day, in accordance with our chronometers, and it's in accordance with it that we'll regulate our daily activities. Is that understood?"

"Perfectly."

"Furthermore, we'll each have our pocket watch, which will be put in accord with the chronometers every day."

"Understood. What about the date?"

"We departed on 25 June 1914; I'll place a calendar beside the clock, on which we'll scratch out one day every twenty-four hours. That way, we'll always know what day and what time it is."

"That's very well organized," said the doctor, "but you haven't told me yet what we'll do in order to know how far away from the Earth or some other planet we are."

"You're about to find out," said the Marquis.

He went to open one of the cupboards in the chamber and took out a pair of prismatic binoculars, the magnification of which was fifteen times.

"This," he said to his companions, "is the instrument for measuring distances. It's simply a pair of the telemetric binoculars that artillerymen use. The ocular lens on the right has a divided micrometer; the number of divisions that an object occupies permits the measurement of its distance."

---

[18] The term *"montre torpilleur"* [torpedo-boat watch] came into use in France prior to the Great War with reference to compact chronometers employed by the French navy.

"But what's the object of known dimensions in this case?" asked the doctor.

"For military uses it's an infantryman or a cavalier. Here's it will simply be the Moon, or Mars, or Saturn, the diameters of which astronomy has furnished for us, or simply the Earth, when we're sufficiently far away for its image to be contained within the instrument's field."

"That's marvelous in its simplicity!" Portier exclaimed.

"And very reliable, especially with celestial bodies, which, given that they're spherical, always have circular images in the binoculars, the diameter of which is easily measurable on the micrometer."

"But what if the sun is hidden by clouds?" asked Thomas.

The three men laughed.

"My good Thomas, there are only clouds around the Earth," the Marquis replied. "Here, there won't be anything to hide the sun's rays from us. In any case, to illuminate the interior of the *Fusée*, we have, as you can see, a particle of virium in a glass tube fixed to the ceiling, and that will suffice."

Indeed, in spite of the terrestrial night in the midst of which the *Fusée* had taken off, a milky light emitted by the virium tube filled the chamber and illuminated objects with a white light that was not fatiguing and very agreeable to the sight.

Thomas declared himself satisfied with the explanation. The Marquis told him, in any case, to prepare the couchettes for the night. The worthy servant carried out the order, saying to himself: *That's all right. To think that I'm going to the Moon! Damn! These things only happen to me!*

Meanwhile, the *Fusée* advanced like a meteor; the disintegration of the virium made though the three orifices communicated to the projectile an acceleration that was certainly more than eleven tenths that of gravity, for the four voyagers felt heavy. Thomas declared that he had "legs of lead" and Portier made the remark to Valsorres.

"What does it matter," the Marquis replied, "as long as it doesn't inconvenience us? We have work to accomplish, and that apparent surplus of weight is compensated by a surplus of velocity. We'll be near the Moon in about an hour and a quarter."

As one can imagine, there was no question of going to bed. Everyone wanted to see the Moon at close range, especially to see the mysterious hemisphere always hidden from the inhabitants on the Earth, who only perceive half of our satellite, always the same.

Already, for some time, the image of the Moon had become too large to be contained within the telemetric field. With the aid of binoculars, only a part of the increasingly close heavenly body could be perceived.

The *Fusée* was progressing, in any case, with a perfect regularity, and the voyage promised to be smooth. The temperature inside the chamber, however, was beginning to drop considerably.

Thomas blew on his fingers..

"Are you cold, old chap?" Espéret asked him.

"Well, yes, Monsieur. It's not that it's cold, exactly, but it certainly isn't warm!"

"Don't worry, Thomas; you'll be warm shortly."

Valsorres went up to the pilot's station, and, by means of a maneuver of the tangential valves, caused the rocket to rote on its axis, in such a fashion that, instead of offering its polished half to the solar rays, it presented its blackened half to them. The effects did not take long to make itself felt. A few minutes after the demi-rotation, the temperature rose inside the chamber and soon reached twenty degrees above zero.

"It's necessary now to maintain that temperature throughout the voyage," said the doctor. "As we're immobile, it won't be too high."

In the meantime, Portier was occupied with the respirability of the confined air. He studied the presence of carbon dioxide with the aid of a special reagent.

"There isn't enough yet to inconvenience us," he declared, after a rapid analysis. And he went back to take his place at the porthole, in order to contemplate the Moon, which now seemed much closer.

It was more than two hours since the voyagers had quit the Earth. The *Fusée* was traveling at a speed of more the sixty kilometers a second. Our satellite allowed more and more details to be seen. With the aid of the lateral discharge orifices, Valsorres manipulated the vehicle in such a fashion that it would pass within forty kilometers of the Moon's surface. At about quarter past eleven, they began to "traverse the disk" of the star.

The voyagers could not weary of contemplating the hemisphere whose sight, until now, had been forbidden to humans. With a photographic apparatus equipped with a long-range lens and a wide aperture, Portier took photographs; before the departure he had found a means of increasing the sensitivity of photographic plates, with permitted him to take pictures with an exposure of only a hundred thousandth of a second. And that sensitivity was not excessive, given the prodigious velocity with which the *Fusée* was moving relative to the surface of the satellite.

The explorers of the heavens had a unique spectacle before their eyes; close at hand, the lunar craters stood out with great clarity, displaying the details of their architecture. They really were craters, on the perimeter of which, at that reduced distance, the lava flows could clearly be seen. Blocks of stone thrown out by eruptions were visible at the feet of the cones; it was a volcanic landscape in all its savage splendor.

Among the craters, some were immense and others small; they seemed to be orientated in chains following determined alignments; between the chains immense areas could be seen covered in soil of white appearance.

"Let's get a little closer," said Portier.

Valsorres activated the lateral valves, and the *Fusée* drew nearer to the surface of the lunar globe.

"But those are plains of salt!" the doctor exclaimed.

They could, in fact, see the scintillation of the facets of the salt-crystals carpeting the beds of those desiccated oceans.

"What a marvelous spectacle" said Portier. "But what can have happened to the water of those oceans before abandoning the dissolved salt that it contained?"

Espéret reflected, and replied: "My dear friend, that water has been 'breathed in' one molecule at a time by the Earth; over the course of millions of centuries, our globe, by means of its powerful attraction, has stripped the Moon of all its gaseous elements, including the water vapor formed by its oceans."

"There's no longer any water on our satellite, hen?"

"Not a trace, any more than oxygen or nitrogen. And that's why the lunar surface, exposed to the sun's rays, must heat up in a frightful fashion. In any case, we're going to clarify that matter. Valsorres, have you brought the bolometer?"

"Yes," said Valsorres. "It's in its box, on a shelf of the fourth cupboard."

Espéret then took out of its sheath the marvelous instrument that permits the surface temperature of a body radiating or reflecting light to be measured electrically. He exposed it to the light reflected by the Moon and turned to his companions."

"More than a hundred degrees!" he exclaimed. "That's barely credible!"

"And yet it's true," said Valsorres. "This time, the figure can no longer be disputed, since we've just made a direct measurement."

But the Moon was already shrinking in the distance; the *Fusée* was traveling at such a velocity that the traversal of the lunar disk had only lasted a few seconds.

Dr. Portier requested a moment of darkness in order to unload his photographic apparatus and parcel up the exposed plates, which would only be developed on returning to Earth.

"And we'll be able to give names to those volcanoes, mountains and seas!" the young doctor exclaimed.

"Certainly, my friend. We'll see them on your pictures, and as their discoverers we'll have the right to be their godparents."

"There'll be the Sea of France," Portier said, "the Valsorres crater and the Espéret mountain chain."

Thomas was listening to the conversation "And won't there be a very small mountain called Mount Thomas?"

"Yes, my dear Thomas, yes, of course!" And, following his train of thought, the Marquis added: "Well give these lunar mountains the names of those we love: Marie, Hélène, Germaine, Travers…"

"…And Zabeth!" said Portier.

"Yes, my dear friend," said the Marquis. "There are, in fact, two adjacent craters, which we'll name Portier and Zabeth."

The doctor reflected, "And at the risk of reviving your chagrin, my friend, we'll give the highest of the mountains the name Philippe, for I have, by virtue of a sort of prescience of the future, the absolute certainty that you'll see your son again."

"May God hear you!" said Valsorres, his eyes moist.

"He will hear me, for he is just."

There was a moment of silence; excessively cruel memories had just been reawakened. After a brief interval, however, Espéret's voice was heard to say: "Look! The Earth! How odd it is!"

They all ran to the portholes.

Indeed, the Earth appeared, illuminated by the sun. For the voyagers, still close to the Moon, there was a "full Earth." Our globe appeared like a world map.

"Let's find France!" said Valsorres.

But France did not appear, even in the magnified field of powerful binoculars. It was the new world, America, that was turned in the direction of the observers. They could just make out the high mountains that run across the new continent from north to south. Only the deserts of the American west and those of South America, free of clouds, were clearly visible; the coast of California was distinguishable by virtue of its contrast with the somber waters of the Pacific.

"And yet that's what the Earth is," said Valsorres, pensively. "God, how tiny it is in space!"

On that note, the voyagers went to their couchettes, except for the Marquis, taking the first watch, who went to install himself in the pilot's station.

He directed the *Fusée* toward the planet Mars.

II. In which it will be seen that, in spite of everything,
things do not always go as one would wish.

The following morning, that of 26 June 1914, the voyagers settled their routines.

The watches of direction were divided between the Marquis, Espéret and Portier. Thomas, reserved for housekeeping occupations, as exempted from that. However, it was decided that he would be taught the essential maneuvers, in order that, if necessary, he could lend his collaboration and be something other than a passive passenger.

The chronometers had been reset; the clock in the chamber and the time on the torpedo watches also served the four men to regulate their pocket watches, which Valsorres had recommended that they do every day; in that fashion they had, in addition to the five timekeepers and the clock, four excellent watches, whose concordance further augmented the precision of time's measurement.

At eleven o'clock, Thomas prepared a substantial meal, formed of ox-tongue, a salad of pickled vegetables and biscuit, all washed down with hot tea and coffee. The Marquis had wisely proscribed alcohol, including wine.

That was not to Thomas' liking. "To think that I, Thomas Renoult, my father's son, will go four months without even drinking a single bottle!" Then he added, groaning: "These things only happen to me."

"No, my old Thomas," replied Espéret, "you can see that it's also happening to the three of us."

"That true, in fact," the fellow replied, not greatly consoled by the remark. Then he concluded with a reflection full of grandeur: "Fortunately, it's for science!"

The four diners did honor to the meal. They drank to the health of absent friends with tea. Then Thomas cleared the table and cleaned the crockery. That was a delicate operation; it was necessary to save water, so the plates were scrubbed energetically with cloths steeped in warm water. As for cooking food, that was done by the heat emitted by an extremely tiny particle of virium under the action of cathode rays.

There remained question of the exterior disposal of the detritus of meals and, in a general fashion, of all the products rendered inevitable by the very life of the passengers, of which it was necessary to get rid at all costs. To that effect, a valve with a double closure had been fitted into the bottom of the *Fusée*. The interior lid was lifted and the waste products were introduced into the cavity thus opened. The valve was then closed again and, with the aid of a second valve, turning like the first and maneuvered from inside, the waste products were allowed to flow outside. It was, in fact, necessary to expel them with a piston traversing the discharge conduit while touching the lateral wall; liberated from terrestrial gravity, those undesirable substances were only any longer submissive to the attraction of the *Fusée* itself, and would have refused to "fall" far away from it.

Life was thus organized regularly.

Valsorres kept a veritable "ship's log," and noted, hour by hour, the events that occurred. Espéret and Portier each made a copy in their notebooks.

"That way," Valsorres had said, we'll each have the means, later on, of recounting he documented narrative of our voyage, even if we're separated from one another someday."

"Separated!" cried Portier. "But what could separate us? Aren't we inseparable?"

"I hope so, my friend," the Marquis replied. "However, I'd prefer to have anticipated everything."

The twenty-fifth passed without incident. The Earth diminished visibly; on the other hand, Mars appeared increasingly large.

On the evening of the twenty-sixth, the diameter of the planet, seen through the instruments, was that of a plate. There is no need to speak of the curiosity with which the voyagers examined the slightest details of it. They had with them a map of Mars drawn by the Italian astronomer Schiaparelli, who had been the first to signal the existence of the famous "canals." They tried, but without any great success, to correlate what they had before their eyes with the indications of the drawing made by the Latin scholar.

"Well," said Espéret, "What about the canals?"

Portier examined the planet with sustained attention.

"I can certainly see a network of straight lines that seem to have centers around which they radiate—but are they canals? With the sun's rays striking them, we ought to see the water that fills them shining, but I can't see anything like that."

Espéret convinced himself of the accuracy of the young doctor's observation.

"Anyway," he said, "We'll pass in close proximity to Mars, as we did with the Moon, and we'll see what there is to see."

The doctor then addressed Valsorres. "Are we going to make a little stopover on Mars? It wouldn't derange our plans: it's on our route, and we could land on the planet for a day or two."

"I've already thought of that," Valsorres replied, "but I don't see any utility in it, nor even any interest. Mars is an old world, much older than the Earth. Perhaps Martians are a myth. In any case, our goal is Saturn; let's go to Saturn first. On the return journey, we'll see whether it's possible to devote a few hours to disembarking on the planet whose inhabitants have caused so much ink to flow on Earth."

"Do you believe in Martians yourself? asked Portier.

"My God, yes," replied the Marquis. "Why not?"

"And on what do you base your opinion?"

"Simply on the identity of origin of Mars and the Earth."

Espéret and the doctor listened to Henri de Valsorres attentively. The latter continued his explanation.

"Mars, like the Earth, is a fragment of the solar nebula detached by centrifugal force. That commonality of origin implies an identity of mineral structure in the composition of its solid crust. In a word, Mars must, from a geological point of view, be similar in all points to our terrestrial globe."

"Perfect," said Portier. "But what about the Martians?"

"Well, the Martian similarly have no reason, in my view, not to resemble the inhabitants of Earth. Having arrived, placed by a superior Force, on a globe similar to ours, they ought, in all probability, to resemble terrestrial human beings considerably."

"Wells, however, imagined strange beings endowed with extraordinary organs, improbable limbs, prodigious tentacles and unsuspected means of locomotion."

"That, my dear friend, is the novelist's imagination," Valsorres continued. "Here, we're no longer in the realm of fiction, but reality. In any case, as I told you only a moment ago, when we return from Saturn to Earth we'll be able to pass very close to Mars, and might be able to land there and see for ourselves what truth there is in the imaginations and anticipation of the celebrated English novelist."

That concluded the little discussion on the subject of Mars. It was therefore decided that they would pass close to the surface of the planet, as they had the previous evening for the Moon, but without pausing to make a landfall there.

Life was now fully organized about the *Fusée*. Thomas, perfectly trained for that function by the doctor, refreshed the atmosphere inside the chamber twice a day. To that effect he began by taking a sheet of asbestos steeped in a solution of potash from the ceiling. By virtue of the large surface thus offered, it absorbed the carbon dioxide expelled from the voyagers' lungs, and transformed it into potassium carbonate. As for the oxygen consumed, that as replaced by heating a certain mass of copper oxide with the aid of virium, which emitted the gas indispensable to the life of the voyagers.

Dr. Portier had combined with that indispensable operation an equally necessary complement. To regenerate oxygen and absorb carbon dioxide is vital, but it is not everything. In addition to carbon dioxide, respiration emits a veritably toxic element discovered by the illustrious Professor d'Arsonval, which he has studied and to which he has given the name of pulmonary poison.[19] It is, in

---

[19] In 1887 the physiologist Charles-Édouard Brown-Séquard (1817-1894), assisted by Jacques-Arsène d'Arsonval (1851-1940), built an apparatus to collect air breathed out by patients suffering from "consumption" (tuberculosis) in an attempt to isolate an infective agent. At a conference on the disease held in 1888

fact, a veritable poison, a dangerous principle susceptible, by its continuous action, of leading, after a certain time, to the death of those respiring it incessantly.

But Dr. Portier had studied the question. As soon as the departure had been decided, he had thought about it and he had found a reagent that permitted the pulmonary poison contained in the air expelled by lungs and confined in the cabin to be completely destroyed. With the aid of a little hand-cranked turbine, he caused the air in the chamber to pass through a tube containing the reagent; that fixed the poison and the air that reemerged was absolutely pure.

That operation, renewed every day, was sufficient to ensure the perfect salubrity of the atmosphere of the *Fusée*.

The day of the twenty-seventh had begun.

They were approaching Mars rapidly, and could perceive the two minuscule satellites of the planet, the two tiny Martian "moons," to which our terrestrial astronomers have given the terrible names Deimos and Phobos. They could be seen rotating around the Martian globe.

"The tides on Mars must be very complicated," said Espéret, who was observing the revolution of the two satellites attentively.

"Yes, certainly," replied Valsorres. "But they must be even more so on Saturn, around which ten moons gravitate, not to mention the ring that constitutes, on its own, the most gigantic of satellites."

"We'll see all that at close range," said the doctor.

Valsorres had gone back up to the direction post, and he maintained the *Fusée* in a straight line with the apparent edge of Mars. Once the route had been thus set, there was no reason to think that the projectile would deviate in any way, and the pilot station could thus be abandoned without any inconvenience, at least during lunch time.

The distance from the plant was diminishing visibly, and the *Fusée*, given its constant acceleration, ought now to be moving at more than eight hundred kilometers a second.

At about four o'clock in the afternoon, it was no longer possible to perceive the entire Martian globe in the field of the instruments. The distance traveled since the departure was measurable by observing the apparent diameter of the Earth with the micrometer. Valsorres had taken the trouble in advance to

---

he claimed to have found such a poison, related to ptomaine, in that air. Although few of the delegates took the claim seriously and no one else succeeded in isolating such a substance, it was an important factor in popularizing the establishment of sanatoria in mountainous regions where the air was pure. It might seem surprising to find Berget repeating the bogus claim in 1922 and crediting it to Brown-Séquard's assistant, but d'Arsonval became far better known as a physicist than a physician, and Berget must have been personally acquainted with him, and d'Arsonval presumably refused to accept that the "discovery" had been an error.

calculate the tables giving he distance in accordance with the apparent diameter of the terrestrial disk, taking account of the movement of translation of the Earth in its elliptical orbit.

The lines that humans had baptized "canals" were visible with the greatest clarity. Not only could the broadest of them be perceived, but, the distance being diminished, one could see a veritable network of secondary canals, transversal relative to the primary one, like the adjoining strands of an immense spider-web.

At six o'clock the travelers ate a good dinner, made of excellent tinned grouse heated and prepared by Thomas—after which Espéret went to take his watch at the pilot station.

Suddenly, he was heard calling to Valsorres. "Henri! Come here! Come quickly!"

The Marquis hurtled up the ladder and joined his friend,

"What is it?" he demanded.

"We're deviating from our route!"

Valsorres was momentarily nonplussed. "We're deviating?"

"As I say. I've taken as a point of direction one of the stars in Orion—the one in the middle of the alignment known as the belt. Now, we set a course, not for that one, but for the one at the extreme left of that alignment. Look for yourself."

Valsorres put his eye to the ocular of the directional telescope mounted in the axis of the *Fusée*, the reticle of which was rigorously fixed in the direction followed by the projectile. He was immediately convinced that the *Fusée* had, in fact, deviated from its course. He manifested his astonishment to Espéret.

"I don't understand it at all!" the latter replied. "I thought I observed a slight deviation four hours ago, but I attributed it to a maneuvering error and I rectified the route immediately. This evening, there's no doubt—we're drifting."

"But that's unimaginable!" said Valsorres.

"Absolutely," said Espéret. "We're not yet in the zone of attraction of Mars, and I'm at a loss in the presence of that deflection inflicted on our route, so rigorously straight until now."

"Indeed! You observed nothing similar in passing close to the Moon?"

"Nothing. I was even struck by the perfection with which our *Fusée* was following the chosen route, without the slightest angular deviation. So I'm not only astonished, but, I must say, even a little anxious."

By means of a maneuver of the lateral escape-valves, Valsorres restored the *Fusée* to its original direction.

Espéret had descended to inform Portier and Thomas of the incident. The latter did not fail to say: "These things only happen to me."

But the thing was happening. It was necessary to yield to the evidence when, half an hour later, Valsorres was obliged to combat a further deviation of the apparatus by means of a new maneuver. It seemed to be subject to a mysterious but certain force that was bringing it toward the planet Mars.

Valsorres was racking his brains trying to find the solution to the enigma. In spite of all his science, he could not find it. Nor could Espéret or Portier.

At about half past seven, the deviation began to become worrying. It was necessary to rectify the route by means of the valves every five minutes.

"One might think that Mars were attracting us with an extraordinary force," murmured the Marquis, manipulating the controls. Then, after a moment of reflection, he turned to Espéret. "Are there, then, forces in the universe other than gravitation?"

Espéret did not reply. He was thinking about the impenetrable mysteries of the infinite too.

At eight-thirty, no more uncertainty was permissible. The deviation was absolutely certain and, what as more, permanent. The planet Mars was exerting an energetic attraction on the *Fusée*.

Valsorres then decided to take extreme action.

"Since Mars appears to be deviating us from the route we want to follow in passing close to it without touching it, let's orientate the *Fusée* frankly in such a fashion as to draw away from the planet directly. Do you agree?"

"You're right," replied Espéret.

"I think so too," said the doctor.

Valsorres then manipulated the valves in such a fashion as to cause the *Fusée* to deviate from its route by ninety degrees, and to draw way from Mars in a straight line, turning its hind end to the planet.[20]

The maneuver of orientation succeeded.

For a moment, the passengers were able to think that they were sheltered from the inexplicable traction of the Martian globe. Then Portier, who was observing the surface of the planet from which they wanted to draw away through the rear porthole, shouted: "We're still getting closer to Mars!"

Valsorres and Espéret raced to look out of the rear porthole, bringing their micrometers to bear. There was no doubt about it. The velocity of the *Fusée* was relenting, combated by an evident attraction emanating from the planet.

Valsorres addressed Espéret. "Since it seems that there's no means of struggling against that unexpected and inconceivable force, let's at least make our preparations to alight with the least risk on the Martian soil, on which we now seem to be condemned to set foot." Then, to himself, he added: "I'm at a loss. Gravity on Mars is four times weaker than on Earth. We triumphed over terrestrial gravity, since we were able to reach space. We passed within thirty kilometers of the Moon without suffering any effect. So what's happening here? What's the matter?"

---

[20] Modern readers will have little difficulty in imagining the fatal effect on the passengers of making an abrupt ninety-degree turn in a vehicle traveling at eight hundred kilometers a second, but even a physicist of Berget's caliber was capable of suffering blind spots in his thought-experiments.

And he maneuvered the disintegration of the virium in such a fashion as to "brake" and reduced the velocity of the descent on to the planet.

At nine o'clock they began to perceive the details of the Martian surface, illuminated by the light of the Sun, already diminished in diameter by distance.

Large patches of dark green were outlined against the ruddy soil, through an atmosphere devoid of clouds. In places, large areas, generally rectangular and darker, allowed a few light fumes to pass. Other areas, even larger, appeared to be absolutely uniform, and did not seem to be covered either by vegetation or by the substance that appeared to constitute the soil of the Martian world.

Except for Portier, however, who was examining all that with the greatest interest, the voyagers were gripped by an indescribable anguish. In fact, the *Fusée* was visibly falling.

In order to augment the efficacy of the braking, Valsorres increased the disintegration in such a fashion that, in spite of the double envelope and in spite of the non-conductivity of the metal of the tubes, the temperature of the cabin was beginning to become intolerable.

Suddenly, Thomas' voice was heard, saying: "That's it! We're going to crash."

A few seconds later, an impact was produced—a mercifully gentle impact, attenuated by the powerful springs with which the Marquis, by virtue of a sort of prescience, had fitted the inferior parts of the Fusée's supports.

The four voyagers, doubtless the first humans who had made the voyage, had arrived on the planet Mars.

*III. In which the Marquis de Valsorres and his companions receive
a surprising welcome on the planet Mars.*

When the *Fusée*, by virtue of its immobility, had demonstrated the reality of the landing—if one can use that word to speak of the arrival on soil other than that of the planet Earth[21]—Valsorres turned to his companions.

"What are we going to do?"

The three men remained silent for a moment. Thomas broke the silence first, and said: "I believe it's first necessary to see where we are."

That was the advice of common sense.

The four voyagers went to the lateral portholes, and this is what all four of them were able to see:

A crowd of a hundred individuals, who appeared to be human, were agitating around the *Fusée*, waving their arms. All those individuals were enveloped in garments that seemed to be very thick, and did not allow their noses or eyes to be perceived. Their hands were covered in bulky gloves, their feet shod in boots that appeared to be padded with a dense lining.

"It seems that it can't be very warm hereabouts!" exclaimed Thomas, at the sight of them.

"I can believe that," said Valsorres, struck by the remark. "If the anticipations of our astronomers are exact, the temperature on the surface of Mars must be quite glacial." After having observed the indigenes again, he added: "Look, that verifies my prognostications. These Martians have a singular resemblance to humans like us."

It was necessary to make a decision, however.

Valsorres ordered Thomas to get four carbines, four pistols and four hunting knives ready, as well as full cartridge belts. In the meantime, the voyagers changed their "indoor" clothes for exceedingly warm garments, over which they put, by virtue of extra precaution, woolen cardigans and shorts. Fur gloves covered their hands.

All four of them felt particularly light.

Before going outside, Portier put the tube of a small manometer over a tap fitment able to communicate with the exterior. He opened the tap and looked at the instrument's dial. It indicated a pressure of only forty-eight centimeters.

"Damn!" said the doctor. "That's inconvenient. If Martian air is formed of the same elements as atmospheric air, and in the same proportions, we won't be able to breathe—or, at least, our respiration will be very insufficient."

"Why is that?" Espéret asked.

---

[21] The French for "landing," *atterrissage*, retains a link with "*la terre*" [the Earth] that the English term does not, hence the parenthetical remark.

"Because, given the feeble pressure, we'll find ourselves in the situation of aeronauts at an altitude of seven or eight thousand meters. And you know that one breathes so poorly at those heights that one dies of it."

Valsorres turned to Thomas. "Bring the small bottles of oxygen and the inhalers," he said to him.

Thomas climbed the ladder that led to "the loft"—that was what he called the upper stage of the *Fusée*, where, along with the provisions, the requested apparatus was. He came back after a few moments carrying respiratory masks, like the ones with which firemen cover their faces when they have to penetrate into rooms filled with harmful gases during conflagrations.

The voyagers fitted the masks to their faces, fixed the bottles of oxygen to their backs, and prepared to leave the *Fusée*.

"Gently!" said Valsorres. "Let's not lose all our nitrogen. Let's decant ourselves carefully through the double panel." They raised the interior panel that closed the exit shaft; the four men penetrated into it and closed the upper panel over their heads. Then they raised the inferior panel and, with the aid of the ladder that they had allowed to slide down vertically, they set foot on the soil of Mars.

Valsorres advanced ahead of his companions toward the individual who seemed to be in command of the group.

With his index finger he indicated the Earth, which then appeared, seen from Mars, much as the Moon appears to us in its first quarter. He made a sign that they had arrived from that distant point.

Would the Martians understand him?

At any rate, the one who seemed to be the leader touched the Marquis' arm with his finger, and, indicating the direction of a sort of mound about two kilometers away, made him understand by signs that he wanted to take him there.

The Marquis turned to his companions. "You're on your guard?" he asked.

"Yes," all three replied.

"In any case," said Espéret, "we're not numerous enough to resist, so let's go with these indigenes.

They set forth, while Thomas exclaimed: "These things only happen to me! Damn, it's cold in this place!"

It was, in fact, very cold.

Dr. Portier, ever curious, had taken a copper case out of his pocket containing an alcohol thermometer; the liquid column in the rube stopped at minus 27 degrees.

"Twenty-seven degrees below zero," he said to Valsorres.

"I can tell," said the latter. "I'm absolutely frozen."

Fortunately, the troop, led by the Martian, marched at a rapid pace.

Thomas, who evidently wanted to do some exercises in order to warm himself up, tried to jump a little, and thrust himself off the ground with one leg. To his great surprise, his effort carried him ten meters into the air.

"There's a thing!" he said, when he had fallen back. "Now I can jump like a flea. Oh, these things only happen to me."

That one also happened to his three companions, and the Marquis immediately replied. "My dear Thomas, don't forget that you weigh three times less here than on Earth; in consequence, spare your efforts. You will, however, do the same tasks."

"Oh, so that's it," said Thomas, simply, having as an absolute principle not being astonished by anything.

The Martians and the four "Earthmen" had been walking for about twenty minutes, and had arrived at the foot of the mound that seemed to be the objective of their journey. The mound was simply a kind of cupola pierced by a few circular openings, each fitted with a perfectly transparent window, for curious faces could be seen behind each one, but the glass had no polish and did not reflect the light.

In the middle of the round openings was a rectangular doorway closed by a metal panel that glinted like gold.

The Martian leader touched a button to the right of the door; the panel pivoted, uncovering the entrance to a passage that seemed brightly illuminated. Then he turned to the Marquis and his companions, and beckoned to them to follow him into the corridor.

Valsorres followed his guide on to the steps of a descending staircase. His three companions marched on his heels; the entire troop of Martians came behind them. They heard the sound of the panel closing again.

The guide paused momentarily. The Marquis took advantage of that to cast a glance around. They had arrived in a sort of circular vestibule, the walls of which were uniformly covered by a layer of pink substance, of the shade that as known in eighteenth century France as "*cuisse de nymphe*." No painting or ornament interrupted the uniformity. Four doors opened into the vestibule.

The Martian made a sign and articulated four sounds. Immediately, his men were engulfed by one of the doors, and every one of them disappeared. The Marquis and his companions were alone with their guide.

The latter headed toward one of the doors, which he opened like the first; he went through, followed by our four friends.

They found themselves in a quadrangular room, the walls of which were hung with rich fabrics. None of the designs were visible that have characterized the successive artistic styles of terrestrial humankind; their charm was a veritable sparkle of changing colors; one might have thought that the textiles were made with mother of pearl with iridescent reflections.

The entire room was illuminated by large bays opening upwards; the daylight was bright, for the sun, its disk reduced by distance, was near the zenith, so it was approximately midday. A very mild temperature reigned in the rectangular room, the air of which was perfumed.

Valsorres looked at all that with astonishment.

The guide made him a sign to sit down, showing him low seats—sofas of a sort—which garnished the four corners of the rom. The Marquis and his companions accepted the indigene's invitation. The guide also signaled to them to take off their respiratory masks. They removed them, and, to their great astonishment, they could breathe perfectly.

They felt very light; the weak gravity on the planet explained that sensation, extraordinary and new for them. Valsorres placed his carbine beside him; it seemed no heavier than an ordinary cane.

The guide had brought closer to the voyagers a small table laden with gray metal goblets ornamented with fine engraving, traced in networks. He filled them with a yellow liquid contained in a ewer, and filled a fifth goblet for himself. Then he made a sort of ritual gesture above the five receptacles and, looking at our four friends, put the cup to his lips and emptied it instantly.

After a momentary hesitation, Valsorres did the same, and his companions imitated him.

The liquor had a bizarre taste; it gave off a heady perfume, as foamy in appearance and piquant on the tongue. Was it special wine? Was it a product of distillation?

Thomas had evidently asked himself the question, for he said: "It's surely not bad, but all the same, it's not as good as a bottle of good Burgundy."

After having drunk, however, the voyagers felt that there were in a state of infinite bliss; their brains seemed more fecund, their ideas clearer, their senses sharper. Their thoughts flew through space and time, pausing above all on the happy memories of their previous existence, leaving the sad memories as if enveloped in a salutary penumbra. Valsorres envisaged his separation from his wife and the abduction of his son as something distant; he saw the future as rosy. Portier, half-closing his eyes, believed that he was in the arms of his dear little Zabeth.

Was it, then, the nectar of ancient mythology that the inhabitant of the planet Mars had poured for them?

The four voyagers were thus plunged in a kind of exquisite torpor when a prolonged sound, not that of a bell or a gong, but a kind of continuous song, simultaneously soft and powerful, became audible.

At that sound, Valsorres and his friends shivered.

Their guide stood up. He beckoned to them to follow him. Then he opened a door situated in one of the corners of the room. The Marquis and his friends followed him. He went down some fifty steps; having reached the bottom of the stairs he lifted up a heavy curtain in order to allow the four Frenchmen to pass through.

They stopped for a moment, struck with astonishment by the extraordinary spectacle offered to their eyes.

Imagine an immense room, more than three hundred meters long, a hundred broad and thirty high.

The walls of that room were papered with the fabrics with iridescent reflections that we have already seen on the walls of the rectangular room. Garlanded with brightly colored flowers, columns connected to one another at the summit sustained the colossal vault that covered the edifice.

A diffuse, indefinable white light, the sources of which were invisible, illuminated all the parts of the immense nave with a milky clarity. One might have thought that the walls, in places that were not covered by the fabrics, were emitting that light, so gentle on the eyes and yet so marvelous in bringing out the sparkling colors of everything offered to the voyagers' gaze.

On each side of the hall there were staged terraces on which an innumerable crowd was standing, formed of men and women, all young and all beautiful. No old men could be seen, or women who were simply "mature." All the men seemed adolescent, all the women young.

The men were clad in short tunics, fabrics of varied, indecisive colors with metallic reflections. The women were covered in absolutely transparent tunics, allowing the sight of their magnificent beauty. Precious stones glittered in their hair, on their arms, their wrists and their ankles; their feet were shod in delicate sandals.

A warm temperature reigned in that immense temple-like space. The atmosphere was impregnated with a suave, subtle and penetrating perfume.

In the middle of the hall, between the steps, was an empty space, like an aisle, covered with slabs of polychromatic stone. At the back, at the end of the aisle, a platform with three stages rose up. The inferior stage was occupied by musicians, about two hundred in number, armed with metallic instruments that seemed to be made of silver. The middle stage was garnished with two hundred women standing upright, their eyes fixed upon one of their number, the tallest, who, beneath a veritable mantle of magnificent red hair, which thus completed her costume, was holding a baton enriched by gems in her hand. Like the women on the steps, these were clad in translucent tunics.

Finally at the very top, on the uppermost stage, sitting on a kind of large throne, was a man with a white beard. Alongside him, a splendid creature was lying on her elbow on a cushion; on her knees she was holding a minuscule elephant the size of a small dog, and playing with its trunk.

At the arrival of the four voyagers, all the members of the audience had risen to their feet and uttered the same cry three times: "Roh! Roh! Roh!"

Then the woman with golden hair had raised her baton.

The musicians had immediately raised their instruments to their mouths. A concert of strange harmonies had begun, with which the voices of the beautiful choristers placed on the intermediate sage mingled.

The man seated on the throne had also risen to his feet. Descending two steps, he gestured to his visitors to come forward.

Valsorres and his friends, passing from one surprise to another, walked slowly along the long aisle between the two rows of steps. As they went, the cries of Roh! Roh!" resounded; then men made hand gestures, and the women threw flowers under their feet.

It must be said that our four friends felt as if they had been transported into another world. Being light, their feet hardly seemed to be touching the floor; the perfumes, the caress of the chords reaching their ears and the sight of those women, all equally beautiful, put them into an indescribable state.

They advanced slowly toward the throne in the midst of the enthusiastic ovations of the audience.

Finally, when they arrived at the foot of the platform, the woman with the gem-encrusted baton lowered it abruptly. The instruments and the singers immediately fell silent.

Valsorres placed his foot on the first step.

Then the man from the throne descended another step; he raised his right hand; a deathly silence fell in the crowd. And, addressing the stupefied Valsorres, he said to him, in the purest French ever spoken: "Marquis de Valsorres, and your companions, welcome to this planet, which I believe your terrestrial astronomers call Mars."

IV. In which the Marquis de Valsorres and his friends perceive that the planet Mars appears to be an enchanted abode.

If anyone ever experienced a paralyzing surprise it was certainly Marquis Henri de Valsorres, on hearing the words of welcome addressed to him by the man who appeared to command that assembly of the inhabitants of the planet Mars.

Espéret and Portier were similarly plunged into profound amazement. As for Thomas, he muttered: "It's true! These things only happen to me."

When the initial moment of stupor had passed, the Marquis addressed the leader and said: "Monsieur, my companions and I are penetrated by gratitude for the sympathetic welcome that we have received on your planet, where we were far from expecting to find such amiable inhabitants, such beautiful women and, above all, our language spoken so purely."

At those words the leader turned to his companion. "Oh, not everyone here speaks French as we two do, but there are a few of us who possess your language completely enough, are there not, Saâh?"

Saâh, directly questioned, turned to the four voyagers, welcoming them with a truly celestial smile.

"Yes, Thaû, we speak the beautiful French language between ourselves, when we want a little repose from the rudeness of ours, which, as you have been able to observe, Messieurs, consists largely of monosyllables."

All of that was said by the marvelous woman in a musical voice, with a great purity of language. Only the pronunciation of the *r*s, which rolled slightly, reminded our four friends of the slight and delightful accent of Rumanian ladies, which further emphasizes the perfection with which they speak French.

Saâh turned to her companion. "But Thaû, don't you think that these seigneurs must be a little weary after that long journey, and that they would be glad to have a little rest, not without having restored themselves with a suitable collation?"

Thaû—since that seemed to be his name—replied to his companion: "I am entirely in conformity with your opinion, beautiful Saâh. Invite our guests to follow us, then, and we will conduct them to their apartments, which we have accommodated to receive them in a fashion worthy of them."

Our four voyagers were going from one astonishment to another.

Thaû and Saâh had stood up. Saâh held her minuscule elephant on a leash, at the end of a chain that seemed to be made of gold. It gamboled behind its beautiful mistress, who said to it: "Come on, Pik, salute these four seigneurs with our most beautiful trick."

The little elephant stood up on its hind feet, and made a kind of salute with its trunk, moving it up and down several times.

"Good, Pik, good!" said the lady. Addressing the Marquis, who could not get over it, she said: "Be my chevalier, Marquis; give me your arm."

Involuntarily, Valsorres obeyed, and offered his arm to the splendid creature, who placed her hand on it lightly. She walked with the dignity of a queen, or even a divinity, and it could certainly be said of her, as the Latin poet put it: *Incessu patuit dea.*[22]

As soon as Thaû and Saâh had stood up, the woman with the ardent hair who presided over the music had made a slight sign. Immediately, the musicians and choristers began the execution of a kind of triumphant song to company the exit of the four voyagers, who followed Thaû, showing them the way.

At a gesture from Saâh, four young and beautiful women had stood up, and accompanied the Frenchmen.

The latter, following their guide, passed under a portal closed by a curtain of rich fabric, and found themselves in a rectangular room, in the center of which stood a table covered in delicately sculpted yellow metal dishes, baskets containing strange things, decanters of pure crystal and magnificently wrought cups.

Thaû and Saâh sat down on soft seats, inviting our four friends to do likewise. They imitated them.

One of the four women sat down beside each of them, and poured him a little of the golden liquid that they had already sampled before penetrating into the great ceremonial hall.

Everything respired the most refined elegance; everything was impregnated with an atmosphere of gripping sensuality.

Valsorres and his friends had plates before them on which their captivating companions placed little cakes of a sort, which were slightly warm. The woman who was serving the Marquis said to him, with a caress in her eyes and an enchanting smile: "Eat, Marquis, eat; you must be very hungry."

The Marquis thanked his beautiful neighbor. "Thank you, Madame; from your hands I would take anything gladly. But what should I call you?"

"My name is Zith," replied the captivating Martian.

"Well, my beautiful Zith, I shall allow myself to be guided by you; you shall be the organizer of my meal."

Thaû addressed the four Frenchmen. "Messieurs," he said, "may I introduce to you those who will be your constant companions during our sojourn on this planet, and who will, I am sure do everything possible to make the hours that you consent to spend here appear shorter. All four speak your beautiful language. You, Marquis, have just made the acquaintance of Zith, who is yours henceforth. But I would be obliged to you for allowing me to know the names of your traveling companions."

---

[22] Virgil, from the *Aeneid*; the quote is usually rendered in a slightly fuller version as *vera incessu patuit dea* [the true goddess revealed in her stride].

The Marquis, indicating, Espéret, said to Thaû: "My friend the engineer Espéret, a scientist of the greatest merit."

Thaû addressed the engineer. "My dear Monsieur Espéret, you have to your right our beautiful Rasôh; she has chosen you herself among your companions, in order to put herself entirely at your service."

At that moment, the beautiful Rasôh passed her left arm around Espéret's neck and gave him a long kiss.

Then Valsorres introduced the doctor. "Dr. Portier, a young and already illustrious scientist, a glory of French medicine."

Thaû turned to the young man. "Your science will be unnecessary here, Doctor. On Mars, diseases are unknown—at least, we have vanquished them and they have disappeared from the planet. You have to your right one of our most gracious inhabitants, the beautiful Daâh."

Daâh had leaned toward Portier. "Oh, my friend," she said to him, meeting his eyes, "I shall be glad to be your companion, and I already feel that I shall love you." As she finished speaking she ran the tips of her slender fingers around the young physician's neck in an almost immaterial caress.

Was it the effect of the beverage he had drunk? At any rate, the shadow of little Zabeth passed before his eyes, but very fleetingly and very distantly.

The Marquis only had Thomas left to introduce. "Our faithful companion Thomas," he said.

"You shall be accompanied here by the beautiful Hina," Thaû said to the worthy fellow.

The latter admired his buxom neighbor, a beautiful and sturdy woman. He dared not show her any sympathy, retained as he was by his master's presence, but Hina made the first advances.

"Come closer to me, my friend," she said to Thomas, "And drink from the cup that I have filled for you." And she held out a cup full of the enchanted beverage.

Thomas let himself go; he emptied the cup, murmuring: "Decidedly, these things only happen to me."

The feast went on. The four women went to take trays from a dresser laden with other dishes, always exquisite, always substantial and always in minuscule portions. They made our friends drink, eating and drinking with them.

Valsorres and his companions were overtaken by a sort of voluptuous torpor. Thaû and Saâh looked at them, smiling.

However, the Marquis had recovered his self-control.

"My dear Thaû," he said to the master of the place, "now that we know who we are, will you permit me to ask you a question?"

"At your ease, Marquis."

"Well, then, tell me, pray, how it is that you, Saâh and our beautiful companions speak French so purely? And tell me, above all, by what inconceivable miracle you knew my name before I had set foot on your planet?"

Thaû looked at Saâh. The latter replied briefly to the master's interrogative glance: "Not yet!"

Then, turning to the four voyagers, she said to them in her musical voice: "We will tell you all that, Messieurs, but tomorrow. Today, go savor the rest that you have earned so well; follow your companions, who will take you to the apartments that have been prepared for you. Tomorrow, when you have been restored by reparative sleep, we will tell you all you desire to know, and we have reserved for you in particular, Marquis de Valsorres, a surprise that you are far from expecting."

Valsorres looked at Saâh with eyes dilated by astonishment and curiosity; but she put a finger over his mouth and addressed the Marquis with such a smile that he did not insist. He followed the beautiful Zith, who drew him gently into a wide corridor, at the end of which a door opened to the left.

Zith ushered her companion through it.

"Oh, my friend," she said, "now I am entirely yours!"

She handed Valsorres a small crystal cup filled with a pink liquid. "Drink, my friend, drink," she said. "Drink half of this liqueur; I will drink the other half."

The Marquis drank half the contents of the cup; Zith drank the rest.

Valsorres suddenly felt as if he were ablaze with a divine fire; it seemed to him that flames were running through his veins; unknown frissons were causing his marrow to quiver, and rose all the way to his brain. He let himself fall on to a long divan.

At that moment, the illumination was attenuated by a light dusk, which enveloped everything with his hospitable and discreet shadow.

V. In which Thaû is seen to give a few details regarding Mars and the existence of its inhabitants.

How long did the sleep of our four friends last? None of them would have been able to say.

When the Marquis woke up, Zith was sitting beside him, waiting for him to open his eyes. She appeared more beautiful than ever, with a smile on her lips and joy in her eyes.

"Zith," Valsorres said to her, "Where are my companions?"

"Your companions are already awake, my friend," Zith replied, "waiting for you to take the morning meal with the four of us, our master Thaû and our mistress Saâh. Look, friend, the sun is already high in the sky."

In fact, through a large bay window open in the ceiling of the room, the sun was visible: a miserable minuscule sun shrunken by distance, which sent to the planet, not the heat, but merely the warmth of its enfeebled rays.

Zith withdrew, and two Martian women immediately came in.

Valsorres abandoned himself to the hands of the two servants. They put him in a perfumed bath, rubbed his skin with the greatest delicacy, smoothed his hair and dressed him in one of the short tunics that the Marquis had seen the day before serving the Martians as garments.

Valsorres was astonished by that.

"But during the time you spend with us," said one of them, "Thaû and Saâh have decided that you won't wear other attire, except that your garments and those of your friends will be richer than those worn here."

As she finished speaking, the two Martian women, kneeling down, put luxurious, admirable embroidered sandals on his feet. Utterly astounded, Valsorres let them do it.

When he was thus adorned, Zith returned, took him by the hand and led him along a corridor that led to the rectangular room where he had taken the welcoming meal the previous evening. Espéret, Portier and Thomas were already there, each accompanied by his amiable guide.

In the warm atmosphere impregnated with perfumes, Valsorres appreciated the lightness of his costume, and understood its practical utility.

A moment later, a curtain was raised and Thaû appeared, holding Saâh by the waist, the latter of almost superhuman beauty.

"Greetings, Messieurs," said Thaû. "Do you feel completely rested from the fatigues of your long journey?"

"Marvelously, Thaû," replied the Marquis, "speaking for myself, and I hope my companions can say the same."

The three men nodded their heads.

"Well then, Messieurs, let us have a morning collation while awaiting the midday meal. Order that we be served, Saâh."

Saâh pressed a button placed on the table. Immediately, four women clad in short violet tunics embroidered with gold brought small plates on large metal trays, each containing a few grams of an odorous preparation.

The Marquis and his friends, following the example of Thaû and Saâh, ate the delicate foodstuffs with the aid of little two-pronged forks, which seemed to be made of gold. Their companions poured the golden liquor that they had already tasted the day before, which they drank with a veritable sensuality. Then a warm brown liquid was served; it was not coffee or tea, but something indefinable and exquisite. Our four friends did not hide the pleasure that its consumption gave them.

"O Thaû, O beautiful Saâh," said Espéret, "I see that on your planet, the pleasures of the mouth are equal to those of the eyes, and those of the senses of smell and touch."

"Well, Messieurs, all those pleasures are at your discretion," said Saâh. "I hope that you will savor them sufficiently to remain among us for some time, and however long the time might be, be sure that it will seem too short to us."

Valsorres stood up; bowing to Saâh, he kissed her hand and said to her: "Madame, your beauty, your grace and your intelligence seduce us to a degree that we cannot express; receive the homage of our gratitude, that of our admiration and of our profound respect."

An exquisite smile illuminated Saâh's lips. She extended her hand to be kissed successively by the four voyagers. Then she addressed Thaû.

"My friend," she said, "the time has come to satisfy the very legitimate curiosity of our guests, to tell them how we learned of their departure and how we knew the Marquis de Valsorres' name."

The four Frenchmen then stretched themselves out on sofas; their companions sat at their feet, holding their hands tenderly.

Thaû and Saâh sat down next to one another in the center of the circle. Thaû then began to speak.

"You're undoubtedly not unaware, Messieurs, that this planet, which you call Mars and we call Raas, is much more advanced than the one from which you come, which you call Earth and to which we give the name Sila."

"We're Silians, then," said Portier.

"Yes, said the beautiful Saâh, laughing. "For us, you are Silians, just as, for you, we are Martians."

Thaû resumed his interrupted discourse. "We passed through the phases that your planet is traversing today a long time ago. For a long time we have developed science to its extreme limits, and our present existence, our entire life, is enabled by the countless applications of the successive discoveries of our scientists. Your astronomers know, we have no doubt, that the duration of a day on our planet is almost equal to the duration of a day on Earth. While you divide the day, I believe into twenty-four hours, we divide ours, equivalent to approximately twenty-four and a half hours, into ten parts. On the other hand, the period of time that you call the year, and which comprises, for you, 365 days, comprises here 687 days, 322 more than on Earth. Our year is, therefore, almost twice as long as yours. Is that correct?"

"Yes, certainly," said Espéret. "But what fills me with astonishment is that you know all these details relevant to the Earth by the names that we have given them."

"Patience; you shall have the key to that enigma shortly. Let me continue. Being further away from the Sun, our planet receives less heat therefrom; the temperature on the surface of our globe is always extremely low, even when it is illuminated by the star, for it is too distant to send us heat in sufficient quantity. Only a scant vegetation, a few meager mosses, now grows in the region of the line that on Earth you call the equator. Our planet therefore cooled faster than yours. There is, in addition, another reason: its volume is scarcely an eighth of that of your globe, and its mass is only a tenth of that of your Earth. For all these reasons, the cooling was much more rapid here than there.

"The conditions of existence of animals became difficult a great many centuries ago and we only conserve a few rare individuals, objects of curiosity rather than utility, Saâh's little elephant is an example."

Saâh smiled, striking her domestic elephant, which rolled at her feet, performing capers.

"In those conditions," Thaû continued, "deprived of the greater part of vegetal and animal resources, and subjected ourselves to an increasing rigorous temperature, we were forced to appeal to all the resources that the genius of scientists were able to create for us, for want of natural resources. More than ten of our centuries ago—which is to say, more than two thousand of your years ago—we made conquests of a scientific order that would certainly astonish you, Messieurs, as scientists.

"Thus, all of our aliments are products extracted for us by chemistry from the mineral substances that constitute the solid crust of the planet. All our garments are of mineral origin, all the objects we employ are, in sum, extracted from our soil. The air we breathe, which does not contain, in itself, enough of the gas necessary to respiration, we have completed by means of the same gas extracted from our minerals."

"Oxygen?" asked the Marquis,

"Ah! You call it oxygen. Well, so be it: we manufacture oxygen."

"That's marvelous! But where do you obtain the energy necessary to develop that industry, which must be prodigious?"

"It's quite simple," replied Thaû. "It's the heat of the molten substances accumulated under the crust, extending all the way to the center of the planet, that furnishes us with the enormous energy necessary to our physical industry."

"What do you call your *physical industry*?"

"The industry that concerns what I believe you call 'electricity'—that which consists of utilizing the radiations of light—and the forces that one of your terrestrial men of genius has called gravitation."

"Gravitation!" exclaimed Valsorres. "So you have also penetrated that inviolable secret! You know its mechanism?"

"Better than that, Marquis," Thaû replied. "We know that it propagates by means of waves, and we have succeeded in capturing those waves and making use of them."

Valsorres was astounded. "Gravitational waves!" he exclaimed, after a momentary silence.[23]

"Yes, gravitational waves. Do you recall what happened to your vehicle when you arrived in proximity with our planet? You observed a deviation of your route; you understood then that an unknown and irresistible force was attracting you to our globe."

"Yes, certainly," said Espéret. "That attraction seemed inexplicable to us."

"Well, you now have the explanation. We concentrated on your projectile a powerful beam of attractive gravitational waves, which was sufficient to paralyze your motive power and forced you to land on Martian soil—which, I hope, does not seem to inhospitable to you."

Valsorres, Espéret and Portier were drinking in Thaû's words; he seemed to them to be a sort of mythological divinity who was suddenly revealing to them unsuspected and unsuspectable mysteries.

After having observed the astonishment of his listener, he continued.

"Thus, everything here, even a part of the air that we breathe, is artificial, and comes from the materials of the solid crust forming the surface of our planet."

"But what about water?" asked Espéret.

"Oh, water! That's our black spot. Water is relatively rare on our little Martian glob, so we use it sparingly and preserve it carefully from the cold that would freeze it. The entire surface of our planet is furrowed by immense tunnels, well covered and sheltered, in which the water indispensable for the life of or inhabitants is protected from the exterior cold and maintained in a liquid state by the action of the internal heat."

"Those are the canals, then!" Valsorres exclaimed.

"Canals, if you wish," replied Thaû. "You've discovered that on Earth?"

"Yes, but we weren't absolutely certain of it."

"It's the exact truth, however. They are indeed canals, excavated and covered over by the industry of the inhabitants. They depart from few basins where several of them meet, and distribute water to all points of the planet."

---

[23] The idea of gravitational waves was proposed in 1905 by Henri Poincaré, who was one of the scientists present at Berget's 1902 duplication of the experiment known as "Foucault's pendulum."

"That's admirable," said Valsorres. "But where are your cities, your houses and your factories?"

"All of that is beneath the surface, sheltered from the external cold. The Martians live, as you put it 'underground,' if that term can be applied to a planet other than your Earth."[24]

"But in that case," said Dr. Portier, "the atmosphere you absorb in your lungs must rapidly become unbreathable."

"It would indeed, without the endeavors of our scientists and the discoveries of our engineers. We have known for a long time how to absorb the deleterious emanations expelled by the lungs of living beings."

"Carbon dioxide?" asked Portier.

"Oh, you call it carbon dioxide?" Thaû replied. "Yes, indeed, I seem to have come across that term. But it's not just that; there is, in addition, a veritable poison expelled into the air by the lungs."

"The pulmonary poison," said the doctor, "discovered twenty years ago by Dr. d'Arsonval."

"You've only known about it for twenty years? Here, we've known about it for more than two thousand. We are able to destroy it and replace it with the aromatic emanations that you might have noticed in the air that you're breathing at present?"

"The perfumed air!" exclaimed Thomas.

"Yes, the perfumed air; it's not simply a perfume that it contains but a veritable balm, preserving the lungs from any unhealthy alteration, at the same time as it destroys the toxic substance expelled from bodies by respiration. In the same way, our aliments, prepared by chemical combinations of the elements necessary to life, contain—in a small volume that does not overload the stomach—all the most active nutritive principles, and also the remedies preventing all diseases; they nourish and preserve simultaneously."

"Oh!" said the young doctor. "Will you show me that, Monsieur?"

"Be tranquil," replied the beautiful Saâh. "Daâh, your beautiful companion, will enable you to visit the places where aliments are manufactured for our inhabitants, as well as the liquids that are their ordinary beverages."

"Thank you in advance, Madame," said Portier.

"I'll continue," said Thaû. "Our beverages are, as you've been able to see, of two kinds: a yellow liquid and a pink liquid."

"Yes, certainly," said Espéret. "Both are exquisite."

"Well, the yellow liquid composed by our chemists is the liquid of maintenance; it's the one that repairs the losses of the organism and maintains it is a perpetual state of strength and youth. We call it tarass."

---

[24] The French equivalent of the English "underground" *sous terre*, translates literally as "under the earth."

"So it's for that reason," Valsorres said, "that all the people here, men and women alike, are uniformly young and beautiful?"

"Yes, Marquis, it's in large measure due to that. As for the other liquid, the pink one, which we call zoreb, we employ it when our organs require a supplementary effort, either of the mind or he body. It procures the forgetfulness of past pains and sufferings, and brings the mind back to a present full of charms You drank it yesterday evening, Messieurs—what do you think of it?"

The four men smiled, while their beautiful companions gazed at them with a keen expression of sympathy.

"But in those conditions, Thaû, your Martians always remain beautiful and strong; they never grow old?"

"Certainly not, Among us, old age is unknown."

"Then people don't die on Mars?"

"Alas, yes," replied Thaû, "people die here, as on Earth, but they die differently; they die without growing old. One morning, or evening, they suddenly fell themselves getting cold, and he limbs refusing all service. Then, they understand that it is the end, and it arrives very rapidly. In less than an hour, it is all over. But until that supreme moment, our existence is passed in youth and pleasures."

Valsorres and his companions were struck with admiration. That victorious struggle undertaken by created beings against the forces of nature, against disease, and against old age, seemed to them to contain the miraculous.

"But you haven't attempted to struggle against death itself, then?" asked Espéret.

Thaû remained pensive for a moment. "Yes, we have tried! But there, it was necessary to realize that we found ourselves in the presence of a Force superior to ours, a Reason superior to ours and a Will superior to ours. Great as we might have become, we feel small in the presence of the Supreme Being that you, I believe, call God. The closer we approach it with our incessantly increasing discoveries, the more it dominates us with its grandeur and its infinity. No, in spite of all our efforts, we have not succeeded in struggling against death."

Vividly impressed, the listeners remained silent after those words from the man who seemed to be the master of Mars. It was Dr. Portier who broke the silence first.

"But in that case," he said, "these ladies, who have the appearance of young women are not as young as they seem. My beautiful Daâh, tell me how old you are, and above all, no cheating."

Without the slightest hesitation, Daâh replied: "I'm seventy-one years old."[25]

---

[25] The subsequent text implies that Daâh is citing her age in Earthly years rather than Martian years, but it is sometimes unclear henceforth whether references to

Portier uttered a loud burst of laughter. "No, my friend! It's a joke, and you're pulling my leg!"

"Putting your…what?"

"Making me believe what isn't so. You aren't seventy-one years old. It isn't possible."

"Yes it is, my friend. Ask my mistress Saâh, who knows my age. She will tell you."

"That's correct," said Saâh, "Daâh has just passed her seventy-first year."

They all looked in amazement at that magnificent creature, who respired strength, youth and vigor.

Thaû saw their astonishment. "I'd astonish you even more, Messieurs, if I told you my age, and that of Saâh, my beautiful companion. If I hide it, it's not out of coquetry; here, one doesn't blush at the years gone by in pleasure; it's to reserve a surprise for you.

Portier then advanced toward Thaû and Saâh. "What I see here would appear supernatural to me if you hadn't prepared me by the announcement of your scientific discoveries, accumulated over the centuries. But that doesn't tell us how you were forewarned about our voyage and how, when we arrived here, you were able to greet the leader of our expedition by his name and title, in his own language."

"Well, Doctor," said Thaû, "you shall have satisfaction. We were alerted to your projected voyage, your departure and the name of the Marquis de Valsorres by messages send by waves."

"By wireless telegraphy!" exclaimed Espéret.

"You call it wireless telegraphy? So be it. Well, it's by that means that we learned your name and about your project."

"Oh, that's too much!" said Valsorres. Explain yourself."

"Patience, Marquis; I shall explain everything, and you shall understand everything."

"years" made by Martians are to their years, or whether the timespans have been tacitly "translated."

VI. In which the Marquis de Valsorres and his companions learn how the Martians speak French so fluently.

Thaû straightened up slightly on the sofa on which he was sitting, and, scanning his listeners with a circular glance, he continued.

"Before telling you how I received the wireless telegraphy messages—to use your term—that informed me of your departure, it's necessary for me to give you a few details about the past of our Martian globe. As I have told you, our planet is much older than Earth; it represents a more advanced evolution, a greater degree of general progress. It is more distant from its origins and closer to its end than your terrestrial globe.

"As I have also said, more than two thousand years ago our scientists made discoveries that yours have scarcely glimpsed and announced. Thus, we have known about your waves for more than fifteen hundred years, and it is with their aid that we communicate between different points on our planet, transmitting words and music directly over distance."

"You've had wireless telegraphy for fifteen hundred years?" said Espéret.

"Yes, Monsieur," Thaû replied. "You understand that, whereas you have only just discovered it, we have greatly improved it. Our instruments of reception are extraordinarily sensitive—too much so that, as soon as you began to emit signals with the aid of waves, we received them here, in spite of the distance."

"That's almost incredible!" said Valsorres.

"It is, however, true," said Thaû. "We rapidly understood that your combinations of short and long signals must represent letters. Then, by means of the art of decryption, of which some of our inhabitants charged with special functions have a marvelous mastery, we reconstituted the alphabet. In that fashion, not one message sent in the French language is lost to us. When attention was paid to you by the Chambre des députés de France, messages were sent to announce that you had requested the money that you were refused; we received those messages. When you had constructed your apparatus, other messages announced your departure, giving your name. We knew it too; we watched out for the moment you quit the Earth, and followed you through the heavens."

"You followed us? How?" Valsorres asked.

"With our telescopes. Oh, we have greatly improved the instruments that you use to see into the distance. By virtue of special artifices, we can perceive rays that you doubtless cannot see, with the result that we were able, given the colossal power of our telescopes, to see the luminous trail that your projectile left in space as it advanced through the obscurity of the heavens."

"And you grabbed us in passing?"

"Yes, as you have seen, with gravitational waves."

Valsorres had risen to his feet. "What you have just told us, Thaû, as if it were a very simple matter, is one marvel more on your marvelous globe; but it doesn't tell us how you learned French. For, in order to decipher the key to the telegraphic signals, it is necessary to know what letters they might represent—which is to say, to know the French alphabet and the French language—and I don't understand how you could have succeeded in that."

"Oh, that is another story," said Thaû. "It's necessary to go back into the past a little, and go back to the year 1786, in your system of counting. I've told you that more than two thousand years ago, our science made gigantic progress. The discoveries you have recently made, which permit you to utilize the energy contained in the atoms that compose substances, were made about five hundred years ago, with the consequence that about two centuries ago, we had in our hands an instrument analogous to the one that has permitted you to reach us, as well as the active matter necessary for its propulsion."

"You've never been tempted to come to Earth, then."

"Yes, indeed. We equipped an engine greatly resembling yours and departed, I believe, in 1787."

"How did you know that date?"

"Our voyagers only knew it afterwards, as you shall see. So, five of our inhabitants departed for Earth. They were completely ignorant regarding the planet Sila, on which they were about to descend. Their voyage, very similar to yours, lasted about four days, at the end of which they found themselves above an immense expanse of water. We have discovered since that you call it the Pacific Ocean.

"As they approached Earth, they only saw that liquid sphere, which seemed to constitute the entire globe. Only a few black dots came to trouble he monotony. A few of those dots seemed to be emitting flames and smoke. Finally, they chose one of the dots at random and steered toward it; they descended there, and found that they were on a desert island.

"At first they were agreeably surprised by the mildness of the climate and the beauty of the trees offered to their eyes, but they traveled the island in all directions, in vain; they found no trace of living beings.

They were about to go back to their vehicle and return to our globe when one of them perceived thin smoke emerging from a sort of wooden hut. He approached it, and then saw a man clad in ragged garments, who began emitting cries of joy at the sight of them.

"How did that man of the white race come to be alone on that island, where he was condemned to die of isolation? That was what subsequent events informed those of our inhabitants who had attempted the voyage. Naturally, the man did not understand the language of our people, not they his. In spite of that, by means of signs, he made them understand that he wanted to go with them. He thought that they had come in a ship.

"Our five Martians took him to their projectile then and showed him the heavens, in order thus to indicate whence they came, and that they were about to return in the same vehicle. The man hesitated momentarily, but he made his decision. He returned to his hut with two of us and showed them a few objects which he evidently desired to take with him. Among those objects were two rather large creates containing books and instruments.

"Our Martians helped him to transport all that to their machine; then, all five of them and their new companion commenced the return journey to the planet, where they arrived without accidents on the fourth day, bring back an 'Earthman.'"

"With the consequence," said Valsorres, "that we aren't the first Earthmen who have set foot on Mars?"

"As you see."

"And what became of that Earthman?"

"Wait; you shall know. The man seemed very learned and highly intelligent. Thanks to the use of gestures and signs, the Martians who were in daily contact with him, as well as their wives and daughters, learned rapidly to understand his language, as he learned theirs. He then took a few children of both sexes and undertook to teach them to read and write his language.

"That man was a Frenchman, an officer in the navy of King Louis XVI. Having departed with the expedition of the celebrated navigator La Pérouse,[26] he was the sole survivor of that unfortunate shipwreck. He had drifted ashore on a raft of sorts. He had collected wreckage, among which were two crates of books, one of which contained an astonishing work entitled the *Encyclopédie*.

"I shall not prolong this story with unnecessary detail; I shall simply tell you that, when a few of our Martians had taken cognizance of the French language, they found it so beautiful, elegant, clear and precise that it was adopted by the elite of our inhabitants. By way of the *Encyclopédie*, we were therefore informed of the general state of affairs on Earth and of your terrestrial sciences at the moment of your year 1787. I must admit that the sciences, on Earth, were in a rudimentary state, almost non-existence, so to speak, by comparison with their development among us.

"That is how we were able to obtain precisions regarding the past of your planet, how we learned the French language, and how many of us now speak it purely. You will, Messieurs, I hope, refresh our language; if some of our expres-

---

[26] Jean-François de Galaup, Comte de La Pérouse (1741-1788?) was a famous explorer commissioned by Louis XVI to lead an elite scientific expedition around the world, in order to complete the Pacific explorations of James Cook. He sent back abundant information from various landfalls but his two ships vanished after leaving Australia. A subsequent expedition sent in 1791 to investigate found nothing, and it was not until 1826 that the fate of the ships, wrecked in the vicinity of Vanikoro, was discovered.

sions leave something to be desired, be good enough to inform us of it; far from being offended, we would be grateful for it."

"Thank you, Thaû, for having recounted these events. But permit me to ask you a question."

"Please do."

"Do you know the name of that naval officer?"

"Certainly. He was, he said, an ensign in the Royal Navy, and his name was Vicomte François de Ressigny."

"De Ressigny!" cried Valsorres. "But the Ressigny family is related to ours!"

"I know. In the papers that he left his children..."

"He had children, then?"

"Yes, Marquis. He never wanted to return to Earth, although the offer to take him back there was made several times. He took a companion on Mars and had two children by her: a son and a daughter."

"Are those children still alive?"

"Wait. The son, who devoted himself to scientific research in one of the great workshops in which we carry it out, is unfortunately dead, of an accident impossible to foresee, but the daughter is still alive."

"Oh! Thaû, put me in her presence so that I can embrace that celestial cousin, whom I am encountering such a providential manner."

"You have her before you, Marquis. That daughter is none other than my beautiful companion, the admirable Saâh, who reigns with me over all the inhabitants of this planet. Saâh, embrace your cousin, the Marquis de Valsorres."

Saâh had risen to her feet, and fell into Henri's arms.

After that first embrace, the Marquis, whose astonishment surpassed all possible limits, addressed Thaû again.

"King Thaû, if my relative arrived here in 1787, when did he marry?"

"About twelve or thirteen years later, in your year 1800 or thereabouts. He had always measured 'years' in the terrestrial manner."

"But when were his children born, then?"

"I believe that the son was born in 1802, the daughter—which is to say, Saâh—in 1805."

The Marquis looked at his cousin with veritable amazement. "But then, my dear cousin Saâh, you would be..."

"A hundred and nine years old, in terrestrial years, yes, my dear cousin," she replied, addressing an enchanting smile to the Marquis, which uncovered the double row of pearly teeth behind her vermilion lips.

"A hundred and nine years old! But that's incredible!"

"It's true," added the admirable creature, laughing, "that it's scarcely more than fifty-eight Martian years."

But the Marquis could not get over it, and he turned to Portier. "Well, Doctor, a hundred and nine years old! What do you say to that, my friend?"

217

"I don't say anything," said the young scientist. "Like you, I'm amazed; that's all I can tell you."

Valsorres turned to Saâh. "Just now, Thaû mentioned papers left to his children by my relative, Vicomte de Ressigny?"

"Yes, my cousin," Saâh replied. "We'll show them to you in due course. There's mention of his remaining family on Earth, and the Marquis de Valsorres is mentioned as being a cousin. So, when the wave messages told us of our project and your name, Thaû and I were particularly pleased by the thought that we were about to meet one of our terrestrial relatives. That is why we took the liberty of deflecting you from your route and constraining you to land here."

Henri kissed Saâh's hand, and then said: "But to get back to our cousin de Ressigny, your father, you say that he never wanted to return to Earth?"

"Never," relied Thaû. "Oh, Marquis, that is because life, in the conditions in which we live here, is not how you appear to live on Earth, according to the accounts of Monsieur de Ressigny and the *Encyclopédie*. Here, there are all pleasures, all joys, no maladies and no infirmities; life is prolonged, thanks to the beautiful discoveries of our scientists, in perpetual youth, for an average duration of two hundred and fifty years."

"Two hundred and fifty years!" exclaimed Portier. "You live for two hundred and fifty years?"

"On average, yes: two hundred and fifty Martian years, I mean, which is about five hundred terrestrial years. But our scientists have done better; as I told you, they have suppressed diseases. The body conserves its youth, its strength and its beauty until the end; one dies almost abruptly, but without having known the horror of old age and decrepitude. That is why Monsieur de Ressigny never wanted to return to Earth, and why we have dispensed with making a further voyage ourselves."

The Marquis then addressed Thaû.

"Cousin—permit me to give you that name—I am progressing from astonishment to astonishment. I am burning with the desire to know, in more detail, the past of your planet and its present organization, for I presume that its entire life is not concentrated in that superb hall where a few thousand inhabitants gave us the welcome that we received here. I beg you, on behalf of my companions and myself, to satisfy our curiosity quickly."

"My cousin," Thaû replied, "your wishes will be granted, and you shall know, by means of a brief account, the past of our planet Raas, which you call Mars. We know, from reading the *Encyclopédie*, that Mars was the god of war among the ancient peoples of the Earth. Alas, our unfortunate planet has justified the appellation that you chanced to give it only too well."

"You have had wars?" asked Valsorres.

"As far back as our history, transmitted by writing, permits us to go, we see that the inhabitants of Mars—I shall call it that henceforth, for your benefit—have been divided into two nations, those of the North and those of the South.

"As you know, the sun appears to us smaller by half than it does to you, and sends us scarcely a quarter of the heat that it sends to Earth, so the temperature at the surface of soil is extremely low and the vegetation very poor. The first inhabitants, therefore, sought refuge in deep caves, in order to protect them from the cold. How did their industry develop? That is a mystery for our historians, for, as far back as their research extends into the past, they always find traces of an advanced industry. The first Martians certainly knew fire and metals.

"In order to live in a milder temperature, they had hollowed out habitations under the ground, and it is the subterranean existence now perfected by us that our ancestors already lived. The few rare animals that populated the planet could not suffice to fed its inhabitants; very rapidly, they became skillful chemists, and realized twenty-five or thirty thousand years ago the aliments prepared directly from mineral elements, which now constitute, as you have been able to ascertain by sampling them, our unique and substantial nourishment. It is the same with our beverages."

"Ah!" said Espéret. "You've known the secrets of chemistry for more than twenty-five thousand years?"

"Yes, Monsieur—except that today, everything has been greatly improved. Our ancestors already knew them, however in a sufficient fashion to satisfy the necessities of their alimentation. It is the conquest of the natural deposits containing the raw materials of that nourishment that led to our first wars. The people of the North possessed more deposits permitting the artificial constitution of aliments; those of the South coveted them. Hence the terrible struggles that took place between twelve and fifteen thousand years ago. It was the people of the South who prevailed, and for about eight thousand years an absolute, unique, hereditary monarchy ruled the planet, bringing an era of incessantly increasing prosperity, thanks to a skillfully directed organization. But as the arts were perfected and books multiplied and propagated their ideas..."

"Ah, you discovered printing!"

"No, not in the sense you understand it on Earth. We write on very thin metal sheets, and by means of a special method that we will show you, we can reproduce what we have written in as great a quantity as we wish.

"So, I was saying that as books spread among our inhabitants, ideas of independence germinated in the minds of many of them. No one wanted to work any longer; the inhabitants lacked everything. The most profound poverty reigned over our unfortunate globe, the prosperity of which was rapidly reduced to nothing by the sequence of events."

"There was a revolution?"

"Yes. The instigators took possession of the sovereign and put him to death. They then proclaimed a State in which all the inhabitants were to be equals, to have everything at their disposal, and never to work. Then all the discoveries of our scientists, and all the progress accomplished in the course of the previous centuries, were annihilated. Barbarity invaded our globe again.

"The Martians, once so fortunate, knew famine and all its horrors; it was an intolerable regime. Thanks to that regime, in two hundred years Mars lost the benefits of eight thousand years of continuous prosperity, labor and progress. The inhabitants had almost returned to the savage state, to the extent that they had almost lost the current language. It was, therefore, the beginning of the end.

"It was then that an energetic man emerged from the crowd debased by misery and privation. His name was Russ. By means of his communicative ardor, his example and his indomitable courage, he drew the majority of healthy men to fight against those who were tyrannizing our people. The most ferocious of the latter were put to death, the others surrendered, after having recognized what a terrible adventure they had embarked on in such an unfortunate fashion.

"That happened about three thousand years ago. Russ then took power and organized our world in accordance with the principles that still rule it today. Under his impulsion, the planet knew a veritable rebirth. It is from him that all the great projects date that brought us to our present condition."

"And what is that State?" said Valsorres.

"This one," replied Thaû. "On Mars, all the inhabitants are born, live and die equal."

"Oh," said Espéret. "You've arrived at the regime of equality?"

"Yes, there are neither rich nor poor among us. There are no idlers and everyone works, in the same way that everyone savors the same pleasures and the same amusements. Some work with the brain: they are the scientists and artists. Others work with their hands: they are the laborers. But the latter are not considered as inferior to the former. All are penetrated by the idea that they contribute equally to the general wellbeing, albeit by different means, and they work as hard as they can."

"That's admirable!" said Portier.

"Isn't it?" said Espéret.

Thaû continued. "That equality is translated in a very simple and natural manner: everything belongs to everyone. We have no desires, for as soon as a Martian wants something, he or she has only to go to the immense storehouses where all the products of our industry are accumulated.

"Ah!" said Valsorres. "That's true socialism."

"What are you saying? Socialism?"

"Yes, that's what we call, on Earth, the regime after which everyone sighs, but which is so difficult to realize among us."

"Why is that?"

"Because, on Earth, we always have struggles, divisions between citizens, which our parliaments can never settle."

Thaû reflected. "Parliaments did you say? You have Parliaments, then?"

"Yes, of course."

"Well, here, we have no parliaments. The government has all the powers, and it uses them to ensure the continuation of the regime of equality and wellbeing that obtains the happiness of our inhabitants. Thanks to a very widespread education, all our citizens understand the interest they have in assuring order, and observing the general conditions, so exceptions are rare. We have few misdemeanors and even fewer crimes."

"But if the order is troubled, what do you do?"

"We have what I believe you call on Earth the constabulary."

"Yes, we called it the constabulary in the eighteenth century; today we call it the police.

"Well, so be it. We have a small corps of police. Thanks to the rapidity of transport on our planet, it can move very rapidly to any point on our globe, and it is sufficient to maintain public order and repress any excesses that might be produced, wherever they emerge."

Thaû paused momentarily.

Then the Marquis de Valsorres said to him: "But, my cousin, how do you conciliate that principle of authority with the monarchic form of your government?"

"It was conciliated of its own accord after our last great crisis. The people understood that they needed a unique leader, and the unique leader, once elected by the acclamation of all, similarly understood that only an absolutely egalitarian regime could ensure universal happiness. The fact of having a unique leader, recognized and accepted by everyone, eliminates all competitions—and besides, as I told you, we have no parliaments and no politicians."

"But are there not public orators susceptible of drawing the people with subversive speeches?"

"We have no orators. On Mars, speeches are forbidden. An orator is, in effect, a man who wants to impose his way of thinking on others; he is thus attacking their liberty. Here, all the inhabitants, even the laborers who carry out the hardest labor, are sufficiently educated for it to be pointless to try to insinuate a thought into their minds that is not their own."

"What about the newspapers, then?"

"The newspapers limit themselves to announcing news, describing discoveries, recounting important events and eulogizing the dead. They never publish any stories that would tend to impose any opinion on their readers, whose intellectual liberty they respect too much."

"That is a very remarkable general State," said Valsorres. "Do you think that it is stable and that that it will last?"

"I don't know," said Thaû. "For the moment, the present regime appears to be firmly established, and its continuation seems assured, at least for quite a long time. Perhaps crises or new revolutions will be produced later and will modify or transform the present state of affairs. That we can't foresee. But our inhabitants, instructed of the history of the past, know the state to which our first crisis brought our planet; they understand how grave the consequences of a new civil war would be. I don't say that no regime better than ours can exist; perhaps you have one on Earth; but, given the doubt, we're content with the one we presently have."

"That's evidently wisdom," said Valsorres.

"Isn't it? And wisdom based on long experience. Believe me, Messieurs, in this matter above all, a little experience is worth infinitely more than a great deal of theory."

Our four friends had listened to Thaû's story with sustained attention. Dr. Portier, addressing the king, said to him: "How is Martian society organized, then King Thaû."

"It's quite simple. To govern the whole planet there is an absolute sovereign; that is me, who reigns with my beautiful Saâh, your cousin. Our children will inherit the right to our dignity and our power. Around me are six ministers and four governments, each of which is at the head of one of the regions of Mars."

"They must have a considerable task, then."

"Not as much as you might think. First of all, the surface area of Mars is scarcely a quarter of that of Earth. Then, the rapidity of communications is such that there are, so to speak, no longer any long distances for our inhabitants."

"What are those means?"

"There are gliders that fly, in a sense, over the surface of the water enclosed in our innumerable covered canals,"

"So your canals really exist?"

"Yes; in that, at least, your terrestrial astronomers were not mistaken. Thanks to those canals, traced following the arcs of the great circle on the surface of the sphere, journeys from one point to another are easy and rapid. The circumference of Mars is only half that of Earth, so the distances are shorter, and our four governments are broadly sufficient to their task, which is, in sum, less burdensome than one might think at first."

"Can I ask you, then, how the family is organized?"

"The family? In a manner of speaking, we have none. The inhabitants come together of their own accord, living together at the whim of their respective inclinations. When one of those unions produces a child, the parents are free either to abandon it to the State, which raises it, or to keep it with them, on condition that it receives the same education as the State provides.

"In any case, given the difficulties of life on Mars, we have limited the number of children. Every woman must have at last two children, and at most three. If she has more than three children, the children additional to three are rightfully the property of the State, which ensures their education in conformity with heir aptitudes, but the mother never sees them again. In that fashion we succeed in maintaining the number of inhabitants stationary; otherwise, the planet could no longer nourish them.

Valsorres spoke then. "You have, in fact, realized a remarkable social state. But how is it organized from the economic point of view?"

"It's very simple. First of all, we have no commerce, everything being everyone's, and in consequence, no finance and no money. Property being general, so to speak, Martians have nothing to envy their neighbors, since they have a right to possess the same things, on condition they carry out conscientiously the share of labor that reverts to each of them. Having no commerce, we have no temptations to fraud or exaggerated benefits. Theft is also very rare and is only exercised, occasionally and exceptionally, on precious stones."

"Oh," said Espéret. "Precious stones don't belong to everyone, then?"

"No. They're the only thing that can't be shared, because they're so rare on the planet. They belong to those who find them. Our women are very desirous of them, and the few misdemeanors that we have to repress almost all stem from that."

"And how do you repress them? Do you have tribunals?"

"Yes; in the region of each of the four governments, there is a tribunal. It's a assembly of twelve inhabitants appointed by their peers and presided over by the governor. That tribunal pronounces sentence, not in accordance with laws that are necessarily out of date as soon as they are made, but in accordance with the common sense of those called upon to judge."

"And what if the accused deems the judgment unjust?"

Then the matter comes before me. Together with my six ministers, we constitute a supreme tribunal, the sentence of which is definitive and without appeal."

Our four friends remained pensive at the explanation of that social system, so new for them.

Portier broke the silence, and addressed Thaû. "It is, therefore, only the possession of precious stones that can break—temporarily, at least—the equilibrium of Martian society, so perfect from the triple viewpoint of liberty, equality and fraternity."

"Yes, liberty, equality and fraternity are, in fact, the basis of our social life, except with regard to two categories of citizens: actors and philosophers."

"Oh?" said Espéret, curiously. "Actors?"

"Yes," Thaû replied. "Those people, indispensable to our recreation and our pleasure, always wanted to break equality, because they thought themselves superior to everyone, even to our most skillful and most laborious workers, and even our most admirable scientists. When they arrived in a public place, they raised their voices, only talking about themselves, and talking constantly. Furthermore, they were always arguing with one another, each one claiming to have more talent than the others. It was a veritable obstacle to the maintenance of our egalitarian regime; so we put it in order.

"Actors no longer go out. They're enclosed in a vast palace, where they enjoy all the luxury and desirable wellbeing, but they have to live there together.

The doors of their dwelling, carefully guarded by policemen, only open to let them go to the various theaters at which they perform, where they're taken under escort. They're brought back in the same fashion when the performances are over. Every month they elect a leader who is responsible for order in his domain.

"In addition, the women, many of whom are very beautiful, are terribly jealous of one another."

"Ah!" said the curious Espéret. "Your actresses are very beautiful?"

"Yes, Monsieur," Thaû replied. "You can judge for yourself, for we shall soon have great celebrations, where you will see them appear. As for the men, they spend their time declaiming, quarreling, and, above all, playing."

"Playing? What do you mean? Performing plays between them?"

"No, playing games of chance, in order to try to obtain the precious stones for which the actresses are so avid. And I have no need to tell you that the games often lead to unfortunate incidents, almost the only ones produced on our globe."

"But if they don't go out, can people at least visit them?"

"Yes, certainly. The ladies receive their visitors very amiably and in a very welcoming fashion. They accept the homages that flatter their vanity with pleasure, as well as the little presents that accompany them. That, my dear Marquis, is the sole exception to our egalitarian system."

"But you mentioned philosophers," said Valsorres, "and you haven't talked about religion."

"Religion?" said Thaû. "We have none. We believe that there is a Supreme Being, an infinite Intelligence and Power, the Cause of everything we see. Once a year, at the new year, all the inhabitants gather in temples to render collective homage to Him."

"And that's all?" asked Valsorres.

"That's all. There are, however, among our scholars a few of the specialists that are, I believe, called philosophers on Earth."

"Yes, philosophers," said Espéret.

"These philosophers try to explain what becomes of us after death, but some say that everything is finished when one dies and others say, on the contrary, that everything begins again, and those are not in accord regarding the manner of recommencement. So, the people in question are regarded as dangerous. They are made to live in a special dwelling, and when they shout too loudly, they are put in close confinement. Then they calm down for a while.

"In addition, scientists all have their particular installations, in order to devote themselves to their research, and when that is finished, it is exploited in the subterranean workshops where our workmen toil, and where the heat of the core of the planet is utilized to fabricate everything. Whenever you wish, Messieurs, we can enable you to visit all of that; I hope that you'll find it of some interest."

"I believe so," replied Valsorres.

"Certainly," said Espéret and the doctor, in unison.

Only Thomas grumbled, privately. "If only there were a factory of good wine! That would suit me. To think that I'm condemned to live in a place where there's no wine! Damn it! These things only happen to me."

VII. In which Valsorres, Espéret and the doctor are able to observe that the scientists of Mars are more advanced than those of Earth.

As Thaû had made the offer to them, our three scientists had eagerly accepted to be initiated into Martian discoveries.

"You only know the history of terrestrial science up to the epoch of the *Encyclopédie*, which is to say, the end of the eighteenth century," the Marquis had said to the sovereign of the planet. "We'll make you a gift of a more modern encyclopedia, the illustrated *Larousse*, which will bring you up to date with the state of humankind in all the branches of its knowledge at the present time."

In fact, they gave Thaû a copy of that great reference book, which they had brought with them in the *Fusée*.

Their host was very appreciative of that present.

"You see, Messieurs," he said to them, "We appreciate the French language at its high value, but although we speak it fluently, we scarcely know its writers. Monsieur de Ressigny's crates, saved from La Pérouse's shipwreck, only contained the *Encyclopédie*, books of mathematics, and a few literary works by La Fontaine, Molière and La Bruyère."

"Well, my dear cousin," Valsorres replied, "the library of the *Fusée* isn't very rich, but it contains modern works that will interest you; you'll see the writings of Chateaubriand, Victor Hugo, Alexandre Dumas, Balzac, Paul Bourget, Anatole France and, in particular, the works of the modern Molière, Georges Courteline, where you'll find humor and perfect language."

And things had passed thus, to the great joy of Thaû, and above all of Saâh and our voyagers' beautiful friends. Meanwhile, the latter had commenced their scientific visits.

To begin with, Thaû had taken them to the workshops where the alimentary substances necessary to the life of the Martians were prepared from mineral elements extracted from the soil of the planet.

Portier opened his eyes wide on seeing the operations that were being carried out before his eyes.

In the hands of the Martian chemists, the mineral matter, reduced to its simple elements: hydrogen, oxygen, carbon, nitrogen, sulfur and phosphorus, permitted the synthesis of all the albuminoid substances, fats and sugars. By means of successive carefully measured concentrations, the scientists produced aliments that, in a small volume, contained all the alimentary principles indispensable to the maintenance of the human machine, without weighing down the stomach.

The most remarkable thing was that the preparations were not made in laboratories but in veritable subterranean factories. It was, in fact, necessary to furnish aliments to the entire Martian population, and that, according to Thaû, amounted to nearly a hundred million individuals. The enormous workshops were, therefore, distributed in different parts of the planet.

Those aliments not only contained nutritive principles, but also antiseptic and curative principles discovered thousands of years before by the physiologists and biochemists of Mars. Thus at the same time as they were nourished, the Martians absorbed the substances that preserved them from disease and old age, conserving their youth, strength and health until the brink of the grave.

One preparation that attracted Dr. Portier's attention particularly was that of beverages, which as explained to him in all its details by the director of the colossal alimentary service. The director spoke French very well; his name was Tiss. He was assisted by a physiologist, who also spoke our language, and was named Zouk.

It must be said that, in spite of the French language, long days went by before Portier was able to comprehend the explanations of his Martian colleagues. That is because they only understood the scientific French language that existed in the epoch of Diderot and d'Alembert's *Encyclopédie*, which was their only terrestrial document.

In that epoch, except for mathematics, the sciences were in their infancy, and the knowledge of the solar system stopped at Saturn. The Martians were therefore ignorant of the names that chemists had given in the nineteenth century to the various substances they had prepared; they did not even know the names of phenomena discovered in optics, thermodynamics and electricity, even though they had known the phenomena for much longer.

Between scientists, however, understanding is always reached eventually, especially in the presence of facts and things. A month after his entry to the factory, Portier, up to date with everything, had assimilated with a rare intelligence all the discoveries of Martian science, of which he had become one of the luminaries. The Martian scientists admired him; Tiss and Zouk considered him a great master, and told him so without jealousy.

His days passed thus, in work and discovery; the young scientist was passionate about it, all the more so because, by virtue of the daily absorption of the two beverages prepared by the Martians, he felt the same beneficent effects as them.

The yellow liquid, tarass, animated the nervous system, augmented physical strength at the same time as the intellectual faculties, and thus operated a conservation that was equivalent for our three friends to a veritable rejuvenation.

As for the pink liquid, the zoreb, its effect was very different; it procured the gradual forgetfulness of the past to the advantage of the present and the future. Thus, Valsorres only any longer saw the people he had left on Earth as if through a veil of mist. His wife appeared to him as a sort of divinity, inhabiting some distant paradise from which the idea of her reached him; but that memory, although pleasant, did not involve any regret. Even the abduction of his son, his dear Philippe, was no longer presented to his memory as a dramatic event calling for vengeance, but as an incident lost in the fog of the past.

It was the same for Portier, in whose eyes the image of little Zabeth, although so dear, became increasingly blurred, in a distant nebulosity.

Only the scientific work retained the attention of the three scientists, and when their day of assiduous labor was over, after spending the evening in the company of Thaû, Saâh and a few notable Martians, when they went back to their apartments, where the atmosphere, warmed and perfumed by the art of the chemists, permitted them a full and delightful respiration, they abandoned themselves unreservedly to the charms of the existence shared by the delightful companions chosen for them by the sovereigns of the planet.

While Portier devoted himself ardently to the study of the enormous progress of physiology, Valsorres and Espéret were impassioned by the conquests of mechanics and industry.

It was into the veritable entrails of the Martian soul that Thaû had enabled the two engineers to penetrate. To begin with he had shown them the formidable establishments where the energy necessary to activate life on Mars was produced.

Naturally, everything was done by electricity—but what a difference there was from our earthly electricity! First of all, the current did not require machines and dynamos. A long time ago, the Martians had realized the direct production of electricity; they were only unaware of the name that we gave it, and Valsorres told them that. They obtained electrical energy by means of the immediate transformation of caloric energy furnished by the central heat of the planet.

Shafts excavated by generations of workers plunged into the entrails of the globe to the point where the temperature was sufficient to produce a sufficient electromotive force in bimetallic elements placed in juxtaposition. That current activated powerful transformers, which launched electric waves all over Mars. The Martians were able to direct, capture and concentrate those waves, which we presently employ in order to activate ultra-sensitive detectors for the purposes of wireless telegraphy. They made better use of them than we make of luminous waves, using them for the instantaneous transport of energy, and all the vehicles that flew over the waters of the vaulted canals were powered by those waves, as were all the aircraft flying through the Martian atmosphere for long journeys, which had no need to carry reserves of energy, since they captured that sent to them along the route by power stations.

Espéret was astonished by the metallurgical exploitations. The rarest metals—iridium and palladium, for example—were in use on Mars. Knives and tools were made of iridium, and thus immune to oxidation. Gold was a domestic metal there, with no other value than its inalterability. It served to make household utensils. It was the same for platinum. The only precious metals were silver and copper, the latter alloyed with a metal unknown on Earth called ravek, which rendered it inalterable.

All those metals were extracted from their minerals with the aid of electric furnaces. The minerals themselves, extracted from the subsoil by workers, were transported in extremely rapid wagons through wide vaulted corridors that connected the factories with one another and with the junction points of the canals, where there were "ports."

The two engineers were also ecstatic before the factories in which the metals were manufactured, where they were transformed into utensils and objects of every sort. Nothing could have given them an idea of the prodigious ingenuity and the incredible perfection that presides over all those processes. They were overwhelmed by them. And when they penetrated into the secret laboratories where explosives were manufactured they were even more astounded.

Not only were the Marians familiar with radium and virium, to which they gave other names, but they had also succeeded in extracting from the central nucleus, while condensing the emanations, a compound a thousand times more energetic than the virium of which Valsorres and Espéret were so proud. They compared it with a specimen of their product, taken from the provision of the *Fusée*, and were obliged to recognize that they had been far outdistanced by the scientists of the planet, who had veritably penetrated and utilized the secret of the structure of atoms and their constitutive energy.

But what astonished them more was the printing.

Books were made of thin sheets of an alloy of nickel and iridium that was almost untearable. The metallic surface on which the impression was made received a special preparation; a photographic image produced by quartz lenses rendered achromatic by their combination with other lenses of spar, was projected on to the prepared sheet, and the image of the characters thus projected was reproduced in an indelible fashion. Simple contact with another sheet furnished a second copy, and so on.

To give a practical demonstration of that marvelous method, 15,000 copies of the eight volumes of the *Larousse* that Espéret and Valsorres had given to Thaû were produced in ten days and distributed to all the Martians who spoke French, who took possession of them avidly.

There was, however, something that provoked even more admiration from Valsorres and Espéret, and that was Martian astronomy.

Thaû took both of them to the observatory situated on the highest mountain on Mars, at an altitude of 2,710 physes. Valsorres had, as you might think, compared the length of the physe with that of the meter that he had aboard the *Fusée*, and found that a physe was 1.78 meters, which gave 4,823 meters for the height of the mountain, significantly greater than that of Mont Blanc. As the diameter of Mars is less than half that of Earth, that was equivalent to an earthly observatory installed on Mount Everest, the highest peak in the Himalayas.

There, under the direction of a scientist, the astronomer Rash, a swarm of Martian women worked, all youthful and pretty, clad in the transparent gauze that allowed all their beauty to be divined, permitted by the constant warmth of the artificial atmosphere in which they lived.

In that entirely closed observatory, the sky was viewed through openings fitted with glass of marvelous transparence and clarity, without having to suffer from the cold, which would have been mortal, especially at that altitude.

All the women—one cannot say "young women" because there was no apparent aging on Mars[27]—worked assiduously; some observed, on vast unpolished panels, the images of heavenly bodies projected by powerful optical apparatus; others devoted themselves to calculations that they carried out rapidly in an exclusively mechanical manner.

There were no telescopes, properly speaking—no long tubes to the extremity of which it was necessary to apply the eye by adopting uncomfortable positions. The images of heavenly bodies, the clarity of which was augmented by means discovered by the Martians of capturing and reinforcing undulations of every sort, were painted on checkered sheets where all measurements were carried out with the utmost rapidity.

Valsorres was amazed when he was shown the Earth, the image of which, thus projected on the screen, was more than sixty centimeters in diameter; it was a veritable world map. But the clouds of the terrestrial atmosphere prevented the sight of the surface of our distant globe almost completely; only a few points of Australia and southern Africa could be identified by our scientists in the course of their first visit to the observatory.

What astonished them was the sight of the minor planets, the minuscule globes orbiting between Mars and Jupiter. On Earth we know about nine hundred of them; from the Martian observatory more than six thousand could be seen. It was like an army of mobile stars in the midst of the stars of the sky.

Our two scientists could not tear themselves away from that spectacle. However, the astronomer Rash had another reserved for them. He led them to a larger screen and, showing them another luminous disk, said: "This is the planet Hour, which you call Jupiter on Earth."

Valsorres and Espéret gazed tirelessly at that marvelous spectacle. So that was the giant planet of the solar system; it was a world still in a viscous condition, the considerable flattening of which translated its great velocity of rotation; it was a globe enveloped by dense clouds, on which the day lasts ten hours and the year eleven years. And around it they saw an army of satellites strung out; not only were there the nine satellites that we know visible to the naked eye, but ten more smaller ones were discernible, which brought to nineteen the number

---

[27] In fact, that very sensible observation does not prevent the authors from referring to Martian "*jeunes filles*" subsequently, even with respect to characters whose advanced ages have been established, but I have refrained from translating the phrase as "young women" except in instances where it does seem to imply literal youth.

of moons that must illuminate the Jovian world, and must produce tides in its oceans of a complication that would defy the calculations of our astronomers and hydrographers.

But Valsorres and Espéret were not yet at the end of their surprises. While they were observing Jupiter, two of the men, at a signal from their chief, had orientated a second objective lens, the image of which they received on another screen. Rash took the two scientists by the arm and led them in front of the bright surface.

"The planet Nidh," he said, simply.

The planet Nidh! But that was Saturn, the objective of their voyage, toward which all their ambitions were extended. Oh, how beautiful it was, the marvelous planet, enveloped by its ring of light, floating in space around its equator. The dark clouds could be seen that covered it almost entirely; only tiny fractions of the Saturnian surface could be glimpsed through chinks in the cloud from time to time, which disappeared very quickly, hidden again beneath other clouds.

And around the ring, the shadow of which was projected obliquely over the central sphere, a host of satellites could be seen gravitating, a host of moons that must add their light to that of the ring, to brighten Saturnian nights with an unparalleled illumination.

There were Rhea, Dione and Tethys, discovered in the seventeenth century; there were Mimas and Enceladus, discovered by Herschel in 1789; there was Titan, discovered by Huygens in 1655, Iapetus, which Cassini observed in 1671, Hyperion, discovered in 1848, Phoebe, whose discovery dates from 1898, and Themis, found in 1904. But the marveling Valsorres saw a further fifteen smaller satellites serving as a cortege to the ten lords just listed, and constituting, with the ring, a kind of crown of glory that surrounded the planet with its eccentric orbs.

Oh, how subject the Marquis was to the influence of that poetry of the infinite, only provided by the contemplation of the celestial world! How his thought pierced the clouds that enveloped the globe of Saturn and traveled to the strange soil that must constitute the surface of the mysterious planet! How he saw, in his imagination, the giant vegetables and the bizarre beings that were the manifestations of life on that world still in formation!

Espéret was subject to the same fascination as Valsorres in the presence of the image of Saturn, which took the form on the screen of a luminous circle more than a meter in diameter; like him, he explored in thought the unknown soil on which he and his friend had planned to plant the flag of France.

How distant those audacious projects already were!

Meanwhile, the two women had aimed another objective lens at another point in the sky, and had received the image of a new planet on a checkered screen.

"Vasa," said Rash, simply

"Vasa?" asked Valsorres.

"Yes, the planet that comes after Nidh."

Valsorres looked at it and, addressing Espéret, said: "Uranus."

It was, in fact, Uranus, discovered by Herschel, projected before the eyes of the two friends, escorted by its four satellites. In contrast to Jupiter and Saturn, of which the actual number of satellites was greater than the number known on Earth, only four could be seen: the four known to our astronomers, called Ariel, Umbriel, Oberon and Titania.

But it was written that our two scientists would pass the solar system in review. Rash touched their arms and showed them another screen on which another luminous disk about thirty centimeters in diameter was projected.

"The planet Yath," he said.

Valsorres looked at Espéret. "Neptune?" he asked his friend.

"Certainly," the engineer replied.

The two men gazed with ardent curiosity at the planet in question, an object of current observation for the Martians, which the powerful genius of Le Verrier, with the aid of calculation and celestial mechanics had revealed to the inhabitants of Earth before it could be observed telescopically.

It was seen to be escorted by a single satellite; it was rather pale, for the sun, very distant, only sent it an insufficient light; even so, they could make out parallel strips, doubtless clouds, covering the entire surface.

Thus, all the elements of the planetary world had filed before the eyes of Valsorres and Espéret. They were about to thank Rash for the marvelous spectacle that he had enabled them to witness when the two women signaled to them that there was something else to see.

The two scientists followed them.

On a screen sheltered by a sort of hood designed to interrupt the exterior light, a pale disk was projected, the image of which was about five centimeters in diameter.

The two men turned to Rash and interrogated him with their gaze.

"Zook," said the astronomer, pointing at the image.

Espéret looked, curiously.

"Yes," Rash added, "the planet that comes after the one you just called Neptune."

"Oh," said Valsorres, simply.

So they had before their eyes the key to the enigma that was exciting all the astronomers of Earth. The unknown planet suspected and foreseen by Le Verrier—who, without being able to perceive it, had given it the name of Pluto—was there before their eyes. Its image, faint but clear, was projected on a screen.

And around its mass, a unique but enormous satellite a quarter the size of the plants itself, could be seen gravitating. It was, therefore, a "double system" that terminated the solar system.[28]

The two scientists could not weary of gazing at what no terrestrial eye had been able to see before them.

Espéret was the first to emerge from his contemplation,

"And after that?" he asked Rash.

"After that," replied the Martian astronomer, "there is doubtless another planet. Three of our women are in the process of calculating the elements, with the aid of an integration machine, and the first results permit us to hope for another sphere, but until now, we have not been able to see it,

Valsorres and Espéret had risen to their feet. After having saluted Rash and thanked his gracious and savant collaborators, they followed Thaû. He conducted them to a rapid "descender," with brought them own to the level of the waters, and from there, a glider took them back to the palace in a matter of minutes.

"Well, Messieurs?" Thaû asked, "What do you think of our astronomers?"

"I say, my dear cousin," Valsorres replied, "that we Earthmen are simply ignorant, and that their science confounds us."

---

[28] It is, of course, pure coincidence that the dwarf planet Pluto, discovered some years after the publication of the present novel, in 1930, was eventually discovered to be part of a binary system with its largest satellite Charon, discovered in 1978.

*VIII. In which it can be seen how the Martians conserve
the history of their past.*

One morning, Thaû went into the Marquis de Valsorres' apartment, just as the latter was about to emerge in the company of his beautiful and inseparable companion Zith.

"What fortunate motive brings you, my dear cousin?" he asked his visitor.

"I have simply come to keep a promise that I made to you some time ago," said Thaû.

"What is that?"

"To show you, other than in a cold narration, the past of our planet and the events through which it has lived."

Valsorres looked at the Martian king curiously.

"You have a means of reproducing past events?" he asked, curiously.[29]

"Nor reproducing them in the true sense of the word, but at least a living image of them: not only the appearance of things and people but the movements and the words produced then, as well as various accompanying sounds."

Valsorres was already heading for the door. "How eager I am, cousin, to see this new marvel." He and his friend both followed Thaû to the rectangular room, where Espéret, with Rasôh, Portier, with Daâh, and Thomas, with Hina, were already gathered. They were all standing around Saâh, forming a circle of which the beautiful sovereign was the center.

The latter stood up when Thaû and the Marquis arrived. She held out her hand to her cousin, who deposited a respectful kiss on it, and said to him: "So, my dear Henri, you're going to see the history of our country."

"Yes, Saâh. It is one marvel more into which we will be initiated, and I'm impatient to see it."

Thaû turned to our friends and their companions. "Well, Messieurs, let's go. It's quite a long way from here."

They all followed the king. Preceded by two men who were waiting for him at the door of the room, he went down a long sloping corridor or approximately two hundred meters. They arrived at a door, which one of the two guides opened.

Our friends then found themselves, we dare not say "in the open air," since life on Mars was entirely subterranean, but in a vast plaza with a very high vault. Many inhabitants were circulating there; some were carrying parcels, other

---

[29] In this line and the next half dozen, thirteen individual words are indicated as missing in the copy of the text I have, I have inserted some that are obvious, and have improvised likely inclusions to bridge the other gaps.

pushing little three-wheeled carts in front of them, which were both light and robust, on which bales were stacked.

They were all heading toward a distant point, at which a large expanse of water could be seen.

"The port of the palace," said Thaû, indicating it to his guests.

Valsorres and his companions gazed, astonished. It was, indeed, a port, in the strict sense of the word. Boats were lined up along an immense quay in large number. But the port had nothing in common with our terrestrial ports.

First of all, the boats appeared to be so flat on the water that they only seemed to have two dimensions. They seemed, in fact, to be almost entirely lacking in height.

Some of the boats were only carrying merchandise; others were taking on passengers. None of them was fitted with a mast. They simply carried a kind of turbine situated at the front, which rotated in the air, powered by a machine that received its own power from electric waves radiating throughout the air, received by a special collector.

Several of the boats departed while our friends were approaching the edge of the quay. At first their departure was very slow, but scarcely had they arrived in the middle of the harbor than they placed themselves in the axis of a broad canal adjacent to it, and then launched forth at such a high velocity that they were completely out of sight in a matter of seconds.

When King Thaû arrived, escorted by our four voyagers, there was a stir in the crowd, which parted respectfully.

"I see that your subjects have a great deference for you," said Valsorres.

"My dear Marquis," Thaû replied. "In respecting me they're respecting themselves. In regard to them I am only the descendant of the chief that they gave themselves freely. I therefore incarnate in my person the ensemble of all the citizens of Mars; in consequence, in honoring me with their homage, it is to themselves, in the final analysis, that the homage reverts. And that is only just."

Thaû drew nearer to the guide.

A large boat, richly decorated with polychromatic ornaments, was moored along the wall. A man descended from it and came toward the arriving group. He saluted Thaû deferentially and his companions with affability.

"Is everything ready, Rufo?" asked the king.

"Everything is ready, O Thaû," the man replied, in excellent French.

"Then let's embark, Messieurs."

Taking Saâh by the hand, Thaû set the example by climbing aboard the boat. Our four friends followed him, each accompanied by his friend. When they were all aboard, Thaû said a few words to the man in command of the boat. Immediately, the mooring rope that retained it to the quay was cast off. The forward turbine was activated, and the boat advanced slowly into the middle of the harbor.

"Let's go down into the lounge," Thaû said to the voyagers.

They all went down into a low-ceilinged room beneath the deck.

Scarcely were they installed there than the boat, steered into the axis of the canal, launched forth. In a few seconds its speed had increased to the point of becoming vertiginous.

Valsorres and his friends looked out through the lateral windows; such was the rapidity of their progress that they could not see anything of the objects before which he nautical vehicle passed.

Thaû perceived their astonishment. "It's completely pointless, my dear friends," he said to them, "to fatigue your eyes seeking objects to look at; you won't see anything, given that we're navigating on a completely enclosed canal."

"At what speed are we traveling?" Espéret asked.

Thaû reflected momentarily. "According to what you've explained to me," he replied, "what you call a kilometer is the forty millionth part of the circumference of the Earth. It is, therefore, similar to a twenty millionth part of the circumference of Mars, the diameter of which is approximately half that of your globe."

"That's correct."

"Well, then, we must be traveling at two hundred kilometers an hour—I mean one of our Martian hours, which is equivalent to more than two of yours. In terrestrial measures, we're traveling at a little over five hundred kilometers an hour."

Valsorres and his companions were being carried, therefore, at that terrifying velocity.

After twenty minutes or so the machine slowed down and ended up stopping completely.

"We've arrived," said Thaû.

The boat had stopped at the quay of another harbor. The voyagers disembarked. They were awaited by functionaries, who led them along several broad avenues to a vast building, which they entered.

First they went into a small square room, which had divans around the perimeter. Thaû invited them to sit down.

When they had all taken their places on the soft seats, Thaû said to Valsorres: "My dear cousin, you are going to relive, in a few hours, the history of our past, which will unfurl before your eyes, showing you the events that happened, the individuals who were their authors, while enabling you to hear all the sounds that accompanied them, in order that the resurrection of the past should be complete for you."

"How is that, my dear Thaû?"

"Like this, my dear cousin. How do you perceive the events that are happening around you?"

"By means of the eyes and ears, of course."

"In other words, by means of waves—luminous waves and sonic waves—that strike the retina of your eye and the tympanum of your ear."

"That's correct."

"Well, do you think that those luminous and sonic waves are ever lost?"

"No," Valsorres replied, "but although they're not lost, they're at least dissipated, and it seems impossible to reconstitute them in an efficacious manner."

"That's where you're mistaken, my dear cousin. Our scientists have searched for that means of reconstitution, and have found it."

"What? You have a means of regenerating the luminous and sonic waves that were emitted in times remote from the present?"

"Yes."

"That's marvelous!"

"Not as much as you think. For our Martian scientists, at least, it wasn't difficult. You'll be able to judge for yourself. In order to be captured the luminous waves only require a surface sensible to the impressions of the various radiations that constitute them. You're in accord with me on that point, aren't you?"

"Perfectly. It's on that principle that we've based the art of photography."

"Good. Several centuries ago we found a way of making what you call photographs, but instead of making them immobile, we make them animated."

"We have that too, on Earth. It's called cinematography. It's a marvel initially conceived by the physiologist Marey, who m made use of it to analyze the elementary movements of locomotion. Later, it was exploited commercially under the name I cited."

"Very good!" replied Thaû. "And how do you capture the images of moving bodies?"

"On a long strip of a flexible, transparent substance covered in a layer of a substance sensitive to light."

"Perfect. Does it require great lengths of it?"

"Yes, hundreds of meters to reproduce a scene of some duration."

Thaû reflected momentarily. "I understand," he said. "Evidently, it's one solution. But here, I think, we found a better one a long time ago. We realized, in an extremely small and perfect form, the marvelous organ that is the eye of certain living beings that have almost disappeared today from the surface of our planet, but which exist in large numbers on the surface of the Earth. I've seen in the *Encyclopédie* that you call them insects."

"Ah! You've reproduced the insect eye artificially?"

"Yes. It wasn't without difficulty, but in the end, our constructors, aided by seamstresses whose work was extremely meticulous, succeeded in obtaining that delicate object. In these conditions, an artificial 'insect eye' placed before any scene receives on the surface where the episodes passing before it are designed an image that, examined subsequently after being fixed on a plate, not only reproduces the scene but its relief."

"Its relief, you say?"

"Yes, to put it another way, on a surface sensitive to light, we obtain by that means a reproduction that, to the eye that examines it through a similar system, presents a length, a width and a depth."

"It's a three-dimensional image then?"

"That's right. But we go even further. The image thus reproduced was immobile. As our insect eye is very small, it is of very reduced dimensions itself. Thus, it only occupied a minuscule place on the surface to which it was attached. Then we had the idea of causing that surface to rotate in a continuous and rapid fashion. That way the successive images are placed next to one another in a spiral traced on a vast disk. When the disk is rotated with the same velocity that it had when it was being imprinted, one has a exact reproduction of the entire scene, with its characters, its dimensions, its depth and its exact duration."

"It's necessary, then, to have these disks and these insect eyes in the presence of the scenes to be reproduced?"

"Certainly—but on Mars we always have them in quantity. All important events are fixed in the way and can be reproduced at will."

"I understand and I admire," said Espéret. "But what do you do with respect to the sounds and words?"

"Exactly the same thing, except that, instead of having a disk coated in a substance sensitive to light, we have one, turning on the same axis as the other, that is covered with a substance sensitive to sonic vibrations. A reversible system then reproduces the sounds, when the disk is rotated, by the same mechanism that registered hem. In consequence, by looking through the insect eye and listening simultaneously to the sounds emitted by the sonorous disk, one has a reconstitution in space of the entire scene.

"It's both simple and marvelous," said the doctor.

"Yes, Messieurs, and you can even see a reproduction of your arrival on Mars."

Thaû gave an order to a man standing behind him, and made a sign to our four friends to follow him. With their companions, they followed the king and queen, who took them into a vast room where light, without being completely absent, was nevertheless greatly attenuated. A kind of crepuscular gloom reigned here.

The spectators were invited to sit down at a circular table, in the center of which was a rather voluminous apparatus in the form of a broad cylinder. In front of each of them was a very special optical instrument; one might have thought that it was a large diamond sculpted with an infinity of microscopic facets.

Thaû turned to his guests. "While explaining the principle of our apparatus," he said, "I told you that the images and sounds were recorded on disks; in reality it's on large cylinders that the double inscription of light and sound is made. In that fashion, the recording can be much longer, and can thus reproduce a scene of much longer duration. Now, pay attention, Messieurs; it's about to begin."

Everyone looked attentively at the center of the apparatus placed in front of them.

A slight sound was audible in the midst of the general silence; it was the cylinder commencing its rotation. While turning, it descended with every turn, its axis being borne by a screw moving along a fixed groove. The spectators were then able to see extremely curious scenes.

First, there was the king's palace.

Officers were circulating there actively, carrying orders whose tenor was audible. Women, elegantly adorned, were heading for the queen's apartment, the door of which was guarded by twelve women of great beauty, armed with small halberds whose points seemed to be made of gold.

Then, suddenly, a sort of excitement was manifest among the individuals circulating in the corridors of the palace. They stopped, questioned one another, and listened. A vague rumor was audible, which seemed at first to be coming from far away and then drawing closer and closer.

"The arrival of the insurgents," said Thaû.

The king and queen were then seen emerging from their apartments. The queen, of great beauty, was followed by several maids of honor; the king, with a long spear in hand, was in the middle of a large group of officers carrying weapons of bizarre form, the nature of which escaped our four friends completely.

"What do they have in their hands?" Valsorres asked his cousin.

"You'll see and hear," relied Thaû.

Summoned by one of the officers in the king's retinue, soldiers had come running, armed in an identical fashion.

Then, one of the doors of the gallery as forced, and a howling crowed precipitated into the palace.

The king made a sign.

Immediately, the soldiers and the officers lowered the weapons they were holding in the direction of the insurgents. A click was heard; the first rank of the invaders fell, as if mown down. They were replaced by a new crowd following the first. The soldiers lowered their weapons for a second time; there was a further hecatomb, and hundreds of cadavers strewed the floor again.

Three times the attempted invasion was rendered; three times it was repelled in the same fashion.

"What, then, are the weapons they're using?" asked Espéret.

"They're engines that I believe you call cannons on Earth," Thaû replied.

"Cannons? But they scarcely make the sound of a whiplash, and yet the wounds their projectiles inflict seem to be mortal."

"Yes, that's true. With the aid of an electric current, they launch little condensers charged with a considerable quantity of electricity."

"And how can those charges be maintained without escaping into the surrounding air?"

"Thanks to an insulating substance of a special nature, which our chemists succeeded in fabricating a long time ago. It's that insulator which permit us to have the electrical industry that we have; otherwise, it would be impossible, with the high voltages that we use. But look, Messieurs!"

The crowd was still continuing to invade the palace. The dead were piled on the dead, and the defense appeared to be victorious, when a Martian taller than the others, a sort of giant, suddenly surged forth behind the king and laid him out at his feet, splitting his skull with an enormous ax that he wielded as if it were a feather.

On seeing the king fall, whose presence had animated them, the officers and soldiers uttered howls of anguish, to which the terrible howls of the insurgents responded. The latter were still arriving, ever more numerous and ever more ferocious.

A group of officers had gathered around the queen in order to make a rampart of their bodies. They fought with the energy of desperation. So long as their weapons could be supplied with projectiles, it was possible to believe that the queen might escape the fury of the revolutionaries, but the ammunition ran out, and the heroic officers could no longer combat the thrusts of spears and swords. They could not continue the battle for long. One after another they fell under the blows of their ever-more-numerous enemies.

Finally, the queen found herself alone in the presence of her ferocious assailants. For an instant, the latter were subjugated by the dignity of her attitude and the majesty of her person. But the giant who had felled the king launched himself toward the queen and, seizing her by the hair in order to draw her head back, slashed her throat with a single stroke of a large cutlass.

That was the signal for a bloody orgy. The men forming the queen's escort were murdered pitilessly; their bodies were profaned with a terrifying bestiality, in the midst of howls that had nothing human about them.

The spectators were breathless; they watched that terrible scene in the most profound silence.

Valsorres was the first to speak. "Thaû! Enough, enough! That frightful spectacle has lasted long enough for us. Have it stopped!"

Thaû gave an order, and the scene was interrupted.

"That," he said to our four friends, "was the first act of our great crisis, of which I previously gave you a brief account. Isn't it terrible, Messieurs?"

"Yes, certainly," replied Espéret. "That, however, is what is reproduced in all analogous crises. We too have had that in France."

"Ah!" said Thaû. "But I didn't see an account of it in the *Encyclopédie*."

"No, you couldn't have seen it there, for the events occurred in 1789, and especially in 1793, whereas he final volume of the *Encyclopédie* was published in 1780."

"And the crisis that you had was equally bloody?"

"Yes," said Espéret. "But the patriotism of the French effaced, by the acts of heroism that were the consequence of it, the horror of the internal crisis. Attacked by Europe entire, France faced up, alone, to all the nations in coalition against her. With improvised generals and armies, she was able to confront her enemies victoriously and triumph over the peoples who had united to subjugate her."

While Espéret was speaking, the Martian in charge of the operation of the apparatus had substituted a new cylinder for the preceding one.

"Now, Messieurs," said Thaû, "After the crisis, here is the calm; after the destruction, here is the renaissance. Look."

They all fixed their eyes on their little "visors" and this is what they saw:

In an immense room, staged on two gigantic platforms, an innumerable crowd was uttering enthusiastic acclamations: "Roh! Roh! Roh!"

Saluted by the cries of an entire people, accompanied by the strains of a triumphal march executed by a numerous orchestra, a man advanced, followed by a compact group of officers clad in splendid costumes.

"Russ," said Thaû, simply.

"Russ the savior?" asked Valsorres.

"Yes, the savior and regenerator of Mars."

The "savior" continued his march, to the sound of trumpets. The men lowered their weapons before him; women extended the richest fabrics beneath his feet. Joy was legible on all the faces. Slowly, Russ mounted the steps of the throne, on which he sat down. Then a group of soldiers brought a troop of men in chains before him. They prostrated themselves at the foot of the throne, faces to the floor.

Russ made a sign. A great silence reigned in the audience.

Then the "liberator" addressed a brief speech to the assembled people, and, turning to the soldiers who were escorting the prisoners, he gave them a rapid order. They detached the bonds that had enchained the captives.

"Russ, generous and magnanimous, is pardoning them and setting them at liberty," Thaû said to his friends.

In fact, the prisoners rose to their feet; they kissed Russ' hand; the people uttered cries of admiration.

"And it's from that moment on," Thaû continued, addressing his quests, "that order has reigned on Mars; the regime of complete liberty, general equality and absolute fraternity established by the liberator summoned by the people to the hereditary government of all, assures our inhabitants a perfect happiness in the midst of unprecedented prosperity."

"Fortunate Martians!" said Dr. Portier, sententiously.

The movement of the cylinder had stopped.

"Messieurs, now I will enable you to relive your disembarkation on his globe You're going to see the very moment when, for the first time, you set foot on the soil of our planet."

Thaû gave an order to the man operating the apparatus. The latter changed the cylinder and set the machine in motion again.

Then Valsorres, Espéret, Portier and Thomas, completely bewildered, saw a scene representing the Martian soil in the open air. A hundred inhabitants, dressed like Eskimos, were grouped in the middle of an arid plain, devoid of water and vegetation. They were pointing their fingers at the sky.

Soon, an object appeared, which seemed to fall slowly on the planet, spurting flames through orifices pierced in its inferior part.

"But that's the *Fusée!*" said Thomas.

"Yes, my friend," said Thaû. "It's the *Fusée*. Here it is, alighting on the soil of Mars."

In fact, the *Fusée* set down gently and safely on the Martian soil, on its three iron supports; the flexion of the powerful springs that terminated its legs was visible, which caused the telescopic tubes that prolonged them to reenter slightly into their interior.

Then the Martians grouped around the vehicle, waving their arms.

"She looks good, our *Fusée*," said Portier.

"Doesn't she?" replied the Marquis.

Then they saw the inferior panel of the machine open; a ladder emerged, which was lowered to the ground, and along that ladder our four friends were able to recognize themselves descending the rungs, dressed in the costumes of polar explorers, armed to the teeth, with respiratory masks over their faces.

Then there was the first contact with the Martians, the departure for the entrance to the palace in the glacial atmosphere of the planet; then there was Thomas, who, in order to warm himself, wanting to adopt a galloping gait, made a leap that took him several meters into the air.

"Oh, unlucky me!" said Thomas, recognizing himself. "Look, my little Hina," he went on, putting his arm around his lovely friend's waist, "you see that fellow jumping? Well, that's me."

Hina replied to him with an affectionate kiss.

"Now, Messieurs, I could enable you to see one of our great festivals."

"Oh, you have great festivals?" said Valsorres.

"Yes, we have the festival of the new year, we have the festival of labor, the festival of the provinces, the festival of the canals and the festival of the factories. But as you'll see one of those celebrations soon in person, I believe that there's no point in showing you in images what you'll appreciate much better in reality."

And on that promise from Thaû, our four voyagers rose to their feet. Accompanied by their charming friends, they followed Thaû and Saâh to the boat, which took them back to the port of the palace in three quarters of an hour.

As he went back to his apartment, Valsorres said to Thaû: "Allow me, my cousin, to express my admiration for the remarkable manner in which you have conserved the history of Mars."

"Isn't it, Marquis?" replied Thaû. "It's history without historians. That way, we're sure that it isn't adulterated."

IX. In which the reader will see that our four voyagers have, after all, something to teach the Martians.

A few days after that historic session, Saâh said to the Marquis de Valsorres: "My dear cousin, until now you've scarcely had any distractions on our distant globe, and you and your friends must be very bored."

"Oh no, Madame" said the four voyagers, in unison.

"My dear cousin," Henri replied, "how could we find the time long when the presence of our beautiful friends makes it pass so quickly?" As he spoke he raised the perfumed hand of his exquisite companion, Zith, to his lips.

The latter responded to that caress with a tender kiss.

The Marquis continued: "And then, frequently, we've had the joy of dining with you, and of savoring, along with the sight of your unequaled beauty, the irresistible charm of your always sparkling intelligence."

Saâh smiled, while playing with her little elephant.

"Thank you, Messieurs, for the flattering judgment you've expressed of me; I attribute the honor of it, in large part to your charming companions. But I'll return to my idea. Until now, you have only had austere pleasures on Mars. As scientists, you're evidently impassioned by the discoveries made by our physicists, chemists and astronomers, but the joys that you've savored thus are a little too scientific; you have hardly known anything of our artistic distractions."

"That's true, Madame," replied Espéret, "and as regards myself, I must admit that I find the music somewhat lacking."

"Good," replied Saâh. "That's one confession."

Portier spoke in his turn. "And I, Madame, being less of a music lover than Monsieur Espéret, would like to enjoy the sight of beautiful works of art, paintings, sculptures and drawings executed by your Martian artists, who must, in that regard as in others, be well in advance of ours."

Saâh reflected for a moment. "My dear Espéret," she said, "with respect to music, you can have every satisfaction. We have remarkable musicians here; they compose works that transport me even though I know almost all of them. And our performers have a skill that, I believe, would be difficult to equal."

"We have had a sample during our triumphal reception on the day of our rival," Espéret replied. "Although your music seemed strange to me, it left an impression of intense charm and sensuality."

"Oh," Saâh replied, "our music doesn't proceed by the same rules as yours."

"You know them, then, Madame?"

"But yes, still via the *Encyclopédie*. Our chords are much more numerous than ours, for we proceed, not in semitones, like you, but in quarter-tones. Thus, we have an incomparable richness of harmony."

"However," said the engineer, "that must correspond to very great difficulties in instrumental execution."

"Yes, evidently, but the difficulties do not frighten our artistes. They begin very young, and you know that people live for a very long time on Mars; until the very end, we conserve all our physical and intellectual faculties. Furthermore, we have mechanical executions."

"Mechanical executions? You make music without musicians, then?"

"Exactly. The composer writes his work with the aid of certain signs, geometrical in form, combinations of dots grouped in accordance with determined rules. These dots are reproduced in dents in long strips of metal, and those strips, placed before a machine moved by what you call electricity, sends the necessary air into the instruments, with the desired intensity and duration."

Valsorres looked at his friends.

"But in that case, we're not as backward on Earth as one might think. We have a very interesting, and simultaneously very simple, little instrument that we call a gramophone."

"A gramophone?" asked Saâh, curiously.

"Yes, the name is formed from two Greek words that signify 'writing sound.' The sounds are recorded on a disk, and the vibrations of the imprints engraved on it are reproduced by agitating a membrane bearing a very fine point at its center, which follows the relief of the impression."

Saâh manifested the sharpest astonishment. "Oh, I'd like to see and hear that little apparatus."

"That's easy, Madame," Espéret replied. He turned to Thomas. "Thomas, my friend, dress for the North Pole, as you put it, go to the *Fusée* and bring back the small gramophone, with the provision of disks."

Thomas got up, followed by his faithful Hina.

The conversation between the queen and her guests continued.

"That's it for music," said Dr. Portier, "but what about painting and sculpture? Thus far, I confess, I haven't seen a single specimen."

Saâh reflected for a moment. "My dear doctor," she said, in her musical voice, "there's a simple reason why you haven't seen any paintings or statues."

"What is it, Madame?"

"Simply because, on our planet, which is rather old, we have neither painting nor sculpture."

Portier was greatly astonished. "What, Madame? With a civilization as advanced as yours, you've been able to live without knowing those admirable arts?"

"We knew them once, thousands of centuries ago. The first beings that lived on our globe, before the birth of all industry, reproduced, in lines engraved in stone, the figures of animals now disappeared, and those of their companions in existence."

"Well, was the rudimentary art not perfected by science?"

"Very little, and this is why. The rigor of our climate caused almost all vegetation to disappear from our soil. Only along the line that I believe you call the equator were a few paltry mosses able to germinate and live, with difficulty. We have no trees, and no visible water; we are therefore ignorant of what you Earthmen call 'landscapes.'"

"But what about reproductions of the human figure?" Portier interjected. "What about historical painting?"

"Well, my dear doctor, in that regard, painting and sculpture would be quite unnecessary. If I have understood what the authors of the *Encyclopédie* say, the painter ought to strive to reproduce beauty so as to conserve the memory of it. It is the same with sculpture. Now, what is the point of reproducing one beauty on a world where everyone is beautiful? Why seek to conserve the memory of youth in a world here everyone remains youthful in appearance until they die? Why reproduce, in marble or in bronze, forms often imagined by the artist, when it is sufficient to look round in order to see living individuals as beautiful, and even more beautiful?"

And Saâh, combining action with words, had got up from her seat; she stood before the eyes of her guests, superb in her incomparable beauty, clad in her rich costume, superb in her marvelous jewelry.

Our friends admired her silently.

Thaû had come in during that scene and had heard the end of the conversation.

"Isn't it the case, Messieurs," he said, "that painting and sculpture are unnecessary when one has living models of such perfection before one?"

"That's true," replied Valsorres. "But not everyone has the unequaled beauty of my cousin."

"Oh, other Martian women scarcely cede anything to her; I believe your companions ought to have proved that to you."

Saâh had just let herself fall back softly on the cushions. Addressing Valsorres she went on: "And as for historical painting, you have been able to take account, my cousin of how our manner of conserving the images of past events renders it unnecessary."[30]

At that moment Thomas returned with Hina, bringing the gramophone, which he deposited on a table in front of the queen.

"What is that?" asked Thaû, curiously.

"It's a gramophone," Henri replied. "It's an apparatus that reproduces very simply sounds, songs, music and speech."

"Quickly! Quickly!" said Saâh, clapping her hands impatiently. "Make it work, my cousin!"

---

[30] It is possible that the limitations of this notion of the nature and necessity of visual art provoked some reaction among the readers of *Le Petit Parisien*, as the authors return to it at a later point in the serial, in an argumentative fashion.

Valsorres wound up the machine. He put an impressed disk on the platform, ensured the contact of the needle, and started the movement. Initially, a slight scratching was heard.

"Is that it?" asked Saâh. "It's not very agreeable."

The scratching finished. A pure voice became audible. It was the beautiful duet from *Samson et Dalila*.[31]

Thaû, Saâh and the four Martian women listened with a keen interest.

When the piece finished, Saâh cried: "Oh, again! Again!"

Valsorres wound up the apparatus again and played the piece a second time.

"That's marvelous!" said Thaû. "What's remarkable about it is its simplicity. There's no mechanism."

"No," said Espéret. "The sounds are recorded and reproduced in themselves, with all their nuances."

"And are the sounds of instruments reproduced as well as those of voices?" asked Saâh.

"Judge for yourself, my cousin."

Valsorres selected another disk, on which the Soldiers' March from Gounod's *Faust* was recorded, plated by the celebrated band of the Republican Guard.

At the first sounds of the brass instruments Thaû stood up and moved with the rhythm, prey to an indescribable enthusiasm. Saâh and our friends' four companions shared his admiration. It was the omnipotence of rhythm that was manifest in a victorious fashion in those people, although they were so cultivated.

When the march had finished, the Martians demanded another encore.

Thaû had sent Hina to fetch the "musical director." The splendid creature who had conducted the orchestra on the stage when our friends arrived on Mars, whose golden hair formed a veritable mantle, came into the room. They were all struck by her splendid beauty. Espéret could not take his eyes off her.

"Look, Zoloh!" said Saâh. "Listen to the music that they make on Earth."

In the presence of the new arrival, who watched everything he did very attentively, Valsorres wound up the mechanism again, and the Soldiers' March was executed once more.

The beautiful musicienne was sitting in front of the gramophone; one might have thought that she was drinking the sounds. Her head in her hands, she was plunged into a sort of ecstasy; she did not move a muscle. When it had finished, she said, in the finest French: "How beautiful that music is!"

Valsorres addressed Thaû then. "Well, my cousin, that's a small revenge of Earth on Mars. We have, therefore, taught you, who know everything, something new. We have revealed an art unknown to you."

---

[31] The opera by Camille Saint-Saëns, with a libretto by Ferdinand Lemaire.

"Yes, my dear Marquis. Yes, your music is more beautiful than ours, just as your language is more beautiful that the language of Mars. And I'm wondering how that can be."

Valsorres reflected momentarily. "I think, Thaû," he said "that it is because we have the admirable thing called 'Nature.' Your aged soil is not longer anything but a mine of raw materials. Everything here is artificial, including, very nearly, the air you breathe. You live underground; you're unaware of the view of large open spaces, the blue of the sky and that of the ocean. You don't have the harmony of things that enchants the eyes and goes directly to the soul, where it stimulates the noblest emotions. You don't have the trees of our forests, the wheat of our fields, the verdure of our meadows or the flowers of our gardens. You don't hear the murmur of springs or the hum of insects; you don't know birdsong.

"All of that, you see, is the perpetual hymn that Nature sings to the Creator. All of that is what inspires musicians and poets; all of that is what gives birth to masterpieces."

"However," said Saâh, "we have amour."

Valsorres tilted his head. "Yes, amour; you have amour, that's true. You have it in its sensual form. But here, it's realized too easily. You're unaware of ardent amour, amour frustrated, vanquished amour and victorious amour, the amour that makes people commit crimes and accomplish miracles. That's our amour, our Earthly amour. And confess, my dear cousin, that it has its value!"

Saâh was thoughtful, as were the beautiful Martian women who surrounded her.

After a moment's silence, the queen said: "So, my dear cousin, if amour is something that has to be tormented in order to be complete, it doesn't procure you happiness?"

"Yes, my cousin. There isn't only ardent, passionate amour—tormented, as you put it—there's also calm, tranquil love, made of the esteem and reciprocal affection of two beings who unite themselves. Although it's a little less 'artistic' than the other, that amour, you see, it's a pure and noble amour, a healthy and holy amour. It's the amour that is the rock on which the admirable thing is built that is the foundation of our society."

"And what is that?" asked Saâh.

"It's the family," replied the Marquis de Valsorres.

"The family!" said Thaû and Saâh, in unison.

"Yes, the family, the nucleus of our social condition. The family is the center in which the life of the past is summarized, in contact with that of the present and that of the future. The family is the location in which the qualities of the race are jealously conserved and faithfully transmitted; the family is an oasis in the desert of life. In the midst of the somber storms of existence it's a corner of blue sky that appears, with a cradle for an altar."

Valsorres paused momentarily, prey to a keen emotion, which his friends shared.

Evidently, at that moment, in spite of the forgetfulness that Zith poured him with his daily beverage, a reminiscence of the past had just traversed the obscured horizon of his memory like a bolt of lightning in a somber sky, and inspired dolorous recollections.

After a brief silence, which his listeners respected faithfully, he continued.

"It's thanks to the omnipotence of the family that France has been able to traverse the most terrible internal crises. It's that to which the wealth of our homeland is due, for family life deflects vain pleasures, which are as dear as they are dangerous. It is in family life that a father and mother find the purest joys, around the child who summarizes the virtues of yesterday and in whom the parents strive to prepare those of tomorrow. And it's the family, in sum, that constitutes the element of something even more noble, more elevated and greater..."

"What, then, is this greater thing than the family of which you've just made us a moving depiction?"

"It's the fatherland," said Valsorres, rising to his feet.

Instinctively, as if impelled by an invincible force, his three companions had risen to their feet at the same time.

"Yes," he continued, in a grave voice. "The fatherland is the family of families, the greatest family of all; it's what summarizes the riches, the joys and the hopes of all he families united. It's for the fatherland that the great geniuses of our laboratories toil without hope of gain; it's for the fatherland that, when the time comes, mothers give their husbands and their sons, sisters give their brothers, and fiancées sacrifices the elect of their heart. For, without the fatherland, they all sense keenly that there would no longer be an ideal and that the noblest sentiments would be extinct in the human heart.

"Oh, the fatherland! What a magical word to provoke noble actions, to give birth to heroisms, to stimulate devotions! The fatherland is the glorious mosaic of which every fragment in a shard of the past, and to which every effort of the present will add a new tile in order to augment its future splendor. The fatherland is art, science and poetry; the fatherland is yesterday and tomorrow; the fatherland is everything."

Valsorres stopped.

His companions had tears in their eyes. Had they too just glimpsed, through a clearing in the mist that enveloped their memory, the image of France, already so distant, of those they had left behind and who were perhaps spending days full of anxiety and despair, waiting for them?

Thaû advanced toward Henri. "I can see that you love your fatherland, my cousin."

"Oh, yes, I love her.[32] I love her more than my mother, for she is my mother's mother; she is the mother of us all, and all of us ought to devote ourselves to increasing her glory and grandeur, as we ought to sacrifice everything save for honor to her when she is menaced. *Honor, fatherland*: those are the words that are in letters of gold on all our flags, and imprinted in an ineradicable fashion in the hearts of all our soldiers."

The Marquis had let himself fall back on his seat. Thaû and Saâh had exchanged a furtive glance.

At that moment the beautiful musicienne stood up and addressed Espéret. "Monsieur," she said, "permit me to take this away." She pointed at the gramophone. "I'll return it to you tomorrow."

"With pleasure, my beautiful artiste," the engineer replied "I'll show you how it works."

Espéret showed the captivating creature how to wind up the apparatus, how the disk as placed, and how the needle was applied.

Zoloh left, thanking him with an enchanting smile, and taking away the gramophone held preciously beneath her alabaster arm.

Our four friends got up to take their leave of the two sovereigns, and, followed by their faithful companions, they returned to their respective apartments.

When they had gone, Saâh said to Thaû: "Well, wasn't I right to conceal from them the war between France and Germany, news of which the waves have transmitted to us?"

"Why?"

"Because, animated as Henri is by an ardent love for his fatherland, he would have wanted to return to Earth immediately, in order to take his place in the first rank of her defenders...and we would have lost him, and his companions, whose arrival on our old planet has brought us a new element, from another world."

---

[32] It is one of the quirks of the French language that *patrie* [fatherland] is a feminine noun, so that the fatherland is "she" when personalized.

X. In the course of which the reader will see how festivals are organized on the planet Mars.

The following evening, the beautiful Zoloh, he superb creature who directed the organization of Martian festivals, brought the gramophone back to Espéret, addressing all her thanks to him.

"I've made all the disks sing," she told him, addressing him with an incendiary gaze. "Our workmen will try to reproduce the instrument; as for our musicians, I'll try to enable them to play the pieces that the apparatus has allowed us to hear. Thank you again, Monsieur."

Espéret had taken the hand of the beautiful creature, but she disengaged it, laughing, and that laugh uncovered the thirty-two pearls of her mouth.

That evening, at dinner there was no talk of anything but music.

"Do you know," said Saâh, "that our precision workers have already set to work?"

"To do what?" asked Valsorres.

"To copy your gramophone—that's what you call it, isn't it, my cousin?"

"Yes, Saâh."

"And not only do they want to copy it, but to improve it."

"Oh, really?"

"Certainly. Our physicists found the invention admirable, especially because of its great simplicity, but they think that the sounds it produces are not intense enough, and they intend to augment the power of the apparatus considerably."

"Then they're working already?"

"Yes, and the chief of the research laboratory, Zuk, hopes that on the occasion of the Festival of the Provinces, which takes place in four days' time, he'll be able to make the pieces recorded on your disks heard, but played with much greater power, by the Martian gramophone."

"That's marvelous," said Espéret.

"We'll await it with impatience," said the Marquis. "So there will be a festival in four days?"

"Yes my cousin," said Thaû. "I was just about to inform you of that, in order that you can liberate yourself from any engagement of work for that day."

"Well, my dear cousins," replied Henri, "that's agreed; it will be a pleasure for us to attend the festival."

"You'll attend it, moreover, by our side," said Saâh. "The entire planet now knows about our sojourn among us. To see all four of you will be, for our inhabitants, one of the great attractions of the solemnity, to which, by reason of that circumstance, we count on giving an even greater splendor than usual."

"What is the Festival of the Provinces, Madame?" asked Portier, addressing the queen.

"It's a festival that brings together, once a year, the representatives of the four provinces that form the divisions of the planet Mars. In the course of the festival, the youngest men devote themselves to bodily exercises and competitions of strength and skill. The youngest women perform dances in which they compete in grace. Finally, children march and perform collective exercises that show the degree to which their physical education has progressed. In addition, the most intelligent among them read literary pieces that they have composed.

"After those manifestations of the activity of our provinces, actors and prestidigitators give the united crowd a spectacle that they enjoy greatly, while the musicians, conducted by the beautiful Zoloh, whose beauty had such an impact on Monsieur Espéret, will perform their most appreciated pieces."

Four days later, the moment of the Festival of the Provinces arrived.

From early morning, innumerable gliders poured a compact crowd on to the quay of the Palace port, radiant with gaiety and enthusiasm.

Special boats brought companies of men or women, clad in a uniform fashion. Numerous groups of children, conducted by their masters or mistresses, mingled their cries and laughter.

All these assemblies, guided by soldiers charged with maintaining order, were conducted to the immense enclosure where the festival announced by Saâh was to be unfurled in all of its splendor.

We shall try to give an idea of that gigantic "hall."

Imagine a colossal rectangle with rounded corners. The rectangle was more than six hundred meters long and four hundred meters wide, with a height of at least fifty meters.

The seemingly continuous vault that covered it was supported by a hundred slender perforated columns made of a metal analogous to steel, the upper extremities of which were united by garlands consisting of pieces of colored fabric, the sparkling hues of which had the most pleasing effect on the eye of the spectator.

The entire room was illuminated by a diffuse light, for which no apparent source could be seen. One might have thought that the light emanated from the drapes that covered the walls and the ceiling that covered the immense enclosure.

In the middle of the vast quadrilateral stood a stage a hundred meters long and eighty wide, on which the exercises present by the inhabitants of the various provinces were evidently going to be performed. A large aisle ending at a vast portal pierced in one of the sides of the quadrilateral led to the stage, reached by stairway of twenty steps.

All around the platform were terraces on which seats were disposed. Nearly three hundred thousand spectators could be accommodated there.

In the middle of the file of terraces installed on the longer side of the quadrilateral was a box covered with an awning formed of fabrics of unimaginable richness. It was there that Thaû, Saâh, the men and women of their retinues, and our four friends were to take their places. At the foot of the box, on other terraces disposed in a horseshoe in front of the stage, were the seats reserved for the musicians.

On the day of the feast, early in the morning, all the seats were already occupied. The inhabitants of the provinces who had come for the festival were pressing at the portals. The inhabitants of the capital, which was called Nuro, occupied the terraces at the back. The festival was to commence at midday. The musicians entered an hour earlier, and their beautiful conductress went from one to another giving her final instructions. Then came the procession of actors, who arrived escorted by policemen and were installed in the large area reserved for them under the stage before going up the steps and appearing in all their splendor before the eyes of the public.

Then, a few minutes before the commencement of the ceremony, workers brought a kind of large square crate furnished with six enormous funnels, analogous in their approximate dimensions to those of hunting horns and orientated in six different directions.

The beautiful Zoloh had immediately had that apparatus installed on a large tripod placed in front of the little stall from which she was to direct the orchestra, whose members were beginning to tune their instruments.

The murmur of the crowd had become intense. Everyone was waiting impatiently for the commencement of the festival.

Suddenly, a powerful gong produced a grave and intense vibration, the waves of which continued for a long time. The curtain that closed the back of the box opened and Thaû appeared, holding Saâh by the hand, resplendent in her superhuman beauty.

At that sight, all the spectators rose to their feet and uttered in unison the enthusiastic cry: "Roh! Roh! Roh!"

Behind Thaû and Saâh came the four provincial governors with their female companions, dressed in magnificent costumes. Then came our four voyagers, accompanied by their delightful friends, also clad in splendid attire. After them there were the officers of Thaû's retinue and the women of Saâh's.

When the sovereigns had shown themselves, the beautiful Zoloh, dazzling under the mantle of her golden hair, raised her baton. Immediately, the musicians, putting their instruments to their mouths, commenced a triumphal march.

"But that's the Soldiers' March from Gounod's *Faust*!" Espéret exclaimed.

Saâh, who had heard him, turned toward him. "Certainly, Monsieur. It's one of the pieces that your little gramophone revealed to us."

"But that's incredible, Madame. What! In five days your musicians have been able to learn that work, to the point of executing it with such perfection?"

"It wasn't difficult for them. They're so skillful! And their director is such a consummate artist."

"And so beautiful, Madame."

"Isn't she, Monsieur?" said Saâh, with a smile.

Meanwhile, the march from *Faust* ended, in the midst of the enthusiastic cries of the crowd.

The Martians, who only knew their own music, made of complicated chords, were amazed by the revelation of the mysterious force of rhythm, which appeared to them suddenly.

Thaû advanced to the edge of the box then, and made a sign that he wanted to speak. A profound silence was immediately established.

The king addressed a few words to his people, among which the word Sila was distinguishable several times; you will remember that Sila was the name by which he Martians designated the Earth.

When he had finished, the crowd burst into cries of joy, repeating the word "Sila" with an indescribable enthusiasm.

Then Saâh, taking Valsorres by the hand, led him to the balustrade of the box, with his three friends. The cries and ovations redoubled. The four Frenchmen bowed in response that triumphal welcome, of which they understood nothing.

It was Saâh who revealed the cause of it. "Thaû told the spectators that it was you who brought the music here that transported them with admiration. That's why our inhabitants are uttering such abundant acclamations in your honor."

Thomas claimed his share of that. He held his dear Hina by the waist, murmuring: "That's all right. These things only happen to me."

But everything comes to an end, even ovations.

At a signal from Thaû, soldiers opened the huge doors at the back. Then a troop of young men were seen advancing, numbering about a hundred, who came along the central aisle at a run, with a prodigious agility, and launched themselves like squirrels on to the stage, where they stopped abruptly, facing Thaû and Saâh, who saluted them with a gesture of infinite grace. Thaû and Saâh had stood up to return their salute.

The contests commenced immediately.

The young men were divided into four teams, wearing shorts of different colors: blue, red, yellow and green. Saâh explained to Valsorres that they were the colors of the four provinces whose representatives were about to measure themselves against one another in pairs.

The contests began with an encounter of the red team with the green team. Twenty-five athletes, of a statuesque beauty, represented two of the Martian provinces, Or and Phes. The wrestlers, in parallel lines, advanced to meet one another and immediately gripped one another round the waist, making every effort to throw one another to the ground.

Portier, a great lover of sports, followed the combat attentively. He noticed that several wrestlers whose shoulders had touched the floor got up and measured themselves against their standing adversaries once again. He asked Thaû the reason.

"In order for a wrestler to be put out of the contest," the king replied, "it's necessary that he be completely turned over, belly to the ground. Only then do the judges declare him vanquished."

In spite of the skill and vigor of the athletes involved, the wrestling match finished fairly quickly. The green team was clearly superior; of the twenty-five men of the red team, nineteen had been felled. A stroke of a gong announced the victory.

It was then the turn of the blue and yellow teams, from the provinces Tet and Prou. The contest was more brilliant and more closely disputed. It lasted much longer. The blues put up a magnificent defense and the yellows were only victorious by a single point, having felled thirteen of their adversaries while twelve of their own had been put down and rolled over.

It remained for the two victorious teams to compete. The greens advanced against the yellows. The latter, doubtless better tested by the resistance of the blues they had just fought, immediately demonstrated a evident superiority. Seventeen greens were put down, against only eight yellows. The team from the province of Prou was therefore triumphant.

All the victors—which is to say, the seventeen athletes who had felled their antagonists—were then conducted to the royal box by an officer. They bowed before the sovereigns, to the acclamations of the delirious crowd, and received from Thaû's hand a sort of pennant covered with signs embroidered in glittering thread, borne on a shaft terminated by a metal ball as shiny as gold.

When they went back to the foot of the stage and passed between the terraces charged with spectators, there was an indescribable ovation. The women, especially, distinguished themselves by their extreme enthusiasm. Several of them tore off their jewels and threw them to the victors, accompanied by smiles and blown kisses.

When the tumult of the manifestation had finally died down, Thaû stood up and gave a new signal. The beautiful musicienne then headed for the instrument with the six funnels that had been placed before her, and pressed a button. Then commenced the execution of the celebrated mazurka from *Coppelia,* one of the masterpieces of Léo Delibes.

At the strains of that marvelously rhythmic music, the spectators rose to their feet; they stamped their feet in cadence in order to follow the movement of the piece, simultaneously so captivating and so gracious. It was no longer enthusiasm; it was madness.

The audience turned to the royal box, uttering cries of "Sila! Sila! Roh! Roh!"

Saâh turned to our friends and said to them: "It's to your music that those thanks are addressed. Take a bow, Messieurs, salute; they're asking for you."

The four friends advanced to the edge of the box and saluted with their heads and hands, in the midst of indescribable ovations.

Valsorres then asked Thaû: "But, my cousin, how were your workmen able to construct such a powerful and perfect gramophone so rapidly?"

"Oh, it wasn't very difficult for them," Thaû replied. "I promised you five days ago that our workers would make that construction. You can see that they've succeeded."

"Yes, certainly, and beyond all expectation."

When the piece finished, Thaû made a sign.

The great portal at the back opened, and a veritable swarm of women, all very pretty, and as gracious as one another, came lightly to take the place on the stage that the wrestlers had previously occupied.

"The dancers," said Saâh, simply.

The mistress of the orchestra, the beautiful Zoloh with the golden hair, had raised her baton.

Then the musicians commenced the execution of a slow chant with complicated chords, appropriate to surprise the ears of the Earthmen. The rhythm was slow and barely indicated, and the quarter-tone intervals that constituted the basis of the harmony rendered the general ambiance entirely nebulous.

To that rhythm, however, the dancers commenced their steps.

They were all clad in short, near-transparent tunics that fell half way down the leg. Their feet were should in rich cothurnes of a sort, covering their ankles with great finesse. Bracelets of precious metals circled their arms, and golden girdles tightened their waists slightly beneath their breasts. Some of them wore rings on their fingers in which gens of various colors glittered.

In spite of the slowness of its pace, the dance was strangely sensual. The dancers all inclined their bodies in unison, and let themselves fall to the ground, rose on one knee, and then straightened up, agitating their white arms above their heads, with a infinite grace. At other times they came together in concentric circles, those in the middle standing on the knees of a group of their companions, the following circle standing on the ground, the third kneeling, and the fourth extended in an attitude of amorous lassitude. One might have thought it the living corolla of a gigantic flower; and the tunics, with sparkling and indescribable reflection, rendered that comparison even more exact.

The cries and the stamping feet of the audience indicated the admiration of the spectators for that unique spectacle.

Our four friends marveled, and did not hide their pleasure—but Thaû turned toward them. "Wait, Messieurs," he said to them. "You haven't seen anything yet."

"What!" said Espéret. "There's something better than that? But I don't believe that's possible."

"That is, however, what is about to happen."

At that moment the dancers separated, in order to arrange themselves in a vast square along the edges of the sage, their faces turned toward the center.

Then, from a trap-door situated under the boards, an almost immaterial creature sprang, and, launching herself into the air with a leap of nearly ten meters, she fell back like a bird on to the carpet.

"That's the queen of the dancers, little Thé," Saâh said to Valsorres.

The orchestra had fallen silent. Only four musicians continued to play, blowing into flutes of unequal length, accompanied by a drum with a muted timbre that provided he melody with rhythm, while a carillon of little cymbals, brushed by a sixth artiste, added the coloration of its silvery tones.

Then, under the action of that rhythm, which, slow and solemn at first, accelerated incessantly, tormenting the little artiste, as it were, she commenced the strangest, most captivating and most unimaginable dance.

Almost lying down it first, she underlined the allure of the music by means of barely perceptible movements of her exceedingly delicate body. As the musicians' rhythm accelerated however, the movements followed their cadence. Raised on one knee, she described curves in the air with her arms, always allowing a truly celestial smile to wander over her lips.

Finally, she was entirely upright. At first, without changing location, she executed movements of an ideal grace; then, as if drawn by the music, which hastened its pace, she began to dance.

What was that dance? It was impossible to tell.

As light as a bird, she seemed not to touch the ground. The leaps she made, and which, by virtue of the weak gravity of Mars, lifted her ten meters into the air, appeared to be executed without the slightest effort. Always smiling, always with an unequaled grace, she flew through the air like a dragonfly in spring.

And when, eventually, the rhythm of the music, accelerating more and more, took the agitated form of an almost savage tarantella, she began to spin with a rapidity that became vertiginous,

Finally, in a last bound, leaping higher than she had done before, she described a sort of parabola and came to alight in front of the sovereigns' box, before whom, like the personification of beauty, charm and talent, she bowed slowly, in a gesture in which there as simultaneously an infinite grace and an almost royal majesty.

Superhuman acclamations saluted the end of that unparalleled dance. The other dancers bowed before that omnipotence of a talent so superior that it rendered any sentiment of jealousy impossible, and they were the first to wave their arms to salute their incomparable star.

Valsorres turned to Espéret. "Well, old chap," he said, "you're an habitué of our Opéra and the foyer of dance-halls; what do you say to that?"

"I don't say anything," said the engineer. "I'll limit myself to admiration, without even trying to find words adequate to express my admiration."

Saâh had heard Espéret's response. "We're going to have her come up to the box in order to congratulate her and offer her a little present," she said. "And you'll see that our little Thé is as delightful a woman as she is a dancer."

Saâh made a sign; two women from her entourage came forward. She said a few words to them in a low voice; the two women bowed, went down on to the stage and each took Thé by one hand in order to lead her to the sovereigns.

The dancer came down between her two guides and entered the royal box. Thaû advanced toward her and kissed her hand, while Saâh took off the richest of her rings and put it on the finger of the little dancer, who was not wearing any jewelry, and embraced her, with all the marks of the greatest amity.

At that spectacle, the cries of enthusiasm redoubled: "Roh! Roh! Roh!" uttered by two hundred thousand throats. One might have thought that the walls of the immense hall were about to collapse.

Espéret had approached Thé.

"My dear Thé," Saâh said to her, "may I introduce Monsieur Espéret, one of the four inhabitants of Sila who have been kind enough to visit us. He's a great connoisseur in matters of dancing, and he declares that what he has just seen surpasses anything he could have imagined. He desires to compliment you himself in the beautiful French language that you speak so well."

Espéret then advanced toward the little dancer.

"Mademoiselle," he said to her, "you are not a dancer, you are dance itself; you are not a graceful woman, you are grace itself; you are not an artiste, but artistry made woman."

Little Thé evidently relished that compliment, of which she sensed all the sincerity. She extended her pretty hand to the engineer, who deposited an ardent kiss thereon, and who, after that homage, could not take his eyes off the almost immaterial creature.

"Oh," said Thaû, "our little Thé is the spoiled child of all the Martians. Every time there is a celebration, even in the most distant town in our provinces, Thé brings to it the attraction of her unequaled talent and grace. She is as learned as she is artistic." The king turned to Valsorres. "Yes my cousin, Thé knows everything, as she would astonish you by the extent of her astronomical science, just as she would astonish Dr. Portier by her vast knowledge of anatomy."

After having bowed with a charming modesty, Thé returned to take her place among the dancers, who executed a kind of quadrille, to the sounds of the orchestra, with the star in their mist. At the conclusion, the little ballerina was carried like the steeple of a bell-tower to the summit of a pyramid formed by the combined bodies of her companions.

That was the apotheosis.

Then Thaû made a sign, and the gong resounded three times. It was the signal for the intermission.

Men and women carrying large ewers went along the terraces pouring each spectator as "festival liqueur," which was received in a small cup with which each was furnished. Then men brought little warm cakes in baskets, which tasted exquisite.

Thé had been invited to take her refreshment in the royal box. She conducted herself there with a charming ease and modesty. Our four friends were impressed by the artiste's distinction

"How can so much intelligence and grace be united in a single creature?" Valsorres asked Saâh.

"Thé is, indeed, a exceptional creature," the queen replied. "First of all, know that she's a child of the planet."

"What does that mean?"

"Thé was orphaned at a very young age. Her father and mother wanted to bring her up themselves, as was their right, but, unfortunately, they both perished in an inexplicable accident that happened on one of our canals when one glider collided with another. You will understand that, given the speed at which they travel, nothing remained either of the boats or the passengers."

"Yes, indeed."

"Then, since her parents had died in the catastrophe, the State took charge of Thé's education, but it was quickly perceived that she was no ordinary child. With a penetrating intelligence, she understood even before her masters had finished explaining. She learned and retained everything with the greatest ease; today she's a young woman."

"Oh," said Espéret. "She hasn't yet had a husband?"

"No, Thé is still a virgin. She's only sixteen years old—sixteen Martian years, I mean. She's the idol of all the Martians but she hasn't wanted to listen to any of them. An artiste, she's uniquely consecrated to her art."

"But is she, like all actors," Espéret asked, "required to live in the sort of reclusion in which you force them to live for the tranquility of the inhabitants?"

"No, and this is the only exception we've made to that absolute rule. But we made it with the consent of all the actors. They're so conscious of the superiority of their little comrade that they proposed themselves that she be removed from the petty everyday intrigues that are the element of their special existence. So Thé lives in the palace; but she remains a good friend to all her comrades, and goes to spend time with them every day in a small house that she occupies in the actors' quarter, and to give them, with one or two of her dances, the notion of her incessantly renewed art. In addition, for two years she has been the mistress of choreography who organizes and regulates all the ballets, like the one you saw performed before you a few moments ago."

"My cousin," Valsorres said, "you've explained how Thé has been taught all the arts and sciences, but who can have educated her in her own art, dance, with a degree of perfection that, it seems to me, cannot be surpassed?"

"Who? No one. Thé, as a dancer, is self-made. She had seen the dances, already so beautiful, that we have on our planet. She then decided to devote herself entirely to that art; but it's her, and her alone, who has conceived those extraordinary steps which she alone was able to conceive and which she alone is able to realize."

Espéret remained thoughtful, and could not take his eyes off the little ballerina, who addressed the most intoxicating of smiles to him.

The intermission ended.

Thaû stood up; the gong sounded.

The dancer had quit the platform in order to take her place among the other individuals.

"The children!" said Saâh, simply.

In fact, through the large portal a double row of children, adorable and perfectly beautiful little boys and little girls, entered, clad in richly colored fabrics. In perfect order, they advanced to the stage, here they lined up with a remarkable discipline.

Portier gazed at the splendid little beings, wonderstruck.

"How can you have such beautiful children, Thaû?" he asked. "They're all equally accomplished, from the physical point of view."

"It's quite simple," said Thaû. "We've eliminated all physical flaws from the surface of Mars."

"Ah!" said the doctor. "And how have you done that?"

"I told you before that our scientists had succeeded in battling disease, but there are certain hereditary maladies that can't be eliminated by a direct cure. So we got rid of them by preventing those afflicted by them from founding a family and passing them on to their descendants. We constrained them to live in isolation. In that fashion, they died without transmitting to others the defect with which they were afflicted, and we arrived at having an absolutely healthy population, exempt from all general infirmities and, in consequence, strong and beautiful."

"That's admirable," said Portier, "but very difficult to realize!"

"Difficult? No, my dear doctor. It's sufficient to want it. My predecessors wanted it. The people understood that the determination in question was for the general good, and it was followed by the effect. But the children are beginning their games. Watch.

Like the wrestlers previously, the children were grouped in accordance with their provinces. They accomplished the most astonishing exercises in gymnastics and flexibility, and rhythmic dances. It was a charming spectacle, from the sight of which the entire assembly seemed to obtain an extreme pleasure, which was manifested by applause and the prolonged stamping of feet.

Finally, the little girls, two by two, carrying baskets filled with knotted ribbons of the most various colors, launched themselves in the direction of the royal box, blowing long kisses from the tips of their little fingers to the two sovereigns, who responded in the same fashion.

The gong sounded; the orchestra attacked the trumpet march from *Aïda*.

Espéret looked at Thaû.

"That's still the music from your disks," the latter replied. "The beautiful Zoloh has had her musicians learn it, and you can see that they aren't acquitting their task badly."

In fact the execution was perfect. The trumpets, above all, had a strident tone and notes of mathematical accuracy.

There is no need to describe the enthusiasm that greeted the execution of that celebrated piece. The entire audience turned toward our four friends, crying: "Sila! Sila!" They were obliged to stand once again and render a salute.

The gong resonated for the final time.

"Now," said Saâh, "this is the most enjoyable part of the festival. You're going to see tricksters, Messieurs."

"Really?" said Valsorres, curiously. "You have prestidigitators?"

"What did you say?"

"Prestidigitators. It means 'people with nimble fingers.'"

"That's right—that's what jugglers and conjurers are called in the *Encyclopédie*, I believe."

"That's correct, my cousin."

"Well, my dear cousin, you're going to see what the prestidigitators of the planet Mars can do."

In fact, ten men and four women had gone up on to the stage. A large table had been installed here, and a sort of crate containing various objects.

One of the prestidigitators saluted the sovereign and pronounced a few words.

"He's announcing the trick he's going to perform," Thaû said to Valsorres. He's going to do the *marvelous hat*."

The man, clad in a tight costume decorated with brightly colored embroideries advanced toward the edge of the stage and asked for a hat. A member of the audience gave him his own. It was a soft had made of a sort of supple felt.

The man on the stage took it, turned it over and over, and inside out. When everyone was convinced that the hat had not been "doctored," he placed it on the table and touched it with a long wand. He lifted it up, giving the impression, by the effort he seemed to be making, that the hat had become heavy. To general astonishment, he turned it over, and a veritable heap of metal disks fell out of it, which clinked against one another as they escaped.

The members of the audience stamped their feet joyfully. The man thanked them, and signaled that he had not finished.

A second dose of metallic disks was added to the first, and then a third and a fourth, to such an extent that after a few minutes there as a huge pile on the table. But that was not all. The artiste plunged his wand into the pile, agitating and swirling it as if he were trying to dissolve sugar in a glass of water. As he swirled, the heap of disks diminished, as did their dimensions. After a few moments, it had disappeared entirely. The acclamations redoubled. The man made a sign that he wanted to speak, and, addressing Queen Saâh, he asked her where her little elephant was.

The queen, who had had it on her knees a moment before, looked, and observed with amazement that her little animal had disappeared.

Then the man, lifting the hat, which was a little stouter than before, turned it over on the table. The little elephant came out of it, trumpeting as loudly as it could and waving its trunk.

The amusement of the audience was manifested noisily. Thaû and Saâh gave the foremost example.

The prestidigitator bowed and stood side, giving way to the four women.

As gracious as possible in their short black gauze tunics with silver embroidery, they each picked up four balls of shiny metal, which the beam of a spotlight, directed at them, caused to scintillate like as many luminous rockets.

They began to juggle, initially all executing the same movement, and afterwards throwing the balls to one another, which, illuminated by the radiant beam, gave the impression of a veritable rain of shooting stars.

Nothing can convey an idea of the grace, dexterity and precision with which that exercise was performed so prettily by the four delightful creatures.

Valsorres, Espéret and Portier were watching and admiring conscientiously. Thomas murmured: "Damn it! To think that I, Thomas Renoult, the son of my father, have seen such things! Truly, these things only happen to me."

The pretty jugglers, saluted by the acclamations of the audience, went to sit down on the seats reserved for them. Then the five men who had not yet done anything stood up, advanced to the middle of the stage and began truly implausible acrobatic exercises.

Favored by the low level of Martian gravity, they launched themselves into the air, and they threw one of their number back and forth, who seemed to be flying from one shoulder to another, like a bird in an aviary leaping from one perch to another.

The voyagers from Earth watched the spectacle with astonishment and admiration.

But that was not all. The prestidigitator returned to the table. He made a sign to the prettiest of the jugglers. She came forward, leapt lightly on to the table, and sat down there cross-legged. Then the prestidigitator extended a large veil of blue silk over her, which enveloped her entirely, and then tapped it with his wand.

The veil collapsed, completely limp. The woman had vanished.

The whole thing had only lasted five seconds.

As the crowd stamped and howled with joy, the prestidigitator pointed with the tip of his wand at the seat that he had caused to vanish had just quit. She was sitting in it.

Then there was madness. All the members of the audience were on their feet, shouting, applauding and uttering acclamations of every sort.

Meanwhile, Thaû rose to his feet.

In a few words, he thanked the representatives of the provinces for having come in such numbers to the festival; he thanked and congratulated the artistes who had illustrated the gathering with their various talents; and, taking Saâh by the hand, he descended from the box in order to go to the large portal, passing through the middle of his subjects.

Our four friends followed him, each with his companion.

Scarcely were they at the foot of the steps of the box than a triumphal song burst forth, executed by the orchestra, conducted by the beautiful Zoloh, mingling the energetic tones of instruments with the powerful voices of singers.

Valsorres stooped, seized by a sharp emotion.

"The *Marseillaise!*"

Saâh put her arm under his. "Yes, my cousin, the *Marseillaise*; it was on one of your gramophone disks. I've seen how much you love your fatherland, and I asked Zoloh to have your national anthem played by all her musicians, thinking that it would be agreeable for you to hear it here."

It was, indeed, Rouget de Lisle's hymn, but executed as it had perhaps never been executed on Earth. Valsorres, Espéret, Portier and Thomas had stopped. Thaû and Saâh had imitated them, waiting before leaving until the song of triumph had concluded.

When they went through the great portal, Thaû said to Valsorres: "Well, my cousin, are you satisfied with the fashion in which the Martians are able to play your music?"

Valsorres only replied to Thaû with a vigorous handshake, and a respectful kiss on Saâh's pretty fingers.

But they walked on ahead of him in order to reach the palace, and did not see that the Marquis de Valsorres was weeping.

XI. In which it will be seen in what circumstances Thomas found his master.

One day, after his dinner without wine, Thomas was lying on a sofa beside his faithful Hina, who was looking at him with a certain anxiety.

"What a melancholy expression you have, my love," she said to him.

Thomas made no reply.

"Truly," she insisted, "you look very sad."

Thomas still did not react.

"Are you asleep?"

"No."

"Are you ill?"

"No."

"Are you annoyed? Have I done something to irritate you?"

"No."

"Tell me, then, my friend, what's upsetting you."

"What's upsetting me, my chicken, is that I'm bored."

"Oh," she said, with an indescribable expression of affectionate sadness. "Oh, my friend, you're bored and I'm beside you." And a dolorous contraction altered the smile of her beautiful face.

Thomas perceived the chagrin that he had caused his friend.

"I beg your pardon, my little Hina, for distressing you like that," he said, "but what do you expect? It's stronger than me. I'm bored, I'm bored and bored again in your sad country."

"How can you say that about our planet, where one can savor all pleasures at will?"

"Oh, let's talk about your planet," said Thomas, with ill-contained anger. "It's nice, your planet! A planet where I find everything that I don't desire, and nothing that I love."

Hina looked at him with tears in her eyes.

"What about me?" she said, in a tremulous voice.

"Oh, you, my little Hina, are my only consolation. If I didn't have you here, I'd have swallowed one of the drugs in the *Fusée*'s pharmacy a long time ago to put an end to my existence."

"In sum," asked Hina, "for what are you reproaching my country?"

Thomas let all his long-suppressed rancor burst forth then.

"What do I reproach it for? Well, first of all, having no newspapers."

Hina looked at him in astonishment. "Newspapers?" she asked. "But what would be the point, since news items are posted at every street corner in enormous letters during the day and luminous ones by night?"

"First of all, in order to read them, it's necessary to know Martian."

"But my soul, I've taught you a few words, and it's only a matter of teaching you a few more."

"Agreed," replied Thomas. "With you, besides, I'd take all the lessons you want to give. But even if I knew Martian, your news is never anything but news, and what's more, news of here, and I miss the feuilleton."

Hina opened her eyes—magnificent eyes—wide. "The feuilleton?" she said. "What is a feuilleton?"

Thomas reflected for a moment.

"The feuilleton, my little darling, you see, is the soul of the newspaper. It's an interesting, impassioning, palpitating story that is recounted, like that, in little morsels. In every issue, which appears every day, there's a part of the story that's being told."

"It never finishes, then?"

"Yes my chick, it finishes, but, you understand, when the story is a really good yarn, one takes it to heart. Then one waits for the next day's issue with the greatest impatience, and all day long, one thinks about what's going to happen to the characters in the story, to the persecuted young woman or the courageous young man who loves her, and who finds, in the midst of his amour, the most frightful circumstances provoked by wicked people who want to do him harm!"

"Ah!" said Hina, curiously.

"Yes. And then, when it's finished, when one sees that the worthy people can finally be tranquil, when one sees that the brigands are unmasked, that the villains are punished, then one understands that there is, after all, a justice, and one feels better, and encouraged in doing good."

"I'd never have believed that!" replied the beautiful Martian.

"That's because you've never read a feuilleton, my little sugar-plum. Look—a supposition. You're in Paris; you read *Le Petit Parisien* every day."

"What's that?"

"*Le Petit Parisien?* No! Where do you come from? You don't know *Le Petit Parisien?*"

Hina writhed with laughter. "How do you expect me to know *Le Petit Parisien*, me, who has never left the planet Mars?"

Thomas was struck by the justice of that observation. "That's true," he said. "You can't know *Le Petit Parisien*, Otherwise you'd have seen the fine feuilletons it publishes! All the men, women and young women in Paris palpitate with emotion in reading the fine stories of Charles Mérouvel, René Vincy, Arthur Bernède and Jules Mary, and they experience the greatest emotions in that reading."

"Really?"

"It's as I tell you. And do you want to know something? Well, if I ever return to Earth and someone recounts that I, Thomas Renoult, son of my father, have come down on this sacred ball, that I've known a woman as beautiful and as good as you there, my little Hina, and that I've seen what I've seen, well, that someone could make a fine feuilleton for *Le Petit Parisien*, and, as true as my name's Thomas, there'd be a lot of people who'd read it."

Hina was sensible to the compliment, and manifested her pleasure by a tender kiss, which she gave her friend. She added: "And yet, you're bored, you miss the newspapers. What else?"

Thomas had become somber again. Hina resumed her interrogation. "Anyway, it's your own fault. Why don't you go out?"

"Go out!" cried Thomas. "Go out! To do what, damn it? To see what? Roofs and mountains, and only on condition of dressing for the North Pole, it's so cold in his damned place!"

"But I'm not asking you to go outside," said the beautiful Martian. "Anyway, you know that when you go to the *Fusée* I always go with you."

Thomas took Hina's head in his hands and kissed her for a long time. "Yes, my soul, you're always with me, I know. But after all, when one goes out, there are no trees, no grass and no water."

"Water! There's water in the canals!" said Hina.

"Oh, yes, let's talk about your canals! And no autobuses, no trams, no taxis. Nothing! Nothing! Not one plant! Not one flower!"

"You're forgetting our hothouses, where the most beautiful plants have been conserved."

"Yes, but underground! Everything's underground here. You don't live like intelligent creatures, you live like moles."

"Oh, my dear Thomas, how unjust you are!"

Thomas collected himself momentarily. Suddenly, he let out a cry from the heart. "If only there were bistros!"

Hina questioned him with her gaze.

"Yes," Thomas went on, "bistros—which is to say, charming places where one can drink, smoke and play cards..."

"I don't understand," she said.

"You can't understand, my little darling. You don't know those delightful places."

"You amused yourself there a great deal, then?"

"Oh, yes, I amused myself! Here!" He took Hina by the waist and sat her on his knee. "Listen, my kitten. When I was free in the evening, I went to the café-concert."

"But we have concerts here too."

"That's true. Except, the music at your concerts puts me to sleep. Or I went to the cinema. Yes, yes! I know what you're going to say, that you have them here too, cinemas, and fine cinemas. But it's not the same thing as ours; back home, there we funny fellows: Charlot, Max Rinder, Rigadin, and others. And then, after that, I went to Père Mansuy's, who kept a nice little bar near the Gare Montparnasse. And there, with a few comrades, we drank beer to kill time, playing a little auction manille. And while playing manille we smoked a good pipe, and we spent a pleasant evening.

"Oh it's a long way away, Père Mansuy's bar! And the manille! And the tobacco! And the beer! There's tea here, but it's not a drink, tea, it's a medicine! So, I'm bored—during the day, that is, for in the evening, my little Hina, you're here, and beside you, I forget everything, only to think of the pleasure of having you beside me."

Hina reflected.

"But then, my great friend, what is it that your happiness lacks? Is it only that game of manille, as you call it?"

"Oh, yes, just a little manille. That would be paradise!"

"Well, my darling, perhaps I'll be able to satisfy you."

"You'd do that? Hina of my heart...."

"Yes. For you, what wouldn't I do?"

"You have cards, then?"

"No, but isn't it with cards, as you call them, that you make those complicated figures all day long on the big table in our room, which you call *patiences*?"

"Yes that's true; I brought four packs of cards with me."

"Well, get your cards and come with me. I'll take you to a place where you might find friends who'll play with you. Come, my love."

Thomas put two packs of cards in his satchel and followed his beautiful friend.

They left the palace.

After walking for about twenty minutes through streets full of people, they arrived at a vast enclosure, the wall of which was pierced by a small door. Two policemen were on duty to either side of that door.

Hina went past the policemen, greeting them politely, and, followed by Thomas, went into a large vestibule into a much larger area, where one might have believed that they were in the open air, in a vast garden, with trees, lawns and flowers.

On entering the actors' palace by the little door of which he had noticed. Thomas had begun by grimacing. "Another rat's nest!" he had muttered between his teeth. But when he had penetrated into that garden, he could not dissimulate his profound astonishment.

"I'll be damned!" he said. "Trees!"

Hina rejoiced in her friend's surprise.

"Yes, trees and flowers!" she said, laughing.

Thomas raised his head and looked up in the air. "But, God forgive me, I can see blue sky with white clouds!"

"Indeed," replied his friend. "You see, we have trees and flowers on our planet too."

Thomas spotted a magnificent red carnation and, bending down, extended his hand in order to pick it by breaking the stem.

The stem resisted. Thomas persisted; his finger slid along the slender support of the flower and encountered the petals. Alas, at that contact, the flower vanished; it disintegrated instantaneously, and nothing remained of it but an impalpable shiny dust.

The worthy fellow was heartbroken. "Oh!" he said. "They're artificial flowers, then?"

Hina laughed uproariously. "Yes, my soul," she said. "In the actors' palace, everything is artificial: the flowers, the trees..."

"What? The trees too?"

"Yes, the trees too."

"Incredulously, Thomas approached the trunk of a magnificent palm tree, which extended its shade over a bright green lawn.

The palm tree was cold to the touch; the tree was made of hollow metal, admirably painted; its leaves were similarly made of metallic substance, analogous to tinplate.

He raised his head. "And the sky...?"

"The sky, my friend?" Hina replied. "The sky is painted on the vault of this immense cupola, with its blue color and its pink and white clouds. Here, as I've already told you, everything is artificial, everything is painted."

"And I was already rejoicing in being in the open air! Oh, misery! These things only happen to me!"

Meanwhile, Hina had taken her friend's arm and had taken him into a small rectangular room where there as a woman.

"Spad?" she asked her.

"He's here," the woman relied. "Would you like to see him?"

"Yes, if he can come; I'd like to have a word with him."

The young woman put her mouth to a kind of cornet. A moment later a door opened and a man appeared, who advanced toward Hina, smiling.

The beautiful Martian took him by the hand. "Look, Thomas! You're going to make the acquaintance of one of the finest artistes on Mars, the skillful Spad, to whom you'll be able to teach the game you like so much. Then he'll teach it to a few of his friends; that way, you'll be able to find here the pleasure that you're regretting so keenly.

Thomas and Spad shook hands.

"You know," said Hina, "Spad speaks French well enough."

Thomas sat down with his new friend at a little table. Hina looked at him sympathetically. Our worthy friend took a deck of thirty-two cards out of his satchel.[33] He laid them out on the table and explained the suits and values to his

---

[33] Manille is played with a "piquet deck" in which the lowest ranking card is the seven. The ten outranks the court cards, and is scored at five points for the pur-

new friend, whose eyes, sparkling with intelligence, followed the Earthman's explanations with the keenest attention.

The lesson was a little long, for Thomas not only had to explain his favorite game to the Martian in all its details, but also the manner of counting and marking the points.

Spad had listened religiously to the explanations he had been given. When he got up, he simply said: "Thank you, Thomas. I understand perfectly."

And in fact, with his penetrating intelligence and prodigious faculty of assimilation, Spad, the Martian artiste, now knew the game of manille as well as his teacher. In fact, he knew it even better, and he was to prove that the next day, as the continuation of his story will demonstrate.

Spad took his leave of the couple.

When he had gone, Hina said to Thomas: "Well, friend, are you content now? You'll be able to play your favorite game."

"Yes, my dear little Hina. You're an angel."

And, taking her arm, he left the actors' palace with her, showing his pierced plaques, which the policemen on duty at the exit checked with the most rigorous manner.

That evening, after dinner, when he went back to his apartment with his friend, the worthy Thomas felt a little more joyful.

"To think that, in two days' time, I'll be able to play manille," he exclaimed. "If only, at the same time, I had tobacco to stuff Josephine"—that was what he called his pipe—"I believe I'd begin to regret the Earth a little less."

Hina drew nearer to him. "What do you call tobacco? Is it the black herb of which you had a few packets when you arrived?"

"Yes, alas. They've gone…and long gone."

Hina made no reply.

Two days later, after lunch, she took her friend to the actors' house again. They were due to meet there the three Martians initiated by Spad into the game of "auction manille."

Before departing, the worthy fellow had, to be sure, asked one question: "What are we going to play for?"

They could not play for money, because there was no money on Mars. They could not play for beans, because there were none of those either.

On the off chance, Thomas put into his satchel a few louis d'or that he had brought in the *Fusée*, a few silver coins and a few sous. Then he went into the small drawing room where he had made the acquaintance of his new friend Spad two days earlier.

---

pose of bidding for the total number of points aggregated by number of tricks a player believes that he can take, the ace scoring four, the king three, the queen two and the jack one.

The latter was there with three other Martians, whom he introduced, one after the other, to Thomas and Hina.

"Boss; Past; Zori."

Hira greeted each one with a smile. Thomas generously granted them three handshakes.

"We can begin," said Spad.

The five men sat down around the table. A wooden bowl was placed in the middle. Hira sat on a large cushion next to the players.

After shuffling the cards, Thomas asked Spad: "What are we going to play for?"

Spad reflected momentarily and said: "What can you play for?"

Thomas put his hand in his satchel and brought out the coins, which he set out on the table.

The players passed them around and examined them curiously.

The gold coins interested them greatly, and the copper coins too, but what excited their curiosity most of all were the silver coins.

They returned the money to Thomas. Then Spad said to him: "Here, we don't have pieces of metal like yours, but we have things that we consider very precious and for which we wager between ourselves."

And he threw on the table a series of iron disks the size of a five franc piece, at the center of each of which was a small diamond.

"These," he said, "are our usual stakes. If you wish, inhabitant of Earth, we'll agree what your pieces of metal are worth, with regard to ours."

The four Martians consulted one another briefly in their own language. When they were in accord, Spad said: "This is what we propose. "You small pieces of silver are each worth two of our plaques; the larger ones are worth five, and the largest ones of all are worth ten. As for your yellow pieces, we regard them as each being worth one of our plaques, and your pieces of blackened metal"—he meant the sous—"the same."

Thomas replied that he accepted. Privately, he was joyful. To barter a twenty-sou piece for two diamonds each worth at least a hundred francs, a thune for ten of those plaques and a simple sou for one diamond-bearing plaque seemed to him to be unexpected good fortune, all the more so as he counted on taking advantage of his long experience at the game to aid luck to turn in his direction.

There was one shadow over the picture: the louis d'or were each only estimated at a single plaque, which only rated them at five hundred per cent, but fortunately. Thomas only had seven louis, whereas he had thirty silver coins and thirty sous.

The players agreed to divide each plaque into ten parts, represented by small round pebbles.

As the game was about to begin, Hira approached Thomas and handed him a little packet, which the worthy fellow opened. An exclamation of joy emerged from his throat. "My pipe! Josephine! And tobacco!"

Hira had, in fact, brought a small bag of a dried herb, yellow in color.

Thomas stuffed his pipe and asked for a light. Spad took a little apparatus out of his pocket from which a flame sprang, which the smoker approached to his pipe.

"Damn! That's good. Oh, my little Hina! You're truly an angel from heaven!"

And he drew voluptuous puffs from Josephine.

"Evidently, it's not tobacco, but that doesn't prevent it from being damnably good! Oh, my dear little Hina, come and have a kiss."

He kissed his friend tenderly and said: "Let's go! The day's beginning well." Then he turned to his four competitors. "Now we're getting there. Forward ho!"

And he murmured in a very low voice, looking out of the corner of his eye at the diamond-studded plaques that he already considered as his property: "It's true! I'd never have thought such a thing could happen to me, Thomas Renoult!"

Turning toward his opponents, he said: "You know the rules of the game, don't you?"

"Perfectly," Spad replied, on behalf of his three fellows. "Each player puts a unit in the kitty; then, the cards having been dealt, he asks for the points he thinks he can make. If he succeeds, each player gives him a unit, reckoning from twenty, and he takes what there is in the kitty."

"That's it, Messieurs. I'm at your orders."

Each of the Martians put a unit in the bowl placed in the middle of the table. Thomas thought delightedly about the extraordinary profit that he was about to obtain from the little game.

The cards having been dealt, Boss, who was the first, said quietly: "Twenty-five."

How well they know how to count in French, Thomas thought, and immediately added: "I say twenty-six."

"Twenty-seven," said Past.

"Twenty-eight."

"Thirty," said the Martian.

"Thirty-five!" cried Thomas.

No overbid having been made, they played the hand. Without the slightest difficulty, Thomas made the figure he had requested, and more.

Wait, wait, my old Martian, he thought, looking at Spad. *I'll show you what a Parisian is.*

And the game continued.

Gradually, the bids rose, for the Martians, irritated by seeing Thomas win almost every hand, became increasingly audacious. Our friend's face was radiant.

He looked at his hand. "Fifty-four," he said.

"Fifty-five," replied Boss.

Thomas tapped the table and cried: "I ask for the general."

"The general?" asked Spad. "What's that?"

"Oh, that's true," said Thomas. "I forgot to tell you that when one asks for the general, one plays first. If one takes all the tricks, the other players pay seven units and one picks up the kitty."

"And if one doesn't succeed?"

"Then one has to pay each player seven units and double the kitty," Thomas replied, and then added, with an air of great nobility: "But I can't abuse your ignorance, and this time, I won't ask for the general."

The Martians, for who Spad translated those words, inclined deferentially before Thomas. The latter said, majestically: "We're all like that in France. Then, looking at his hand again, he said: "Fifty-six. No more bids? Adjudged!"

Thomas's grandeur of soul was handsomely recompensed; he made one point more than he had specified, and the heap of diamond-studded disks that he was beginning to accumulate in front of him increased sensibly. Furthermore, "to make the money" at the Martians' request, he exchanged his copper, gold and silver coins, for the needs of the game, for the agreed number of precious plaques—with the consequence that all the diamonds were before him, while Spad, Boss, Past and Zori only had in their hands a share of his coins. Again, Thomas won back almost all of them, as a result of a sequence of fortunate coups.

A lucky streak! he thought. *The streak of streaks! I've have more than a hundred thousand francs, for sure. It's true. These things only happen...*

He was interrupted by Spad, who, passionate about the game, so new for him, said: "Well, are we continuing?"

"Certainly!"

At that moment, he four Martians exchanged a rapid glance that Thomas did not see, and immediately, fortune—capricious and changing fortune—appeared to abandon our friend abruptly.

The previous conqueror lost several hands. Wanting to give his adversaries a lesson in deportment, he continued with a smile. But the ill luck persisted and he began to become serious, playing with an admirable prudence.

In spite of that prudence, he saw the heap of his disks melt like wax in the African sun.

Then he played slowly and apathetically.

His adversaries noticed that. "Are you tired, Thomas?" Spad asked.

"Yes, a little. Perhaps it's this fake tobacco going to my head," he said, indicating his pipe.

"It's said," replied Spad, having learned it from the *Encyclopédie*, "that a great emperor of your country, having made many conquests, didn't want to make any more, for fear of losing his enormous booty again afterwards."

"That's the Emperor Charles...the Great," said Hina, showing off her knowledge of French history.

"Well," said Thomas, with dignity, "It won't be said the Monsieur Espéret's man of confidence played Charlemagne on the planet Mars. Let's continue Messieurs, please."

The Martians inclined, and the game recommenced.

Capricious fortune seemed, momentarily, to smile again on the French champion; after a few alternatives of gain and loss, it even appeared to abandon the Martians entirely. Beaten in every encounter, they could not succeed in single coup, and Thomas was privately jubilant on seeing the coins and diamond-studded disks of his adversaries accumulate in front of him and fill the kitty in the middle of the table.

Oh, that kitty! Full to overflowing with precious plaques, how covetously he gazed at it, but with the near-certainty of success. The possession of all those diamonds was a fortune!

He silence, observed religiously until then, became, if possible, even more profound.

Boss dealt the cards. Spad stopped him and said: "If my count is correct, there's a sum of 1,285 units in the kitty."

"Yes," said the players.

Thomas slowly lifted up his hand. When the six cards were arranged, he was dazzled. He had the ten of hearts, the ace of hearts, the king of hearts, the jack of hearts, the ten of diamonds and the ace of diamonds—which is to say, an almost complete certainty of taking all the tricks."

"I bid twenty-five," said Boss."

"Twenty-six," said Past.

"Thirty," said Spad.

"Forty!" cried Zori.

Thomas waited for his turn to speak. The worthy fellow made considerable efforts to prevent his emotion betraying itself in his physiognomy.

"I ask for the general," he said.

The Martians inclined.

Thomas played and took the first three tricks without the slightest hesitation, but he was suddenly seized by a frightful anguish and cold sweat pearled on his forehead.

The queen of hearts, which, naturally, ought to have been taken by one of the superior cards that he had just played, had not fallen.

I've lost! he thought. And he sensed himself going pale.

The four Martians looked at him impassively.

"I've lost," he said, in a low voice, playing the jack of hearts. And, in fact, the triumphant queen of hearts covered his unfortunate jack.

"You have to give us seven units each and double the kitty," said Spad then, addressing the unfortunate.

Having emptied his bowl, Thomas paid each of the Martians seven units and then, pale and trembling, murmured in a strangled voice: "Excuse me, my friends. I didn't think such a coup could happen...and I don't have enough units on me to double the kitty."

The Martians looked at him, smiling. "You can pay us tomorrow," Spad said to him. "Do you want to continue the game?"

"Oh, no!" said Thomas. Turning to Hina, who had witnessed the entire tragicomedy as a spectator, he said: "Let's go, my beauty, it's time to go home."

He saluted his four competitors, saying to them: "You'll be paid tomorrow."

But how was he to acquit his debt? He had lost all his gold, silver and sous—everything! He had nothing left.

"How pale you are," said Hina, affectionately.

"It's nothing! It's doubtless the tobacco I smoked, to which I'm not yet habituated. It will pass. Have no fear."

As they were traversing the courtyard with the artificial trees they perceived Espéret, who was strolling there, his arm tenderly linked with that of the little dancer, the ravishing Thé.

For his part, the engineer had perceived his valet.

"Look," said Hina. "There's Monsieur Espéret calling you."

Thomas approached rapidly.

"What are you doing here?" his master asked him.

"I've just been playing manille," replied Thomas, piteously.

"Ah! From what I can see, luck hasn't been very favorable to you. Anyway, my dear Thomas, you know the proverb: unlucky at cards, lucky in love. Isn't that so, Hina?" And, taking the arm once again of little Thé, who seemed delighted to be at his side, he disappeared with her in a path of the tinplate park.

Thomas and Hina, leaving the actors' palace, returned to their apartment.

Dejected, Thomas fell on to a divan, his head in his hands.

Suddenly, an idea occurred to him.

"What do those men do with whom you enabled me to play?" he asked his beautiful friend.

"They're jugglers."

"Jugglers! Performers of tricks!"

Yes. Didn't you recognize one of them, Zori, who was on stage at the Festival of the Provinces?"

Thomas was flabbergasted. "Oh. what a fool I am!" he cried. "They've turned me over!"

At that moment someone knocked gently on the door. Hina went to open it. A pretty little girl appeared carrying a little packet. "For Thomas," she said, smiling sweetly. And she left, making a gracious curtsey.

Thomas opened the packet, which contained a little box. He lifted the lid curiously, and uttered a cry.

His gold, silver and sous appeared to his eyes inside the magic box, and, even more astonishing, five iron disks, at the center of each of which was a diamond. Five of the precious plaques that his adversaries had used as stakes accompanied his coins. The consignment was accompanied by a note, which read:

Spad, Boss, Past and Zori, to their friend Thomas, in order to be forgiven for the trick they played on him.

XII. In which it will be seen that Martians can love with as much passion as the inhabitants of Earth.

"My cousin," said Thaû to the Marquis one day, "you now know almost everything that we have to show you on our little planet."

"Little!" replied Valsorres, "Oh, small in dimensions, but great in discoveries."

"That's so," said the king. "Anyway, you have been able to see how we have captured natural forces, but you still know very little about the arts that flourish, or rather, have flourished, on our Martian globe."

"Indeed," replied the Marquis. "Of your present arts I only know the music and dance. The latter is, moreover, very remarkable. But of painting I've only seen the ancient images traced on the walls of caves by your primitive inhabitants, and I confess that they seemed very rudimentary."

"That's true," said Thaû. "However, independently of those paintings, which date from such a remote era, we possess others, very beautiful, that go back to an era already distant."

"And for what reason has that art fallen into neglect?"

Thaû reflected momentarily. "Quite simply because our artists, having arrived, in a certain epoch, very close to perfection, wanted to do 'something different' at any price. Then they gradually drew away from the verity that is, fundamentally, the great inspirer of art. In gradually going astray on that fatal route, they arrived at painting such horrors that the art of painting became an affair of fashion and pure convention."

"Is that possible?"

"Yes, indeed. Then they represented human figures with combinations of rectangles and triangles. They claimed to be retracing the settings in which the characters were located by combinations of various patches that looked like the tracks left on the painting by a cat that had walked through the colors. Then the intelligent Martians, understanding that painting had become a simple affair of mad fantasy, left the naïve and the imbecilic to wax ecstatic before the monstrosities that were submitted to them. And in the end, the imbecilic and the naïve ended up blushing in their turn at their stupidity, with the consequence that painting, thus degraded, ended up being forsaken completely, and disappeared without a trace.

"But how is it." said the Marquis, "that you haven't had what we call a *renaissance*?"

"We've realized it in living beings.

Valsorres looked at Thaû in astonishment.

"You're surprised, my cousin," the king went on. Nothing is truer, however. As I've explained to you, we have succeeded in vanquishing disease and eliminating hereditary defects. We have thus obtained generations of Martians of an increasing physical perfection."

"That's true; your fellow citizens are admirable."

"What is the point, then, of reproducing on canvas what is living perfection? And then, do we not have the reproduction of life that we have shown you, and which perpetuates the memory of people and events?"

"That's true too."

"So, painting had become unnecessary on our globe, and it disappeared. But it isn't the same for dramatic art."

"You have a literature of the theater?" said the Marquis, curiously.

"Yes."

"It must be very interesting. For, amour being free, or very nearly, on your planet, you don't have the resource of perpetually putting it to contribution, as is done for the dramatic works performed in our theaters on Earth."

Thaû reflected momentarily. "Your theater, then, reposes on the fragile basis of amour?"

"Yes, except for some plays that recall historic events…repeatedly."

"We have those too," the king replied. "They're very ancient, and go back to the era when our inhabitants were only beginning to penetrate the mysteries of nature."

"And since that distant era?"

"We only produce plays capable of developing intelligence, beauty or great sentiments."

"On those conditions, you can't have a very large number of works."

"We have as many as necessary, for in that domain as in others, nothing unnecessary is done here."

"That's not like Earth," replied Valsorres, and added: "May I ask a question?"

"Go ahead."

"In what manner are your new plays judged? Do you have what we on Earth call 'critics'—which is to say, writers capable of appreciating, with more or less competence, the value of the works performed and the artists who perform them?"

"No, but we have judges."

"Judges?"

"Yes. There are Martians who are only occupied in reading written works and formulating their sentiment regarding them. If they seem to them to be perfect from all points of view, the works are performed."

"And in the contrary case?"

"They're burned. But since the theater appears to interest you, would you like to witness one of these days, in my box, the performance of one of our ancient dramas?"

"Certainly, and with pleasure."

"I won't propose that you hear one of our new works, which would un-doubtedly be devoid of interest for you, whereas our ancient dramas ought to be much more similar to those put on in your theaters."

"I accept gladly, my dear cousin."

"Until tomorrow evening, then," said Thaû. "In the meantime, go and visit your cousin Saâh, who claims that, taken over by your scientific work, you've been neglecting her somewhat."

The Marquis shook the king's hand and went to pay his respects to his beautiful cousin Saâh.

The following evening, accompanied by Dr. Portier, he went to the actors' quarter, went into the theater, and was introduced into the royal box. Thaû and Saâh were waiting for them there, and gave them the most affable welcome.

The queen was clad in a tunic of black lace on which golden spangles scin-tillated. Her magnificent hair was circled by a diadem, the magnificent dia-monds and emeralds of which glinted under the action of the lights illuminating the hall.

While chatting, the Marquis sitting to Saâh's right, gazed at that immense nave. No theater on Earth could have given a similar impression of beauty, rich-ness and splendor. All the places were occupied by Martian men and women, who had donned their finest costumes and their most dazzling jewelry. Although the men and women were all good looking it was not in an identical fashion; there was a variety in the beauty that further enhanced its charm and captivating quality.

Naturally, Valsorres was accompanied by his beautiful friend Zith, stream-ing with jewels, and Portier had the lovely Daâh on his arm.

After having pointed out a few notorious Martians who were in the hall, the king designated with his gaze a large box in which there were numerous individuals. "The tribunal of dramatic judges," he said. And he named some of them to his guests. "Look, there's Briss, Ant, Boy, Bid, Gin, Ad, Noz, Flé, Gif, Sch, Bou...and two women who are also theatrical judges, Col and Mend."

Valsorres looked at the individuals in question. "They don't have the pre-occupied and somber faces of our Parisian critics," the Marquis said to Portier.

"That's doubtless because they know that they don't have to deliver a re-view of the work tomorrow."

"Now," said the making to his quests, "permit me to explain the play to you, which, written in the Martian language, will be almost incomprehensible for you.

"A king of Mars, one of my very ancient predecessors—for the drama is set in the epoch preceding our great revolutions—had married a young woman of great beauty. The queen was as ambitious and as authoritarian as the king was simple, modest and mild, while being endowed with a great intelligence."

"Fortunately," said Portier, "for those qualities are often the prerogative of poor intelligence."

"On Earth, perhaps, but not here," said Thaû. "Now, the king in question, weary of being treated with scornful indifference by his spouse, took a mistress, and fell madly in love with her, for that woman, to who he was able to open his heart, communicate his thoughts and make his projects understood, was, for her part, in admiration before her royal lover, in whom she had rapidly recognized a veritably superior individual."

At that moment, the door of a box placed at the back of the theater opened, and to the great surprise of the Marquis and Portier, they saw their friend Espéret enter it, who had refused to accompany them.

As soon as he was introduced into the box, the engineer had respectfully kissed the hand of an exquisite creature who was already there. At a gesture from her, he sat down beside her.

"Isn't that Monsieur Espéret?" said Queen Saâh.

"Yes," replied Thaû, "with the dancer Thé."

Saâh looked at the couple attentively. "Poor Monsieur Espéret," she said, in a soft voice.

"So, I was saying." Thaû resumed, continuing his story, "that the king's mistress, who is the hero of the story, was gripped by the most ardent love for him; it was a veritable passion. The queen didn't take long to be informed of it, and conceived a sharp chagrin in consequence. Obedient to the impulsion of her violent nature, she attempted to break her husband's liaison by violence. Having failed by violence, she tried to succeed by cunning, but she had no more success. She went so far as to strive to appear amiable and meek. But, the king having resisted her caresses as he had her violence, fearing an eventual abandonment, she resolved to employ the supreme means; she had her husband assassinated."

"On Earth," said the doctor, "one generally does it oneself."

"And, left alone on the throne," queried the Marquis, "she doubtless had a long and happy reign, and died leaving history the memory of a great and glorious sovereign?"

"No, because, her mind invaded by remorse, and incessantly pursued by the memory of the crime she had committed, she came to an atrocious and premature end."

"When I return to France," said the Marquis, "I'll give the subject of that play to one of our great authors; he'll make a masterpiece of it—a modern masterpiece, of course."

Meanwhile, Valsorres and Portier, informed of the gist of the drama, followed the course of the action that unfolded before their eyes with the keenest interest. They appreciated, with as much surprise as admiration, the powerful, sober and subtle performances of the great artistes interpreting the work borrowed from the history of Mars.

The audience was quivering; at the end of each act its members testified their enthusiasm for the acting by cries and stamping their feet. The latter, advancing to the edge of the stage, bowed repeatedly to the spectators who were acclaiming them abundantly.

In the meantime, Espéret, who cared very little about the spectacle unfolding on the stage, was talking to his beautiful neighbor in a low voice. An enchanting smile was sometimes sketched on the exquisite creature's face.

The attention of the Marquis having been provoked by a gesture on the part of the queen, he looked in the direction of the box occupied by the little dancer Thé.

"Your friend Espéret seems preoccupied," said Saâh.

"Indeed," replied the Marquis.

"He seems to be violently infatuated with Thé."

Valsorres smiled. "Oh," he said, "everything will sort itself out, for on your world of delights, everything ends up sorting itself out, doesn't it?"

"I doubt it," the queen replied. She had known for some time, in fact, that the great engineer adored the little dancer, and that all his prayers and supplications had remained quite futile. Thé had refused absolutely to belong to the Earthman."

Meanwhile, hidden in the depths of another box, her face veiled, hidden behind a tapestry, a woman was weeping. That was the beautiful Rasôh, Espéret's friend. You will remember that it was she who, of her own free will, had chosen the engineer in order to be his constant companion during his sojourn on the planet. In living thus with that superior man, Rasôh had, without suspecting it, ended up loving him with all the force of her soul. Her affection, incessantly satisfied by the presence of the cherished individual, had only burst forth when she perceived that her friend was interested in another woman and was courting the little dancer Thé.

Yes, Rasôh, the beautiful and cheerful Rasôh, was in love! Rasôh was jealous! Rasôh, the joy of Saâh's court, was shedding the bitterest tears, like a simple amorous woman of the Earth from which her infidel friend came.

When the spectacle concluded, Valsorres and Portier took their leave of the sovereigns and headed for the exit in order to be able to encounter Espéret and try to obtain some clarifications, but they waited in vain.

Following the little dancer, the engineer had left the hall via the stage, and had accompanied the young woman to the small apartment she occupied in the actors' domain.

"Follow me, friend," she said to him, when they had arrived.

Espéret thought for a moment that he had arrived at the realization of his dreams and finally reaching the termination of his anguish. With joy in his heart, he went into little Thé's abode.

On penetrating into it, it was impossible for him to dissimulate the astonishment and admiration that he experienced. Never, even on that extraordinary planet, where luxury seemed commonplace, could he have dreamed of such a residence.

Each of the rooms of the apartment was garnished with furniture both precious and elegant, made of a substance imitating the appearance of ebony, encrusted with designs in a yellow metal that shone like gold. Dressers with finely sculpted doors, and tables of an infinite artistry, were encountered everywhere. Low seats laden with cushions covered in the richest fabrics and the most delicate embroideries seemed to invite repose. The smaller room that served as the dancer's boudoir resembled an admirable flower of which the little artiste was the center, so rich and bright were the drapes and tapestries that ornamented it.

A sweet, exotic, intoxicating perfume floated in the air.

"Oh, Thé," exclaimed Espéret, "what a jewel-box you live in. But the casket is worthy of the jewel it shelters!"

He sat down at his idol's feet. He devoured her with his eyes, and she, for her part, let a gaze of infinite softness fall upon him.

"Thé!" the engineer said to her. "Thé, my soul, my life. No, I can't believe what you repeated to me just now!"

"It is, however, necessary to believe it," she said, with melancholy.

"No, Thé! I can't believe that, free and independent as you are, you refuse to become my companion, my lover, my wife."

"It is, however, necessary to believe it."

"But why? Why?" the engineer repeated, taking her head in his hands, "Why?"

Thé remained silent for a moment. Then, after a moment's thought, she said: "Listen, Espéret, listen, my friend. I'm suffering..."

"You're suffering, Thé?"

"Yes, I'm suffering at the thought that you can be so unhappy because of me, at the idea that your amour for me is dominating all your intelligence. But if it can calm your chagrin, I can tell you that never—never, you hear—will Thé belong to a man other than you."

Espéret looked at her with dolorous astonishment.

"Yes," she went on, with a great sadness in her voice, "you, who have come from an unknown world, who have dared with your companions to attempt what no one before you had attempted—which is to say, to venture into the infinity of the immense heaves—are the only one that I would have loved if..."

"If...?"

"...If I hadn't made an oath always to remain chaste and to dedicate my life to art forever."

"But..."

"Yes, my friend, I know what you want to say to me. Well, no...no. Thé will not betray her oath, even for you...whom I love," she said, with a profound sigh.

Espéret wept, his head in his hands.

The little dancer went on: "No, Thé will remain faithful to her promise, faithful to the art to which she has given herself, body and soul. If I have learned everything that one can learn, if I have studied everything that one can study, it was in order to glimpse in the art more than it was believed could be seen there-in…it was to penetrate the mystery of souls."

"The mystery of souls?"

"Yes. I wanted to know for what reasons, by virtue of the influence of what immaterial forces, certain special beings, certain exceptional creatures, exercise on all those who surround them an irresistible fascination, a complete power, an absolute domination; why they radiate around them a charm that nothing can resist."

"And…you know now?"

"I believe I know. And, friend of my soul, if I'm not mistaken, the name of Thé will remain immortal and will be pronounced until the remotest centuries, and those who live in those distant times will speak with admiration of the little dancer who will then be no more than a pinch of impalpable dust!"

Thé had stopped, and had become pensive; tears were pearling on the rim of her long eyelashes, and her gaze was lost in the distance.

Espéret could not weary of admiring that strange creature, the unique woman who was speaking to him thus. On seeing that forehead, so pure, that face, so pretty, those large dark green eyes, that opulent gilded hair, those coral lips, between which a double row of pearls shone, that nacreous and transparent skin, and that supple and delicate body, he could not believe that that beauty, never having belonged to any man, would disappear into death and be extinguished forever.

"Thé," he said, throwing himself at her feet, "Thé, if you knew how I love you…!"

"I have told you, my friend; I love you too, but only as I can love, with my soul. Don't ask me for anything more. Nothing!"

Espéret saw such a glint of resolution shining in the dancer's eyes, such a willful gleam, that he fell silent. He lowered his head and wept silently.

Then, on seeing tears flowing from the eyes of the man she considered to be the hero of Space, she leaned toward him. Slowly, she deposited a tender and chaste kiss on the forehead of the man who loved her, and whom she also loved.

Under that unexpected caress, the engineer shuddered. Getting to his feet, he extended his arms to grasp his idol. But the arms only encountered empty air, the dancer Thé had disappeared.

The unfortunate fellow went back to his apartment in the palace, slowly. He swallowed cup after cup of the liquor that "gave forgetfulness," and, falling on to his bed, he fell into a heavy slumber.

While he was sleeping thus, a door-curtain lifted and a woman appeared.

It was Rasôh.

His loving friend looked at him for a long time with eyes full of tenderness, and, kneeling at the foot of the bed, covered the infidel's hand with kisses.

When the engineer woke up, he perceived his companion.

"You, Rasôh?" he said. "You?"

"Yes, me," said the gentle creature. "Yes, me, whom you don't love, and yet, who has always loved you; me, the flesh of your flesh and the soul of your soul. Me, who has come to save you."

"To save me? Do you think that's possible?"

"Yes. I'll save you by means of my amour, by my affection, by my devotion. Yes, I'll save you, I for I'm suffering too much in seeing you forget your friend Rasôh."

"You're suffering, you say? That seems strange to me. With your light character, similar to that of all your sisters, you cannot and ought not to suffer."

"Do you think so?"

"Yes, I think so. And if you're suffering, you can drink this." He showed her the flask of pink liquid.

Rasôh took it from his hands. "You've drunk it," she said, "and yet..."

"But I'm not a Martian. I haven't been, like your brothers, habituated to this liquor since childhood, and it doesn't act on me as it acts on you."

Rasôh looked at him intently. "And what if I weren't drinking it anymore?" she said. Espéret made a gesture of astonishment. "What are you saying?"

"The truth. I no longer drink the liquor of forgetfulness."

"Why? Why not?"

"Because," she said, gazing at him with eyes filled with amour, "in seeing you, in hearing you, in living with you, I understood that there was a difference between us, a distance that I wanted to eradicate."

"So?"

"So, I wanted to become a woman similar to the women of your homeland, of the Earth that you've quit."

"But that's impossible, Rasôh!"

"It's true, however." And after a long pause she added: "For a year, I haven't been drinking anything but water."

Espéret shivered.

"So," she went on, "for you, for love of you, because of you, I've known the love of the women of Earth; I've known their joys, their happiness, their intoxications. And today, I know their cruel dolors, I know all their sufferings, and I've savored all their bitterness."

"You're jealous?"

"I love you."

He took her hands, gently.

"Oh," she said, raising her beautiful eyes, moist with tears, toward him, "don't feel pity for me, but come back to me...and I'll be so happy!"

283

The Earthman, the man who was so well able to dissimulate his most secret thoughts, reappeared.

"But Rasôh, I still love you," he said.

"No," replied the faithful Martian woman. "No, it's Thé that you love, and it's for Thé that you're sacrificing me."

Espéret reflected momentarily. "And what if I were?" he said. "Wouldn't I be doing what all the Martians do?"

"You're not a Martian."

"But what are you, then, Rasôh?"

"What am I? A woman! A woman who loves you!"

She pronounced the last words with an emphasis so profound, and an emotion so great, that he understood, then, the immense amour that his companion felt for him.

"Pity me, Rasôh," he said, caressing her beautiful hair. "Pity me and forgive me if I've made you suffer. But I swear to you that I'm no longer the master of my will, that I'm carried away by a force against which all resistance is impossible, and that I can't...no, that I can't not tell you what I would have liked to hide from you at any price."

The poor woman had risen to her feet. "That's all right, my friend," she said, sadly. "I've understood."

She headed for the door.

"You're leaving me?" he said.

"Yes."

"You'll come back, at least?"

"Perhaps."

And, lifting the door-curtain, she disappeared.

Meanwhile, the Marquis and the doctor, anxious about their friend after what they had learned and what they had seen, had gone to the king's apartment.

Thaû saw them immediately, and received the confidence of their anxieties on the subject of the engineer. Then he said to them, smiling: "Have no fear, Messieurs. Don't worry about your friend. On our planet, there is not and never has been a tragic end to an amorous adventure."

"But there is on Earth," Valsorres exclaimed, "and our friend Espéret isn't a Martian."

"That's true. Believe me, though, calm your alarms. And to tranquilize you entirely," the king said, in taking his leave of them, "I'll tell you one thing: if it becomes necessary. I'll look into it."

While our two friends were in the king's apartment, Rasôh went to the apartment of the dancer Thé, into which she was introduced immediately.

Thé came to meet her and invited her to sit down "I've guessed the motive for your visit, Rasôh."

Rasôh replied in a dull voice: "Thé, my friend Espéret is suffering and desolate. Because of you, he's unhappy and desperate. I would never have believed that amour could make someone suffer so much."

"He's a man of Earth," said Thé.

Rasôh looked at the dancer. "And what if I told you that I'm suffering as much as, or more than, him?"

"I wouldn't believe you."

"What if I affirmed that my nights are sleepless, and that my eyes are always full of tears?"

"I wouldn't believe you. What! You, a Martian woman, can suffer from amour, and from amour for an inhabitant of Earth?"

"I'm no longer a Martian."

"What are you, then, Rasôh?"

"What am I? I'm Espéret's wife."

"I know that."

"But what you don't know is that for him, I would quit everything—our homeland, our sovereigns, my sisters, my memories—and I'd go with him to Earth, to distant Sila, if he wanted to take me there."

"You'd do that?"

"I'd do that."

Little Thé had taken Rasôh's hands in hers. She met her eyes with her own pure gaze. After a pause, she said to her. "You're troubling me profoundly, my friend, by telling me about your chagrin. I'm suffering from your suffering and I share your dolor."

"But you alone can make that suffering cease!"

The dancer reflected momentarily. She appeared to make a grave resolution. Then, leaning toward Espéret's companion, she clasped her in her alabaster arms and kissed her tenderly.

"You shall be satisfied, Rasôh," she said to her. "Listen to what I'm going to tell you. But this, I'm telling to you alone. To you alone I'm confiding a redoubtable secret. Swear that you will never reveal it to anyone—you understand, not to anyone in the world."

And slowly, in a low voce, she revealed the mystery of souls; she gave her the secret of the invincible charm that she had discovered, and which gave her the absolute power she could exercise at will over all those who approached her.

When she had finished, Rasôh threw herself at her knees.

"Thé," she said to her, "you are the noblest creature that exists. You are the greatest of all our sisters. What you are doing for me is sublime."

"Yes, Rasôh, for you," Thé replied. And she added, in a dull voice: "For you...and for *him*."

Two large tears fell from her beautiful eyes on to the forehead of Espéret's friend.

Days had passed, and more days.

Valsorres and Portier had tried all means to distract Espéret and extract him from his melancholy, but neither the prospect of the most brilliant fêtes or the proposition of the most captivating scientific endeavors succeeded in tear the engineer away from the memory of his little dancer.

She, however, remained invisible.

When the beautiful Rasôh encountered our two friends, she did not hide from them either the profound chagrin she was experiencing or the anxiety that the somber sadness of her dear Espéret was causing her.

After a few days, the engineer could no longer stand it. Determined to try anything to see Thé again, no matter what the cost, he was going to the actors' quarter when one of the women in service at the gate told him that he little dancer wanted to see him.

Mad with joy and emotion, he headed for the small house that she occupied. As he approached it, however, he observed with surprise that the young woman's dwelling was brightly lit, and that couples were going into it one after another.

Then he decided to penetrated into his idol's sanctuary.

As soon as Thé saw him she advanced toward him, her hands extended and her face smiling.

"Oh, my friend," she said to him, in her musical voice, "I'm very glad to see you here and to be able to converse with you one last time."

And, leaving her guests, among whom were Dr. Portier and the Marquis de Valsorres, who came to shake their friend's hand, she drew him into a small drawing rom.

Espéret looked at her passionately. "Why are you hiding?" he asked her, in a voice trembling with emotion. "Why do you no longer want me to be able to see you?" The orchestra that was playing in one of the dancer's reception rooms made a muffled accompaniment to his plaint. He went on: "Have you forgotten, then, that away from you I'm suffering to the point of despair?"

She looked into his eyes for a long time. "No, my friend, I haven't forgotten. I haven't forgotten anything. But now I can tell you that your pain will cease."

"No!"

"Yes, since the cause that gave birth to it will cease."

He looked at her, stupefied. "What do you mean, Thé? Oh, I'm afraid of understanding you. You're driving me mad!"

Thé took him by the hand. "You'll find out."

She took him into the room where the guests were. With an extreme surprise, he then perceived his faithful companion Rasôh, who advanced toward him, smiling, more beautiful than ever, with spring in her face and the sky in her eyes. She seemed completely changed; she seemed a different woman from his friend of previous days.

"How cheerful and happy you seem!" he said to her, with a smile full of irony.

"Yes, I'm happy, my friend...very happy," she added, looking at him with an expression of the most profound tenderness.

He was very surprised by the gleam in her eyes; in her company, he felt as if strange effluvia were brushing him with an almost immaterial contact; he felt invaded by an entirely new sentiment. But, perceiving Thé chatting with Valsorres, Portier and a group of Martians, he no longer thought about anything but his idol.

The latter made him a sign to approach; he went to her, and her interlocutors stood aside discreetly.

He repeated then to the little dancer, perhaps for the thousandth time, the ardent words that expressed his amour. But she listened to them smiling. At a sign she made, all the guests withdrew, with the exception of Valsorres, Portier and Rasôh.

Then Thé addressed Espéret. "My friend," she said, "I have told you, and I repeat, that I love you as much as I can love anyone—but that isn't sufficient for your soul of an inhabitant of Earth. And in the meantime, one of my sisters is desolate because you are abandoning her. I don't want your suffering to continue."

Espéret made a despairing gesture.

"Wait, friend," she continued. "In order for happiness to return to both your souls, I shall disappear, and you will never see little Thé again. Between you and her I shall put an unbridgeable distance. Later, when you have returned to the distant world that saw your birth you will only remember that for you, because of you, the little dancer who loves you..."

"What are you saying, Thé?" roared Espéret. "You said 'who loves you...'"

"...Or who loved you, has delivered the secret she had extracted of the mysterious nature of souls, and which was to render her name immortal throughout the centuries, to the person who was suffering because of her."

At that moment, Rasôh had fallen to her knees before Thé, whose visage was resplendent with a celestial beauty. "Thé," she cried, kissing her hands, "I swear to you that your secret will die with me and that no one will ever know it."

"Adieu, friend," said the dancer, disengaging herself from Rasôh's embrace and extending her hand to Espéret. "Adieu...forever."

The engineer was devastated.

"Oh, not to see you again, not to hear your voice again...oh, The! Oh!"

But Thé, in an exquisite caress, took Espéret's head in her small hands, deposited a long kiss on his forehead and then, indicating Rasôh, said: "Love her well, my friend. She has a noble heart; she is worthy of you and she will be able to make you forget the woman that you will never see again."

And she disappeared, leaving her friend crushed by dolor.

The Rasôh drew the despairing unfortunate outside the house where he had just experienced the greatest pain of his entire existence.

Then, days succeeded days and weeks succeeded weeks.

Little by little, Espéret saw the radiant image of Thé fading into an indecisive mist. It was still an exquisite memory, to be sure, but which was translated by a gentle and consoling sensation instead of imposing itself by means of dolor and bitter regrets.

And at the same time, his sentiments for Rasôh became more vivid.

At first there was gratitude and a profound sympathy; then came a great affection, and that affection did not take long to give way to a powerful amour for the faithful friend who had consoled him in his trouble and who united herself with him in all the ardor of an ever-present amity.

Rasôh was radiant. She was swimming in happiness. She knew the reason for the phenomenon that was being accomplished in her friend's soul, but she had sworn to little Thé never to reveal the secret by means of which she was to reconquer the soul of the infidel forever, and she kept her word.

Valsorres and Portier were delighted by their friend's "mental cure." They had resumed their insouciant and free existence.

One day, Thaû asked the Marquis for news of Espéret, whose visits had become rarer.

"But my cousin," Henri replied, "Espéret is in love with Rasôh to the highest degree, and savoring an unequaled happiness with his friend. Then, after a momentary pause, he added: "How right you were, Thaû, when you said that everything sorts itself out on your delightful world!"

"Wasn't I? And your friend Espéret is no longer thinking about Thé?"

"I believe that Rasôh's touching tenderness has enabled him to forget the little dancer with whom he was once so infatuated."

"I'm certain of it," said Thaû.

"That's veritably extraordinary," murmured Portier. "How can it be explained that such a sincere and violent passion was able to vanish so rapidly? I don't understand it! In truth, it beats me!"

"That," replied Thaû, "is little Thé's secret—who, admit it, showed herself to be truly heroic in the circumstances. That secret is now Rasôh's, and be sure, Messieurs, that she isn't a woman to reveal it to others."

XIII. In the course of which we shall see how Thomas and his companions quit the hospitable planet.

We have seen our three scientists in their visits and in their studies; to them, seduced by the beauties of scientific research, the time seemed short; they observed, they studied and they worked during the day, and in the evening, the company of Thaû, Saâh and their friends relaxed them from their daily labors, while the food and drink they absorbed gave them strength, youth and forgetfulness of the past.

They had no thought, therefore, of quitting their enchanting abode.

But was it the same for Thomas? That is what we are about to see.

By virtue of his arrival on Mars, the good Thomas had been abruptly elevated from the condition of domestic to that of bourgeois. An amiable and beautiful companion did her best to make the time of his sojourn seem brief. In spite of all the pleasures that he savored without reserve, however, in spite of the warmth of the embalmed air that he breathed, and which permitted the Martians to wear lighter garments than his own, in spite of the tobacco that his friend had procured, and in spite of the manille that he had taught his new companions, Thomas was bored.

Visits to factories had no attraction for him. On the other hand, he frequented towns, centers of habitation; there he lingered in places of pleasure, where his status as a guest of Thaû and Saâh opened all doors to him. Accompanied by his inseparable Hina, he was seen in all the places where people amused themselves.

He had quickly learned a few words of the Martian language, and like a native, he was able to address the women he brushed in passing with the engaging remark: "Mohr wicki pour hasa can stichel!"

But as we have said, Thomas was bored. Thomas found the time long, and what made him find it even longer, above all, was the privation of his favorite drink, wine.

Yes, Thomas missed Burgundy and Bordeaux, the red and white wines that had rendered his sojourn on Earth so pleasant. He had tried in vain, in all science, to make do with the pink and yellow liquids, tarass and zoreb, that the beautiful Hina served him; he did not find them "uplifting" and preferred to stick to pure water, which at least reminded him of something terrestrial.[34]

As for nourishment, Thomas was one of those people who place the pleasure of eating above the need to be nourished. Now, although the food that was

---

[34] The authors appear to have forgotten which of the two liquids is which, although there was a certain amount of confusion when they were first introduced.

served to him was nutritious, it was small in volume; in brief it "went down too quickly." and that was not to the worthy fellow's liking.

In consequence, not absorbing the pink liquid, Thomas was not rejuvenated, and, not absorbing the yellow liquid, he did not forget. Alone of the four voyagers, he had kept before him his watch and his notebook. He wound the former carefully, and every day he marked another figure on the paper. He therefore knew how long he had been on Mars and how long ago he had quit the Earth.

Several times, he had tried to talk to Espéret and the Marquis about it, but they, absorbed in their impassioning studies, had sent him away. So the only consolation that worthy fellow had was dressing from time to time in his "North Pole outfit," as he called it, and going with Hina, dressed in the same fashion, to spend a few hours in the *Fusée*, which was still in the place where it had touched down on the planet. It was necessary, in order to get there, to leave the warm subterranean dwellings and brave the cold of the Martian atmosphere, but Thomas imposed that constraint on himself in order to spend a few quarter hours, as he put it, in a corner of the Earth, which he regretted deeply.

Over time, his regrets became an obsession, and Thomas natural cheerfulness felt its effect. His brow only cleared in the presence of Hina's affectionate smile, but whenever his companion went away, he became melancholy and pensive again.

Then he began to look for means of extracting Espéret, the Marquis and Portier from the double seduction of intelligence and pleasure that was exercised upon them by the existence they were leading. He racked his brains to succeed in that, but he could not find any, and despaired of achieving the slightest result. He saw himself condemned to end his days on that planet, where Earth only appeared as a tiny grain of luminous rice, and glimpsed with terror the endless sequence of days without wine that extended lamentably on that soil, otherwise so hospitable to him and his masters.

The seemed to have forgotten the Earth and those they had left behind there; they were no longer thinking about anything but the present, they no longer had any other concern than their scientific work, or any other pleasures than the company of their friends or the splendid fêtes in which Thaû and Saâh invited them to take part.

And thus the days, the months, and even the years passed and fled.

The month of March 1918 arrived.

Thomas could no longer stand it. He ruminated an escape plan, and by dint of cerebral mastication, he ended up conceiving one and preparing its realization he greatest secrecy.

In the course of one of his visits to the *Fusée* he had brought back a small bottle that he had borrowed from the on-board pharmacy. It was a powerful anesthetic potion, odorless sand tasteless, prepared by Portier, which had the advantages of chloroform without the inconveniences. The young physician had found the formula himself, had experimented with it carefully before the departure and had often talked about it, describing the method of its employment.

Thomas remembered all that precisely; he also knew that the awakening of the sleeping subject could be provoked instantaneously by the respiration of a little chlorhydrate of ammonium; by virtue of living in the laboratory, the worthy fellow had, as you can see, picked up a "smidgen" of chemistry.

Then he prepared the execution of his project.

One evening, after a great fête, in the course of which there had been dancing, in which, in which the three scientists and their friends had taken part, they had returned to their apartments and, vanquished by fatigue, had not taken long to fall into a deep sleep.

Then Thomas, accompanied by the faithful Hina, who had been completely subjugated and had become his minion, went into the rooms in which his three companions were sleeping and made them respire the soporific liquid.

When they were thus anesthetized, Thomas, aided by Hina, dressed them "for the North Pole" and the worthy fellow and his companion carried the three sleeping friends, one by one, through the deserted tunnels to the exit door. In a final journey, they transported their rifles, pistols and knives. Thomas had taken care to mix a few drops of his potion with the drinks of the two guards on watch, so that they too were deeply asleep. When the three scientists were taken into the vestibule of the exit, Thomas went to open the door behind which he had placed a small handcart, under the pretext of bringing back various objects from the *Fusée*.

Then, aided by Hina, he loaded the Marquis, Espéret and the doctor, still asleep, on to the vehicle and transported them to the *Fusée*.[35] Still with the aid of his faithful friend, he caused them to pass successively through the ascension shaft, and from there into the interior of the chamber.

Then he came back and took Hina in his arms, tenderly.

"Come with us!" he said to her, pointing at the sky.

Hina gave him a long kiss. "My friend," she said to him, "I will follow you wherever you wish. Where you go, I will go; where you stop, I will stop; where you live, I will live; where you die, I will die."

"Come, then."

They went into the chamber, all of whose panels they closed with care.

You will recall that Thomas, without being charged with the direction, had nevertheless been gradually initiated in the maneuvering.

He was not stupid, the good Thomas. He had remembered everything perfectly; every time he had returned to spend a few hours on the *Fusée*, he had made sure that he controls were in a good state.

---

[35] The authors seem to have forgotten that the two-kilometer journey to the rocket is impossible without breathing apparatus, because of the low atmospheric pressure.

As soon as the panels were closed, he activated the transformer and the cathode ray tube. Then he took a pinch of radioactive powder from the virium reserve with his lead spoon, and put it in the combustion chamber; after that he directed the beam of cathode rays himself, concentrated by a quartz lens.

A violent hiss was heard and the vehicle trembled. Thomas increased the dose of virium; the *Fusée* rose up lightly. Then he activated the other two combustion chambers and the projectile quit the Martian soil with a velocity that increased progressively.

Thomas looked out though the rear porthole.

"Adieu, Mars!" he said. "Adieu, my old ball!"

It was thus that he quit the planet where he had lived for four years.

Scarcely had the *Fusée* been launched into space that Thomas thought about waking his companions. He made them respire the emanations of ammonium chlorhydrate, but it was necessary for the operation to be repeated, so profound was the slumber provoke by Portier's anesthetic.

Finally, the Marquis was the first to open his eyes.

"Where are we?" he asked, gradually collecting his thoughts.

"On the way to Saturn," said the worthy fellow.

The Marquis recognized Thomas. "Oh, it's you my old Thomas. But where the devil am I?"

Still under the influence of the Martian beverages, the Marquis had not recovered completely his memory of the past.

"We're in the *Fusée*, our good *Fusée*, Monsieur le Marquis, and we're finally going to arrive at the destruction of our voyage in the heavens, Saturn."

"Saturn?" asked the Marquis, as if emerging from a dream. Then, perceiving Hina, who was waking Espéret, he asked: "Who's that?"

"That's Hina, Monsieur le Marquis, my Martian companion, whom I've brought with us—and you can thank her, the brave girl, for without her, I wouldn't have been able to get you out of there."

"Get us out? We're no longer on Mars?"

"No, Monsieur le Marquis no. I repeat to you, we're on our way to Saturn and its ring...you know, the ring of light."

At that moment, Espéret came round. Hina occupied herself then with the doctor.

The engineer manifested the same amazement. It required a full quarter of an hour for him to recognize the *Fusée* and understand that they had escaped from Mars, thanks to his faithful Thomas.

Finally, Dr. Portier woke up in his turn.

When the three scientists were able to stand up, Valsorres said to Thomas: "Explain to us, in sum, what you've done and how you did it."

Thomas sat down bedside Hina and said: "Messieurs, what I've done I did for you, for your families and for your country. You were blockaded in that accursed planet where one never saw the open air and where the scientists had captured you by means of your weakness. They made you eat and drink a heap of drugs that made you forget the Earth and the people you left behind there. Me, I ate but I didn't drink, so I didn't forget anything and I found the time long, counting the days."

"You counted the days?" said Espéret.

"Yes, Monsieur, and I continued to reset the watches."

Valsorres, Espéret and Portier looked at one another, stupefied. "And how long did we stay on Mars?" asked the Marquis.

"Exactly three years and nine months, Monsieur le Marquis."

"Nearly four years!" said the three men, in chorus.

"No less, Messieurs," replied Thomas, simply.

The Marquis was thoughtful. His memory was coming back to him now. He thought about the dolor that his wife, his sister and his aunt must be feeling, in the belief that they were irredeemably lost.

"But tell us how you were able to succeed in getting us out of that prison where we were so comfortable," said Espéret.

Thomas then told the story of the escape. He described the ruse he had employed, stressed the precious collaboration that the devotion of his companion Hina had furnished, and how, thanks to the woman's muscular vigor, they had been transported to the *Fusée*.

But how were you able to make the vehicle depart?"

"Oh, that was easy, Messieurs. I've often watched you while you operated the machine, and I just did the same. Only now, it's necessary for you to put your hand to the wheel, for, about navigating through the stars, it's necessary to admit to you that I don't know anything."

The three men shook the worthy fellow's hand cordially, and embraced Hina affectionately. The latter took off her North Pole costume, as Thomas called it, but, like the most elegant of Parisiennes, she had "nothing to wear," so she dressed like a man in Espéret's clothes, those that fit her best.

When Hina was dressed in that fashion, she turned to the three men and said: "My friends, I want you to take away one last benefit from my planet Raas; this is what I succeeded in bringing, secretly."

She took out a square bottle from a little bag; it contained a dark pink liquid; uncorked, it spread a characteristic etheric odor. The four men looked at it uncomprehendingly.

"It's the concentrated principle of zoreb, the pink liquid that conserves youth. With one drop in a measure of water, you can make a beverage that prevents the person drinking it from aging. There's enough here to make more than a hundred thousand does of zoreb; you'll remain young and strong, and you'll think that you owe your youth to your friend Hina, whom you'll all love as much as one another."[36]

Very emotional, the four men clasped Hina in their arms again. Immediately, they made a beverage with a liter of water and a drop of the elixir, which Dr. Portier measured carefully with a drop-counter.

They immediately felt restored and refreshed; their thoughts were clearer.

Valsorres was the first to take stock of the situation.

My friends," he said, "let's resume our interrupted journey; let's finally go to Saturn."

"Let's go to Saturn!" replied the voyagers.

And Valsorres, climbing up the superior ladder, found his reference points among the stars and, activating the lateral valves, directed the *Fusée* toward the Ring of Light.

---

[36] The authors also appear to have forgotten the entire subplot regarding the fickle Espéret's violent infatuations and their strange consequences, to which no further mention is made in the present story. That might have occasioned some reaction from the feuilleton's readers, as both Rasôh and Thé make a belated and somewhat apologetic reappearance in the sequel, *Le Loi de Mars*.

PART FIVE: THE RING OF LIGHT

I. In which we see the Fusée *after a few encounters, finally penetrate the Ring of Light.*

The *Fusée*, therefore, was en route for Saturn.

The voyagers felt embarrassed from the physiological point of view. That was because, for four years, they had been living on a planet on which the intensity of weight was only half what it is on Earth.

Now, abruptly, not only did they find themselves back in the conditions of their terrestrial weight, but in even more aggravated conditions. You will remember, in fact, that Valsorres had regulated the expulsion of gas in such a fashion that the projectile was animated by a constant acceleration equal to eleven tenths that of gravity.

Thus, the first moments of the second part of the voyage were marked by a kind of lassitude, general fatigue and torpor. The organs of the conquerors of space needed to acclimatize gradually to that new gravitational regime.

It was then that they appreciated at its full value the importance of the elixir brought by Hina. Thanks to a few glasses of a slightly more concentrated beverage, our friends were able to overcome the muscular fatigue resulting from the excess of weight, and gradually, they found their condition absolutely normal again.

In any case, the beautiful Hina was the joy of the voyage. Always cheerful, always in a good humor, she lent herself to all he asks the she accomplished with the greatest intelligence and a marvelous dexterity. Provided that her dear Thomas was content, she was satisfied. She understood how to cook marvelously, and that by veritable instinct, for on Mars, she had not devoted herself to that occupation at all, being part of Saâh's retinue.[37]

During one meal that was taken board the *Fusée*. Portier asked her: "I'd like to know what Thaû and Saâh thought on seeing that we had decamped?"

It was Thomas who replied. "I didn't leave like a boor," he said. "I left a letter on the table of Monsieur le Marquis' apartment addressed to Monsieur Thaû and Madame Saâh, to tell them the reasons for our departure."

"What?" said Espéret. "You wrote a letter?"

---

[37] Oddly enough, Hina does not seem to be affected by the sudden increase in her weight, after a lifetime of adaptation to Martian gravity, and seems to thrive on it.

"Yes, Monsieur le Marquis," said Thomas, modestly. "Oh, not without difficulty; I had to redo it several times; it was when I came with Hina to take a little rest in the *Fusée*. Finally, by dint of hard work and searching the dictionary, I finished up turning out a letter and I put it in an envelope addressed to your Martian cousins. Anyway, I kept a copy here."

He addressed his friend: "Hina, go fetch the piece of paper I put in the desk drawer."

Ever obliging, Hina got up and came back to suit with her friends with the requested sheet of paper, which she handed to the Marquis.

The latter unfolded it and read:

"My dear cousin Thaû and my beautiful cousin Saâh...."

"What! You impudent phenomenon! You permitted yourself to write in my name!"

"Well, Monsieur le Marquis, I couldn't ask you to do it, since you were too well pinched by the Martian scientists and the beautiful Martian women; and then, too, I couldn't write in my own name."

"The animal has an answer for everything," said Espéret.

"In any case," Portier observed, "Thaû doesn't know your handwriting."

"That's true," said the Marquis.

He continued reading the letter:

"My dear cousin Thaû and my beautiful cousin Saâh.

"When you receive this letter we will be far from your globe, where you have accorded us a hospitality that we shall never forget.

"You have given us all the satisfactions of science and you have rejuvenated us by means of the most refined pleasures. And above all, by revealing to us that there was a relationship between us, you have made us penetrate into a family atmosphere, which we could not have hoped to find on a distant planet..."

"But that's very good, your letter, my old Thomas," said the doctor.

Thomas lowered his eyes modestly.

Valsorres continued reading:

"It is not without regret that we are quitting you, my dear cousins; it is not without melancholy that we are separating from our beautiful and charming companions, Zith, Rasôh and Daâh. Tell them that their memory will never quit us.

"We are taking with us Hina, who has not wanted to quit her friend Thomas, We shall thus have one of your people with us, with whom we can talk about Mars, its princes and its inhabitants, when we have returned to the midst of our own people.

"Au revoir, my dear cousin Thaû; I kiss your hands, my beautiful cousin Saâh.

"Henri, Marquis de Valsorres."

When the Marquis had finished reading, he turned to Thomas. "You know, you old brigand, that's quite well turned. I certainly wouldn't have done any better. You've said everything that was necessary, as it was necessary to say it. How the devil did you learn to compose a letter like that?"

"Well, Monsieur le Marquis, I've read a great deal; then, I was trying to write, and when I write, I think otherwise than when I speak."

"Oh, you write, rogue?"

"Yes, Monsieur, and I've even put in a notebook, day by day, everything that happened to us on that planet."

The three men looked at one another, laughing.

Thus, thanks to the worthy Thomas, they had what none of them had thought of ding: a diary of their sojourn on Martian soil.

"Thomas," said the Marquis, "you're a truly worthy fellow; I congratulate you and I thank you. And Henri de Valsorres shook the good servant's hand warmly.

Meanwhile, the voyage continued at lightning speed.

Espéret, who had increased the dose of virium, counted on reaching a velocity of a thousand kilometers a second. It is true that it augmented the acceleration and, in consequence, the apparent weight of the voyagers, and hence produced a surplus of fatigue for them, but thanks to Hina's marvelous elixir, that fatigue was supported lightly, and the pioneers of the heavens did not feel any lassitude.

The distance of Saturn from the Earth is about seventeen times that of Mars, It would therefore have been necessary to anticipate thirty-four or thirty-five days of travel with the acceleration anticipated at the start. But since the voyagers could support a greater acceleration, it was necessary to take advantage of the windfall and go at a greater velocity.

They rendered thanks to Hina for the good idea that she had had.

Nevertheless, an incident occurred that caused a slight delay to our friends' voyage.

Between Mars and Jupiter, a veritably swarm of tiny planets circulates, forming a sort of ring; terrestrial astronomers presently know a few more than nine hundred. The largest are a few hundred kilometers in diameter, the smallest a few dozen at the most. Valsorres and Espéret had certainly anticipated traversing that ring of small heavenly bodies, but they had relied on the data known on Earth.

If one takes the distance from the Earth to the sun as a unit, the distance to Mars is approximately 1.5, and the mean distance of the asteroids 2.5. Our two scientists, therefore, had not expected to encounter the first of the tiny planets until at least a day and a half after their departure from Mars. However, they had scarcely quit Martian soil for twenty hours when Espéret, who was on watch, uttered an appeal for help to the Marquis.

The latter ran to the watch station. With his finger, Espéret showed him a bright globe that seemed to be approaching the *Fusée* with great rapidity. Valsorres immediately changed course by means of the lateral valves.

He was just in time. The globe passed very close to the projectile—so close that, by virtue of its attraction, it imprinted an abrupt deviation upon it, which the voyagers felt.

"Damn!" said Espéret. "Is that a minor planet already?"

"I believe so," said Valsorres. "At any rate, it merits the term minor; it's scarcely three or four hundred meters in diameter."

"But what astonishes me," said the engineer, "is to encounter one so close to Mars."

Valsorres reflected. "It's surprising, evidently," he said, "But it's necessary for us to expect other surprises too. Our terrestrial astronomers know about a thousand of these little bodies, but their observation is difficult. The smallest that they've been able to observe with their equatorials, with great difficulty, still have a diameter of a few kilometers, whereas the one we just saw only had a few hectometers, and is certainly invisible from Earth. There are doubtless many similar ones—and look, here comes a second one."

In fact, a second bright globe was rapidly approaching the *Fusée*. It was necessary once again to change the latter's route in order to avoid the encounter with the celestial body, which would have been disastrous. It went past the projectile with a vertiginous velocity.

Espéret had picked up a pair of prismatic binoculars of large magnification. He aimed it at another bright dot that appeared to the right and was visibly growing. "And there's a third," he said.

Given of the impossibility of observing it during its transversal passage, because of its excessive velocity, he observed it head on while it was approaching the vehicle.

"That one must also be very small; it looks exactly like the Moon."

Valsorres had also picked up his binoculars. "My word, yes," he said. "Craters and 'seas.' One might think that it were a miniature of our satellite."

"Look out!" exclaimed Espéret.

Valsorres only just had time to activate the lateral valve; the planeticule had just passed only a few kilometers away from the *Fusée*. And other globes could be seen in the sky, in immense numbers.

"Aha!" said the Marquis. "Is it a game of bowls?"

It was more than a game of bowls; it was like a volley of gigantic grapeshot launched by a colossal army; the two men required all the quickness of their eyes and all their mental composure to maneuver in the midst of the celestial machine-gun fire. It was necessary not to be distracted for an instant.

In an hour the *Fusée* encountered more than a thousand asteroids, some that they veered to avoid, and others that passed above, below or alongside them.

Two hours after the first encounter, they saw one of the planets that was much larger than the rest.

"That must be Ceres," said Valsorres.

"I believe so," said Espéret. "It's big enough."

Indeed, a planet truly worthy of the name was approaching; it did not intersect the trajectory of the *Fusée*. The two scientists observed it as it drew closer.

"Can you see?" said Espéret.

"Yes," Valsorres replied.

They were both examining the visibly growing body curiously.

"Active volcanoes!" said the Marquis.

It was correct; jets of fame were spurting from the surface of the planet; under the pressure of its igneous core, lava was breaking through the crust, doubtless of excessively feeble thickness, and spreading over the exterior in terrible eruptions.

The two scientists could not take their eyes away from that majestic spectacle.

Portier had come to join them. "Look out!" he cried. "Here comes another planet!"

Valsorres recommenced the play of the valves. The planet that it was necessary to avoid was tiny enough, but what rendered it veritably curious was that it was escorted by a flock of minuscule satellites, of which the largest, illuminated by the already distant light of the sun was scarcely thirty or forty meters in size. As for the planet itself, it might have been three kilometers in diameter.

Valsorres and Espéret were struck by astonishment.

"So," said the Marquis, "there are worlds on decreasing scales. Jupiter and its satellites are a miniature of the solar system; but this is a further reduction of it, on an infinitely smaller scale."

"Yes," said Espéret. "And to think that that reduction goes all the way to the atom, which is itself a solar system in miniature, formed by a central nucleus around which, like as many infinitesimal planets, the mysterious electrons gravitate that modern physicists have conceived, and out of which they have made such a fecund theory."

For four hours the two scientists had to redouble their attention. During that interval they were able to observe more than three thousand asteroids, and as they had only cut one part of the ring, Valsorres estimated their probable number at more than twenty thousand. You will remember that the Martian astronomers had given them the figure of six thousand.

"That's something that will make astronomers dream when we tell them on, our return," said the Marquis, simply.

The *Fusée* had taken about six hours to traverse the whole of the ring of minor planets. It was now heading for Saturn.

Espéret had talked about stopping on Jupiter "in passing" but Valsorres had opposed it.

"Jupiter isn't in conjunction with Saturn at the moment," he said. That would impose a detour that would double the length of our journey. We'll pass relatively close to the giant planet; we'll therefore be able to photograph it in conditions unknown on Earth. That's already a great deal."

Three days later, in fact, they passed within a relatively short distance of Jupiter, and saw the disk, flattered by centrifugal force, increase in diameter as they got closer. Valsorres then set up his photographic telescope in order to take pictures of the enormous globe, the nineteen satellites of which, gravitating around it, could be seen with the naked eye.

While Valsorres was taking photographs, Espéret and Portier examined the disk of the planet with their most powerful binoculars. It seemed ten times larger than the full Moon appears to us. They saw the bands of thick cloud in its atmosphere. They saw the mysterious "red spot" that intrigues the astronomers of Earth so much. At that short distance, however, the red spot was resolved into a veritable seed-bed of individuals spots, very close together but nevertheless distinct. The other mysterious spot, the "perturbation," was also visible, which took on the characteristic appearance of a dappled sky at that limited distance.

What was the composition of those patches, which stood out so distinctly against the clouds of the Jovian atmosphere? A mystery, for all those who could not or did not want to traverse the layer of those clouds and descend to the surface, doubtless still hot, of the gigantic planet.

Meanwhile, the *Fusée* sped onwards, without encumbrance.

The disk of Jupiter shrank with distance. That of Saturn, by contrast, was increasing in a sensible manner. From one day to the next it was seen on a larger scale, and with simple binoculars the ring and the ten principal satellites were clearly visible; it was even becoming possible to glimpse a few of the fifteen other, much smaller moons, that the astronomers of Mars had shown to Valsorres and Espéret.

Six days after passing within the closest distance of Jupiter, Saturn appeared as a globe whose diameter was more than twenty times that of the Moon seen from the Earth. A magnificent spectacle was offered to the voyagers who perceived, in all its dazzling splendor, the admirable Ring of Light that surrounded the planet with its resplendent halo.

The concentric circles of the ring were visible, as were the great bands, doubtless made of thick cloud, that envelop the planet parallel to the plane of the ring, and now the twenty-five satellites could be observed: the twenty-five moons that must illuminate the nights of the immense globe with their varied crescents.

Valsorres and Espéret no longer quit the ocular lenses of their binoculars. With the aid of the micrometer, the Marquis continually calculated the distance that separated him from the globe toward which his efforts were extended. Already, the image of the Saturnian disk surpassed the limits of the instrument's field; they were beginning to get very close to it. To the naked eye, the planet appeared to cover almost half of the sky.

Valsorres began to make preparations for the arrival, for with the enormous speed of the *Fusée*, deduced from measuring the decreasing dimensions of Jupiter, our voyagers must have been traveling at nearly twelve hundred kilometers a second. He therefore carried out the maneuvers of rotating the *Fusée* end for end; henceforth, its base was turned toward the globe of Saturn. In spite of that rotation, however, its center of gravity continued to move in the original direction, irrespective of the cessation of the propulsive jet. A few moments later, however, the Marquis brought the gaseous discharges back into play, this time operating in the opposite direction, beginning to brake and slow down the progress of the *Fusée*.

The latter was now drawing closer to the planet. Valsorres wanted to land it above the ring, in its northern hemisphere. Already the *Fusée* had the ring to the left; its structure could be observed in marvelous detail. It was made of an infinity of juxtaposed corpuscles, in such numbers that their ensemble gave the impression to the naked eye of a continuous surface.

After an hour of constant deceleration, the *Fusée* began to penetrate into the dense clouds of the Saturnian atmosphere.

The moment was critical.

Valsorres could not perceive the surface of the planet. He assumed that the thickness of its atmosphere must be in proportion to the diameter of the dusk, and, by comparing it to the terrestrial atmosphere, he estimated it to be between two hundred and three hundred kilometers.

In order to avoid a brutal and disastrous impact, therefore he had to slow down the descent of the *Fusée*, which, now solicited by the attraction of the planet, was submissive to the gravity exercised by it.

Portier had the idea of consulting the special barometer, the elastic tube of which could be put in communication with the exterior. A few minutes after the entry into the clouds, the instrument showed a pressure of 340 millimeters. That pressure increased slowly.

"We're not falling rapidly," observed the young physician.

"So much the better," replied Espéret. "Let's slow down even further."

Valsorres augmented the braking by discharging gas.

"Six hundred and ten millimeters," said the doctor.

"Slow down further!" said Espéret.

The velocity diminished again, so that ten seconds later, the barometer only marked 620 millimeters.

"That's good," said the engineer.

That feeble speed of descent was maintained; the barometer rose to 750, then 760, then 770 and then 780.

"Damn!" said the Marquis, "There are high pressures on this planet. We can't be far from the Saturnian surface.

But the *Fusée* was still falling through the clouds.

"Seven ninety-two millimeters," said Portier.

The Marquis slowed the descent forcefully by an energetic braking. The barometer rose slowly to 799 millimeters. Then there was a sort of clearing in the clouds. Thomas, who was observing though the inferior porthole with Hina, shouted: "Look out! We're arriving."

Valsorres released an even more energetic jet.

The *Fusée* suffered a slight shock, and remained immobile.

The voyagers had arrived on Saturn. They were finally at the terminus of their audacious expedition; they could legitimately consider themselves as the first humans to have penetrated the interior of the Ring of Light.

II. In which we see how the Marquis and his companions made contact with Saturnian animals.

The Marquis de Valsorres had not chosen the location of his landing on Saturn at random. He knew that the planet takes more than nineteen years to travel the orbit that it describes around the Sun. During half of that period one face of the ring is illuminated, and during the other, that same face is obscure. He had therefore directed the *Fusée* in such a fashion as to land in the northern hemisphere of the planet; in 1918 the north face of the rings was receiving the pale light of the distant sun, and the immense girdle that surrounds Saturn was projecting its shadow in the southern hemisphere. In those conditions, he was not at risk of finding himself in the zone of the shadow produced by the interposition of the rings.

Scarcely had the *Fusée* set down on Saturnian soil than the voyagers were at the portholes, all their eyes gazing at the aspect of the "earth of the heavens" that was the object of their ambitions.

They were able to observe that the daylight was very faint. The Sun, which, had it been visible, would only have sent about a hundredth of the light it sends to Earth, because of the distance, was hidden by an atmosphere charged with clouds as well. Whatever part of the day it was, the surface of the planet was only illuminated by a kind of gray twilight, which gave a general tint of sadness to objects, and a melancholy character to the landscape.

"Let's go down!" Thomas cried.

"Yes," the Marquis replied, "but not before the doctor has studied the conditions of respirability and temperature of the Saturnian atmosphere, which might have a few surprises in store for us."

Portier had not waited for Valsorres to make that reflection in order to begin his determination. Through an orifice fitted into the wall of the *Fusée* he had first pushed the reservoir of a long thermometer, whose divisions could be read inside the vehicle. After ten minutes, the level, which climbed rapidly, became stationary.

"Thirty-eight degrees," said Portier.

"Thirty-eight degrees!" Espéret repeated. "But that's a tropical temperature."

"Yes," said the Marquis. "That can't be attributed to the Sun's rays. I've calculated what the temperature ought to be in accordance with the distance of the world. If the conditions were the same as on Earth or Mars, it ought to be in the region of a hundred degrees below zero."

"A hundred degrees of frost!" said the doctor.

"At least," said the Marquis. "And yet you find thirty-eight degrees of heat; that shows us that the high temperature of Saturn's atmosphere comes from the ground. That must be of relatively fresh date, and must only constitute a thin crust around the matter in fusion that forms the central mass of the planet."

"That's probable," said Espéret.

"It's certain," the Marquis continued. "The nights will therefore be as warm as the days on this enormous globe, since the high temperature that reigns here isn't due to the alternating appearances of the sun. Now it remains for us to know the composition of that atmosphere before risking our lungs in it."

Portier was in the process of analyzing the Saturnian air.

To begin with, he had extended a long metal tube through the orifice that had served for the extrusion of the thermometer, terminated by a glass tube, which caused the exterior air to bubble into a bottle with two small tubes, into which it was drawn by a pump. The bottle contained a solution of a calcium salt. As soon as the first bubbles of Saturnian air had passed into the solution, it rapidly became turbulent.

"There's a large quantity of carbon dioxide," observed the doctor.

"What do you call a *large quantity*?" asked Valsorres.

"I'll tell you when I've measured it. At first sight, though, I estimate the proportion at one per cent at least."

"One per cent! But in our terrestrial atmosphere, there's only one three-thousandth, at the most."

"That's correct; so the atmosphere of this planet contains at least thirty times as much as ours."

Portier continued his trials. After having collected a certain volume of air, he analyzed it in a test tube, absorbing the oxygen by means of pyrogallic acid and potash.

"I find a little less oxygen than in terrestrial air," he said. "Nineteen per cent instead of twenty-one."

"Fortunately, that deficit will be compensated by the greater pressure," Espéret remarked.

"Yes," replied the doctor. "Our lungs will have almost the same quantity as on Earth."

"We can go out then?" asked Thomas.

"Yes, old chap. Prepare our weapons, and let's be on our guard here. I can see enormous vegetables, as the doctor foresaw, and I have an idea that those vegetables must shelter animals no less enormous."

Thomas climbed into "the loft," as he called the superior chamber, and came back after a few moments carrying three repeater carbines, a double-barreled express rifle, four hunting knives and four pistols. He was also carrying a double-barreled shotgun for Hina, as well as a hatchet, which the robust woman, dressed as a man, passed through her belt.

The basal panel was opened and the five voyagers descended one after another on to the Saturnian soil, after having closed the orifice that served the *Fusée* as a door behind them.

Before venturing over the surface of the planet, Valsorres stopped them and took a small compass from his pocket. "My children," he said, "it's necessary that we can find our way back to our vehicle easily. Now, we can't rely on the sun for guidance; it's invisible, hidden by the clouds. Furthermore, our excursions will have to be of short duration."

"Why?" asked Portier.

"Because the duration of the planet's rotation about its axis, instead of being twenty-four hours, like that of Earth, is only ten and a quarter hours, not even half of ours. We've landed on Saturn a little above the plane of the rings, which is to say, near its equator. Thus, we can expect about five hours of daylight and five hours of night."

"That does indeed limit the duration of our excursions," said Espéret. "But my dear Henri, you spoke of finding our way back to the *Fusée* easily. What do you have to fear on that subject?"

"I simply fear having difficulty orientating ourselves. I've brought a sensitive little compass with me. Well, look!"

The voyagers grouped around the Marquis curiously. The needle of the compass seemed to be motionless.

"But that's because it's orientated toward the north of Saturn," said Espéret.

"We'll see."

The Marquis approached the needle of the compass to the blade of his knife. The needle deviated, but did not return to its initial position immediately when the knife was taken away.

"Damn!" said the engineer. "That's annoying."

"However," said Valsorres, "if the Earth has a magnetism, Saturn, whose primal origin is the same, ought to have one too."

"Unless the origin of our terrestrial magnetism in uniquely due to the Sun. As this world is at a much greater distance from it, its action is much weaker."

Suddenly, the doctor exclaimed: "It moved! It moved!"

In fact, the needle of the little compass shifted—slowly, to be sure, but manifesting a distinct movement of orientation. After a slow oscillation of about twenty seconds, it stopped in a sensibly fixed direction.

"Magnetic north," said the Marquis.

"Yes," replied Espéret.

"Well, then," said the doctor, "we're not entirely disorientated. We have only to take the bearing of the *Fusée*."

"There's a simpler way," said the Marquis. "Since we have no reason to go in one direction rather than another, let's simply march in the direction of the needle; in that way, our route will always be marked."

"That's perfect," said Espéret. He pointed his finger at a sort of hill that was distinguishable against the gray background of the Saturnian sky. "That hill is in a northerly direction. Let's march until we reach it."

That is what was decided,

Valsorres took the head of the columns, with Espéret and Portier next. Thomas and Hina brought up the rear.

The sun must have been rising, because the light appeared to be slightly augmented as the voyagers walked. Several times, Valsorres turned round and, taking the *Fusée* as a reference point as long as it was in sight, he made sure that the magnetic needle was quite constant.

"What do you fear, then?" Portier asked him.

"I feared that the magnetic elements might be very variable, but I see nothing of the sort, and I'm satisfied."

The voyagers, lightly dressed because of the temperature, were advancing slowly and awkwardly over marshy ground. The heat was stifling, the air visibly charged with a enormous quantity of water vapor; the humidity was manifest in multiple ways.

Fortunately, the *Fusée* had landed in a sort of meadow forming a clearing, but all around that clearing, gigantic vegetables were visible. It was not, however, a forest, strictly speaking; it was a sort of immense thicket. Mosses that came up to the waist of the voyagers covered the ground with a continuous layer, above which the stems of immense ferns rose up at intervals.

Portier bent down continually to examine a leaf or a stem.

"Gymnosperms," he said.

And, in fact, the crowns of cedars and pines could be seen, which showed that, in spite of the distance from the sun, the effects of climate were making themselves felt. In spite of that, it was the cryptogams that were dominant, and the ferns attained enormous dimensions, which Portier estimated at more than twenty meters for some of them.

As the voyagers advanced the vegetation became thicker. Under the vaults of foliage, the heat and humidity formed a stifling atmosphere. Fortunately, the passengers of the *Fusée* were only wearing shirts and trousers tightened by leather belts; otherwise they would not have been able to go on.

Thomas had shown Hina how to use her hunting rifle, and by firing her weapon twice at a target, which she had not missed, his devoted companion had proved her intelligence and her skill.

After an hour, they had not yet perceived any living being, whether quadruped, biped or bird. Portier, who was examining with increasing attention the vegetation that unfurled before his eyes, made a remark whose justice struck Valsorres and Espéret.

"One might think that there's a mixture of the Primary, Secondary and Tertiary eras here, for these ferns are characteristic of the Primary Era, while these cedars, pines and palm trees clearly belong to Tertiary times."

The two scientists, formed by the admirable geological education of the École des Mines, could not help confirming that observation, However, Espéret added: "That's true, but we haven't yet seen any specimens of fauna, and who knows whether the animal kingdom might have a few surprises in store?"

"Yes, who knows?" replied Valsorres.

That surprise did not take long to materialize. Only a few minutes had gone by when Thomas shouted, loudly: "A rabbit!"

"A rabbit? Where?" said Valsorres and Espéret, in unison.

"There," said Hina, pointing at a bush that seemed to be agitated by the presence of a hidden animal.

All five of them ran toward the indicated spot and beat the plants with the butts of their rifles. A small quadruped emerged, not much larger than a rabbit, hopping on is hind feet.

"It's a kangaroo!" said Portier.

"No, my friend," Valsorres replied. "It's a specimen of the small marsupials that were the first mammals to appear in the Secondary Era. But look, there are others."

Indeed, a troop of five or six of the little jumping quadrupeds fled from the new arrivals. Thomas had taken the double-barreled rifle with which she was armed from Hina's hands, but Portier stopped him.

"Don't shoot, Thomas," he said "It's unnecessary."

Thomas raised the barrel of the gun again and returned it to Hina. "Why not, Monsieur?" he asked.

"Simply because it's unnecessary. We have enough to eat in our bags, and it's not worth the trouble of killing for the pleasure of killing. Later, we'll see about varying our diet, if we see the necessity of doing so."

The voyagers seemed to have arrived in a region richer in animals. They had only taken a few more steps when a flying creature the size of a chicken rose up in front of them, uttering raucous cries.

Portier watched it flying heavily.

"A pterodactyl," he said, simply.

It was, in fact, one of the flying reptiles with a lizard's beak and the wings of a bat that were the first inhabitants of the air in the Secondary Era. Valsorres and Espéret followed it with their eyes. Suddenly, the latter uttered an exclamation of astonishment.

Another flying creature, a bird this time, with veritable feathers, had also risen up like a pheasant before the hunters. Slightly larger than the previous one, it had a beak in which teeth could be distinguished. It had a veritable tail prolonging the vertebral column, garnished with feathers.

"An archaeopteryx," said Valsorres.

"Yes," Espéret replied. "This really is a Secondary fauna."

"In that case," said the Marquis, "Let's expect to see some specimens of the giants of that epoch."

"At least they can't be hiding in the vegetation!" said the doctor.

"At any rate, let's have our rifles in our hands and let's not separate."

The five voyagers marched in a compact group under the somber crepuscular light coming from the ray of the distant Sun diffused by the thick atmosphere of Saturn.

Suddenly, Hina extended her arm to the right. "Oh!" she said. "Oh!" She could find no other words to depict, I shall not say her fear, for that energetic creature was effortlessly courageous, but her astonishment.

Her four companions looked in the indicated direction, trying to search the semi-darkness of the forest. They were anxious.

Portier spoke first. "It's truly a monster," he said, in a low voice.

It was, indeed, a monster, one of the gigantic saurians that pullulated on Earth at the end of the Jurassic epoch, the terrifying dimensions of which surpass all imagination.

The individual that was approaching was at least thirty or thirty-two meters in height. A ridiculously small head crowned that enormous body, which was supported on a sort of tripod formed by its two hind feet and a formidable tail. Two forepaws, much reduced, served to grip the upper parts of the trees that provided its nutrition.

"A brontosaurus," murmured Portier.

Valsorres and Espéret gazed with wide eyes. "It's more like an atlantosaurus, an individual of the largest species," said the Marquis. "Don't worry; these great herbivorous saurians, stupid beasts, have very small brains. I don't think there's anything to fear."

The five voyagers hid behind the trunk of a stout tree. analogous to one of our cypresses. Motionless, they held their breath.

The enormous animal passed within a few meters of them, fortunately without seeing them. Its head surpassed the summits of the tallest trees; its gigantic feet sank into the damp soil. It went on its way, crushing plants and saplings underfoot.

Suddenly, it uttered a strident cry, to which another cry responded. The voyagers looked in the direction from which the second howl had come, and were struck by fear. Another monster was advancing toward the first. It was not as big, scarcely ten meters tall, but whereas the former, being a herbivore, was not very redoubtable, the second, equipped with a enormous maw armed with terrible teeth, was frightful to behold.

Portier, Valsorres and Espéret were mute with horror. Thomas held Hina tightly in his arms. Curiosity, however, prevailed over fear. Valsorres examined the ferocious monster, which headed toward its enemy with huge strides. The latter, deprived of any means of defense, ought to be easy prey for the terrible carnivore.

"A ceratosaurus," the Marquis whispered to Espéret.

It was, indeed, one of those treble animals. The head, much larger than that of the brontosaurus, was surmounted above the nose by a trenchant horn in the form of an ax; its maw, which it opened in order to roar, allowed the sight of a formidable armament of sharp conical teeth.

It launched itself toward the brontosaurus, whose huge size prevented it from fleeing through the trees. First it placed itself beneath the underside of its victim, head down; then, raising its neck abruptly, it sank its horny tusk into the belly of the unfortunate saurian, which began to moan, shedding veritable torrents of blood, along with its entrails.

The brontosaurus fell.

Then the ceratosaurus launched itself upon its victim, and, with a single movement of its terrible jaw, it cut clean through its enemy' neck, a little beneath the head.

The combat was over; the feasting began, bestial, extraordinary and repulsive.

Valsorres and his companions watched that scene of carnage and ferocity, mute with fear.

Evidently, the victor was overjoyed by its triumph, and intoxicated by the blood of its victim.

What happened then? Did it catch the voyagers' scent? Had the latter made some sound that betrayed their presence? At any rate, the enormous carnivore, raising its head, sniffed abruptly, and then, suddenly turning to one side, hurled itself toward the left of the little troop, at the extremity at which Dr. Portier was standing.

The latter uttered a cry: "Help me! Help!"

Fortunately Valsorres had not lost his composure. He raised his express rifle and rapidly took aim. It was necessary not to think of hitting the monster in the body; in addition to its scaly skin, the thick mass of its flesh would have defended against the Marquis' bullets. It was necessary to hit the head.

The beast extended its forepaws toward the doctor; its sharp claws were almost touching the young physician's body when a shot rang out.

Valsorres had just fired; his reliable weapon, guided by his infallible eye, had done its work. The bullet had entered the monster's eye. It collapsed; its brain smashed, alongside the unconscious Portier.

The Marquis and Espéret ran to their companion.

"He's alive!" cried Valsorres.

Meanwhile, Hina had gone as far as a pond, from which she brought back a cloth soaked in water. She bathed the doctor's face. He recovered consciousness.

"Well, my dear Portier," the Marquis said to him, "You've come back from far away."

Portier looked around and perceived the corpse of the ceratosaurus.

"Fortunately," he said to his companions, "you're good shots. Thank you, my dear friends."

"Thank the Marquis," replied Espéret. "He hit the monster in the eye. I would have been absolutely incapable of it."

The five voyagers sat down on the trunk of a fallen pine. Thomas had taken a little bottle out of his bag containing peppermint cordial, which he mixed with a little water in an aluminum goblet, and which he made the doctor drink.

The later already felt much better. Fortunately, he had not received any wound.

Valsorres turned to his companions. "Let's go back to the *Fusée*," he said. "After that excitement, we need a little rest."

"Oh yes," replied the doctor.

The five rose to their feet.

"Permit me," said Portier, "to take away a souvenir of my aggressor."

And the doctor, leaning over the cadaver of the ceratosaurus, set about removing one of the formidable teeth from its jaw. There were sixty-six of them. By dint of effort, and with Thomas' aid, Portier ended up extracting one of the teeth. It was conical in form and twelve centimeters long, including the root.

Once in possession of his trophy, the doctor followed his companions, who, guided by the compass, after half an hour of marching, eventually found the clearing at the center of which the *Fusée* stood. They reentered it with a indescribable joy and, before going to sleep, did honor to the meal that Thomas improvised artfully, with Hina's help.

Thus passed the first day on Saturn.

III. The reading of which will demonstrate that primitive humans might be more advanced than one might believe at first.

Our five friends were fast asleep; they were sleeping so soundly that after the five-hour Saturnian night they finished a terrestrial night of a further five hours. When they woke up, night had fallen again on Saturn, and the night was accompanied by a terrible tempest.

Under what influences has the atmospheric masses of the planet been disturbed? Not under that of solar heat, which was evidently too enfeebled by distance. The clouds, however, swept by a terrible wind, raced raggedly above the voyagers; squalls blew violently, almost bending the tall stems of the gigantic ferns all the way to the ground.

Valsorres and Espéret watched that unleashing of the elements with an evident curiosity; the cloudy mass was sometimes somber to the point of being black, and was sometimes brightened by a kind of pale light that gave it a less Stygian tint.

At one moment, the tempest tore the nebulous mass.

"Oh!" cried Valsorres. "Oh, look, my friends!"

Portier, Espéret, Thomas and Hina raced to the portholes.

"How beautiful it is!" said the doctor.

It was, in fact, beautiful, in the full sense of the term.

Through the rent made in the cloudy layer, the sky showed—but what a sky!

An immense luminous arch analogous to one of our terrestrial rainbows, occupied a third of the firmament. Its width, reduced by its inclination, was nevertheless considerable. Darker circular bands divided it into concentric zones.

"The ring!" said the doctor.

"Yes, the Ring of Light. There it is in all its glory."

Valsorres had taken the *Fusée*'s most powerful optical instrument, a small refracto-reflector telescope, short in length but magnifying two hundred times. He directed it toward the ring.

Suddenly, he summoned Espéret.

"Here! Look!" he said to him.

The engineer put his eye to the ocular lens. "That's truly incredible!" he exclaimed.

Portier looked in his turn. "But that's a chaplet of minuscule planets; one can see the larger beads distinctly."

It was, in fact, a veritable medley of spherical corpuscles, but a prodigious medley composed of an infinite number of elements. Compared with that formidable mass of solid spheres, the swarm of minor planets that the voyagers had traversed in coming was nothing but a desert.

Espéret, who was looking at the rest of the sky, called the attention of his companions to something no less remarkable. Seven moons—seven of the twenty-five satellites of Saturn—showed above the ring. A few of them were moving with sufficient velocity for their movement to be directly perceptible without the intermediary of any instrument.

Portier had picked up a photographic apparatus and had already taken four or five pictures of the ring and the satellites when the rent in the clouds effected by the wind closed up again.

"Fortunately," said Valsorres, "we've be able to enjoy that marvelous spectacle and take pictures that are indisputable witnesses to the fact."

"Yes, replied the doctor. "Let's bless the tempest that procured it for us."

Valsorres remained pensive, however. "It's the origin of the tempest that worries me," he said. "If it isn't solar heat, what could have caused it?"

Interrogated directly, Espéret replied: "Perhaps a formidable manifestation of internal heat, perhaps a terrible volcanic eruption that destroyed the atmospheric equilibrium."

"It must be that," said the Marquis. "In any case, it's worrying. Evidently, the crust of Saturn, still young, must be shaken by numerous convulsions, and if ever there was an occasion to say that we've been sleeping on a volcano, it's now."

The night finished rapidly, and as soon as morning came, the five voyagers, furnished with food supplies and well armed, left the *Fusée* again.

"Since we found marshy terrain in the direction we followed yesterday," said the Marquis, "perhaps we'll find firmer ground and a more advanced fauna in the opposite direction, where we can see a few hills."

"Yes, perhaps," said Espéret.

They set forth, therefore, with Valsorres and Espéret in the lead, followed a few paces behind by Portier, Thomas and Hina. The vegetation was just as luxuriant as in the marshy zone. Nevertheless, as they progressed, the giant ferns, so numerous in the terrains that our geologists have called primary and secondary, became rarer. Palm trees replaced them, with pines and enormous cypresses. The firmer ground was covered with veritable grasses.

Birds—veritable birds—flew over the branches of trees and filled the air with deafening cries. Little marsupials like those that Thomas had mistaken for rabbits were hopping in the grass, and fled as the voyagers approached.

Everything, therefore, seemed to indicate a more advanced fauna. The problem arose in the minds of the two scientists, in a troubling manner, of the coexistence of animals that corresponded, on Earth, to such different ages.

"What I can't account for," said Espéret, "are those trees with deciduous foliage, in an atmosphere where, because of the distance from the sun and the dominance of clouds, the change of the seasons must scarcely be sensible."

"That's true," replied the Marquis. "But are the sun's rays, if one considers them purely from the calorific point of view, really the only factors affecting vegetation?"

"I don't believe so," riposted Dr. Portier.

The two scientists turned toward him.

"You know," the young physician continued, "that very remarkable experiments have shown the influence of electricity on vegetation."

"Oh, certainly, and the results are more than convincing."

"Well, how do you know that what we attribute, in terrestrial vegetation, to the action of luminous and calorific rays emitted by the sun might not be the result of electrical radiations that it sends us in a permanent fashion?"

Espéret and Valsorres looked at one another.

"In that case," Portier continued, "as those radiations are not blocked by clouds, like luminous rays, they would arrived at the surface of Saturn, and permit all the phases of the most varied vegetation there, like that we see here."

The two scientists could not help admitting the justice of Dr. Portier's opinion. In any case, no other reasoning could explain what they had before their eyes at that moment, so they rallied without hesitation to the young physician's way of seeing.

During the following days the five voyagers made daily excursions to explore the region of Saturn in the middle of which they had descended. They certainly did not have the pretention of exploring the immense globe of the planet—a globe more than 745 times as voluminous as Earth—in its entirety; they simply had the ambition to study the vegetal and animal life there, and to bring back a few mineral specimens of its soil.

The five voyagers, instructed by the terrible adventure that had nearly cost Dr. Portier his life, always marched in a compact group, with Valsorres, Portier and Espéret most often at the head, and Thomas and Hina bringing up the rear. They were always armed and alert.

The characteristic of the landscapes they explored in that fashion was a great richness of vegetation. As the three scientists had observed, the plants of three geological eras visibly coexisted. As for the fauna, they had mostly encountered gigantic representatives of the Secondary Era.

In order not to be limited in their excursions by the short duration of the Saturnian day, they had taken a light tent, under which they spent the night for several days in succession. They accustomed themselves to dividing up their sleep in accordance with the duration of the pale light that constituted day on the surface of Saturn. They had traveled thus for four days without encountering any other mammals than a few small marsupial hoppers, and no other birds than the archaeopteryx.

One evening, they were in their tent, in the process of eating a frugal meal prepared by Hina. The atmosphere was absolutely calm; no sound troubled its tranquility. After their meal, the voyagers lay down on a bed of ferns and went to sleep under the guard of the Marquis, who took the first watch of the night, his carbine under his arm.

While searching the surrounding darkness with his gaze, Valsorres was pensive. He was thinking about the years that had gone by amid the delights of Mars; his memory often stopped their momentarily, with complaisance. He smiled on seeing again, in his imagination, his beautiful friend Zith, his cousin Saâh, and King Thaû. He also dreamed, in a rapid vision, about the factories of the planet, the Martian astronomers and their discoveries.

Then his thoughts went further back, all the way to Earth, and he perceived, as if in a dream, the cherished individuals he had left behind, and who must believe that he and his companions had disappeared forever: his wife, his dear Marie, who must be mourning him as well as her son Philippe; his sister; and Aunt Hélène.

His imagination voyaged thus through space and time, the two infinities that the Creator has given as limits to human thought. The silence that enveloped him was truly frightful; it required a strong nature like his not to be impressed by the idea and sensation of being alone, with his four sleeping companions, on that distant "earth of the heavens," so distant from our globe, lost in the immensity.

Suddenly, in the midst of the general silence, he thought he distinguished a vague hum, a kind of continuous murmur.

He lent his ear to it, with redoubled attention.

One might imagine that it's the sound of the sea, he thought.

The more he listened, the more he was convinced that it was the ocean. It really was the continuous murmur of waves coming to break on rocks or on a beach; it was the characteristic sound of surf, albeit enfeebled by distance.

He took careful note if the direction from which the indication seemed to be coming. He went back into the tent to wake Thomas, who was due to take his turn on guard for a hour, and waited until the following morning to communicate his discovery to his companions.

As soon as it was light he told them about the incident.

"Oh," said Espéret, "if it's the sea, a Saturnian sea, what discoveries we might be able to make there."

"Yes," said Valsorres, "perhaps there we'll find living specimens of the fauna of the Primary Era."

"Certainly," said Dr. Portier. "In all probability, in fact, life must have begun to make its appearance in the oceans, at least on Earth. And I remember the fine lectures of Professor Joubin on that subject, in his course at the Oceano-graphic Institute in Paris."[38]

"And isn't there a very original theory," said Espéret, "that sees sea water as the origin of the liquids of the organism?"

"Yes, that's the theory of Dr. Quinton.[39] According to that scientist, our tissues and organs were once impregnated, so to speak, with the salt water that is the origin of our existence as living beings."

"However," Valsorres reflected, "If my memory is reliable, liquids like blood are not isotonic with sea water and don't have the same osmotic proper-ties, strictly speaking."

"That's true of the present water of our terrestrial seas," said the doctor. "The water of our oceans contains approximately thirty-five grams of salts per liter, on average. But the primitive oceans must have contained less; the stream-ing of running water, in fact, continuously increases the salinity of the seas with dissolved elements that they pour into it, while the total mass of the water di-minishes gradually."

"According to you, then, my dear friend, the seas of Saturn ought to be less salty than those of Earth?"

"I think so. Anyway, we'll soon see."

Thomas had dismantled the tent with Hina's aid. The voyagers gathered around the Marquis.

"That's the direction from which the sound came," he said, indicating a point on the horizon in a south-easterly direction. "It's therefore toward that point that it's necessary to march in order to arrive at the seashore."

The little troop set forth in the indicated direction.

On the way, Portier collected plants. What interested him most of all was being able to capture a few insects. Thus, he caught a ladybird measuring five centimeters in length, and photographed, for want to being able to carry it be-cause of its size, an enormous dragonfly, which made a terrible buzz as it flew reminiscent of an automobile engine, which had a wingspan of at least eighty centimeters.

As our friends advanced, the sound of the sea became increasingly distinct. Two hours after their departure, they were at the top of a cliff, and at their feet, an immense sea extended as far as the eye could see.

---

[38] Louis Joubin (1861-1935) was a sometime colleague of Berget's, and held a chair at the National History Museum in Paris from 1903 onwards. He was in charge of the educational program at the Oceanographic Institute.

[39] René Quinton (1867-1925) published *L'Eau de mer, milieu organique* [Sea water, the organic matrix] in 1904. On the basis of his theory he developed a "marine plasma" for injection into patients suffering from various conditions, which had considerable success, for the same reasons that an ordinary saline solution now plays such an important role in emergency medicine.

They had stopped before that magnificent spectacle. The sea was calm; it was the surf of little waves that came to die on a shingle beach garnishing the foot of the cliff.

Followed by Thomas, Portier was already getting ready to climb down, clinging on to asperities in the rock. Espéret stopped them.

"Wait!" he shouted at them. "Don't go down yet."

"Why not?" asked the doctor.

"Because you don't know whether it's low tide or high tide, and you might be surprised by the rise of the water before you have time to climb back up."

Portier and Thomas came back to their companions. They decided to call a halt and have lunch overlooking the sea.

"All the same," said Thomas, "to think that this is a sea without boats. To think that I've seen that! These things only happen to me."

The voyagers had commenced their meal, but scarcely had they attacked a piece of smoked tongue than Valsorres stood up.

"You're right," he said to Espéret. "The sea is rising now."

"How do you know?"

"Look at that pointed rock that is almost covered by the water. I noticed it when we arrived, twenty minutes ago, and it emerged by two meters; now only its summit is above the water."

"In that case," said Portier, "I can't explain the rapidity with which the sea is rising."

"But my dear friend," replied he Marquis, "it's quite simple, and you'll understand immediately."

"I'm listening."

"You know that on Earth, the tide is the result of the propagation of a liquid wave raised and propagated at the surface of the sea by the attractions, sometimes concordant and sometimes opposed, exercised on the water by the Moon and the Sun."

"Yes, I know that."

"It's the action of the Moon, which is closer to us, that is predominant. So the interval between high tides on two consecutive days isn't twenty-four hours but twenty-eight hours fifty minutes, which represents the period of rotation of the Mon around the Earth."

"Yes, I know that too."

"Well, here, because of the distance of the Sun, the attraction of the star is ineffective on the waters of the seas of Saturn. Only the lunar attractions subsist. But what attractions! Don't forget that there are twenty-five moons around this planet."

"Yes, not to mention the ring."

"The ring ought not to intervene, for it represents a mass at a constant distance. But what complicated tides the twenty-five moons must engender on the

Saturnian surface, with their alternatives of conjunction and opposition! And look, the demonstration is about to be made."

In fact, the water level, which had just risen so rapidly, was already beginning to go down. The rock pointed out by the Marquis emerged above the waves again, and the sea level went down so rapidly that its movement of descent was appreciably to the eye.

The three scientists watched that astonishing spectacle, and less than twenty minutes later, the level of the Saturnian ocean, after having dropped, began to rise again.

"It's a veritable vibratory movement," said the Marquis.

"Yes, almost," replied Espéret.

Meanwhile, the voyagers had observed, on the face of the cliff, a line marking the level of the highest tides. That line, therefore, indicated the level to which one could venture without peril.

They descended on to a little shingle beach accumulated the foot of a rocky cove. Portier bent down to examine the seashells left by the tide on the edge of the shore. The young scientist picked up new shells one after another. Suddenly, he exclaimed: "Belemnites! Belemnites! Come and see, Marquis!"

Valsorres and Espéret came running. Portier held out to them two marine creatures; they really were belemnites, cephalopods analogous to our cuttlefish of the French coast, characteristic of the Secondary Era.

"And we'll have live ones—or, at least, ones preserved in formaldehyde— to show at the Académie des Sciences when we return."

Valsorres looked attentively at his feet. His companions saw him bend down curiously and examine an object on the strand.

"Well, my dear Portier. I've been even luckier than you," he exclaimed. "You've only found belemnites; I've captured a trilobite."

And the Marquis picked up from amid the pebbles a crustacean about twelve centimeters long, rolled up into a ball like a woodlouse.

The three scientists examined it with the keenest curiosity. Espéret turned it over between his fingers. "Yes," he said, "it really is the trilobite characteristic of Primary times, one of the first truly organized creatures that lived in the seas—at least in our terrestrial seas. Here are its three parts, the head, the thorax and its posterior appendage, the pygidium."

Valsorres turned to his companions. "Well," he said to them, "this confirms my initial impression: species that are separated on Earth by enormous intervals of time coexist on Saturn. Oh, if only we could explore this Saturnian ocean with means analogous to those employed by the Prince of Monaco in his magnificent campaigns, in the course of which he explores the oceans of the Earth. What any extraordinary harvest we'd gather!"

"But what monsters we'd be at risk of encountering on these oceans!" said the doctor. "Look at those we've already seen on the surface of the planet."

317

"That's true! We certainly ought to encounter plesiosaurs and ichthyosaurs here, all the large marine animals of the Secondary Era. And if we ventured forth over these unknown waves, borne by a frail boat, we'd run the risk of being sunk by one of those terrible beasts."

Meanwhile, Valsorres continued examining the shingle, on which waves were arriving capable of bringing creatures which their rapid retreat would prevent from fleeing.

His attentive search was not in vain. He bent down and picked up from a hollow in the rocks a fish brought by the rising tide that had not been able to escape when it went down.

"An armored fish!" he exclaimed.

Portier and Espéret ran toward him.

It was, in fact, one of the primitive fish, with scaly armor and vertebrae that were not ossified. It was one of the inhabitants of the sea characteristic of the Primary Era; added to that of the trilobite, its capture left no possible doubt. The three scientists were jubilant; the animals they had just found were veritable treasures from a scientific point of view, not to mention that Portier had made an ample harvest of globigerina, radiolaria and a host of little mollusks abandoned by the tide on the strand where they were searching. He had also collected a bottle of sea water in order to analyze it.

The short Saturnian day was, however, coming to an end. It was Thomas, less preoccupied than his companions with scientific curiosity, who called attention to that.

"Messieurs," the worthy fellow said to them, "it's getting dark. I believe that it's time to return to our tent, prepare supper there and make our preparations for the night, which falls very quickly.

The advice was sage; everything followed it. The little troop resumed the route to the clearing where the tent had been pitched. Thomas and Hina led the way.

Suddenly, the latter bent down and picked up an object that had struck her sight and showed it to her companion.

Thomas took it, examined it and immediately took it to the Marquis.

It was an empty twelve-bore cartridge case, made of red cardboard. Hina observed that it fit perfectly into the chamber of her rifle.

Valsorres was stupefied. "You haven't fired a shot, Hina?" he asked.

"Not one," replied the beautiful Martian.

"Anyway," said Espéret, "we don't have any cartridge cases of that color; all of ours are made of green cardboard."

Valsorres was plunged in astonishment. "That's incredible!" he said, after a moment's silence.

"What is?" asked Espéret.

"That men have arrived on this distant planet before us."

"Do you think that's what has happened?"

"Germans! Certainly, yes. It's that accursed Osterwald, or one of the Paschwitzes who've pursued us with their hatred and jealousy. Oh, if that's it, and we find ourselves in their presence here, woe betide them!"

"Let's go back to the camp," said the doctor. "We'll examine that cartridge case by the light of our lamps."

They arrived at the tent. While Thomas prepared the evening meal, Valsorres lit an acetylene lantern and examined the empty cartridge case found by Hina.

It was, indeed, a twelve-bore cartridge with an elongated copper base. On that base it bore a mark tamped into the metal: *Waffen werke "Pluto" Spandau.*

That removed all doubt. It was a cartridge case of German manufacture.

So, the Marquis saw his projects deflowered. Others had arrived on the planet Saturn before him, and those others were Germans!

Oh, how he regretted the years lost on Mars, those years spent in scientific research, it is true, but also spent in the most refined pleasures; those years during which he and his companions had lost all notion of time; those years which, without the vigilance and common sense of Thomas, would still be continuing!

Espéret too had a face darkened by sad thoughts. Only Portier envisaged the situation with composure.

"Since we've found that empty cartridge case after a few days' march," he said, "the Germans can't be far away from the place where we are. Let's redouble our prudence during our excursions. And if you take my advice, we'll go back to the *Fusée* as soon as possible. It's our general headquarters; it's around the *Fusée* that we ought to spread out in future."

The advice seemed sound; they decided to follow it.

Supper was morose; the night was agitated for the sleepers. Valsorres could not close an eye, and, getting up from his bed of ferns, he went to relieve Hina, who was taking her turn on guard, saying to her: "Go to bed, Hina. I'll watch in your place, for it's truly impossible for me to sleep."

The next day, after an abbreviated sleep, the five voyagers, doubling their pace, headed toward he place where they had left the *Fusée*. They had been careful, following Thomas' advice, to mark the outward route they had followed with visible reference points, which simplified the return itinerary considerably.

On the evening of the fourth day, they arrived at their hospitable projectile and installed themselves therein with a veritable satisfaction.

Portier hastened to put the "living fossils" he had brought back in formaldehyde, after which they held council on the subject of what to do next.

Valsorres proposed returning to the shore of the sea, to the place where they had found the cartridge case.

Espéret opposed it. "First," he said, "it's necessary to try to encounter indigenes. Given the general aspect of the flora and fauna it appears to me to be impossible that we won't find humans here, even if only in an almost savage state.

Then, at least by means of signs, we can discover whether humans have trod the soil of his planet before us."

The advice seemed good, and was followed.

The next morning, having got up early, our five voyagers quit the *Fusée*, of which Thomas had carefully closed the panel and screwed in all the bolts. Espéret. Portier and Thomas were armed with Winchester automatic carbines, Valsorres was carrying a redoubtable express rifle, Hina her double-barreled shotgun. Everyone had, in addition, a pistol and a hunting knife. Hina alone carried an American hatchet passed through her belt.

They followed a direction different from the one that had led to the Saturnian ocean. They marched in a compact group, Valsorres and Hina in the lead, Thomas, Espéret and Portier following behind.

On the way, and without drawing away from the little column, Portier made an ample harvest of rare vegetables. His box was already full, and he was beginning to confide the surplus of his crop to Thomas when Hina, who was marching in front with the Marquis, signaled to her companions to stop.

They all stood still, Hina had loaded her gun; the four voyagers imitated her.

In fact, it was necessary keep their eyes open again. Through the trunks of the trees, in the feeble light of the Saturnian day, bulky forms could be seen that were moving heavily and seemed to be digging in the ground with their jaws.

The travelers looked carefully, and this is what they saw.

A group of three animals was in front of them, no longer giant saurians characteristic of Secondary times, like those they had seen before in the marshy depths they had explored, but enormous mammals.

The largest of the animals was certainly six meters tall and more than eight meters long. Imagine an elephant, but an elephant equipped with a very short trunk and whose tusks, instead of curving upwards, curved downwards: such was the formidable creature of which three specimens were agitating a few meters away from the voyagers. It was the dinotherium, of which the fossil skeleton had been studied by Cuvier, who had named it thus after discovering its remains.

Valsorres shouldered his express rifle.

Espéret stopped him. "Don't shoot," he said.

Valsorres questioned him with his gaze.

"Look there—a little further on!"

The Marquis looked in the indicated direction.

Humans! Veritable humans, armed with clubs, about ten in number. They were leading a herd of pachyderms analogous to horses in terms of size and appearance. Valsorres recognized them as living representatives of a species extinct on Earth, hipparions, evidently domesticated as beasts of burden by the strange herdsmen who were driving the animals ahead of them.

But what herdsmen! So they were the inhabitants of this distant planet! They were the Saturnians with whom the Marquis' dream was to enter into relations! They were, if they were associated with the animals with which they lived, the "Tertiary humans" whose past existence was so much discussed on Earth by paleontologists.

Valsorres gazed at his "peers" with an intense emotion.

They were of short stature, thickset and compact, with a short neck, a receding brow and a prominent lower jaw. Their limbs were covered in long, thick hair; unkempt hair covered their heads, and solid white teeth appeared in their mouths. They walked with their knees bent inwards; their very long arms were equipped with enormous clubs. They were clad in animal skins that covered them partially; their feet were bare; no adornment or decoration was visible, even on those who appeared to be women.

Around the troop, small mammals were gambling, similar in size to our dogs and in form to hyenas. Those little quadrupeds similarly seemed to be obedient to the primitive humans, for at certain cries uttered by the latter they immediately returned to their masters.

Valsorres, Espéret and Portier could scarcely believe the reality that surpassed their most ambitious dreams: that coexistence of humans with animals not only identical to those of Tertiary times but also those far more ancient, of Secondary and even Primary times, since trilobites were to be found in the Saturnian ocean.

It was necessary to make a decision, however, and to act.

Valsorres understood that the dinotheriums were not redoubtable, since they were watching impassively as the humans filed past them. He therefore made a sign to his companions to follow him and advanced rapidly to meet the Saturnians.

The latter's dogs immediately signaled their approach with cries that were yaps rather than barks.

The humans of the planet, surprised, stopped and looked around. They quickly perceived the five voyagers and stopped, having their dogs gather their herd. Then one of them, probably the chef, advanced toward the Marquis—who was marching slightly ahead of his companions—and, raising his left arm above his head, gave voice to a guttural sound that can only be expressed by the letters: "Grookso."

Slinging his carbine over his shoulder, Valsorres extended his arm toward him and touched his hand.

The indigene bowed, with a second guttural cry. Then he turned to his fellows and pointing at the Marquis, pronounced the cry he had uttered before for a third time.

Then Valsorres pointed at his four companions and said, to him, introducing them: "French!"

The indigene only replied with a single word: "Kraa!" And that word was repeated by the other nine Saturnians, in chorus.

Meanwhile, the "planetary" gazed curiously at the five individuals who ought to have been new to him. But what struck the voyagers was that they did not appear to manifest in their presence the astonishment that almost all primitive humans show in the face of a civilized being equipped with the implements of his civilization. Thus, the knives that impress the savage peoples of the Earth's surface so greatly did not appear to astonish them, not the five rifles that our friends were carrying.

Portier was visibly troubled by that indifference, inexplicable in his eyes. He was wondering privately whether these were humans or superior apes when Hina, who never ceased to gazes attentively at one of the indigenes, whom she supposed to be a woman, uttered an exclamation of astonishment.

On that creature's wrist she had just perceived a sort of little bell suspended from a ribbon dyed in three colors.

She showed it to Thomas, then to Valsorres,

The latter uttered a cry, or rather a roar: "Malediction!"

The three colors on the ribbon were black, white and red. They were the German national colors.

*IV. In which the Marquis de Valsorres is seen to make
a disturbing discovery.*

The Marquis de Valsorres was dumbstruck with amazement.

After a moment of immobility, he showed the ribbon and the trinket suspended from it to Espéret and Portier.

"Before that second proof there's no more doubt," said the engineer. "There are, or there have been, Germans here, and they arrived before us."

"That's incontestable," replied Portier. "In any case, we can be sure that they didn't land on Mars, Thaû and Saâh would have said so."

"Quite so," said Valsorres, "but what is certain is that they've come here *before us*, and that, in consequence, we're burned. Damnation! Damnation!"

And the Marquis, holding his head in his hands, sat down on a tree trunk, in the presence of the bewildered indigenes.

Portier, however, had pulled himself together.

It was a matter of obtaining details, as far as possible, regarding the arrival of the intruders on Saturnian soil. The thing was not easy, given that the inhabitants, veritable savages in the most primitive state, did not even appear to know the most elementary articulate language. However, the doctor did not hesitate for a moment.

He approached the woman with the tricolor ribbon and, pointing at it with his finger, he made an interrogative gesture.

The woman turned toward the chief; the latter responded with a sort of grunt and turned to the west, indicating a direction of the horizon with his extended hand.

Portier extended his hand in the same diction; the indigene moved his head up and down; and it is necessary to believe that the sign in question is instinctive in all human beings, for, among all the peoples of the Earth, it means "yes." Was it the same, then, among the Saturnians?

Portier renewed his interrogation and received, in response, the same sign for a second time.

Then emboldened by the success of his first communication with the inhabitants of the planet, he extended his open raised hand toward the chief, and started counting on his fingers.

"One? Two? Three? Four? Five?"

At the fifth sign the indigene stopped him.

Portier then repeated the same gesture, the five fingers of his hand splayed.

The savage nodded his head.

"There were five!" he said.

The indigene touched his arm, touched four fingers successively, raised his hand above his head; then, having lifted the fifth finger, he lowered his hand to the level of his abdomen.[40]

Portier looked at him uncomprehendingly. The savage repeated his mime.

It was Hina who found the key to the enigma. "He doubtless means that there are four big people and a fifth much smaller."

"That's right," said Portier, struck by a sudden illumination. Then, turning to the man, he raised his hand four times to the level of the heads of his four companions, and, a fifth time, bending down, he made the gesture of touching the head of someone smaller.

Yes, yes, said the indigene, nodding his head.

Valsorres was increasingly stupefied. "So, these bandits are five in number, four big and one small?"

"Without a doubt," said the doctor.

"But it's the height of the small one that astonishes me," said Espéret. "According to that man's gesture, it's a child."

"I'll make sure of it," the young physician replied. He recommenced his interrogative mime, specifying by the number of digits raised, that it was a matter of the fifth stranger.

The Saturnian man repeated his affirmation and, lowering his hand, he stopped it horizontally at the level of the doctor's stomach. It really was, therefore, a matter of a child or a dwarf.

Valsorres could no longer stand it.

"Let's go, my friends," he said to his companions. "Let's go find these filthy Germans and order them to submit to us, or else..."

"Or else what?" asked Espéret.

"Or else we'll kill them. We came here as conquerors; we find usurpers. They want war; they can have it. There are five of them, it seems? Well, there are five of us too. We'll do battle, if necessary, and we'll vanquish or perish."

"Let's not be too hasty," said the prudent Espéret. These Germans will surely be alerted to our presence here. As you've already supposed, and as I believe too, it's certainly a matter of Baron von Osterwald or someone in his entourage, one of those accursed von Paschwitzes whose hatred pursues you from generation to generation, but these people must be on their guard and well armed. It's necessary for us to surprise them if we want to have them at our mercy."

"What? Are you afraid of them, my old comrade?"

---

[40] Five separate words in this paragraph are indicated in the text I have as missing. I have inserted two that are obvious and improvised likely substitutes for the others.

"Certainly not, but I want to have all the advantages on our side. Here, we're the only Frenchmen on an earth of the heavens. We find Germans here; they must disappear or we must disappear; there's no middle course."

During this discussion, Thomas and Hina began a conversation by means of gestures with the Saturnians, who were beginning to become more familiar. One of them touched Thomas' carbine with his finger and mimed pulling the trigger, exclaiming: "Boom! Boom!" Thomas immediately came to recount the incident to the three scientists.

They saw it as a confirmation of their hypotheses. Evidently, the savages had seen the Germans shoulder their rifles and fire at some beast of the planet.

"Messieurs," Espéret continued, "the savage's gesture supports what I said just now: let's be prudent. We have a machine gun with us; let's take it with us on our reconnaissance expedition. We can persuade two of these planetaries to carry it for us, if necessary by making them a little gift."

"What?" asked Portier.

"Simply the little gramophone that we brought, which is in the *Fusée*. We'll make a sign to these men to come with us, we'll enable them to hear the instrument, and indicate that it's for them. Then we'll find two who'll carry our machine gun, our provisions and our ammunition."

"That's an idea, in fact," said the Marquis.

Dr. Portier, who was definitely the expedition's interpreter, turned to the Saturnians. By means of gestures, he invited them to follow him.

The savages looked at one another momentarily. Then the chief, after uttering a few hoarse sounds, made a sign to six of them, who drew away with the hipparions. With three of his men, he followed the voyagers.

Valsorres and Espéret marched in the lead. Portier followed them with the four "planetaries." Thomas and Hina brought up the rear.

After an hour's march, guided by his compass, Valsorres arrived in the small clearing where the *Fusée* was. He turned to the men of the planet and showed them he machine. They approached it curiously, and circled around it.

Then the chief, advancing toward the feet supporting the apparatus, raised his hand in the air and made the gesture of someone climbing a ladder.

"Aha!" said Espéret. "It appears that he has already seen something analogous, for our *Fusée* doesn't seem to astonish him much."

Meanwhile, Thomas, detaching the ladder leaning against one of the struts and applying the upper extremity to two hooks situated beneath the panel, and he began to unscrew the bolts.

The panel was soon opened, and Valsorres, followed by the faithful servant, penetrated into the interior of the projectile. He came out a few moments later holding a square box surmounted by an aluminum cornet, in the center of which was a disk of hardened rubber; that was the gramophone.

Summoning he savages, he placed the instrument on the ground in front of them, wound it up and started the disk. The "phono" then commenced the celebrated popular tune *Viens Poupoule!*

The amazement of the Saturnians was indescribable. They knelt down in order to have their ears closer to the instrument; then they moved their heads to the right and left, following the cadence of the orchestra reproduced by the apparatus. Finally, they began to utter strident cries and, standing up, all together, they performed an unimaginable saraband around the gramophone.

Thomas and Hina clutched their sides, laughing.

When the song had finished, Portier turned the disk over and started another piece; it was the march from *Fatinitza* by Franz von Suppé.

The indigenes' amazement was redoubled.

Then Portier made them understand that the apparatus was for them. He showed the chief how to wind up the mechanism and put the disk in place. With the dexterity of an ape, the savage imitated the doctor's gestures and succeeded, without the slightest difficulty, in making the instrument sing.

Immediately, the Saturnians' gaiety became delirious.

Portier took advantage of that to have them carry the machine gun that Thomas and Hina had gone to fetch from the *Fusée*, with a tripod and several sacks of cartridges. Thomas had also brought a few tins of food, of which he had made two solidly tied-up bundles.

Then the doctor loaded all that on to the robust shoulders of the primitives, and, Thomas having closed the panel again, the five voyagers resumed their march in the direction in which the chief had made them understand that the mysterious strangers were to be found.

The chief marched very rapidly, in advance of the troop, carrying his phonograph carefully. His three companions remained well in rear, with our five friends.

"You see, my dear Portier," said the Marquis, "that phonograph, which the savage is obviously going to show to the Prussians, will serve to put one over on them."

"How's that?"

"It's quite simple. The apparatus has an America trademark, but fortunately, the disk is German."

"What about *Viens Poupoule?*"

"Well, *Viens Poupoule* is a French café-concert adaptation of a popular song that had a great success in Germany, which, sung to the same tune, is called *Komm, Karolinchen!* And the other piece, on the reverse side of the disk, is one of the most famous military marches from beyond the Rhine."

"I understand."

"With the consequence that, on seeing that disk, the Germans will believe themselves anticipated, not by Frenchmen, but by other Germans; they won't be suspicious, and that's an advantage for us."

"Perfectly reasoned."

And the voyagers continued their route.

On the way, they flushed out animals whose species were much closer to contemporary terrestrial species. The fact struck Espéret, who said to the Marquis: "Once again I note with astonishment the coexistence of living beings that on Earth, based on their fossil remains, were separated by millions of centuries. I don't understand it at all."

Valsorres reflected. "In my opinion, though, it's quite simple. "On Earth, which is closer to the Sun, the alternation of the seasons, much more marked than on this planet, must have had a considerable influence on the evolution of species. The progressive diminution of water vapor in the atmosphere cooled it gradually and brought us to the present state of things.

"On Saturn, by contrast, it's the central heat of the planet, transmitted through the crust, which is the almost unique factor of the elevation of the temperature; the Sun, reduced to the apparent dimensions of the head of a large pin, is too far away for the warming of its rays, enfeebled by distance, to have a preponderant influence. The evolution of species has therefore happened in a continuous fashion, in the same conditions of temperature; so, we witness this coexistence of the flora and fauna that, on our world, serve to differentiate the geological eras."

For want of anything better, it was necessary to admit the Marquis' explanation.

Meanwhile, our five friends, guided by the three savages carrying the machine gun and its support, had made progress. They had arrived, while marching through trees, at the summit of a small mound that hid the terrain situated beyond it.

The three Saturnians turned to the voyagers and, without a word or a cry, showed them an object situated in a rather large clearing occupying the center of a ring of small hills.

Valsorres, Espéret, Portier, Thomas and Hina were mute with surprise.

In the center of the clearing stood a kind of shell, absolutely similar to the *Fusée*. Alongside that shell a pole was planted, at the top of which floated a flag with three horizontal bands, black white and red.

"The German flag," said Valsorres, stifling a cry of rage.

Espéret had loaded his carbine. "Let's go, my friends," he said. "Forward, and let's attack those enemies, who have disputed our conquest thus far."

But Portier stopped him with a gesture.

"No need, my dear friend," he said. "We have something better to do."

Espéret looked at him interrogatively.

"Yes. Their shell is doubtless empty, and the five Germans who occupy it must be on an excursion."

"So?"

"Well, the simplest thing for us to do in their absence, is firstly to pay a domiciliary visit to their machine, which might perhaps enlighten us regarding many things."

Valsorres and Espéret approved the doctor's idea, and they set about realizing it immediately. It was decided that Valsorres and Portier would penetrate into the German shell, whose inferior hatch must open by unscrewing he bolts. Thomas still had the wrench in his bag, and the operation ought not to present any difficulty. In the meantime, the machine gun would be set up. Espéret, Thomas and Hina, with the two Saturnians, would remain on the mound, hidden in the bushes, in such a way as to be able to fire at the Germans if the latter came to attack the Marquis and the doctor and seek to dislodge them from their machine.

The plan, as you can see, was well made.

Only Thomas had an objection, or, rather, a proposal. The worthy fellow requested that a French flag that he was carrying in his bag, carefully folded, be hoisted to the top of the pole, instead of the German flag that was floating in the breeze.

Valsorres opposed that; it was necessary not to alert the Germans by any visible manifestation, who ought to return to their shelter without any suspicion.

Thomas therefore accompanied the Marquis under the feet of the machine; iron crampons permitted him to climb up to the panel, which could be distinguished clearly, closed by six bolts. Thomas unscrewed the six bolts and pushed the panel upwards. It unmasked a shaft equipped with a ladder.

"That's good, my old Thomas," said Valsorres. "Return to your post next to the machine gun, and all three of you mount good guard.

And the Marquis, accompanied by Dr. Portier, climbed up the ladder. A second panel, simply closed by a catch, blocked the upper extremity of the shaft.

Valsorres turned the catch and penetrated into a large circular chamber, illuminated by portholes and by an unpolished globe that spread a diffuse milky light.

In the middle of the room, sitting on a folding chair, as a seven-year-old child clad in European clothes. The child was weeping.

At the sight of Valsorres, the little boy initially had a movement of fear; but the Marquis approached him and said, gently: "Don't be afraid, my little friend. You're with good people here, who will protect you if you're in danger, who will love you if you're alone, and will direct you if you're lost."

The child raised his head. His beautiful blue yes radiated frankness, but dark circles that bordered them gave an impression of sadness and dread. He said to the Marquis: "Sprechen sie Deutsch?"

"Ja," replied Valsorres, visibly moved. And, expressing himself in German, in which he was fluent, he started questioning the little boy.

V. In which we rediscover both Dr. Frank and Graf von Paschwitz.

"What is your name?" the Marquis asked his little companion.

The child hesitated momentarily. "Wilhelm."

Valsorres looked him in the face. "Have you no other name?"

The child bowed his head, and shook it.

"How did you get here? Do you know where you are?"

The little boy replied, naively: "Still in the home of Graf von Paschwitz."

"Where is Paschwitz?"

"In Silesia."

Valsorres reflected profoundly, and while thinking, he gazed at his little interlocutor. He was struck by the child's distinction, the slenderness of his hands and feet, the profound blue of his large eyes and his limpid and frank gaze.

"That's not a little Prussian!" he said to the doctor.

"I don't believe so either," the later replied.

An idea had struck the mind of the Marquis, which took on substance. "Have you been in the home of Graf von Paschwitz for a long time, my little friend?" he asked, softly.

"I don't know," the little boy replied. "Perhaps three years, perhaps four, perhaps more...I don't know."

"And were you there with your mother?"

"I have no mother," he replied, somberly.

Valsorres was breathless. "Is she dead?"

"I don't know. One day, I kissed my *maman* before going to bed. I woke up,. I was in a big car, then a big boat, then, after that, another car. Then, always with the Graf von Paschwitz."

"And your *maman*? Do you remember your *maman*?" asked the Marquis, taking the boy's hand.

The child reflected. "Oh, she was beautiful. She was very beautiful. And she was kind. She kissed me before I went to bed, and in the morning, when I woke up, she was there, and kissed me again. Poor *maman*!"

"And your papa?"

"I don't have a papa any more, since I've been with the Graf von Paschwitz."

"But before? You don't remember him? Think hard, my child, my dear little friend. Try to remember."

The boy lowered his head, and, by means of a great effort of memory, appeared to be searching the past with difficulty.

"Yes, that's true, I had a papa, a good papa, who bounced me on his knee in the evening, because, during the day, I didn't see him."

"Why didn't you see him?"

"Because he was always shut up with another monsieur in a big house at the back of a big garden, with Thomas."

Valsorres uttered a roar. "With Thomas? With Thomas, you say?

The child looked at him, astonished by that violent interrogation.

"Yes, the good Thomas, who pushed me in a wheelbarrow."

Valsorres devoured the little boy with his eyes. Suddenly, he said: "Philippe! Philippe!"

The child shivered. "Who called me Philippe? Yes, I remember now. That's what my *maman*, who was so pretty, called me, and my papa, who was so good...Philippe."

"It's me, my dear child, who called you Philippe, because it's your name and I'm your father!" And Valsorres, his eyes full of tears of joy, hugged his miraculously rediscovered son to his bosom.

As for the doctor, he did not try to hide his emotion.

"How you've grown, my Philippe," said the Marquis, caressing the child. "How beautiful you are!" Then, after a moment's silence: "But tell me, my little Philippe—you no longer speak French?"

The child lowered his head. "When I arrived...out there, I spoke...differently, but the Graf forbade it. I only had to speak German."

"But you didn't know it!"

"It was taught to me. Oh, how I've been beaten to make me speak German. They didn't give me anything to eat unless I spoke German. I was very hungry, sometimes."

Valsorres had got up, his fist raised. "Oh, a curse, a triple curse on those who made my son suffer! Woe betide them!"

The child put his arms round his neck. "And my *maman*? Will I see her soon too, Papa. my *petite maman*?"

"Yes, my Philippe, you'll see her, your *maman*, and she'll be very happy to kiss you, my dear child."

While Valsorres, entirely given to his joy, could not take his eyes off his son, Portier made a rapid inspection of the cabin where they were. His attention was attracted by a cupboard whose door was ajar, in which several drawers could be glimpsed. Portier opened one; it contained papers, including letters.

The doctor riffled through them rapidly, and uttered an exclamation of surprise. "Look!" he said. "Here's news, my dear friend."

Valsorres turned round; the young physician handed him two letters. He scanned the rapidly. One was addressed to "Graf W. von Paschwitz"; it was signed "your sister, Emma." The other was addressed to the same Paschwitz; it was signed "your brother-in-law, Baron Lymstroem."

Valsorres slapped his forehead. "Oh," said said, "into what labyrinth of treasons and turpitudes have we fallen? Aunt Hélène, dear Aunt Hélène, you were right!" Then, after a moment's reflection, he said to Portier: "So this

Lymstroem is the brother-in-law of the execrable Paschwitz. In consequence, his wife..."

"Yes, my friend; the beautiful Baronne Lymstroem must be the sister of Graf von Paschwitz..."

"Who is Philippe's kidnapper. Oh, but now that we've found the victim, we'll be able to punish the guilty party in his turn. Oh, woe betide him!"

Valsorres had taken his son on his knees. "And out there, my little Philippe, what was your life like?"

"Working from morning till evening. In the morning they made me study books that said that Germany is the first country in the world, the one that ought to dominate all the others and rule the world. Then I went to eat."

"What did you eat, my child?"

"Lard, cabbages and beans, and I drank a little beer. In the afternoon they made me work with a blacksmith; I filed and drilled bits of iron. The Graf often arrived and said: 'How goes the young son of a dog?' In the beginning the smith told him when I hadn't worked well. Then I was locked in a dark room with black bread and water. And in the evening Baron came and I was whipped hard."

"Oh, the bandit!" said Valsorres.

"But the smith was a good man, He understood that I was beaten when he said something; then he didn't say anything anymore, and in secret, in the afternoon, he sometimes gave me a piece of chocolate. And it went on like that until a short time ago. Then they put me in this big machine, and we stayed in it for a long time. Then, one day, we went out. But I think we're still at the Graf von Paschwitz's home, except that the trees aren't the same..."

"You sometimes get out of here, my dear child?"

"Yes, almost every day; but when the others go away with their rifles, they leave me all alone here, with canned beef, biscuit and water. Oh, I was very bored when you came, Meinherr."

"Don't say Meinherr anymore. Call me Papa."

"Yes, I sense that you're my papa. And I recognize you now, when I look at you. It's you who kissed me at night, before I went up to bed, with Thérèse..."

"You remember Thérèse! But what are you going to say when you see Thomas?"

"Thomas! My good Thomas! Is he here?"

"Yes, dear child, he's a few paces away; you'll see him soon."

"Oh good!" said he child, joyfully.

Portier continued his investigations. He discovered a photograph on which he had no difficulty recognizing the laboratory at the Château de Valsorres. The cathode ray tube and the transformer were in their place on the big table. In the background, the dials of galvanometers could be seen.

He showed it to the Marquis.

The latter started. "These rogues got in everywhere!" he exclaimed. "For that's definitely our laboratory, the electrical measurement room. I even recognize one detail: one of the wires of the Crookes tube in straight, the other twisted in a spiral. Oh, they're master spies! But how were they able...?"

At that moment the Marquis was abruptly interrupted by Portier, who took him by the arm and put a finger to his lips in order to tell him to be quiet, pointing to the hatch pierced in the floor of the cabin, which gave access to the interior.

Valsorres sat his son down on the folding chair and instructed him to be quiet. Then, with Portier, he hid behind a small table. The two men had their pistols in their hands.

After a moment, a head appeared in the opening, and then a man, hoisting himself up the ladder, penetrated into the room.

Perceiving the child, he launched himself toward him brutally and said: "Son of a dog! You've opened the panel in spite of my prohibition. You'll see what that will cost you!"

And, putting down his rifle, he reached out toward the poor child, his arm raised, ready to strike him brutally...when suddenly, he saw two men aiming pistols at him.

One of them shouted: "Hands up, Dr. Frank! You're at our mercy."

Dr. Frank attempted to pick up his rifle, but Portier had rapidly taken possession of it, while Valsorres said to him: "One word, one move, and you're dead!"

Dr. Frank let himself fall into a folding chair, murmuring a blasphemy. While the Marquis held him under the barrel of his pistol. Portier brought his hands behind his back and made it impossible for him to make a gesture.

"Tie his feet," Valsorres ordered.

Portier put a rope around the German's legs.

"Now, my dear doctor," said the Marquis, "it's the two of us. Would you like to chat a little? It will be amusing. We must have many interesting things to say to one another."

The German looked at his two guards with eyes full of rage. He made no reply.

Then little Philippe said to the Marquis: "That's not Dr. Frank. That's Graf von Paschwitz."

Valsorres had an instant revelation of the truth.

"Oh, my dear Monsieur, you afford yourself the luxury of a dual personality! You're Dr. Frank in Paris and Graf von Paschwitz in Prussia!" And. bowing twice before the wretch he addressed two ironically solemn salutations to him. "So," he continued, "you're the brother of that beautiful Baronne Lymstroem, whom we never suspected of being the sister of the celebrated Dr. Frank. My compliments—your sister is an accomplished beauty. And how is your dear brother-in-law, Baron Lymstroem? I hope he's in perfect health?"

Frank—or von Paschwitz, as you wish—rolled his eyes furiously; he was foaming with rage at being taken thus "in his burrow," like a simple rabbit.

"So we've come to take a little tour of the good planet Saturn, in order to plant the flag of the excellent Kaiser Wilhelm there! My God, how proud that great Emperor will be when you present yourself before him, triumphant! You'll be awarded the highest distinctions of the Empire. All my compliments, Monsieur. You've certainly earned them."

If looks could kill, the one that Frank darted at the Marquis would certainly have slain him.

But Valsorres did not stop. "And see what pitiless ill luck pursues you: you kidnap young Philippe de Valsorres—which, in parentheses, might do you a bad turn when we take you back to France—and now the child is taken back from you by his father in the very place where you brought him in order to put him out of range of any search! My poor Graf, you really have no luck. And to complete the misfortune, you've let yourself get caught like a vulgar rabbit and tied up in your own vehicle. No, that's veritably too unlucky."

The Marquis changed is tone then. "Now, Master Brigand, enough pleasantries. What do you think we should do with you?"

The German made no reply.

"We're outside the law here, submissive to the only justice we have to recognize, which is God's. And we're going to judge you."

"Say that you're going to murder me!"

"It's not that; at the most it would be an execution. But in any case, it won't be done without judgment."

At that moment, Portier, who had not intervened in the discussion, advanced toward the Marquis and pointed to the hatch. "Someone's coming up!" he said.

Immediately, Dr. Frank, uttering a veritable howl, shouted with all the force of his lungs: "Help! In the name of the Emperor!"

At the same moment, a man appeared in the opening of the panel, holding a repeater carbine, which he aimed at the Marquis. But Portier was watching; his pistol, directed by a sure hand, launched two bullets, and the German fell, his skull shattered.

Meanwhile, at the sound of the shots, Espéret, Thomas and Hina, understanding that their friends were under attack, brought the machine gun into play. The two Boches outside, who were preparing to climb into their machine, were scythed down in the blink of an eye.

Then the three auxiliaries, forming a rescue squad, emerged from their ambush and ran to the German rocket. Espéret, who was in the lead, darted an anxious glance into the interior of the cabin.

Valsorres welcomed him, and hugged him to his bosom. "Look!" he said.

Espéret recognized the bound prisoner. "Dr. Frank!"

"Or Graf von Paschwitz—your choice, old chap. Yes, the prize is good. But look further.

In the meantime, Thomas and Hina had penetrated into the chamber. Espéret looked at the child.

"Don't you recognize him?" asked the Marquis.

Espéret examined the small boy; but the latter, having perceived Thomas, had got up and went to throw himself in his arms.

"My good Thomas! Don't you recognize me?" And the child, recovering his mother tongue as if by magic, expressed himself in French.

"Oh, Monsieur Philippe, Monsieur Philippe!" said the worthy Thomas, hugging the child to his heart. The fellow did not seek to hide large tears of joy.

"Philippe!" said Espéret. "Philippe! Is that possible?"

"Yes, old friend," the Marquis replied. "God, in his eternal justice, has permitted this miracle. And if we've recovered the victim, we also hold the torturer. The Graf von Paschwitz is ours."

Hina witnessed this scene without comprehending it.

"Well explain it all to you later, my dear Hina," Thomas said to her. "In the meantime, it's an act of justice that is going to be accomplished."

Thomas and Hina, on the Marquis' order, took the cadaver of the Prussian killed by Portier down the ladder and sent him to join the two who had been scythed down by the machine gun bullets; then they climbed back up to the cabin.

The five voyagers and the child stood in a circle around Dr. Frank.

Valsorres spoke. "Dr. Frank, do you admit that you are guilty of having abducted young Philippe de Valsorres, here present, from the Château de Valsorres?"

Frank did not reply.

"Your silence is a confession," the Marquis said to him. He continued: "Dr. Frank, do you admit that you are guilty of having sequestered and maltreated young Philippe de Valsorres, here present, for four years?"

The accused remained silent.

"Here," Valsorres continued, "we have the testimony of the victim. Speak, my Philippe, and tell us everything."

Then the child, expressing himself in German, told the story of the existence he had led since his abduction.

"What have you to respond?" asked the Marquis, when the child had told the story of his suffering.

The German was obstinate in his silence.

"You have nothing to say? You admit, then, that you are guilty. But that's not all. Do you recognize these letters?"

The Marquis put before he wretch's eyes the letters that Portier had shown him, along with others, even more edifying, which the doctor had found in the drawer, and which bore Bettina's signature.

At the sight of the letters, the German experienced a shudder that he could not dissimulate. He understood that he was doomed.

"Ah! You see, Master Spy, that we hold all the proofs of your infamy. So it was you who introduced into my sister's home, as a chambermaid, this Bettina, who spied on your account?"

At Bettina's name, Thomas had shivered. "Bettina!" he said "Oh..." The worthy fellow could not say any more but, overwhelmed by shame, he lowered his head piteously.

Valsorres perceived his trouble. "What's the matter, my good Thomas?"

Thomas summoned up all his courage. "It's just, Monsieur le Marquis, that it's perhaps me who's the cause of everything. That Bettina, you see, bewitched me...and once, she even had me so wound up that I had a rendezvous with her in my bedroom..."

"In your bedroom, wretch!" cried Espéret. "She was able to get into the laboratory, then?"

"Oh, Monsieur, I don't know; in any case, I didn't see anything, I can swear to that. But if she got in, it was surely then. I remember...she made me drink cognac...which had a funny taste..."

"That's it. She put you to sleep, and while you were asleep, she pulled off the coup. So it was her who took the photographs we found here." Valsorres reflected. "But then, it must have been her who put Philippe's nurse to sleep, in order to abduct him afterwards, and the nurse of my sister's children. Oh, the wretch!"

Thomas held his head in his hands. "And to think that it's because of me that all that happened! Oh, Le Bris told me to be wary of Bettina! Damn! Damn! These things only happen to me!"

"Console yourself, my good Thomas," said Valsorres. "You can see that it's all forgotten, from the moment that Philippe threw himself into your arms. He recognized you; he remembers the walks in the park for which you used to take him, pushing him in a wheelbarrow."

But Thomas was inconsolable.

It was Hina who restored his aplomb. "My dear friend," said the worthy woman, "Since these Messieurs tell you that it's nothing, why are you tormenting yourself?"

Valsorres had turned back to Dr. Frank. "So you have no response to make to this triple accusation?"

The accused remained silent.

"In that case, we'll go discus your fate. Thomas, Hina, stay with this rogue, and if he makes the slightest move, kill him like a dog with a pistol shot."

Thomas placed himself to Frank's left, his pistol in his hand. Hina stood to the bandit's right, holding her hatchet firmly.

"Don't worry, Messieurs," she said. "We're here!"

The three men and little Philippe went down the ladder, and found the three Saturnians, who were waiting for them, astonished by what they had just seen.

"What are we going to do with that brigand?" asked Valsorres.

"Shoot him!" replied Portier.

Espéret made a gesture of protest. "No," he said. "Even though we'd have an absolute right, since he threatened us, let's not substitute ourselves for the law. We'll take the swine back to France, where he committed his crimes, and deliver him to the law of our country; he has a lot for which to answer in that regard."

Valsorres raised an objection, however. "I fear the material difficulty," he said. "Our vehicle was designed for four people. We already have six, since we're taking back Hina and little Philippe. Will we have enough potash and copper oxide to be able to ensure our respiration during the return journey, and enough water and food to ensure the subsistence of three extra people?"

"We have the reserves of the German vehicle," replied Portier. "Tomorrow, we can make an inventory of them, and remove what's necessary in order to be amply provided for our return voyage."

"Before anything else," said the Marquis, "let's lower that accursed flag and hoist the French flag in its place."

Portier hastened up the ladder in order to go in search of the national flag that Thomas was carrying in his bag. He told the two guards to bring the prisoner down.

Thomas and Hina untied his legs. Frank descended without resistance. When he was down below he gazed wrathfully at the cadavers of his three companions, and simply said: "Oh, Messieurs the French, you do things well!"

Meanwhile, Thomas got ready to hoist the flag. Hina was holding his hunting rifle.

"Hoist!" commanded Valsorres.

"Fire!" ordered Espéret.

And while the French tricolor flapped in the Saturnian breeze, two rifle shots rendered it the honors. The inhabitants of the planet looked on, completely bewildered.

"Now, the judgment!" said the Marquis.

The five voyagers and the child faced the criminal.

"Graf von Paschwitz, or Dr. Frank, you have been found guilty of child kidnapping, sequestration, treason and espionage. We have the right to condemn you to death and execute you here, under the eyes of God, who sees us, who judges us and who absolves us. But it is necessary that your crime should be expiated in the place where it was committed. We shall take you back to France, where you will be delivered to the law of our country. Have you anything to add for your defense?"

336

Then Dr. Frank, speaking slowly, expressed himself in these terms: "Marquis de Valsorres, I am in your power. I can, therefore, only submit to the law of the stronger. But remember this: yes I hate you! My father, on his death-bed, had me swear, along with my sister Emma, now Baronne Lymstroem, that I would never allow that hatred to be extinguished. Well, it never will be. Wherever I am, wherever you might be, while I am alive, that hatred will pursue you, and your children. Take that as a promise, such as a Paschwitz knows how to make, and how to keep. I have spoken."

And he fell back into his mutism.

It was then decided that Frank would be left in the German vehicle under the guard of Hina and Portier. The latter would make an inventory of the provisions of all kinds that could be found there.

Valsorres, Espéret, Thomas and little Philippe set forth to return to the *Fusée*. Valsorres navigated by means of the compass.

After half an hour the little troop encountered the Saturnian to whom they had given the gramophone. The man prostrated himself before his new friends, whom he evidently regarded as divinities. Valsorres lifted him up and stroked his head with a gesture of amity.

Some time afterwards they encountered another herd of hipparions conducted by indigenes. Espéret took several photographs of them, as well as a large group of dinotheriums that they found near the *Fusée*.

Finally, the voyagers regained their hospitable cabin.

"Oof!" said Thomas. "It's better here than in the Boches' place."

The Marquis had unhooked a gilded frame from the wall containing a photograph, and he showed it to Philippe.

"Here, my child," he said. "This is your maman."

The child put it to his lips, and large tears fell from his eyes.

*VI. In which it will be seen how our voyagers made
the conquest of Saturn.*

Early the next morning our three friends and little Philippe set forth in the direction of the German rocket.

Espéret photographed everything he could, in order to take back as many documents as possible. Valsorres never quit his son, of whom Thomas had appointed himself the bodyguard.

After an hour and a half of marching, they found the German shell again, next to the pole at the top of which the French flag now floated.

Portier was waiting for them, having descended from the apparatus. "First it's necessary to bury these three scoundrels," he said, indicating the cadavers with his foot.

"How is the prisoner?"

"Oh, he's quite tranquil. Hina's watching him, and I wouldn't advise him to show the slightest sign of independence. Anyway, he's well secured.

The three men went up the ladder and came down again shortly afterwards with spades. A ditch was dug and the three bodies were thrown into it.

"Let's give them the honor of a cross," said Valsorres. "They were Christians, after all, and the most culpable one isn't underground."

Thomas went to fetch two branches, which they assembled in the form of a cross and planted on the tomb of the three Boches. After removing their hats, the voyagers made the sign of the cross.

"May God receive their souls," said the Marquis, solemnly.

Then Portier gave an account of his inventory. The German machine contained nearly eight hundred liters of water, enough copper oxide to ensure oxygen for more than two months and enough potash to absorb carbon dioxide for the same duration. In addition, abundant provisions of tinned food would ensure the nourishment of the seven passengers. Even more precious, the doctor had discovered, in a thick lead box, a considerable reserve of a radioactive substance that had to be virium. Finally, eight brand new cathode ray tubes were crated up in boxes padded with cotton.

"Well, my children," said Valsorres. "We have only to transport all that aboard our *Fusée*. That will take us a good fortnight."

"Yes," replied Espéret, "but aren't we going to transport these scoundrels' powder and weapons?"

"No, certainly not. We'll leave them for the Saturnians."

"Stop there!" said Portier. "No firearms for the savages. We can leave them knives, axes, spades, pickaxes, saws and nails, but not rifles or pistols. Don't you agree?"

"Yes," said the voyagers, in unison.

Meanwhile, Thomas had gone up to relieve the worthy Hina of guard duty. When he was in Frank's presence, he said: "Well my colonist, are we beginning to master the métier of sausage? How good it is to feel oneself tied to the back of a chair, eh?"

As always, the German did not reply. His arms were untied and he was given something to eat. He ate with appetite and drank avidly, and then returned to his customary mutism.

That entire day and the following days were employed by the voyagers in carrying out the transshipment of provisions. The Saturnians did their best to help them, and that was a resource for transporting the virium, whose lead boxes were extremely heavy. Every evening, they were recompensed by giving them a knife, a saw or some other implement. Then the joy of the primitives knew no bounds.

One of them, more intelligent than the others, had seen Valsorres picking up minerals and putting them in his bag. One evening, he approached the Marquis and, pointing at the bag, made him a sign indicating that he had something to put in it. The Marquis held out his hand. The savage then took a sort of calabash from a fold in the animal skin with which he was covered and emptied it into the Marquis' hands. A few pieces of shiny mineral fell out.

"Oh!" said Valsorres. "Diamonds."

"Diamonds?" said Espéret.

"Yes, and fine ones. Truly, there's a providence. With a few stones like these, we'll go back with the expenses of the expedition, and you, my dear Portier, will have a fine adornment to offer your pretty little Zabeth when you lead her to the altar."

The Marquis thanked the Saturnian with a caress of the hand and a broad smile; the latter made a sign to say that he would do it again—and, indeed, every day, the worthy planetary brought Valsorres five or six diamonds, some large and others medium-sized, but not one small one.

After ten days, during which Frank was always under the guard of one of the five voyagers, the transshipment was concluded. They would then have been able to commence the return journey and go back to Earth.

Valsorres, impatient to see his wife again and bring back her son, rediscovered in such a miraculous fashion, proposed that they depart as soon as possible.

Espéret opposed that plan forcefully. "My dear Henri," he said, "We came to conquer Saturn and take possession of it in the name of France. It's necessary to carry our effort through to the end. We've planted the flag of our country on Saturnian soil, it's true, but one task remains for us to accomplish."

"What?"

"It's necessary to leave, in the minds and in the memory of these primitive beings who inhabit the planet, a durable trace of or sojourn in their midst."

"I don't understand what you mean."

"I'll explain. Let's stay here for another two or three months. We have nothing more to fear from our enemies now; we can therefore be tranquil and act in all security."

"Act to do what?"

"Simply to give these cavemen the first notions of civilization. Let's teach them a few words of French; let's show them how to create resources; let's instruct them in a few elementary crafts."

Thomas interrupted Espéret then. "As for teaching them to speak French, that's already begun," he said. "In the last fortnight, Hina and I have taught them the names of all the objects they've touched: hammer, saw, hatchet. They know how to say walk, eat and drink."

"You're a true colonizer, my good Thomas," said Portier.

"Oh, it wasn't my idea," Espéret's faithful servant replied, modestly. "It was Hina's…like all good ideas, in fact."

"Well," said Espéret, "It's necessary to continue what Hina and Thomas have begun so well."

"But what about Marie, my poor Marie, who thinks I'm dead and lost to her forever?"

"My dear Henri, your wife has been waiting for you in vain, and must, indeed believe that you're lost to her. She isn't expecting you any longer, and our prolongation of our sojourn here won't increase her chagrin at all, while it will permit us to complete entirely the task that we imposed upon ourselves."

Valsorres reflected for some time. He looked his friend in the face.

"You're right, old chap," he said. "You're always right. Yes, we'll stay here for another two or three months, and we'll leave these primitive beings that surround us with the first seeds of our terrestrial civilization."

"Bravo, Henri! Bravo, and thank you."

"When do we start?"

"Tomorrow, and without delay. We'll all devote ourselves to it."

The next day, in fact, Valsorres, Espéret, Portier, Thomas, Hina and little Philippe left the *Fusée* and went, as they did every day, to meet the Saturnians.

Valsorres had taken a small earthenware vase from the utensils of the voyage. He made the Saturnians understand, by means of signs, that he was going to teach them how to make similar ones. The raw material, clay, was to hand. Valsorres had the indigenes collect an abundant quantity. He made molds with a wood saw, and he accumulated a clay paste in the molds that was to constitute bricks.

The indigenes worked with an indescribable enthusiasm. When the number of bricks was sufficient they were disposed on a large fire and baked, after which a kiln was constructed with them. In that kiln, Espéret and Portier fired primitive items of pottery, which he had fashioned crudely but which, once finished, delighted the Saturnians.

All that had taken ten days, in the course of which the fabrication of bricks continued. After the pottery kiln, a lime kiln was built. There was no lack of material; chalk was abundant.

After the lime kiln, Valsorres and Espéret had one further ambition: to teach the savages to make iron. They had taught them how to obtain wood charcoal, by the classic method of our charcoal burners; iron ore was found in large quantity, and primitive furnace following the rudimentary procedure known as the "Catalan method" permitted the Saturnians to manufacture their own iron.

While all this labor was being pursued relentlessly, Portier had studied the flora of Saturn, had recognized fruits there, and had taught the indigenous women to make fermented beverages with their juice. He had also taught them to make butter with the milk of their animals. And, to finish off his activity, he had shown them how to extract from sea water the salt necessary to alimentation.

In the course of "training" the planetaries, they always learned new words of our language; the most intelligent among them, especially the children, under the direction of Hina, began to speak "pidgin."

After three months of that extraordinary colonization, our friends estimated that they could leave the planet to its destiny. Then Valsorres, assembling the Saturnians, made them his adieux. He distributed to them all the knives, axes, tools, pans and utensils that were aboard the German machine. He even gave the one who seemed to be the chief a pair of Zeiss binoculars, showing him how to use and maintain them by means of gestures.

Then the prisoner was taken to the *Fusée*, which was about to quit the soil of Saturn, of which Valsorres solemnly took possession in the name of France before departing. He distributed tricolor ribbons to the indigenes and gave them copies of their photographs, which Portier had taken and of which he had taken a few prints on paper. That present filled them with joy, and it was to cries of "Vive la France" uttered by the rude voices of those primitive humans that the voyagers installed themselves in their vehicle.

Finally, when everyone had climbed into the shell, the panels were sealed by Thomas, and the cathode ray tubes activated.

The disintegration of the virium commenced immediately, slowly at first, and then more actively, and soon acquired a violence sufficient to make the *Fusée* tremble on its supports. Then it lifted slowly above the ground of the planet and began its return journey through the thick atmosphere, bound for Earth, which it had quit such a long time ago.

LE DOCTEUR PORTIER

THOMAS

PART SIX: THE RETURN

I. In which it will be seen that it is not always prudent to leave a wild beast at liberty.

Shall we talk now about the incidents of the return journey? They were almost the same as those of the outward journey. The passage in the vicinity of Jupiter, and the very difficult traversal of the swarm of minor planets, went in returning as they had on going, with the difference that this time, the voyagers had joy in their hearts; they were bringing back Philippe, liberated, with his torturer a prisoner.

When they approached Mars, the question was raised of whether to make a landfall. All the voyagers were of the opinion that it was necessary not to waste time by stopping there.

Valsorres looked at Hina. Did the courageous woman want to return to her natal world? If she desired that, Valsorres would land in order to deposit her there.

But in her turn, Hina looked at Thomas. "My friend," she said to him, "you know that I have already promised you that wherever you go, I will go; wherever you stop, I will stop; wherever you die I will die."

Thomas hugged his companion to his heart.

And it was decided that they would by-pass Mars.

However, Portier made an observation full of justice: "If Thaû and Saâh want to force us to stop on their planet, they have the means to do so, by making their gravitational waves act on the *Fusée*, as they did before."

But Espéret replied that they would not be forewarned of the passage of the *Fusée* by wireless telegraph messages, as they had been on the outward journey, when they had captured radiograms sent on Earth the announce the departure of the expedition.

They therefore passed within view of Mars—but not too closely, in order not to awaken the attention of the Martian astronomers, whose powerful telescopes would have quickly recognized the *Fusée* by the luminous trail that it left behind.

Valsorres, seething with impatience to see once again those he had left behind, pushed the propulsion of his engine to the limit; he reached the limit of the resistance of the tubes to heat, and it was necessary more than once for Espéret to bring him back to a sentiment of prudence.

The question had been raised several times as to whether to utilize Frank's collaboration for various maneuvers. Valsorres had thought of it, and Portier too; Espéret had hesitated—but Hina, with her prodigious common sense, dissuaded them.

"If he's a traitor, he'll betray again," she said. "It's necessary to distrust him."

They therefore distrusted him, and they were right.

His bonds had been removed, given that he could no longer escape. He did not say a word all day, absorbed in somber thoughts. He took his nourishment silently and lay down to sleep on Thomas' bunk when the latter was taking his turn on watch.

One day, about three weeks after the departure from Saturn and a few hours after the passage of Mars, the passengers were asleep, with the exception of Thomas, who was on watch in the cabin, and Espéret, who was at the pilot station.

The worthy Thomas had he joy of thinking that in two days, he would be in France, where he could marry his dear Hina. At that idea he felt very enthused. He told himself that nothing would be better than a "little drop" and, opening the cupboard which the pharmaceutical products were kept, he searched for a bottle that he believed to contain cognac. He poured himself a glass of its contents, after having assured himself, by the odor, that it really was alcohol, and emptied it in a single draught, with an evident satisfaction.

But he had no sooner swallowed the draught that he felt a terrible malaise; he only just had time to sit down, and fell almost instantaneously into a heavy slumber.

From the height of his bunk, where he was not asleep, Frank had seen the scene. Immediately, descending silently, he approached the orifice pierced in the floor through which the cathode rays were launched that provoked the decomposition of the virium. Already he had lifted the trap that closed the deflagration chamber.

An infernal smile was designed on the wretch's lips.

Yes, he was about to provoke at a single stroke the deflagration of the entire reserve of the radioactive substance.[41] Then he would die, to be sure, but he

---

[41] This makes it clear that Frank/von Paschwitz must have known since 1914 that he was in possession of the means to cause a nuclear explosion, but that he had refrained from giving that information to the German military, even though there was a war on. On the other hand, François Bourcelle also knew the secret, and had similarly failed to confide it to the defenders of France. This detail might support the hypothesis that the original version of Berget's part of the story was probably written some time before the feuilleton version, perhaps in 1913 or the early months of 1914.

would take within him in his ruination Valsorres, his son. Espéret, Portier, Thomas and Hina.

He had already approached the tube to the lead cover that he had just raised. One second more and it would have been all over for the *Fusée* and its passengers. But a vigorous hand grasped the bandit by the throat; it was Hina, who, having heard Thomas fall, had witnessed the whole scene.

Bounding from her couchette, the courageous woman had leapt at the traitor's throat, with a cry that woke everyone up: "The bandit! Tie him up! Tie him well!"

Valsorres, Espéret and Portier threw themselves on the German, who was solidly tied up. When he was extended on the floor, Valsorres said to him, prodding him with his foot: "Wretch! That's one crime more for which you'll have to answer to the law of France!"

Then a satanic laugh shook the body of Graf von Paschwitz. "Ah! The law of France! Ah! France! Ha ha ha!"

The astonished voyagers looked at him.

"France!" the German continued, "But it no longer exists!" And, before the stupor of his listeners, he went on: "Don't you know that war was declared by our Emperor on France, England and Russia? When you departed, there was still peace, but our triumphant armies invaded France in 1914."

"Great God!" said Valsorres. "What is he saying?"

"What am I saying? The truth! You're about to learn that, when you land on Earth. When we departed, at the end of 1917, France was finished. A quarter of its territory was occupied by our victorious soldiers, and we'd bombarded Paris. England's navy had been destroyed by our submarines. As for Russia, our gold had bought all of the democratic parties, and a revolution had taken place, to the profit of Germany."

Valsorres and Espéret looked at one another fearfully. "And I advise you not to land in France," the German continued, for you'll find your entire country definitively conquered by our invincible soldiers. Now kill me if you want; I won't say another word."

Valsorres was crushed by the revelation.

Was it not the ultimate bluster of a beaten man desirous of hurling a supreme insult at his conquerors?

But no: the man was speaking with authority; he had given dates, he had cited facts.

And the Marquis was in despair. "War! And I wasn't there! Me, a Valsorres!"

II. Joy causes fear.

We are in the Château de Valsorres.

Is there any need to say what anguishes and sorrows its inhabitants have passed through? The reader will understand them without difficulty.

The Marquise de Valsorres, under the blow of the abduction of her little Philippe, had supported the departure of her husband stoically. She had not expected him to return for five or six months, so she had lived in an isolation that further augmented her chagrin. In vain, her sister-in-law, Aunt Hélène and little Zabeth surrounded her with the most affectionate care.

"You'll see that they'll come back, Aunt," said the young woman. But those affirmations of hope did not succeed in bringing cheerfulness back to the careworn forehead of the Marquise.

Then, in the month of August 1914, as brutal as a thunderbolt, there was the declaration of war.

All the valid men in the château had gone to join their respective corps. Jérôme, the gamekeeper, a sergeant in a reserve regiment, departed for the Eastern Front.

As soon as hostilities opened, the château had been transformed into an auxiliary hospital. Aunt Hélène was the senior nurse, with little Zabeth under her orders, who expended herself without counting the cost. The young woman regretted that her dear fiancée, Dr. Portier, was not there. Oh, how much more devotion she would have furnished had she been under the sure direction of the elect of her heart!

As if by chance, a fortnight before the declaration of war, when the situation was already "tense," Baron and Baronne Lymstroem had left Paris "for a holiday in Switzerland," so they said. And, also as if by chance, five days after the opening of hostilities, Bettina received a telegram from Switzerland summoning her to the bedside of her dying mother. The spy packed her bags; one can easily guess for what destination.

Then there was the invasion with its horrors, and the investment of Paris; the miracle of the Marne came to render hope that had been momentarily lost; France pulled herself together. Her allies aided her in her prodigious effort; the German hordes were halted. But the long war of the trenches began, and the hospital of Valsorres was always full.

Winter had come; the Boches had been pushed back to the Yser; confidence was reborn.

But, alas for the Marquise, time passed without bringing back the man for whom she was waiting with so much anguish.

Eight months had gone by and the voyagers had not returned.

"Patience!" Abbé Travers said to her, in the course of a leave he had obtained after the battle of Flanders, where, having resumed his service, he had become a Lieutenant-Colonel and an officer of the Légion d'honneur. "Patience. They'll require a little time to explore Saturn."

But all that did not console the poor woman.

In the month of March, nevertheless, a joy was given to her; she gave birth to a son, whom she called Henri. The solicitude with which she raised that son goes without saying. She never quit him, day or night. She installed the concierge, Jérôme's father, in the château. Armed with a rifle, the old country-dweller slept in the room that preceded the Marquise's, and a formidable guard dog was also there. The young woman dreaded seeing the kidnapping of Philippe repeated.

The war continued thus.

After a year, the Marquise had lost all hope; she concentrated all her affection on little Henri. She put on mourning, which she never quit. She occupied herself with the administration of her hospital, of which she was the "housekeeper," which permitted her to have her son always with her, from whom she did not want to be separated for a single minute, under any pretext.

The events that had been accomplished in those four years, however, had passed with the rapidity with which only those who lived though that terrible period can know.

Then the dawn appeared after the darkness of the night.

The retreat of the Germans in the month of August 1918 enabled their imminent defeat to be anticipated. Emperor Wilhelm abdicated, and finally, to the sound of bells and the noise of cannon fire, on 11 November 1918, the armistice was proclaimed.

The war was over!

That day, there was a celebration at the hospital of Valsorres.

Aunt Hélène and Zabeth announced the news to the wounded. Those who could get up were invited to celebrate, a glass of champagne in hand, the triumph of our cause. Jérôme, having returned with one leg fewer and one red ribbon more, was among the latter.

Abbé Travers, who had returned the night before with his colonel's uniform, strode through the wards, stopping before every bed with a word of confidence.

In the evening, the Marquise, overcoming her chagrin, gave a great dinner. Her sister-in-law, who was at the château, Aunt Hélène, little Zabeth, Abbé Travers and the deputy mayor were invited, as well as the brave Jérôme and the schoolteacher, Monsieur Barthon, who had returned from the front with a captain's braid and decorated with the Légion d'honneur, after three citations.

Shortly before dessert, one of the chambermaids who were serving at table, replacing the valets who had been called to the front, approached Abbé Travers and whispered a few words in his ear.

The abbé—or, rather, the colonel—went pale, and then extremely red.

"My apologies, Madame," he said; and, throwing his napkin on his chair, he followed the maid.

That simple incident had troubled the guests. However, Aunt Hélène made the observation that nothing was more natural: might not a wounded man have need of the abbé's assistance?

In spite of that, the conversation had fallen silent when the abbé returned and sat down, his expression, not worried, but somewhat embarrassed. He darted an affectionate glance at the Marquise.

"Well, my dear Colonel Abbé," said Aunt Hélène, "What was the cause that disturbed you?"

"Oh, nothing much, Mademoiselle. It's a man who was encountered in a field and who, being a little fatigued, has asked to repose at the hospital. What is curious is his unexpected resemblance to Monsieur Espéret's domestic—you know, the worthy Thomas."

At the name of Thomas, the Marquise had gone utterly pale.

"Oh!" she said. "I want to see that man."

"You'll see him after dinner, Madame," replied Abbé Travers. As if to himself, however, he added: "The resemblance is truly prodigious. I could almost have believed that I was in the presence of Thomas himself."

The Marquise devoured the abbé with her gaze; the latter had picked up his napkin and continued speaking, striving to remain indifferent.

Meanwhile, the chambermaids continued serving with an unaccustomed grace and verve. They were smiling as they presented the dishes. An expression of joy reigned over their faces.

The abbé went on: "It's certain that I'm still wondering whether it isn't Thomas himself that I've just seen. Truly, as a double it's impossible to dream of anything similar."

The Marquise could no longer contain herself. "My dear Abbé, you're putting me over coals. You're hiding something."

"Me, Madame? I'm not hiding anything. I'm simply telling you that I've just seen a man that I could have mistaken for Thomas. In any case, if you don't believe me, go and see him. He's not far away. He's in the consulting room."

Very emotional, the Marquise got up, accompanied by the abbé colonel. Aunt Hélène, Germaine and Zabeth followed her; the young woman's heart was beating as if to burst.

Madame de Valsorres penetrated into the room, faintly lit by a shaded lamp. A man was lying on a divan.

She approached him and uttered a cry. "Thomas! Thomas! Is it really you?"

The man replied, as if in a dream: "Who's calling me? Yes, it's me; it can't be anyone else, given that it's me, of course! It's no longer necessary that people don't recognize me! Damn it! These things only happen to me!"

The Marquise advanced, choked by emotion.

"But in that case, Thomas, you've come back..."

"...From Saturn, Madame la Marquise, from Saturn, and well content, in truth, to be back on Earth. You can even tell the pharmacist that I'm an 'extract of Saturn.'"[42]

"Then Monsieur Espéret, your master...?"

"...Is very well, Madame, and you'll see him in a moment."

Pale with emotion, the Marquise leaned on a table in order not to fall.

"And...my husband?"

"Monsieur le Marquise de Valsorres? He's very well too, thank you, and you'll..."

At that moment, Abbé Travers intervened. "Madame," he said to the Marquise, "Thank God! He has taken pity on your tears, and is returning to you today those for whom you have wept so much."

And the worthy priest, standing aside, made way for Henri de Valsorres, who only just had time to catch his fainting wife in his arms and clutch her to his heart.

Little Zabeth had also fallen, but without fainting, into the arms of Dr. Portier, who covered her with kisses. Finally, Espéret was the last to appear.

Under the caresses of her husband and Aunt Hélène, however, Marie de Valsorres soon recovered consciousness.

"Thank you, God!" she said, raising her eyes toward the heavens. "You have granted my prayer. Thank you."

And the young woman, falling to her knees, addressed a fervent action of grace to the Almighty.

Then, getting up, she returned to the dining room and came back holding little Henri by the hand.

"This is our son, my love," she said to her husband. "He will replace for us the cherished being that was stolen from us by those accursed swine."

The Marquis lifted the little child, who was nearly four years old, in his arms and look at him lovingly.

"He resembles his brother," he said, putting him down gain.

"Alas," said the Marquise, "that resemblance is the only souvenir that remains to me of my poor child."

Then Abbé Travers spoke: "Just now, Madame I told you to thank heaven for having returned *those* for whom you wept. You have only seen one thus far—your husband, but..."

"Great God!" cried the Marquise. "Oh...!"

---

[42] "*Extrait de Saturne*" [Extract of Saturn], also known as *eau de Goudard* after its popularizer, Thomas Goudard, was a solution of lead acetate and lead oxide in alcohol and water, widely used as an astringent until part way through the twentieth century.

And Abbé Travers pushed little Philippe into the poor woman's arms, who threw his arms round her neck, crying: "*Maman! Ma petite maman!*"

One does not die of joy.

After sweet tears shed over so much happiness, one thinks about questioning one another a little, and it was the Marquis who posed the first queries.

"My dear Marie," he said, "can you explain to me why the château is in celebration today? Why is Abbé Travers wearing a colonel's uniform? You certainly weren't expecting us, so…?"

"But my love, because the war ended today, and victorious France is dictating her conditions to vanquished Germany. And that's the reason for this celebration, for which I would never have dared to hope for such a coronation!"

The Marquis turned toward Espéret and Portier. "So it's true, what that wretch told us!"

And rapidly, he told his wife about the capture of Dr. Frank, taken prisoner on Saturn and returned to Earth, and the affirmations he had made regarding the victory of the Germans.

"You've brought him back, then?"

"Yes, my dear Abbé. He's still in the *Fusée*, trussed up like a sausage and under the surveillance of a guard, who doesn't have frost in her eyes."

In a few words, Valsorres recounted the story of Hina, and how much they already owed to the beautiful and courageous Martian.

The Marquise wanted to summon the wretch to appear before her immediately, but her husband dissuaded her. "Soon, my darling, we'll put the bandit in the hands of the law, in order that he can expiate all his crimes."

Meanwhile, the voyagers had gone into the dining room. At the sight of the Marquis, the deputy mayor, Monsieur Barthon the schoolteacher and Jérôme got up and ran toward them with moist eyes. The Marquis shook all the hands, including those of the chambermaids and the former concierge, who had come running on hearing the news.

"Thank you, my friends, thank you, thank you," he said.

Eventually, before his friends, gathered in an intimate circle in the small drawing room. Henri gave a succinct account of his voyage. He described their sojourn on Mars, without dwelling on the details; he recalled that the joys of the scientific discoveries that had been revealed to them very day had taken away their notion of time, which they had also been caused to lose by the beverages that they had drunk. He also told them that it was thanks to Thomas, who had not been distracted by intellectual preoccupations, that they had resumed their voyage to Saturn, taking Hina, who did not want to be separated from her companion.

He retracted his surprise in finding cousins in the sovereigns of Mars. He recounted the episodes on Saturn, the return journey, and how, an hour ago, they had had the joy, thanks to an almost cloudless atmosphere, of being able, first to steer toward France, and then to land in the fields only a few hectometers from Valsorres.

"And," he added, "As 'joy causes fear,'[43] we used the intermediary of Thomas to have us announced by the woman in service, whom we charge with warning Abbé Travers.

In his turn, in a few minutes of conversation, the abbé summarized the war for our voyagers. He told them about the aggression, the invasion the struggle, the alliances, the bombardment of Paris and, finally, the victory.

"And," he said, "admire the divine bounty that has enabled you to return to Valsorres on the very day when the canons were thundering in honor of the triumph of France."

---

[43] *La joie fait peur* [Joy causes Fear] (1855) is the title of a one-act comedy by Delphine de Girardin.

III. In which everything finishes as the reader has certainly desired.

After the first emotions of that unforgettable return, the Marquis de Valsorres thought about his prisoner. He sent Thomas, accompanied by Jérôme and the former concierge to fetch him from the *Fusée*. At the same time, he sent someone to inform the brigadier of the gendarmerie, who arrived at the château with two gendarmes. Valsorres had them placed in the large drawing room, full of light, next to Abbé Travers, still clad in his colonel's uniform, and the schoolteacher, Monsieur Barthon, in his captain's uniform.

Half an hour later, Dr. Frank—or Graf von Paschwitz, as you wish—was introduced between Thomas and Hina, with Jérôme and the former concierge marching behind him.

When he perceived the colonel, the captain and the gendarmes, he laughed sarcastically. "Well! There are still soldiers in France, then?"

"Yes, wretch," Valsorres replied. "Yes, there are soldiers in France, and victorious soldiers. It's in your country that there are no more of them. Can you hear the bells that are ringing and the cannons that are firing? That's to celebrate the victory of France and her allies, and the defeat of Germany. The Emperor and the crown prince are in flight, a republic has been proclaimed in Berlin, and the vanquished Empire is requesting peace. Here, read."

And the Marquis put before the bandit's eyes an issue of a Paris newspaper that had just arrived and was giving the news of the armistice.

"Defeated!" he cried. "Germany defeated! Oh!"

He paraded his haggard eyes over all the people standing before him. Then, putting his hand to his neck as if he were choking, and turning round, he fell heavily on the floor.

He was dead.

The Marquis turned to the brigadier. "My friend," he said, "your work is simplified; justice has been done of its own accord. That man, who was a great criminal toward France and toward us, is dead.

The three soldiers made the military salute.

"We'll draw up a formal statement," the Marquis told them. "The doctor will attest the natural death, as well as all the people present."

The cadaver was taken away.

Then the Marquis summoned the beautiful Hina, who was still holding the now-unnecessary pistol with which she had been covering the prisoner. Madame de Valsorres already knew all that the voyagers owed to that strong and courageous woman. Embracing her affectionately, she promised to assure her of a privileged situation.

The return of the Marquis and his companions had been, as one can imagine, quite an event in the area. They had been seen to depart, the *Fusée* had been seen to launch into the sky, and for four years there had been no news of them; they had been thought lost forever—so when they were seen to have returned "from the stars" people could scarcely believe their eyes.

Needless to say, the Académie des Sciences in Paris gave Valsorres, Espéret and Portier an unprecedented welcome. The three scientists were received in a solemn session, in the course of which the president, who was then the celebrated astronomer Henri-Alexandre Deslandres, the director of the observatory of Sèvres, presented them with the Grand Medaille Berthelot, awarded to them by the learned company as "the most audacious scholars who have ever personified the genius of French science." The Royal Society in London also awarded them the Davy Medal, and the Accademia dei Lincei of Rome held it an honor to receive them as associates.

Two months later, in the old church of Valsorres, Abbé Travers, who had just, as he put it cheerfully, definitively "quit the saber for the aspergillum" celebrated a double marriage, that of Dr. Portier with Mademoiselle Elisabeth Kessler and that of the worthy Thomas with his dear Hina, baptized the previous day. Espéret had been her godfather and the Marquise de Valsorres her godmother.

It was also an event at the Mairie of the little village. The deputy mayor having asked the civil estate of the bride, she replied: "Born on the planet Mars in the month of December 1887." A murmur of amazement ran through the audience; Hina's story had spread through the neighborhood, but no one had wanted to believe it.

Fortunately, a certificate of identity formally drawn up by the ministerial officer and signed by the Marquis, Espéret and Portier, had put everything in order, and replaced the birth certificate that it was impossible for the Martian to furnish.

After the ceremony, the Marquis de Valsorres gathered the newlyweds in the large drawing room of the château. He gave Zabeth, now Madame Portier, a small casket, which the young woman opened. It was filled with diamonds, selected from those that the Saturnian had given the Marquis before his departure.

"Here, my dear Zabeth. You can have a few cut for yourself; the rest will be the dowry that the Marquise and I request your permission to offer you."

The young woman threw her arms around her cousin

Then the latter gave Hina a box, also containing a few diamonds; it was the wedding present that the Marquis was giving his faithful traveling companions.

"And there are also enough to make some beautiful adornments for you, Marie, you, Aunt Hélène, and you, my dear Germaine," he said. "And when all those have been distributed, the rest will pay for the expenses of the *Fusée*'s construction. They're the petty profits of Saturn!"

After a great dinner held at the château that evening, they talked about the planet Mars and the cousins who reigned there. The Marquis de Valsorres expressed aloud a thought that had been haunting him since his return. "Why, since Thaû and Saâh received wireless messages, didn't they tell me that there was war with Germany? I would have been unable to fulfill my duty as a Frenchman and a gentleman on the battlefield and contribute to the defense of my country, like Abbé Tavers, Jérôme, the schoolmaster Barthon and so many others."

It was Hina who replied. "Monsieur le Marquis," said the beautiful Martian. "King Thaû thought about telling you, but Queen Saâh remarked that if you knew that your country was at war, you would quit Mars immediately in order to return to fight. So it was decided to leave you unaware of events on Earth."

"But since our relatives on Mars receive wireless telegrams," said the Marquise, "ought we not, now that we're all in joy, send them an affectionate souvenir through space?"

"You're right, my dear Marie. I'll send them a message, which will only be understood by them."

And the Marquis went to the laboratory, where he had installed a wireless telegraph apparatus long before the war, and launched the following dispatch into space:

To King Thaû and Queen Saâh,
My dear cousins.

I have now returned to Earth, after a voyage to Saturn. We have brought one of your subjects with us, Hina, who did not want to quit her companion, of whom she is now the wife. All of us send you our warmest regards.

My wife the Marquise Marie de Valsorres would like to meet her Martian cousins. Will you not come to see us on Earth? If not, it will be necessary for us to come to your planet to make a second visit!

We all recall with emotion the four years spent on your globe in your dear company; we send you our good wishes, and embrace our cousins in the heavens.

Marquis Henri de Valsorres,
Marquise Marie de Valsorres.

Epilogue

There is scarcely any need to say that after so many events so well concluded, everyone at Valsorres was happy.

Thomas, raised to the rank of steward of the château, occupied an elegant detached cottage with his dear Hina, who, having become the confidante of the Marquise, wore the costumes of the "ladies of Earth" with great elegance.

A few weeks later, the inhabitants of the château were gathered in the billiard room when a chambermaid brought the marquise a letter with a Swiss stamp, which the postman had just handed to her, with another, bearing an Italian stamp.

The Marquise opened the first envelope and read the following:

Friedrichshafen, 24 December 1918.
Madame,
A woman who was executed by firing squad for helping French prisoners of war to escape asked me for the aid of religion and, after making me a confession of her sins, asked me to forward the enclosed letter to you. Now that the war is over, I am sending the letter to you, via the intermediary of a Swiss priest; I have thus accomplished the last will of a repentant sinner, who died a Christian.

Walter Richtofen
parish priest of Frierdrichshafen.

To that letter another was attached, which the Marquise read with an emotion that she did not seek to hide.

Madame la Marquise.
I am to die tomorrow; my death will be the expiation of the crimes I have committed.
In order to have a first sin forgotten, for which Gräfin Emma von Paschwitz, now Baronne Lymstroem, had assured me material impunity, I had entered into the service of that woman and had become her slave. She knew that I had to obey her blindly, and she employed me in the most sinister designs.
She and her brother, Graf von Paschwitz, who called himself Dr. Frank, had a mortal hatred for your family, for what reason I do not know. She and her brother decided to do you all possible harm.
First she placed me as a chambermaid in the home of Madame la Vicomtesse d'Estrelles. I had the mission of spying on everything I could hear in

355

the house of that diplomat and report it to her immediately. When she deemed that I was not bringing her enough information she punished me cruelly with her own hand.

When Monsieur de Valsorres projected his expedition to the heavens, I was charged with procuring for Dr. Frank photographs of the laboratory where Monsieur le Marquis worked with Monsieur Espéret. By abusing the confidence of the valet de chambre Thomas I introduced myself into the laboratory and took photographs that probably furnished Dr. Frank with precious information, as I was abundantly recompensed. If the information I am giving you can be of any use, I will tell you that Baron von Osterwald, whom Monsieur le Marquis saved from shipwreck in the ocean, had returned to an island he had discovered. He no longer found that island, but after a voyage of few days he discovered another...

At that point the Marquis and Espéret uttered the same exclamation.

"Oh, the bandits! They found a second island! That's how they were able to get to Saturn!"

The Marquise continued reading the letter.

"...another, from which they were able to bring back the stones that provided the material necessary for their expedition.

When they saw that, in spite of everything. Monsieur le Marquis would be ready before them, because they had been delayed by their voyage in the ocean, they decided to prevent him from departing, and for that, to kidnap young Monsieur Philippe de Valsorres.

It was me who put the nurse and the little boy to sleep, as well as the nurse and the two children of Madame d'Estrelles; it was me who took the child from his room and took him to an automobile where Dr. Frank was waiting.

All that I know is that the little boy was taken to the Schloss Paschwitz in Silesia. The last time I saw Baronne Lymstroem, which was two years ago, the child was still alive.

That, Madame la Marquise, was my infamy. I was pursued by remorse for my crimes. So, when Baronne Lymstroem left me in Friedrichshafen, as it was close to the Swiss frontier, I tried to redeem my sins and employed my time and my money in helping French prisoners to escape. I have been able to get thirty-seven to Switzerland, but I was denounced, tried and sentenced to death. I will be shot tomorrow morning.

At the moment when I find myself before my Judge, I humbly beg your pardon for all the harm I have done you, and I shall ask God, before whom I am to appear, to bring you consolation by enabling you to recover your child and your husband.

Your unworthy servant,

Bettina Fuchs.

Beneath the signature, the traces were visible of two tears that the eyes of the unfortunate woman had shed.

The reading of that letter had made a deep impression on the listeners. It was Abbé Travers who broke the silence. "She has repented, she has expiated," he said. "May God have pity on her soul!"

The Marquise opened the second letter, the one bearing an Italian stamp.

"It's from Zabeth!" she exclaimed, as she unfolded it.

This is what the second missive contained:

San Remo, 11 February 1919.
My dear cousins,

Édouard and I are staying for a few more weeks on this marvelous coast, which only lacks your dear presence for our happiness to be complete. For, after Venice, Florence and Milan, we still find nature more beautiful than art, and here, nature truly goes to great expense. The blue of the sky rivals that of the sea; it is a joy for the eyes, which quickly becomes, when there are two to savor it, a joy for the heart.

The only annoyance that experience here is being obliged to live in one of those cosmopolitan caravanserais that are always called "palaces" or "metropoles." And the abundance of Philistines that one encounters here is a trifle inconvenient for newlyweds like us, who would prefer discreet intimacy to an overflowing crowd.

Fortunately, we still have excursions, and I beg you to believe that we make use of them.

There followed a long narration of the most interesting excursions.

Before concluding this letter I shall tell you about an event of which our hotel was the theater a few months ago, and which will certainly strike you with astonishment. I only learned about it yesterday, from one of our neighbors in the dining room, a delightful English widow, who would make an excellent companion for our friend Espéret if he decided to follow our example. That lady, whose name is Mrs. Southworth,[44] has been resident in the hotel for six months. She witnessed the drama, but she only told me about it yesterday.

Can you imagine that shortly before the armistice, Baron and Baronne Lymstroem were resident at the hotel in San Remo. The Baron was a diplomat of a neutral country and was installed there with his wife, whose true nationality was unknown.

---

[44] Mrs. Southworth reappears as a character in the second of the three Miral/Viger feuilletons in *Le Petit Parisien*, the speculative thriller *La Bataille de l'or*.

The Baronne expressed Germanophilic sentiments that had offended several boarders at the hotel more than once. On the day of the armistice the cannons of the Italian forts were heard firing and the bells were ringing; everyone ran to the vestibule of the hotel, where dispatches were pinned up. It was victory! Defeated Germany was suing for peace. The Baronne refused to believe the telegrams, which she claimed were false; but that evening, in the lounge, when the newspapers were distributed that announced the news, she had to yield to the evidence. Then she went back to her room.

The next day, as she had not come down by midday, the chambermaid in service, after having knocked in vain several times, decided to force the door. The Baronne was lying on the bed, still clutching in her hand a little crystal bottle. She had poisoned herself.

No one in the hotel was able to explain the suicide, but I, who knew the nationality of the spy, quickly reconstituted the drama. German to the marrow of her bones, she had not been able to support the defeat of her country and had not wanted to survive what she considered to be its shame.

Perhaps she had also learned of the return of our voyagers from Saturn.

In any case, fortunately, she is no longer here, and, as Édouard says: dead the beast, dead the venom.

That, my dear cousins, is all I have to tell you.

In a fortnight we shall be in Valsorres to give you the kisses that, in the meantime, for want of anything better, we are confiding to the post.

Your little cousin,

Zabeth.

When the Marquise had finished reading the letter, she simply said: "Now all the guilty have been punished. All of that somber history is already in the past."

"Yes, Marie," replied the Marquis. "The past wears a widow's veil, the future that of virgins. Let us have faith in the future; it is opening radiantly, for us and for France!"